JAEN

By the same author

WOMEN ARE BLOODY MARVELLOUS!

JUDE

JAEN

Betty Burton

GRAFTON BOOKS
A Division of the Collins Publishing Group

LONDON GLASGOW
TORONTO SYDNEY AUCKLAND

Grafton Books
A Division of the Collins Publishing Group
8 Grafton Street, London W1X 3LA

Published by Grafton Books 1987

British Library Cataloguing in Publication Data

Burton, Betty
Jaen.
I. Title
823'.914[F] PR6052.U69/

ISBN 0-246-13098-9

Photoset by Deltatype Ltd, Ellesmere Port
Printed in Great Britain by
Robert Hartnoll (1985), Bodmin

For the Hampshire Archers
and the Nottinghamshire Burtons

Especially for my father – Leon Archer of Romsey,
my mother-in-law – Jessie Binch of Mansfield, my sister Margie,
and brother-in-law Ben Burton of Shaftesbury;

and for Barbara and David Randall-Holbury,
Andrew Burton and Sheila Begg – Aberdeen;

and not least for "Fancy"
(my cousin Clarice Crabb) of Romsey.

THANKS!

Mic Cheetham who pushed me over a few humps and Patricia Parkin who hauled me from the occasional trough. And thanks, Pen Isaac, for always seeing the funny side (even of dieting and some of my punctuation).

Thanks also to the staff of Portsmouth Central Library for always coming up with what I was looking for.

(And thanks, Russ, for searching around in the guts of the BBC Micro for five thousand lost words, and for forcing the Apple Mac to disgorge words when it would rather have swallowed them.)

Contents

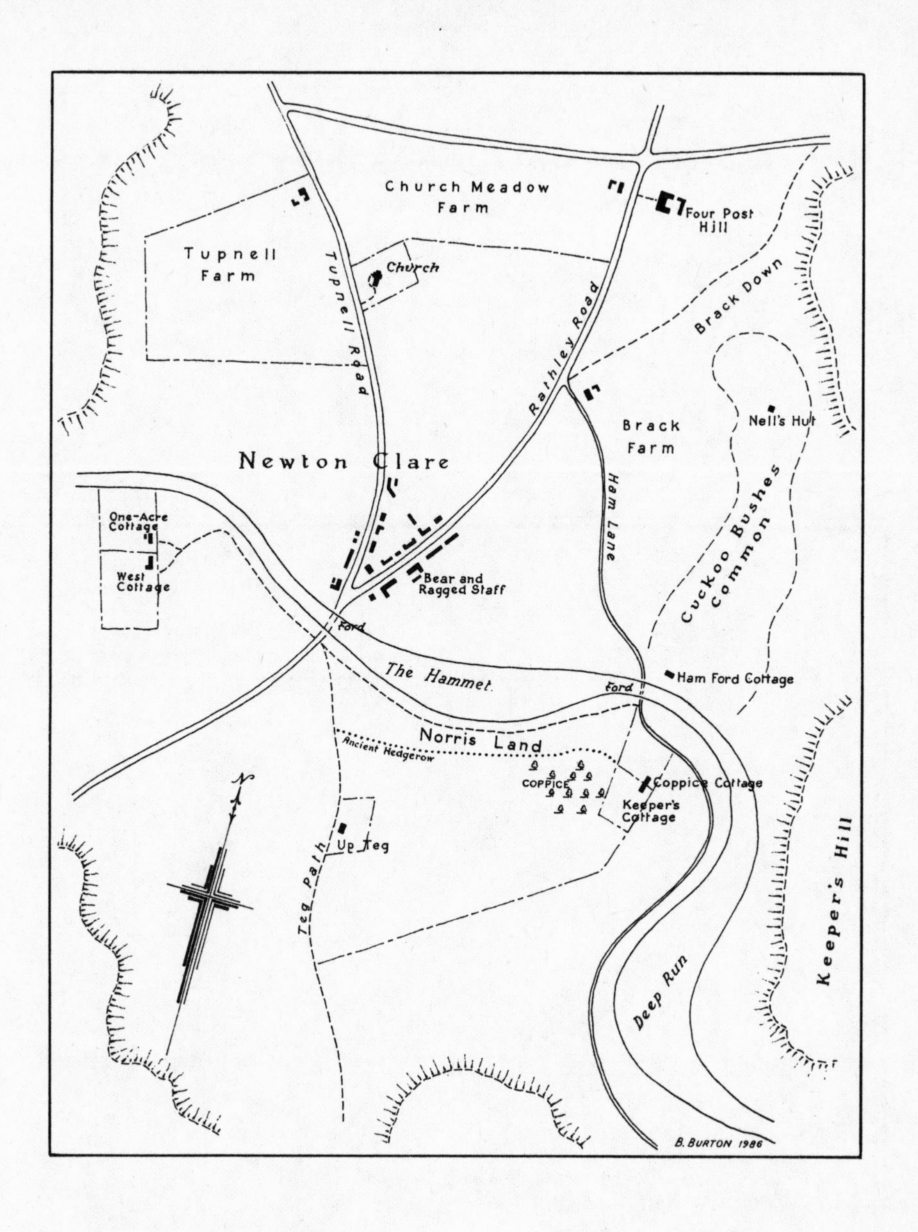

Church Meadow
Farm
Four Post
Hill
Tupnell
Farm
Church
Tupnell Road
Rathley Road
Brack Down
Nell's Hut
Brack
Farm
Newton Clare
Ham Lane
One-Acre
Cottage
West
Cottage
Bear and
Ragged Staff
Cuckoo Bushes
Common
Ford
The Hammet
Ford
Ham Ford Cottage
Norris Land
Ancient Hedgerow
COPPICE
Coppice Cottage
Keeper's
Cottage
N
Up Teg
Teg Path
Keeper's Hill
Deep Run
B. BURTON 1986

NUGENTS

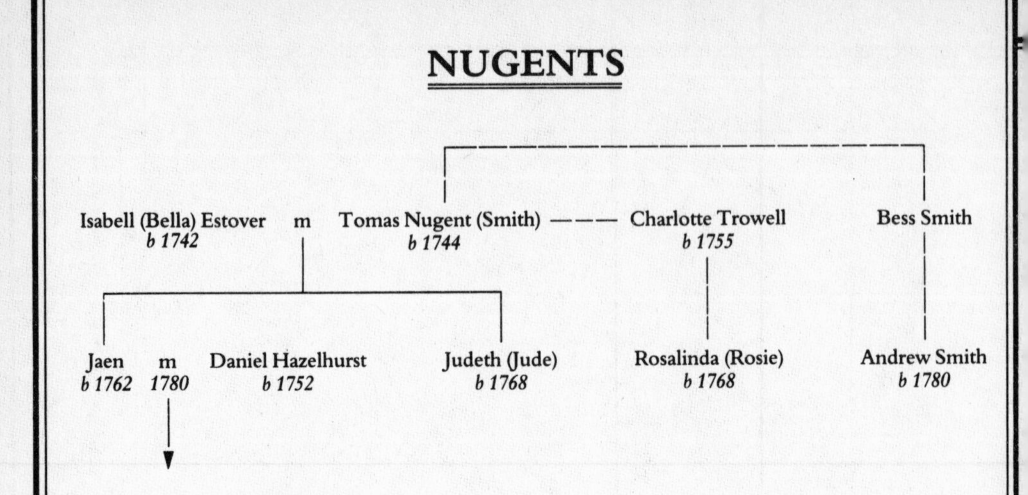

Isabell (Bella) Estover
b 1742
m
Tomas Nugent (Smith)
b 1744
Charlotte Trowell
b 1755
Bess Smith
Jaen
b 1762
m
1780
Daniel Hazelhurst
b 1752
Judeth (Jude)
b 1768
Rosalinda (Rosie)
b 1768
Andrew Smith
b 1780

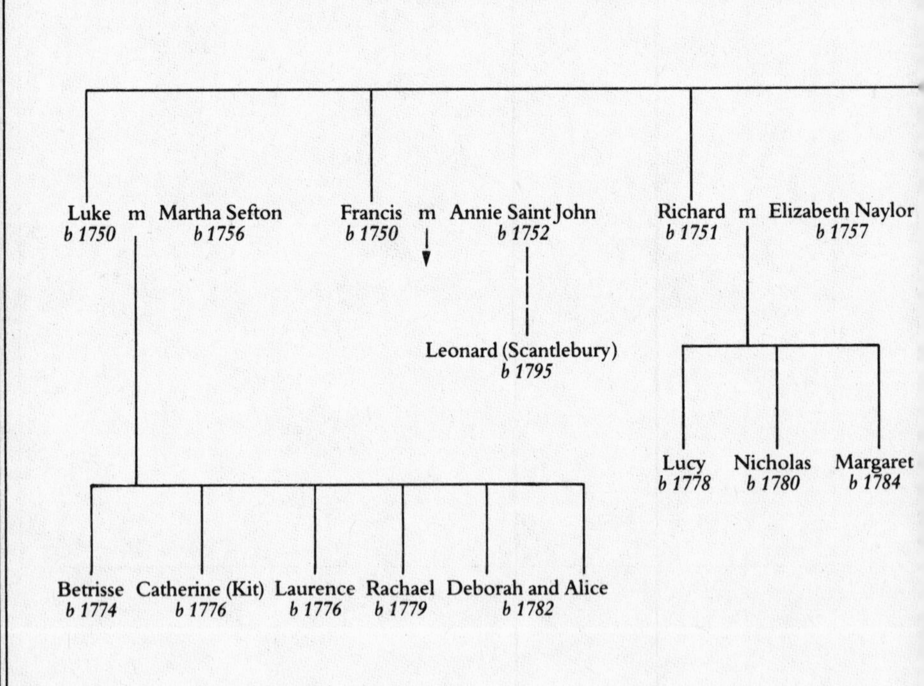

Luke
b 1750
m
Martha Sefton
b 1756
Francis
b 1750
m
Annie Saint John
b 1752
Richard
b 1751
m
Elizabeth Naylor
b 1757
Leonard (Scantlebury)
b 1795
Lucy
b 1778
Nicholas
b 1780
Margaret
b 1784
Betrisse
b 1774
Catherine (Kit)
b 1776
Laurence
b 1776
Rachael
b 1779
Deborah and Alice
b 1782

HAZELHURSTS

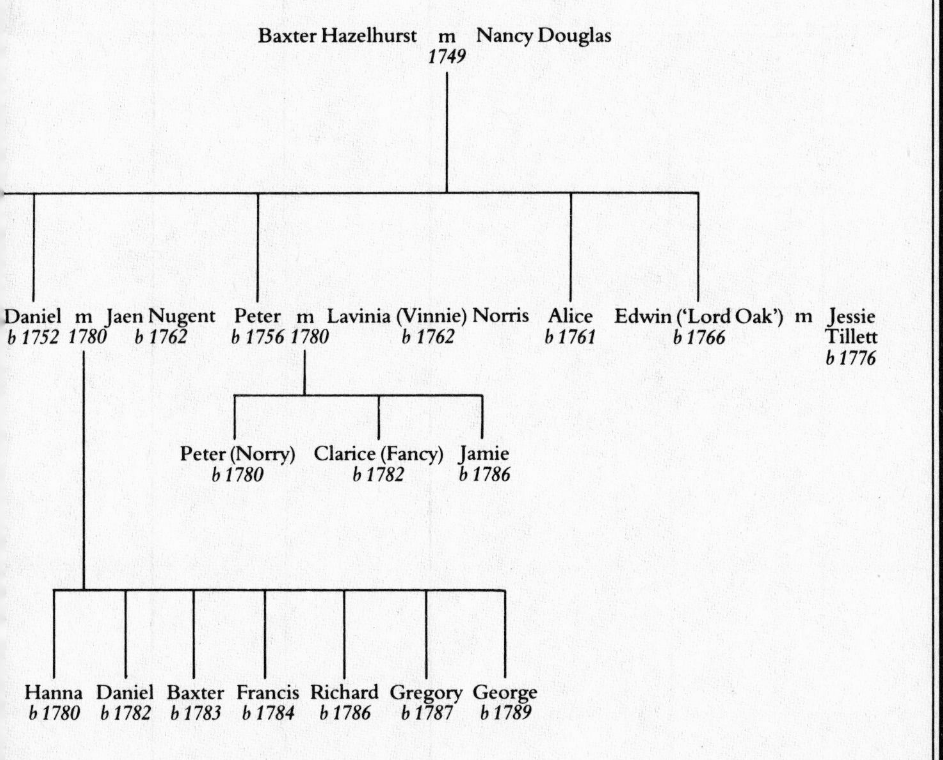

Part One

WEDDINGS

I

1780 – SPRING
Wedding day – Cantle

"JAEN HAZELHURST."

She says it to herself. Jaen Hazelhurst. It sounds strange after being Jaen Nugent for about eighteen years.

In the vestry of St. Peter's, waiting for the writing up to be done, Jaen looks at Daniel Hazelhurst to whom she has surrendered her name in return for a ring and the right to be called Mistress Hazelhurst.

He has not given either ring or name with great enthusiasm, but Bella Nugent, the bride's mother, is known on Blackbrook market for a tongue sharp enough to cut her lip, and for never being bettered when doing a deal. Jaen finds her mother's poker-faced expression a mystery to her, but why should she understand her mother any better today than she has ever done? It is not for nothing that Bella Nugent is called "Master" by her hired hands at Croud Cantle. "She'm a hard'n and no mistake."

At Croud Cantle they all work their fingers to the bone. Toes swollen from frost or heads banging from sun, they work. From dark to dark, every day of every year, they work. Backs breaking from hoeing, ribs tender from days working the breast-plough, they work. And when the dark comes they light oil-wicks and Bella Nugent and her two daughters press cheese or churn butter, then, at their ease, they comb and card and spin and mend and sew their clothes.

Jaen does not come from a family at the bottom of the pile, but nearly so. In Cantle village, as in villages all over rural Hampshire, there are half-starved peasants who would give their right arm to have a bit of land like Bella Nugent has, for since Tomas Nugent went off and never came back, Bella has battled with the Croud Cantle land to keep herself and her two girls above subsistence level. She hires extra labour when necessary because there is a good crop and, because he can turn his hand to any job, she has hired and re-hired old malicious Dicken Bordsell for years.

And now Jaen is going away from Croud Cantle, away from her mother and every bowl, platter and mug that have been her life.

She is going away from Ju.

From Judeth, her sister, six years younger and, until Dan Hazelhurst, the only warm body to have come close to her own. For twelve years Jaen had mothered Ju. But, when it had come to telling Ju that she was going to marry Dan Hazelhurst, that she must leave home, leave Ju and go over to Newton Clare and live at Up Teg farm, Jaen had put it off and put it off until it was too late and Ju heard it from their mother.

Jaen Hazelhurst knows that her young sister is there, silent as she has been for weeks. Jaen has tried to make it up, but Ju deep in her well of misery will speak to no-one.

The groom's mother, Nance Hazelhurst, has for years been sending girls off from the Up Teg farm, with a flea in their ear, girls who claimed that Dan was the cause of them growing big. Most of them were girls hired for turnip lifting or as scullery-maids – nobodies who Baxter Hazelhurst, Master of Up Teg Farm, would never consider suitable mothers for Hazelhurst grandchildren.

But this time Nance told Baxter that Dan should marry the girl. Baxter Hazelhurst knew Bella Nugent and her reputation on Blackbrook market; she was a hard-working woman and decent enough to be associated with the Hazelhursts.

"You take the girl," Baxter told his son.

Anyway, Dan was only two years off being thirty, time he settled down; a man couldn't go on for ever with his feet under his parents' table. Nance Hazelhurst thought if they didn't give him a push now, he would never make a move to get a place of his own. His three older brothers, when they had been in the same boat, had married and were set up with a bit of land and a few hogs running on the commons which their wives saw to, though the main labour of the entire family was put into Up Teg Farm.

The two mothers stand and watch the marriage lines being made; this is their wedding. It has taken weeks and several meetings at Blackbrook to arrange.

Today is a break. Like May-day, Harvest home, Blackbrook Fair or Plough Monday, it is an occasion. After she has provided the

Hazelhursts with food and drink, Bella Nugent will go the mile or so up Howgaite Path to Croud Cantle, the small holding of land she has battled with since Tomas Nugent went off and left her to it, a dozen years back.

Dan follows closely the entry of the marriage being made. Jaen has a secret feel of the hard ring Dan has just slipped on. Not exactly slipped on though, because after the first month in her present condition, everything seemed to swell up, starting from the ankles – sometimes she imagines that she is like one of the pig-bladders that boys fill till nearly bursting then throw over hedges for a lark. By her wedding day it has reached her wrists and fingers and it is still only her fifth month. Whatever shall I be like come August time?

"There." The Parish Clerk puts down the quill.

"What do it say?" Dan asked.

"That Daniel Hazelhurst, son of Baxter Hazelhurst Farmer of the Parish of Rathley, and Nancy Hazelhurst, have married Jaen daughter of Isabell Nugent and the late Tomas Nugent of the Parish of Cantle on April 24th 1780."

Mistress Hazelhurst.

Suddenly, now that she has the title, it seems not to matter. In the muddle of the last few months, the ring, and the protection of married status, have loomed over everything, yet it isn't anything really. A ring that seems already to be embedded in her finger – and the title "Mistress".

2

EVEN IN CHURCH, the Hazelhurst men made no attempt to lower their booming voices and all the brothers jeered and joked in their cheerful-sounding way, the way they always do.

"Come on, Gel, you'm dreaming."

"Bit of a nightmare more like."

Bella Nugent began to look irritable. Jaen guessed that it was because of the way the Hazelhurst Boys tramped into the little vestry as though they owned it. They would, they were like that.

But it took better men than Hazelhursts to out-do Bella Nugent.

"Remember where you are," she said, and The Boys went quiet.

"Ah 'tis the place that wouldn't be here if it wasn't for the likes of we paying our tithes," one of The Boys said. It was meant to be a whisper, but male Hazelhurst voices had no experience of such control.

Twisting inwardly, Jaen waited for her mother's sharp voice, but it did not come. The muscles around Bella Nugent's mouth tightened. Jaen could almost hear the comment her mother had made several times of late: "I met couther famblies in my time."

"Well, 'tis all over here then. What are we waiting for?" As she spoke, Bella turned to Rev Tripp and held out her hand. The gesture was as unexpected as was the realisation that this rough farm-wife was wearing gloves. Tripp felt annoyed at such show and profligacy among the lower orders and hardly knew what to do with the outstretched hand, so he touched a finger and made the sign of the cross at her.

With the wedding pair leading, the party walked from the vestry. It was the first time that Jaen had been with so many of the

Hazelhurst Boys and their wives and children. Old Baxter and his Boys were tall, wide men who revelled in their reputation for their famed Heighth and Breadth, and perhaps it was in an unconscious need to enhance this by contrast, that they all took small women for their wives.

There were six Hazelhurst Boys. Dan was the fourth, or the third according to how you looked at it, Luke and Francis being twins, not that they were alike except in size. They had married from the top down as you might say – eldest first. Now that Dan had got Jaen, there was only Peter of marriageable age, then there was a gap of ten years between Peter and the next, Edwin, who, at fourteen, was no less a man of heighth and breadth than his brothers.

A few Cantle villagers watched as the noisy family came through the porch. In the forefront – because he had known the bride since the day she was born – Dicken Bordsell who had worked at Croud Cantle farm since before Bella Nugent had come there.

"Well now missis," he said to his wife, "young Jaen got herself summit there and no mistake."

To which Mrs Bordsell replied that it was summit she wouldn't fancy for a daughter of hers, but there you are, beggars can't be choosers and the girl should a thought about that munts ago.

Jaen felt smothered by the bodies and voices that surrounded her – all Hazelhursts except for Mother and Ju. Mother was walking just behind, and she caught a glimpse of Ju's wild, red mass of hair and her resentful face, pale and angry – as it had been for weeks. Jaen blinked very fast and clenched her jaws to stop the tears that threatened. In looking about for Jude, Jaen had lagged a step behind Dan.

"Come on then, Mrs Hazelhurst," he said. His brothers roared out their approval as they always did at such times.

Up Teg, the Hazelhurst farm, was some miles from Cantle, on the other side of the chalk-hills that enclosed the Cantle Valley, the valley in which lay Croud Cantle, Jaen's home for all of her eighteen years. Unlike Up Teg, it was a tiny holding of not many acres protected by the great chalk-hill of Tradden Raike.

Because the entire Hazelhurst family had come all that way over from Newton Clare, Bella had arranged for some substantial refreshments and plenty of ale and cider to be put out in the back room of the Dragon and Fount. The inn was a few steps across the green from the church, and inside a few minutes of leaving the vestry, the wedding party and a few others whom Bella had invited to show that she had good connections, were intent on game pies and a dark-brown special brew.

"It's a nice lay-up you done for us, Mistress Nugent, I'll say that."

"Thank you, Mistress Hazelhurst, I just hope there's plenty seeing there's so many and they'm so big. I never seen all your boys before, some on 'm makes Dan look quite small."

"Ah, and there's some more coming on, five on 'm, but only one boy as yet.'

Bella nodded, acknowledging the presence of suckling babes and clod-hopping children.

"I just hope for my Jaen's sake that hern takes a bit after our side – being her first."

"Ah well, what we hopes for and what we gets is two different things. And 'tis my belief anyway a big first one usually makes way for the others to come easier," said Nance Hazelhurst. "But don't you worry about Jaen. I seen all the rest on 'm into the world."

"An' she an't lost a father yet!" Baxter Hazelhurst clapped Bella on the shoulder with one hand and lifted a long draught with the other.

Having done her duty as a woman and mother, Bella Nugent moved herself into a gathering of men and began talking markets and prices.

Seeing her mother like that, Jaen had a swelling of pride that Bella was different, independent, capable – capable as any man. Jaen had been standing on the market at Blackbrook, selling Croud Cantle produce, as long as she could remember. They grew good stuff and Bella knew that she could bargain on that reputation. She liked nothing better than to talk of growing and selling.

The baby flickered a kick – that's all over now, it reminded her. And again she controlled a desire to cry, to run from this great crowd of huge, loud men. She looked everywhere for Ju. Where was she? Gone off up Tradden on her own? Ju had been doing that for weeks now.

Luke, eldest of The Boys – just, having Francis as his twin – said to his wife, "Here, Martha, look at her, happy as a wet hen in a duck-pond."

"And who can blame her? You an't got no idear what your family's like when they'm all together. It's like being thrown into a herd a spring bulls – you'm all shoulders and bellow and snort."

Jaen could not hear what Luke and Martha were saying, but they were both looking at her – she felt that everybody was looking at her, except Dan. Bella was moving about seeing that people had enough to eat; Jaen went to her.

"You seen Ju, Mother?"

"I dare say she's somewhere about."

"She was outside the church, then she was gone – I never saw where she went."

Bella said, "You know she don't like this kind of thing."

"I can't say I blame her," Jaen said very quietly.

Bella threw Jaen a jagged expression that said more than "that's enough a that kind a talk."

"Ah well, it's your duty here, and mine; nobody takes no notice of a girl hooking off. She's probably curled up in some corner somewhere watching a spider making a web or summit – you know what she's like. Here, take some cake round. The sooner they has the cake, the sooner it a be over."

Jaen looked panic-stricken at her mother, and Bella knew that if she didn't clamp down hard, as she had had to do many times over the last weeks and months, then there might be tears.

"Now, I told you, you'll be all right. You an't going far, only over to 'Clare, and that an't hardly no further than Blackbrook market. You a see us often enough. Anyway . . ." Bella began cutting up wedges of dark sticky cake.

All right! All right! I know I made my bed. I know I've got to lie on it. I been told it often enough. I'm the one, I'm the one . . . nothing to do with Dan. I'm the one who has to leave home and everything . . . not him, never the man who has to go to strangers.

Jaen was a past-mistress at pasting a smile over anger and anguish. Her large, wide eyes were bright and her cheeks glowing, and with her gold-red Estover hair, the Hazelhurst family had to admit that she was as pretty a one as ever had married into them.

By eleven o'clock the toasts are done; the jokes that mean nothing to Jaen and Bella made; the casks are empty and the food gone. Jaen's panic and desolate thoughts of leaving Cantle and her mother and Jude have been pushed down. The baby rested, now making in her only little movements which are hardly distinguishable from the digestion of the rich cake and sweet apple wine Dan had insisted that she have to fortify herself for the journey.

Whilst Jude have been there, whilst there is cake and ale, whilst the Hazelhursts are intent on feasting, Jaen still held the last slender threads connecting her to the Cantle Valley, to Croud Cantle, to home, security and dignity. Now the threads shredded and broke.

"Come then, Mistress Hazelhurst, ready for off?" Dan takes her by the elbow and Jaen is pleased at the closeness of the rough cloth of his coat and the warm smell of his sweat.

It will be all right.

As she walks with him in the confusion of a Hazelhurst exit, she plays the old game Ju loves. *It* will be all right. It *will* be all right. It will *be* all right, and so on. The baby objects to the crush in the narrow passageway of the Dragon and Fount, and reminds Jaen that even if it is *not* all right, it is too late now. She has made her bed.

It is time to exchange their farewells. Jaen wonders which would cause the greater embarrassment, kissing her mother who hated that kind of thing? or not kissing her and being prompted to do so by Dan, or worse – by his mother Nance? She brushes Bella's cheeks lightly with her lips.

"Ju *will* be all right now, won't she?"

Bella brushed off the implied suggestion that Jude would continue not speaking to anyone, as she has done since she learned that Dan Hazelhurst had got her adored and necessary sister with a baby. Jude felt betrayed. Jaen knew it. She had known how very much distressed Ju would be at the prospect of their separation, but she had not suspected that she would be so devasted, so angry, so contemptuous of Dan Hazelhurst.

"You leave Jude to sort herself out. There an't nothing you can do."

"She'll like the baby," said Jaen.

"Ah," Bella made herself smile at her daughter, "she'll be like a mother hen, you'll see."

Jaen reached down inside herself yet again to see if it is true, to see whether it is possible that those few minutes with Dan last winter could have brought on all this fuss.

Her thoughts are snagged by the creak and jingle of hay wagons decorated for the occasion with leaves and spring flowers, and drawn by two yoked, wide-horned, red oxen.

"My eye, now there's summit I an't seen since I is a girl," said Bella. "We used to have red oxes like that when our family lived down the West Country."

Baxter looked pleased; he is proud of his old breed of beast.

"It's a tradition that we has oxes to draw at a family wedding. We mostly only keeps them for that these days, don't work 'm much."

Bella recognised Baxter Hazelhurst's boast as that of a thriving farmer, a man with a decent bit of acreage and six sons of great heighth and breadth to work it, a man who could keep beasts just because he fancied them.

Jaen easily interprets her mother's expression – more fool you – and is pleased when, instead of saying so, she slaps the back of a shining beast and hides her opinion. Mother has bitten her tongue a time or two today, but if they don't go soon she will not be able to keep it up.

When the wagons were ready, only Bella Nugent was left outside the Dragon and Fount. A few villagers watched at a distance to see the bedecked wedding carts leave. Watched the taking away of Jaen, the child she got when she had truly loved Tomas Nugent who was long gone, long ago dead. Bella Nugent stood alone and waved.

Waved as though she wanted nothing better in the wide world than to see Jaen drive away with one of they great Hazelhurst tree-trunks. Her pretty daughter who worked the land good as any man, and stood on Blackbrook market charming everybody. Many's the time Bella would have liked to say something nice to Jaen, but it never would come out. Instead it fermented and festered until it exploded as "Oh fer goodness sake!" over some trivial irritation.

3

WEDDING DAY
Up Teg Farm

JAEN AND DAN, seated on a makeshift bench in the leading wagon beside Baxter and Nance, had the place of honour of the occasion. In the bed of the wagon are Martha and Luke and their four children, Betrisse, Kit and Laurie the twins, and the new baby. Martha suckled the baby whilst the others, fagged-out by the excursion and soothed by the familiar boom of voices and the rock and creak of the wagon, slept.

In the following wagon Francis and Annie distanced themselves from one another, Annie sitting with Richard's wife Elizabeth, awkward in her eighth month, France sitting with Richard and jiggling Richard's two-year-old Lucy playfully on his knees. Peter with his arm about Vinnie, whispered about their own wedding day. Edwin chewed leaves and shot plugs at them from the hollow stems of last-year's cow-parsley, deaf to the familiar family arguments about what government ought to be doing, and the new farming methods.

"You never did have no sense when it come to buying a decent ram, our France."

"Hark who's talking. Who pays above coppice price for a pile a hurdles?"

"Lord, an't you never going to forget summit as happened years ago."

"Ah, well . . ."

As the oxen plodded their way out of the village Jaen too is deaf to them. She keeps her head bowed and concentrates upon her shining wedding band so that she shall not see the dissolution of her childhood. But every inch of the way, from the ford at the Dunnock Brook, down Raike Bottom, past Chard Lepe Pond and up, up across the face of Tradden Raike, is so familiar to her that she has no need to look up to know where she is. They reach the pond, which has known their green, childish secrets – hers and Ju's – Jaen knows that if she looks over her left shoulder, she could glimpse the ragged thatch of Croud Cantle.

Croud Cantle with its little acres and orchards, its house-cow, goats and pigs and chickens – and the house with its red-tiled houseplace floor. Croud Cantle, from where she has come a few hours ago – Jaen Nugent, Spinster of the Parish of Cantle in the county of Hampshire. Jaen Nugent is gone, and even if as Jaen Hazelhurst she ever returns to Croud Cantle, it will be as a visitor. Jaen Hazelhurst, wife of Daniel, of Up Teg Farm, Newton Clare in the Parish of Rathley, county of Hampshire, now belonged to Up Teg Farm and the Hazelhursts.

The men, intent on the arguments that are shouted back and forth between the wagons, take no notice of her. The women too seem preoccupied, making the most of the holidaying the other side of the downs.

Even Jude, in unseeing, blind misery, trailing along the bottom of Tradden Raike, does not see her sister's exodus.

Once they were over Tradden Raike Jaen felt able to look about her. The last time she came this way was with her mother when they returned from Up Teg. Bella, for the hundredth time, spitting out her humiliation at the high-handed way old Baxter Hazelhurst tried to treat her when she went to confront him with Dan's obligation to Jaen, Jaen swallowing her humiliation at the same scene.

"They'm a coarse and biggitid lot, and I'd as soon a seen you marry a packman."

It was a figure of speech, for Bella Nugent, although disappointed at the kind of family Jaen had got herself in with, knew almost to a foot the acreage of Up Teg and the security it would provide. That had been in February, the feast of St. Valentine when the birds are supposed to become betrothed, but Jaen had noticed little except the fierce and noisy battles going on among the blue-tits.

And now it was St. Mark's Eve.

Sixty-nine days. If there was one thing Jaen was good at, it was working numbers in her head, necessary if you were a good market trader, starting with counting how many eggs each hen had produced, then how many that made in a month, how much they fetched. Without realising that it happened Jaen had learned, at a very early age, quite complicated methods of calculation. Marrows times pence; twelve carrots to the bunch; bushels, dozens, pounds, stones, rods and acres. And twenty-eight dried beans that Bella had given her. When they had been transferred from one place to another it was time for the rags and tapes – so you don't get caught napping when you'm out in the fields.

Sixty-nine days between St. Valentine's Day and St. Mark's Eve, this day, wedding day. There had been the first twenty-eight days and then another twenty-eight, after Dan had held her warm and close; after he had told her she was beautiful and not to be afraid – and she wasn't, only very happy and a little heady at his touch and the hardness of his muscles and the unexpected softness of his beard.

"You all right, Gel?" Nance poked an elbow at her.

"Oh yes . . ." She smiled to pre-empt any possible further questions. "I was miles away – not used to so much apple wine." Jaen smiled reassuringly at Dan's mother.

Nance nodded off again.

Twenty-eight days of anxiety that something was wrong, then another twenty-eight days. And then telling Bella. That had been the worst part . . . almost the worst. The real worst part was the Hazelhursts. She pushed it from her mind.

They had travelled quite a long way now, six or seven miles. Down the east slope of Tradden and then along the northward curving Wayfarer's Way, the broad rutted cart-track that grew wider as each drover or carrier tried to avoid the churned-up mire of earlier travellers. The children were all asleep; from time to time Jaen felt her own baby trying out its new-found ability to move its limbs. It kicked her sharply in the bladder and she jerked her knees together.

"You want to get down?" Dan asked, rightly interpreting her need.

"No, no, I'm quite comfortable."

"Father, pull over, Jaen wants to get down."

"I don't, Dan, really, I'm all right."

"Time for one anyway," said old Baxter, and halted the swaying, plodding oxen.

Most of the women stayed put, but the men all went a few yards off to relieve themselves of the large gallons of ale and cider Bella had provided.

They'm a coarse lot, Bella had said, and Jaen knew that they were.

There an't no room for fine manners on the land, but there's room for a smidgen of decency, was what her mother always said. And decency to Bella meant not behaving like the beasts in the barn or the fowls of the yard, when it came to things like that. Long ago, she had made the men dig pits well away from the house and put up hurdles round them.

"She's a queer one, and no mistake," was the opinion of Dicken Bordsell on such innovations as the hurdles round the pits, and the rule that no one walk in yard-muck boots on the red tiles of the Croud Cantle houseplace. Dicken and the other men always took their food at the end of the room where there was an ordinary earth floor covered with rushes, like any other kitchen. But to Jaen, never knowing anything different, Bella's standards were not queer, only normal. Bella Nugent had brought them up to wash pretty often too – hair and all. Neighbours said there was summit wrong with her always cleaning things when they wasn't soiled, either that or she must be a sight dirtier than anybody else.

By early afternoon they were on Up Teg land.

Dan's three older brothers who were married had small ordinary labourers' cottages on Up Teg. The wagons stopped to let the women and children down and the rest of the party went on up to the farmhouse. As the farmhouse came into view Jaen awoke to reality.

That place was her home from now on.

Suddenly, the day lost its late-April warmth. The landscape lost its colour. She saw it through murky, unclean glass. Dun colour. Greyness. Black and paleness. Mourning-bleak. The budding crab-apples were not fisting pink buds, primroses had no gleam, swallows taking mud to the house were dull, dull, and the first painted-lady and peacock butterflies of the year were as dusty brown as evening moths.

Jaen shivered.

"Don't worry," Dan said; "we shall be all right when we gets going on our own."

Jaen smiled brightly at her husband.

"I an't worried, Dan. It's going to be nice."

"Well, you a have plenty of company." He laughed. "A lot better'n you been used to over your place. Lord, I never knew how you stuck it. Two women and a funny little gel like your Jude, you must a been like pecketty hens."

The Boys laughed.

"Well then," said old Baxter, "you a have to get used to a yard full a cock-birds round here."

Master Baxter was a rare one for cock-bird jokes. They all roared at their father.

They'm a coarse and biggited lot!

4

NANCE HAZELHURST had played this scene three times before – four really, if she counted herself. A little bit of a thing, with a swelling belly, coming into the big Up Teg kitchen and having to get used to the bull-bellows and the clatter of them, even to the lack of space there always seemed to be when the Hazelhursts were about.

She had been seventeen when Baxter brought her here thirty years ago, not that far gone with Luke and France, but far enough to make her realise that it was this or nothing. As it turned out it hadn't been too bad. At least she had made improvements in the kitchen, the indoor sink, the wheeled spit with the little trained dogs, and lately a new bottle-jack spit, and a whole row of pewter platters on the dresser.

"Come on in. She there's Myrtle helps in the house" – Myrtle bobbed to Dan's wife – "and there's Kath somewhere about. And a course there's Vinnie, and she still does the dairying, and she still lives out there along with the rest of the girls till her and Peter gets wed."

Nance Hazelhurst was a wiry, brown little woman with newt-like movements, fast, sudden, and jerky. Within a minute or two of coming through the door, she had blown up the fire, adjusted the chimney crane, hooked over an iron pot, and generally pattered about seeming to do half a dozen things at once.

"I dare say you a find things a bit different here, but you a soon get used to it. Main thing is, you does things my way. I'm easy-going enough, but Baxter don't like no changes. He likes his same place by the fire, just so much salt in his butter, and his jacket behind the door where he can put his hand on it . . . that kind of thing. So don't go thinking you're helping by doing anything different.

Martha, then Annie and then Elizabeth, they all started off doing things different. He likes things his way."

"I'm use to that. Mother was just the same."

"Ah well, I suppose she's the master at your place."

"Yes, she never stood no nonsense with us or anybody who works there."

"It an't the same when it's men though. I dare say you'll find it a bit funny having to buckle down under a man."

"I expect I shall soon get used to it. Work's work, no matter who tells you to do it."

"Except you an't never had a man to tell you to do none."

The new Mrs Hazelhurst considered for a moment, then smiled but didn't reply, but took the wooden spoon Nance handed to her, and stirred the pot she indicated.

"Do you remember your father?"

"Not much. I was only five. It's his coat I remember; but just when I'm going to sleep, or waking up, I get a real picture of him, then soon as I wake up it's gone. Most likely it's a dream."

Ah well, it would be, thought Nance. She seems a bundle of dreams if you asks me. Miles away half the time. Inside her own head. It's always the quiet ones you have to watch. Let's hope The Boys gets on and mends that roof and her and Dan's out of here before Peter and Vinnie gets wed. Vinnie was just the opposite to this one, Vin probably didn't know she had an inside to her head.

She'd be glad when they were all married and settled down. For the last six or seven years it'd been one after the other tumbling girls in the fields – not that it could a been the fields with this one. Goodness knows where Dan and her found on Pewsey's place in November. Same place as Peter and Vinnie found last January she wouldn't wonder, the hayloft. It was a funny thing, a pile of hay anywhere always seems to set a man off. It was a pity though they didn't wait till they had got a place ready.

Lord knew where they'd find anywhere for Ed when his turn came. There was only so much room on Up Teg, and the little place at Ham Ford The Boys were supposed to be going to mend for Dan really was scraping the barrel when it came to the cottages. Perhaps they'd have to build on. Don't go looking for trouble, let it come and find you.

And, when all was said and done, she was lucky to have had

such a good healthy bunch of sons, and now she had them, she thought the world of them, there were just too many of them. Each time, after the twins and then Richard, she had wished the new one to Kingdom Come, till they were birthen, then once you saw them, give them a name, you soon forgot you hadn't wanted them.

Compared to Croud Cantle, Up Teg Farm was very large and the farmhouse spacious. To Jaen, used to one ground-floor room divided by nothing save the presence of the red floor-tiles, and above a hurdle partition, Up Teg house seemed to be huge and complicated.

At Croud Cantle the sleeping floor was reached by an open-tread stair not much better than a ladder, and the two chambers had no doors, just a coarse-woven draught-curtain. In warm weather, her mother slept in one part and Jaen and Jude curled together on a rough wood-framed cot in the other. In winter Bella Nugent returned to the recess in the kitchen.

At Up Teg, however, there was a staircase made by a joiner and upstairs were several proper rooms, with lath and plaster walls and dormer windows, and each chamber had a door made of planks, with an iron latch.

"I've put your bits and pieces in the Yard Room above," said Nance, and took her up to the room that was to be hers and Dan's until The Boys had seen to the thatching of the little cottage at Ham Ford.

It was a bright chamber, in which a ceiling had been put up. The ceiling had the advantage of warmth, but on the dormer side it prevented anyone taller than Jaen from standing up.

"I said before, it's as well they don't marry tall girls," Nance said. "Baxter reckons he only wed me because nobody else would a fitted."

Jaen smiled, grateful for the older woman's attempt to put her at ease. "It's really nice," she said, wanting to please her mother-in-law. "You been very kind and that. I never thought we should have such a nice room as this."

Nance Hazelhurst, sentimental from remembrances made charming by the passage of thirty years, as well as mellow from the heady very fine apple wine Bella Nugent had provided, thought of her own coming into the Up Teg farmhouse and unexpectedly put her arms about Jaen.

"As long as you'm a good wife, you a be all right. The Hazelhursts have never gone short of much. Even when times is hard, they always seems to do all right. There's always that to think of."

Jaen's nature was to be pliant. She smiled at people. She swallowed any disturbing feelings such as anger or misery. She was gentle.

Bella Nugent had brought her daughters up to hard work and not much pleasure. From an early age, Jaen knew that she was the cause of her mother's sharp manner, and her lack of affection; that there was something estimable in her mother because she always chose to do everything the hard way; that never giving into "soft" feelings was commendable. There were times when Jaen could have cried out with the need for a gentle word or even a hand-pat from Bella.

On the first night at Up Teg, long after Dan had twice heaved himself away from her, Jaen lay wondering about them back home. That morning Jaen had kissed her mother, and had been surprised to find her lips brushing a warm and soft cheek. She tried to remember the feel of her mother's hands but could not recall it, nor when there had been any physical contact between them.

She suddenly thought how strange it was that she and her mother had worked so closely for years without their hands ever touching. There was no reason why they should: churning, hoeing, milking, spinning and all the other jobs needed no contact . . . but other working hands had touched hers.

Dicken's hands, yes, hard, gnarled over her own, showing her, when she was little, the way to hold carrots and rhubarb so as to make a clean pull; Bob Pointer, Rob Netherfield, yes, from time to time during work their hands had met her own in the natural way of people working together, removing splinters and thorns for one another, yes, easy to recall their warmth and strength; and little Johnny-twoey, yes, she had often held his wiry little hands, washed the rolls of dirt from between his fingers before dabbing salve on the blisters he had raised by long hours of clapping boards together to scare the crows, or putting green ointment on chilblains or the cuts he got from sharp flints when stone-picking.

But her mother? no. Even on this day when she had quickly kissed her daughter, they had not touched hands. She had been shaking hands with everybody, but she had gloves on, new gloves she had bought for the occasion, and tried to behave as though she was used to gloves. Only the dugs and teats, only the bristles, only the hair and feathers of the farm-animals ever felt the touch of Bella Nugent's hands.

Jaen curled herself into Dan's back as she had always curled protectively about Ju, hoping for reassurance from the closeness. This was what she wanted, wasn't it. A man. A body to curl around her too. Somebody who would cradle her in their arms and be kind to her and talk to her softly sometimes. And now she had what she wanted – and there were tears gathering in a pool in one eye and trickling into her hair from the other.

How had she come to get herself into this muddle, exchanging the safe, bare little chamber at Croud Cantle, with its smell of apples ripening and rotting in the loft; the soft, limp arms and rough calloused feet of Ju, and the sound of familiar animals, for this enclosed room, for the huge mound of muscle, for strange male breathing and the sounds of beasts who were so unfamiliar that she could not distinguish one from another.

Jaen Hazelhurst was there because she did not know that people can be as hungry and thirsty for affection as for sustenance and drink. She was there because, for a brief moment she had wanted to be supported by the great buttress of his body, to feel light-hearted at his trivial nonsense, to believe that she was beautiful, different, worthwhile. She was there because she had not realised, until it happened, that she could lose control of herself.

She realised now.

Ju loved her, idolised her even, and she loved Ju; twelve years she had loved Ju, and it couldn't ever stop even if they never saw one another again, but that wasn't a kind of "need" love, not like that first time had been, with Dan.

Last November, Jaen Nugent had come to the point where what she needed was somebody to touch her gently, hold her, kiss her, take away an unidentified fear. Unidentified because she did not know that such a fear existed, it was the fear of loneliness. Her inventive imagination used to work magic and fantasy for herself and Jude into the milking, tilling, churning and heavy humping and carrying of everyday life. That imagination, when turned upon a void within herself, created dread and fear which lurked like ghouls behind her pretty, smiling gentleness.

Last November. St. Martin's day, at Pewsey Farm, near the small town of Rathley, not many miles from Up Teg.

The Pewseys had a good reputation for their small flock of Weald Whites, a high-yield breed of goat. Bella Nugent had a reputation for goat-milk cheeses and she wanted to improve their own flock, so she, Bella, had sent Jaen to choose an animal for Croud Cantle. "It's about time you done something like that. You can't leave it all to me."

Jaen had been surprised at her mother's sudden decision, but she did not question it and took the chance to get away from home for a few days with both hands. November was not the best time for walking between Cantle and Rathley, but it was one of the few times when Jaen could be spared.

The Pewseys were distant cousins of the Nugents so Jaen would likely be a welcome visitor if bad weather set in. Perhaps that had something to do with it. "It won't do you no harm to meet a few fresh faces," Bella had said. Perhaps Bella, having prospected locally for a son-in-law, had found none suitable. Perhaps. Perhaps that thought had never entered her head – you never knew with Bella Nugent.

Last November, Dan Hazelhurst rode over to Pewsey's. He had come upon the sight of the slight, pretty, red-haired girl in the pen of goats, dealing with Old Man Pewsey himself, doing a deal like a man, confident, knowledgeable. That vision had roused in Dan Hazelhurst a fantasy, a desire to have a woman who had something about her. There was something about her reminded him of Prancy. She was the dainty chestnut mare all over again. The one who had tossed and kicked and rebelled until she recognised him as master. Nothing before or since had given him as much pleasure as those weeks breaking in the chestnut mare.

Dan Hazelhurst, at twenty-eight, had known any number of girls. Servants and dairy-maids at Up Teg and other farms in and around Newton Clare. He liked a woman to be quick and responsive to his immediate need, like Nell Gritt who, in her hovel mended with old hurdles and roofed with turf, took any man who brought something that would feed her and the silent, twisted man who had been a husband – her husband – before a bull had tossed and gored him back to infancy.

Dan Hazelhurst boasted that there was nothing anybody could tell him about maids or women. He knew that he could charm the birds off the tree. He guessed that Jaen would respond to charm, so he was charming. He thought that she was the kind of girl who would respond to gentleness, so he was gentle. He sensed that she was tinder, so, finding her alone at dusk, looking at the goat she had bought, he created a spark by taking her face between his hands and kissing her. For a minute her passion had burnt more brilliantly than his own. He had been confident that he could get her to return his kisses, but he had not expected such sudden passion. He was as careless of the consequences as he had been once or twice before, ages ago when he had been little more than a youth.

If she had been thirsty for affection, the unexpected draught of physical love had been so sudden and so strong that, after the initial intoxication, it had made her mentally retch. Then, on Christmas morning whilst milking the house-cow, she had physically retched, and there began the bewildering slither down the slope that rushed her away from Croud Cantle, from safety and familiarity – and from Ju.

5

JAEN DID HER BEST TO FIT into the new routine and do things exactly as Nance bade her. Nance had an easy-going nature and, if it had not been for Baxter's likes and dislikes, she would not have minded how anybody did anything, just so long as it got done. But as it was, it was necessary to remember that Baxter preferred one platter to another, to sit this side of the hearth to that; he liked to carve the meat himself, but would never cut bread. That's an 'ooman's job. As far as Jaen knew before she was plunged into this household, people always cut bread as they wished, but Baxter expected bread to be cut ready for him. From time to time he changed his mind about his likes and dislikes, or forgot that he had made a fuss on some earlier occasion. Sometimes Nance would challenge him, but only if she was feeling particularly fed up with his nonsense and she always knew just how far to go.

"For goodness sake, husband, it an't more'n a week ago since you said you can't abide a doughy middle to a loaf, and now you'm saying you can't abide it dry."

"I never said that. In any case there's a difference between not liking a wet middle to a loaf and not liking dry bread."

During the first weeks, whenever Baxter had something to criticise, Jaen immediately flushed and felt guilty. The master of Up Teg hardly ever made reference to her directly, or actually said that she was incompetent, but Jaen was sure that every word of complaint was directed at her.

Unspecific references – "What's this pie-crust then?" And Jaen, whether she was involved in its making or no, would assume that the blame lay somewhere with herself, because his tone indicated that so poor a pie-crust was something he had never encountered until lately, and she was ashamed at letting Dan down.

Sometimes, Nance would defend: "What's a matter with it?" If he was in a bad mood, she would add no more, leaving it open to give vent to whatever bad temper he had brought into the house. But if she knew that it was "just him", showing what was what and who was who, that he was Master in his own place, keeping them all on their toes, she might add, "I can't see there's anything wrong with it." Or if she knew that he was only complaining for complaining's sake, she would be sharp with him: "Be thankful you got a pie at all."

The bickering and complaining were normal family exchange to The Boys. You don't want a take no notice of he – it's only his way, was their attitude once they had become grown men and were working equally with their father.

"But I feel such a fool, Dan. I feel as if I don't know anything when he goes on at me."

"You a get used to it."

But she never did, even though she had been trained in Bella Nugent's hard ways. Back home Jaen knew that although she seldom did anything that reached her mother's standards, she had done as good as anybody else would expect. But under Baxter Hazelhurst's eye, she felt inadequate.

Her one ally was Vinnie Norris.

Vinnie was just eighteen, the same age as Jaen almost to the week. Until four or five years ago, the Norrises had worked a small strip of land that adjoined Up Teg. Then, all in the space of a few months, Vinnie's mother died of the bad lungs that had wasted her body for years, and Vinnie's father pierced his leg on a spike and fatal lockjaw set in. Up Teg, being neighbourly and kin into the bargain, took in the two Norris children, Lavinia and James. Vinnie as milk-maid and dairy-maid, and Jim, with his mother's burning eyes and flushed cheeks, as yard-boy.

Up Teg took in as well the Norris acres.

Vinnie was as robust as Jim was weakly. She was full of spark and life and appeared quite undominated by Baxter or any of The Boys. No matter whether she was muddied from working in the ankle-deep mire, bedraggled from pressing against the flanks of cows or sweating from turning the heavy churn, she seemed always to be lively. Her father had been hefty and stocky, Vinnie was like him.

"There an't no mistaken when Vinnie comes in, she'm like a blimmin heifer."

She seemed to take their comments in good part, as she did the fact that, although she was in effect working her own family land, she had never had a place with the family proper but had slept with the other girls and servants, in a place over the dairy. The tumbledown hovel that had been the Norrises' home had, after a year of neglect, fallen down and was now just a mound of ivy and bramble, with a splurge every spring of gilly-flowers and Molly Norris's wise-woman herbs thriving on the rubble.

Vinnie made no bones about it. She had liked Peter ever since she was a girl, and there was a lot about Vinnie that Peter Hazelhurst liked, particularly her good, solid body and her willingness to clasp him to it at the drop of a hat, as you might say. So when after two years of good luck, and a little knowledge from her wise-woman mother, she eventually did get herself pregnant, neither of them minded much. Now she would be family and anyway it was time Peter settled down a bit.

And the Norris land could properly be considered as Up Teg acres.

When Jaen arrived at Up Teg she was five months pregnant and Vinnie was three, but size for size the reverse looked to be the case.

"You sure you fell, Jaen? I knows a girl who thought she was . . . you know, for six months, but she wasn't. She just started again, but by that time she'd a got wed."

They were in the dairy, just the two of them putting curds in the wooden cheese presses, and for answer Jaen placed Vinnie's hand on her small mound and let Vinnie feel the strong movements.

Vinnie looked amused. "Ah well, you can't get over that, can you, he's a real strong little toad, an't he. It's what I'm waiting for, to feel mine move."

"Don't you mind?" Jaen asked.

Vinnie did not answer instantly as she usually did, no matter what.

"What, mind having the baby?"

"Not only that, don't you mind . . ." What she wanted to ask Vinnie was, didn't she mind the total surrendering of herself to Peter, to having to be, you might say, owned by him so that he had legal rights to do anything he wanted, even if you didn't want him to. But Jaen's nature was to withhold, be private. To say things like that out loud meant admitting them to yourself, making them real.

"I mean, don't you mind . . . like, not being yourself any more?"

Vinnie laughed good-naturedly. "An't much good minden when you been and got yourself poddy. We shall be all right. Peter's all right. Peter's the best of the bunch."

Vinnie, always putting her foot in her mouth. Straight away she was sorry.

"Ah well, I expects we all think that, don't we. Anyway, your Dan's the best looking of all of them, better than Peter. Dan got a real way with him."

And he'd once tried it on Vinnie.

Only once though. For all that Up Teg treated her the same as the hired workers, Vinnie was nobody's fool. She knew the Hazelhursts all right, knew they wouldn't want no trouble between The Boys – because of her father's bit of land.

"I shall tell Master Baxter on it if you don't keep your mitts to yourself," she warned him. Thereafter Dan left the rights to her bodice laces to Peter, and satisfied his self-esteem by telling her she wasn't no oil painting anyway.

From the first Vinnie felt protective toward Jaen. It was funny really, them being the same age. In some ways she seemed really young, yet she knew more than the rest of them put together, and she didn't think anything of going to Blackbrook market. Vinnie had never been to Blackbrook and longed to go there.

Vinnie took to Jaen as she had never taken to anyone. Jaen was different, yet she didn't seem to realise it. Kath and Myrtle too agreed about Master Dan's wife when they chewed her over in low voices on their pallets of bracken on Jaen's first day at Up Teg. "If you put her in a silk gown, you wouldn't hardly know her from a lady."

"The way she stands, with her hands folded."

"And the way she talks – an't she got a nice way of talking."

"Ah. You'd a thought she'd have a hard voice being on the market and that."

Instinct, or perhaps perceptiveness, told Vinnie that Dan's wife had got herself into deeper water than just being married to one of The Boys. Jaen seemed out of her depth, frightened and bewildered. She jumped and started like a deer whenever Baxter or one of the older Boys spoke direct to her, and seemed near on the verge of tears when they started on, like they did to everybody, criticising and that. Especially the old man.

Vinnie was used to him now, and had never been really afraid of him; even when she first came to Up Teg as a girl she hadn't never been scared of him like Jaen was. And it wasn't just him. There was only young Edwin who didn't make Jaen tongue-tied. Why? It was obvious to anybody that she wasn't no ordinary girl. By all accounts she had been helping with the running of her mother's farm for years, as well as having the buying of animals and doing business in Blackbrook market. She must be a sight more clever than Dan Hazelhurst, or any of them for that matter – except Peter, Peter was the clever one of that family – but even Peter couldn't count up things quick, like Jaen could.

Vinnie was lucky it was Peter who took a fancy for her – a serious fancy, he really wanted them to be wed. Peter was all right.

On that first night, the wedding night, when Jaen came to Up Teg, Vinnie hadn't been able to go to sleep for half an hour or more thinking about her. Not once had she smiled in the church . . . not even when the vicar had said "man and wife"; she had just sort of looked to the side, where Mrs Nugent was standing, not at Dan at all. At the feast, she never ate a crumb, and hardly spoke two words all the way back from Cantle.

"I heard Miz Nance say there wasn't no men in Mrs Dan's fambly. It's probably that as makes her jump when they comes shouting in at the kitchen door," was Myrtle's explanation.

Kath had a more lewd suggestion – she always had. The huddle of girls in the out-house had a good laugh at the expense of they-in-the-house, having a laugh at them behind their backs always did you a bit of good.

The better Vinnie got to know Jaen, the more she liked her but the less she understood her. How could she a got herself poddy like that? You couldn't really picture Jaen letting a blimmen hulk like Dan getting his great red hands down her bodice, let alone up her skirt, and you couldn't never in a hundred years imagine her enjoying it, not like herself with Peter. It was funny really, Dan wasn't the biggest of The Boys, but there was something about him that made you think that he was.

In the end, Vinnie came to the only reasonable answer to it. Dan

Hazelhurst had just took her . . . he was like that . . . it was the sort of thing he would do, and she wouldn't a had a chance, hardly up to his chest and looking as though a puff of wind would blow her away.

Vinnie was scarcely taller than Jaen, but she was equal to the Heighth and Breadth of any of The Boys.

6

TOWARDS THE END OF MAY, Vinnie felt the first quickening.

"Is that it, Jaen?"

Jaen agreed that the small flutter was the baby.

"I should a thought it'd been a bit different than a bit of wind, it an't no different than a little ramper running round in your belly after eating peas."

Jaen had begun to establish a place for herself in the dairy. She was good at that kind of work, and it gave Them less chance of picking holes in her; They couldn't say anything about her butter-making, people in Blackbrook had been paying good money for the butter she used to make back home in Cantle.

The two pregnant girls worked there long hard hours, scrubbing, skimming, churning, separating, cooling, patting, pressing and talking.

Talking.

Quiet female voices, talking in the cool, dim outhouse. Low female voices using the ancient language – words strung together in half-sentences. The language whose vocabulary includes intuition, humour, sensitivity, and looks that go in through the darkest dot at the very centre of the pupil. The universal language . . . understanding.

My eyes red?

It hurts . . . but it's better than . . . better than keeping it to yourself . . .

You know?

Don't take no notice of me.

. . . a good cry, you'll feel better.

Don't worry too much.

All kids is like that.
You'll get over it.
I know, I know! Yes. It was the same with me . . .
. . . same with my mother.
. . . same with my old Gran.
Oh, it does you good to laugh.

The language of good women who, from earliest times, said I know, I know. They brewed bitter herbs for one another to expel the rape-child; they made concoctions of oil to hold the wanted child in a fragile womb until it could be born; they impregnated little pads of fleece with lard or butter and told one another it was the best way they knew. If that didn't work and there was another miscarriage, protracted labour or half-formed child, they held one another and said I know, I know, it was the same with me.

Women who had lived there thousands of years before the place became Up Teg, would have understood what went on in the dairy that summer in 1780.

Vinnie and Jaen talked by the hour of the most extraordinary of any human experience, the growing of one being inside another. They stood facing one another as Jaen listened to Vinnie's baby with her hands, then Vinnie felt the more pronounced movement in Jaen, then they each placed a hand on both bellies, comparing.

"Yourn's a strong little toad and mine's only a taddy. Still, it means Peter have to see about getting us a wedding. Mrs Nance says she wants us wed and settled before I'm too far along. But it means a bit of a shift, and I don't expect Master Bax will allow it just at the busy time of year. Yet if we waits till harvest time's over I shall be big as Barney's Barn."

Jaen said, "I reckon you ought to be living in the house, instead of out here."

Vinnie laughed. "Mrs Nance reckons 'tis better for the girls because she can hear every word through the wall, so it's like part of the house. Anyway, it suits me now the weather's hot. I don't know how you can abide being shut up in that end room of a night."

The way Jaen looked for a moment, Vinnie thought that Jaen didn't know how she could abide it neither.

7

THERE WAS SOMETHING about the Yard Room. It was just a room, but it gradually got so that Jaen had to pluck up courage to go in at night. She thought of what Vinnie had said about sleeping out over the milking sheds and dairy.

She remembered summer nights, hot nights back at home. All day the fire from the hearth would rise, heating the brick chimney that was on one wall of their little sleeping chamber, and the sun coming through the small dormer window would take every breath from the air.

On nights like that she and Ju would push their bracken-filled pallets through the little trap and climb into the roof-space. There, on the rough plank floor, with the air coming in through the open brickwork and passing over their naked flesh, she and Ju would lie and whisper in the dark. It was probably not much cooler in the attic, but there was space all around them.

In the Yard Room everything pressed in on Jaen. The steep slope of the roof on the window side and the rough box-like platform on which they slept almost filled the room. It was the Yard Room because its window was above a little side-yard where calves and other small animals were sometimes penned, so that there were always flies and dung-smells and noise. Back home, the animals were not so close to the house. Dan's rough, wool shirt smelled of dust and animals and his own sweat. His hair gave off the strawy smell of the wide field-hat he wore all day, and his great bulk seemed to be just too much for the small space. Yet it wasn't really small, there had been no room except for the kitchen at Croud Cantle as spacious as this.

Like all of them, Dan rose before dawn and worked till there was no light left, and when he slept, he slept heavily.

Until Jaen came to Up Teg, she had never taken but a minute to get to sleep – not like Ju who never seemed ready for sleep and would have talked all night – but these days, tired as she usually was, she was wakeful for hours, then slept fitfully, waiting for the next time when he would stretch his legs and pull her to him, expecting her to put her arms about his neck. But she could not always bring herself to do it. She was not stiff, did not reject him, she accepted that he had those rights which the Law and the Church said were his. His rights to Jaen Hazelhurst's body outruled her own and she never denied him.

About this, they always seemed to be at odds: she did not know how to please him.

During the first week or two he teased her, calling her his goat-girl as he had that first time, when he had been bowled over by her fierce response. That time Dan had wooed her with words that sounded like they had come from a part-song or a glee. He had told her he hadn't ever met a maid or woman like her; that she was like hot coals and frost; that she was an elf-maid who ought always to be loved in the fields and woods. Yet soon after the marriage, when she had gone late one evening into the fields to carry him a drink of cider, and had behaved playfully with him, he had stepped back from her.

"That an't no way for a wife."

She had shrivelled at the crush of his rebuke, and the harshness in his voice. Not that Jaen was unused to having words flung at her; she had been brought up on them, but her mother's voice had never made her mouth go dry. Then later that night he used words to her that she had not expected men used to their wives. It was the language of men or the words that a group of women working together at weeding or gleaning will use to one another occasionally, shrieking raucous laughter.

"That's not a very pretty way to ask, Dan," she had said. "I liked it better to be called something more loving."

"It's the most loving words I know."

He had laughed and teased her into whispering those words of love to him, yet when she had teased him with the same words a few weeks later, he had been surly, telling her it didn't become her to act the Jezebel with a child in her. She had felt guilty and foolish.

Jaen began to hate the Yard Room, with Peter and Edwin and Jim out of view but not out of hearing, and the yard-boys and hired labour in the central roof-space just above.

"You'm like a blimmen pile of fleeces, Gel," Dan said.

"Shh, Dan, don't shout so."

"It's a natural thing, nothing they an't heard before."

When it was over, she could curl into his back without fear of making him desireful and sleep and dream – of Dan lying with dead sheep in his bed.

Many times she tried to remember how it happened, what it was like when she had drawn him to her last November. If she could recall a word or a touch, then she thought she might be able to replay the emotion and be glad that she was a wife. But it was gone.

All that she could remember was that she had been standing there. He had come up and put his hands on her face. Then as he started to kiss her, her breath had quickened and she had felt the spasms that sometimes accompanied her half-waking dreams. She had not even noticed the weight of him upon her. It had happened twice more before she went back to Cantle. She had never suspected that this was the secret, the sin, the forbidden fruit. She had eaten a surfeit of that fruit and could take no more.

She wondered if the answer was, that women's bodies contained only a certain amount of heat, enough to give in to the men from time to time, like the rest of female creation. That didn't seem improbable. She wondered if she had used hers all up in that one great explosion.

When Dan was contemptuous she tried to explain herself.

It's probably because of the baby.

After the baby comes, I shall become a proper wife.

It's bound to take all a woman's strength – carrying.

These all seemed to be good explanations for her unresponsiveness toward Dan.

Dan did not think much of her reasoning.

"Vinnie Norris don't seem to have no trouble that way. Just the opposite. You can't move a sheaf of hay lately without finding her and our Pete. I should a thought you'd a been pleased to have some fun while it can't do you no harm."

Jaen felt guilty that, not only could she not have some fun, but she could not give him the fun that Vinnie was giving Peter.

"It a be all right, Dan. Remember, after the wedding, when we was coming over here in the wagon? You said we should be all right when we gets going on our own. So we shall. It's early days. Soon as I get settled down I shall get back to normal."

Normal. What was normal? Was it normal to be like a setty hen, seeing off all the attentions of the rooster? Was it normal not to know what it was to want a man till you were nearly eighteen, then want one uncontrollably, then go dead again?

But really, Dan bewildered her. She would have given anything to fit in with them all, like Vinnie Norris.

Evidently Dan was not very put out by sleeping with a pile of fleeces. He did his work on the farm and often that summer, when there was a good moon, he went with two or three of the other Boys to work on the roof of the little cottage at Ham Ford, and then up to the Bear and Ragged Staff for several pots of dark-brown ale to wash away the day.

Unlike much of Hampshire, where rich landowners had enclosed much of the arable land, downlands and the commons, many of the villages in the Newton Clare area were still "open". There were still a number of small farms, and commons where a family might run a few hogs or graze a housecow as their forebears had done for as long as memory went. But the new ideas were becoming more prevalent and landowners were following the trend towards engrossing several smaller holdings into a large farm. It had happened in Cantle, where almost everything had been enclosed by the Goodenstone family several generations back and where it was now impossible for any man to set up on his own with a strip of land and a few animals.

On the north side of the River Hammet ford there was a rented cottage which adjoined both the Norris land and Up Teg, close to the commons for the pigs and geese. Once The Boys had finished the roof, Dan and Jaen could start up on their own.

8

HAYMAKING

BY THE END OF JUNE the clover leys whose first shoots had fattened the ewes and lambs in spring were, as The Master of Up Teg decreed, 'about ready for downing'. The red clover bloom was full out and the weather was steady and warm with light drying winds. On many small farms such as Up Teg it was necessary to hire daily labour at hay-making, but Master Baxter and Mrs Nance had produced six strong backs and pairs of arms, and five of them had brought good working women into the family.

It was the first time since they had journeyed over to Cantle to see Dan wed that they had all been together. Martha and Luke and their four children walked across to the main farm with the childless Francis and Annie. France was shouldering the twins, whilst Annie took charge of her favourite, Betrisse, who at six was the oldest of the grandchildren. Martha's youngest, born at the turn of the year, was slung in her mother's shawl.

When they arrived at Up Teg, the men went out into the out-houses to see to the rip-hooks and sickles and the women went into the kitchen to join Nance, Vinnie and Jaen who had already prepared the bread, fat bacon and beer to take out for the breakfasts. Automatically Nance looked Annie up and down for any signs, as she always did to the wives.

"You all right then?"

Annie's mouth tightened. "I'm all right."

"Ah well . . ."

They all knew what she was meaning. Annie felt sure that the servants were looking her over, so were Dan's wife and the girl Peter was going to wed. Annie had been going through this for three years now. It was bad enough losing the baby when it was only a few months along, without them for ever watching, and making her feel so bad not getting another. Every month for getting on three years she had held her breath as you might say to see if it was all right.

Sometimes Annie was sure that it was them for ever waiting for her to fall for a child that kept her so tight, kept her so that France had even clouted her for being such a sour bitch.

She knew she wasn't sour – at least she wouldn't be.

It wasn't as if there were no children to follow on. Luke and Martha had produced four in the last six years, Dick and Elizabeth had two, and now the other two on the way.

Annie would have given her right arm to walk about the kitchen like Jaen and Vinnie, or to sit drinking unskimmed milk and eating fat bacon as she suckled a babe like Martha and Elizabeth. As it was she made do with little Betrisse whenever she had the chance. And there was something about Betrisse, something bright that made you pleased to listen to her, wish that she was your own. The one that Annie miscarried wouldn't have been as old as Betrisse, but in Annie's imagination the lost child always had Betrisse's face, personality, brightness.

With the arrival of Elizabeth there were eight women in the kitchen. Nance moved about in her jerky way, giving orders, firmly placing children who were in the way on benches, seeing that the joints of pickled pork were put out for the big meal and that Kath was doing enough turnips and greens and Myrtle getting the bread-oven hot for the bread that Jaen was setting to prove. Annie couldn't stand it any longer.

"Let you and me be off down with some breakfast for your grandfather then." Annie gave young Betrisse some loaves to carry and she herself took a large can of skim.

"Shall I come back for something else?"

"We a manage," her mother-in-law said. "Give Master Bax his first; we shan't be long here now."

Annie was glad to be out of that kitchen, it was like being in a hen-coop with all of them fussing and clucking away. She knew that as soon as she was out of the door they would all be on about her. As she walked down the slope from the house, she wished that she could have gone on and on down with little Betrisse, down on to the Rathley road, and kept going till they got to Emworthy Bay.

Go to Emworthy, and show Betrisse the glitterish sea. Show

her the place where anybody could live and be happy, where the air smelled different, not green and dungy, not anything like here.

Once, as a small child, she had been taken the thirty or so miles to Emworthy to attend something or other – she could never remember what, probably her great-grandfather's burial – and it didn't matter, what mattered was that somebody had taken her to stand for a couple of minutes at the water's edge and told her, "That there's the sea. Have a good look, it a be a long time 'fore you gets another chance. It goes on for a hundred mile or more," and the young Annie had taken in every detail.

"Shall I tell you about when I was little and I went to see the oyster fishers?"

"Oh yes. I likes that tale. Tell us about the glitterish sea like . . ."

"It was like the night sky had turned the colour of the harebells and had a been threshed so that the stars had fell out like corn, then it changed and it was like the waves was winnowing and the stars was the chaff. What it really was . . ."

"It was the sun shining on the sea-water and making it all glitterish."

As she joined in, Betrisse squinted her eyes inwardly. Aunt Annie had told her the same story plenty of times and she had made her own picture of that place, where there was water that you could never see the other side of, and there was cockle-women and oyster-sellers with great baskets, and boats bringing in baskets with lobsters. Aunt Annie had never said what cockle-women looked like, or what lobsters were, nor boats, but Betrisse knew what she knew. She heard the sound of words like "glitterish" and "air that went to the top of your head", and "baskets with lobsters". And she knew Emworthy, it was the place that made Aunt Annie smile, it was their place. Aunt Annie said "We don't tell none of They about it, Bet."

And Betrisse would never tell. She had few enough secrets that They hadn't ferreted out.

And it was there that Annie would have taken Betrisse, away from the eyes that were always searching for signs, from France wishing for a son, and him secretly always blaming her for losing the first one no sooner they was married. From the never-ending stream of girls parading their swaying bellies, flaunting leaking breasts, taunting swaddled babes.

In the first field, the Hazelhurst men and two hired youths were bent into the same shape as the sickles they rhythmically swathed through the grass and red clover. Already the first cuttings were fading in the sun.

Old Baxter drank from the can and tore the top off a loaf. Annie took up a fork and began lifting and turning the hay.

"Still an't managed it then, France?" Dan said with a nod towards Annie.

"I don't know what it's such a great interest to you for, Dan Hazelhurst," Annie said sharply, "and I should a thought there was enough o' you lot without any more for a bit."

Peter paused in the rhythm of cutting. "You'm a poxy devil, our Dan, you can't never say nothing except it's to say summit," he said.

"What you getting so sharp about. It an't but a joke."

"An't nobody never told you your jokes an't funny."

"You should a been a 'ooman, Pete – you'm too soft."

"A'nt no danger of that with you, our Dan."

Soon, the other women came into the field, and The Boys downed tools and came to take their short breakfast. The morning soon passed: as the sun climbed up, the air grew steadily drier. The men took down the growth of hay and the women followed. There was some coming and going of the women between fields and house, Nance to keep an eye on the servants and the food, and Jaen and Vinnie to feed some of the animals.

"It a be a good take from the two fields," was Old Baxter's estimate. "I reckon we shall have hay to sell off a these two." Each of The Boys had a different idea of what use that money might be put to.

At mid-day the women brought out bread and a round of cheese. A cask of small beer was taken from the cool of a north ditch and for half an hour the quiet of resting labour descended upon the field.

Annie took her bread and cheese and climbed the woody slope that bordered one side of the field. Betrisse had flopped down to sleep and Annie had no desire to see the unlacing of bodices or the half-closed eyes of Martha and Elizabeth as they suckled their infants. She had not noticed Dan's wife go up there, but when Annie reached the crest Jaen was already there, sitting leaning back against a tree staring out away from the hayfield.

"Can't you stand it neither?" she said to Jaen.

The girl smiled and shook her head in a way that could have been yes or no – or yes and no. Annie could not make this one out. Of all The Boys, Dan was the . . . What was he? The most "Hazelhurst" of the lot. Of all of them he had the most of everything that people recognised as being Hazelhurst. True he wasn't the biggest, but he was the loudest, the one who showed himself off the most, argued most, knew everything, knew better than anybody, the one who most prided himself on saying right out what he thought "offend or please", and often he did not please.

"Couldn't blame you if you couldn't stand them." Annie sat down, staring out in the same direction as her sister-in-law. "They takes some swallowing when they'm all together."

The girl smiled again. "It an't that. I wanted to look how far I could see. That's Beacon Hill."

They sat not speaking. Suddenly Annie felt her animosity towards the girl dissolve. She remembered that just below Beacon Hill lay Cantle village where she had come from.

The girl was probably missing her mother, longing for her home again.

"It's where you come from, an't it? Near Beacon Hill."

"Our place is just below . . . my mother's place."

"Dare say you find it different now."

The girl nodded.

They were silent for a few more minutes.

"Miss it?"

"Yes."

"Ah, I know. It was like that the first time I got hired. We never had much to miss, except the company."

"It is that."

Annie gave a little laugh. "You wouldn't think anybody could, not with that great herd always coming and going."

"It's my sister. I miss Ju more than anything I ever knew."

Annie could see the girl was biting her lip.

"I never saw her except for a few minutes at your wedding. I dare say that lot frightened her to death."

"It wasn't that."

The girl did not offer to explain, instead she said, "Beacon Hill is reckoned to be the highest hill for miles; you can see fifty miles or more."

"Could you see Emworthy from up there?"

"Where's that?"

"It's the sea."

"Oh you can see that . . . at least on clear days you can. Portsmouth and that's where the sea is."

Annie's heart leapt at that bit of information.

"Portsmouth isn't too far from Emworthy Bay, more westerly but not far away. What do it look like from up there?"

"It's a shining line. It's like a brightness that runs across just below the horizon. It's the Isle of Wight that you can see on the horizon. Well, that's what we was always told."

"I was at Emworthy once."

Jaen said the right thing. "What was it like?"

It was a long time since Annie had not felt hateful to people, but up there with Dan's wife she heaved a sigh and felt a small warmth in her again.

From below they heard their mother-in-law calling, so together they went back to the hayfield.

"Gossiping?" Dan asked as Annie and Jaen started work.

"Ah not half – and all about the best man of the whole Hazelhurst fambly." Annie laughed – a soft laugh that made Nance and one or two of The Boys look sideways at her.

"You a have to go up Keeper's Hill more often, Annie," said Nance. "It's a treat to see you smile."

Betrisse came to Annie walking stiff-legged and red about the eyes.

"What you done then?"

"Doing what she was told not to," Martha said, "and she cut herself."

Betrisse held out her foot for Annie to see the cut.

"It's still bleeding," she said in a sorrowful voice, then self-pityingly, "and you was up there with her."

Annie picked up the child. "Come on then, I a wash it for you with a drop of skim."

The child's face adjusted itself to the satisfaction of having attention paid to her by an adult.

About three hours after the sun had reached apogee, Nance went up to the house to see that the girls had got supper, their big, main meal, cooked.

"Not more than an hour," she ordered, "then you can get in another four or five hours 'fore it's dark."

At four o'clock all the family traipsed into the hot kitchen, followed soon by the hired hands and maids. Kath and Myrtle ladled out great bowls of broth made with chunks of fat pickled-pork, turnips and apples, and thickened with barley and flour, which Annie handed to the men. Nance cut up four-pound loaves for dipping-in and to go with the cheese and apple-sized onions; Vinnie and Jaen poured mugs of ale for the men; whilst Martha and Elizabeth, as they each suckled their babies, saw that the four children had something to eat.

At last they were all seated around the long table in order, Baxter at the head with Nance on his left. On the master's right ranged in order of seniority Luke (older by one hour), Francis, Richard, Dan, Peter, Edwin and the hired men. Beside Nance, this time not in order of age but ranged by seniority of husbands, were Martha, Annie, Elizabeth, Jaen and, for the first time at the table as one of the family, Vinnie. On down the distaff side Betrisse, Kit, Laurie and Lucy and the female servants.

Except for a short grace by Old Baxter, for ten minutes the only sounds that might be heard were the slurp of broth eaten hungrily, belches, and sniffs from noses affected by the steam and onions.

Betrisse tried to move to sit beside Annie.

"You get back to your place," her grandfather ordered.

Betrisse did as Old Baxter's beetle-browed frown bid her, but with her lip tucked up in objection to having to sit with small children.

"You answering me back?" he barked at the little girl.

"No, Granfer, I never said nothing."

"What's that face for then?"

Only six years old or not, Betrisse was up to him; she stopped her pouting and pulled up her top lip. "It's my tooth what's come loose."

The grandfather looked at his son as though Luke too was still six years old. "You a have to watch that one. She got a sight too much to say for a girl."

Luke frowned at Betrisse who drank her broth and looked as though butter would not melt in her mouth. Baxter rumbled on through his bread and cheese, his full whiskers moving with every word and mouthful. Then, as they all knew he would, as he always did when the entire family was assembled at his table, he expressed his dissatisfaction that neither Martha nor Elizabeth had produced a firstborn son to carry on the line properly.

"Six children between you and only two as can carry on the Hazelhurst name."

The small weakly Laurence and the suckling Nicholas were quite unaware of the expectations of their grandfather, nor did Betrisse, the first grandchild, know that she had been expected to be named Baxter, or that he had put his foot down on the naming of each of the other male children, insisting that it got to be a firstborn to take his name on.

He fixed his eyes on Jaen and Vinnie. "Let's hope you two does better. The land can't run on skirts – he needs britches."

Jaen kept her head bowed over her bowl then glanced the head of the family a complaisant smile, but in her mind she was thinking of her mother. Bella Nugent had for years kept their land and their farm in as good fettle as any man could have done, and had brought up Jaen and Jude to do likewise. They did every job from breast-ploughing with a bag of hay stuffed into their bodices, to hedge-laying and taking heifers to the bull. Neither Bella Nugent's nor her daughters' skirts had proved a handicap.

Bella would have found the separation and seating order at Up Teg extraordinary, and she could never have held back a comment on britches and skirts. Croud Cantle was a good little place. She and her daughters were not only good farmers, they were good market traders too. On Up Teg, they sold only stuff that was surplus to their own needs, but on Croud Cantle, they grew and produced specially for the weekly Blackbrook market. The only rules in Bella Nugent's kitchen were not to walk on her red-tile part with wet muck from the yard.

The meal over, most of them went back to finish off the first field, except for France whose responsibility was the sheep. Jaen and Vinnie and the maids went to do their evening work in the dairy.

Quite late, when they could no longer see in the out-houses and lights had to be lit, France came into the dairy. Vinnie and Jaen had finished and were sluicing down the floor.

If Dan was the one with the most Hazelhurst in him, then Francis was the one with the least. Like the others he was tall but, as his mother always said, "France has got all his heighth in his legs" – the others had their height in their square bodies.

Wherever and whenever there was a local merrimaking or sport, the Hazelhurst sons were in demand. Living as they did in the midst of a rural population which, like its forebears for generations, was ill-nourished, harshly-worked, unhealthy and stunted in their growth, the Hazelhurst men were like another race. Even though many of them had taken small women as wives, it was rare for smallness to be passed on to sons. Old Baxter's grandfather was reputed to stand "six foot six a half in his stockinged feet and it took twelve good men to put him in the ground".

They threw hammers, pulled ropes, hurled rings and pole-vaulted streams, and it was the Master of Up Teg's boast that "me and the fruit o' my loins will take on any team o' twenty from any village in Hampshire".

And it was true, they were a fine sight to see.

Although they were twins, France and Luke were quite unalike. From a distance France was easy to pick out from the rest with their straight brown hair; his hair and beard were black and as tightly curled as a negro's.

"You all finished in here?" France asked.

"Just brushing down," Vinnie answered.

"I be going off then, save Annie walking back up here. Tell Kath not to bother with no supper, I shall have it back home."

"Master won't like that," Vinnie said.

"Ah well, I shall have to risk that."

"The weather's going to hold for quite a few days," Jaen said, "plenty of time to get the other leys cut and dried."

When France was on his own he was often willing to perch on the edge of a bench or something and talk quietly. It was only when he was with the others that he adopted the Hazelhurst manner of loud bombast and argument. Whilst Jaen and Vinnie put away the brushes they talked for a while about the weather, and it ended with his offering to walk with Jaen down to the field so that she could get a breath of air.

Late June, after a warm day.

All day, once the dawn pink had dissolved, the sky had been a blue bowl upturned over the green downs and fertile arable fields of Hampshire. The scent of English summer hung on the air, the combination of the perfume of wild-woodbine and wild-thyme, and from the marshy ground heavy meadow-sweet, put Jaen immediately in mind of the bank at the back of the cottage at Croud Cantle. Their mother never liked night air and threatened Jaen and Jude an early death if they breathed in its dangerous humours. But Jaen risked that death and, on warm nights in early summer, she would open the little dormer window a crack and let in the sweet and savoury perfumes.

Ju would keep jumping into her mind when she was least expecting it. There was nothing Jaen could do about it; everybody was too busy this time of year, but Mother was sure to come to 'Clare as soon as she had the time. It was only natural for girls to leave home and not see their own family sometimes for a year or two at a time. But her mother had said that she would ride over as soon as there was a bit of a lull at Croud Cantle.

It was only seven or eight weeks now before the baby was due. Then Ju would be all right. When she saw the baby she would forget that she was ever upset at being kept out of it all till the wedding was arranged.

A single star had come out now, as France and Jaen walked down to where the sound of the family's voices were coming. The sky on the Kent and Sussex side of Hampshire was indigo and on the Wiltshire Somerset side it was pale violet, rose pink and, low on the horizon, a wipe of orange fire afterglow.

That same bit of orange always lit up one of the windows back home and, when Ju was very little, Jaen would tell her the story of how elves spent all day taking pollen from dog-roses and then threw it at the windows of cottages where somebody had been good that day.

"Shepherds' delight," Jaen said.

"Ah, and mine and all," France said.

They said nothing else to one another until they were nearly at the field entrance. Then, as though he were embarrassed, he blurted out, "I an't seen Annie smile in a long time. Did she say something to you when she was up there on Keeper's Hill? She been very sharp and that since she lost her baby. She been very bitter about you and Vinnie Norris, then there was Martha and Elizabeth before. You can understand. Something must have made her smile."

"We was just talking. Nothing special . . . about being able to see the Solent from Beacon Hill."

They walked a few more steps without speaking.

"She was telling me about when she was little and she went to Emworthy."

"Where's that?"

"Further south. Where they catch oysters."

"And was that all? All you was talking about?" He was awkward and hesitant. "It an't that I'm noseying into your woman's talk or nothing like that only . . . she don't say much to me these days."

"We was just . . . chatting like . . ." Jaen dropped the thread of the conversation and waited for him to pick it up. Suddenly it came to her that within France, inside the manly Hazelhurst frame, was somebody as shy in a way as she was herself; somebody who found it difficult to talk about anything other than what was on the surface, work and the weather. It would be even worse for him, being a man, being one of Master Baxter's eldest sons, one of the men who were looked up to in every way in Rathley parish.

"Was you thinking it was . . . well, about a baby? and she hadn't told you?" Jaen could never have said that to him had it not been almost too dark to see properly.

"Ah, summit like that."

"Oh, France, I am sorry, but it was only about how the sea sparkled . . . it was the remembrance of it that made her smile. You know what it's like. There's some things that don't mean much to anybody except yourself, and yet you would always like to be talking about them, so as to bring them back again for a minute or two."

France made no comment; he seemed deep in thought.

"I was lucky, I always had Ju. She was good at listening." Jaen twisted her knife of guilt. "You could tell Ju anything."

9

THE FIRST CUT OF HAY was all in well before the end of June. Early in July, Luke asked his mother if she would walk over to the cottage sometime and have a look at young Laurie, and take some of her fever physic, which she did that same morning.

She got there too late.

The boy, although at first of a promising Hazelhurst size, had been sickly since birth. Covered in dry patches that nearly drove him mad, he scratched till he bled. They had tried binding his hands when he was little, but once he was running around there was not much that they could do to stop him, except trim his nails often. He went about smeared in goose-grease and chamomile and would stop by any scratching-post and rub his back against it like a little animal. Just after the haymaking one of the open sores had festered and the poison had gone round his small body like furze-fire.

Luke made a box for him and they all went down to the churchyard on Old Baxter's insistence. Some of The Boys thought it was an unnecessary thing to do right at a time when every hand was needed to keep the weeds and insects from the crops, but would not dare say so. Baxter Hazelhurst was still head of the family and his word was law.

"That boy would a been the head of this fambly and he a get proper respect."

Of course Nance did not mention that she had gone alone to bury their daughter. Alice, the one and only girl child she had given birth to, five years after Peter. Alice would have been about the same age as Dan's wife and Vinnie Norris now.

Nor did Nance say anything about Luke and Martha's girl baby, who would a been running about the place by now. Nor yet did she speak aloud the thought that the Master of Up Teg had said that they was making a lot of fuss about a babe what hadn't hardly drawn a breath, when Martha and Nance went to the churchyard with the unbaptised bundle – well, twadden as though it was a Christian burial.

But she thought her own thoughts. You couldn't make a to-do about every baby and child that took sick and died, if you did you could spend half your life in and out of the churchyard; but if she was honest, she couldn't really see why Martha's son was worth an hour of Baxter's time, when Alice had not been.

10

IF TORMENT WAS PROPERLY the punishment for the few spasms of delight that Jaen had the previous November, then she received it harshly during the last few weeks of her pregnancy. The hot August days could not have been better arranged to make her more wretched. Even when, in an attempt to put him off, she showed him her bloated legs, even when the child dropped low, Dan continued to exercise the rights that he had bought with the ring. He no longer complained, he consumed her much the same way as he downed beer when he was thirsty.

She found it difficult to sleep. The air in the close room was still and hot, and she got no relief from the baby's restless movement, and she was in and out of bed a dozen times a night. But it was her legs that caused her most trouble. Each morning when she rose, she would look down at the normal feet and legs that she had had all her life, but within an hour they had so changed in shape that it looked almost as though she wore knee-boots beneath her skin.

"Here, drink this." Nance Hazelhurst seemed to be for ever pushing putting a beaker of something into the hands of Jaen and Vinnie.

"It's only mint," she would say or, It's only raspberry-leaves, only evening primrose or only bladder-wrack. And Jaen did as she was bid.

Vinnie would often spit out the stuff no matter what dire consequences Nance threatened would attend at the birthen.

Earlier in the year, Jaen made swaddling bands and soaked them in diluted dung to start the bleaching. Now that they had been washed in the running stream and laid out in the sun they were sweet and white.

It seems to Jaen, as she takes the finished cloths from the bramble bush, that here is some proof that the baby is now whole. It too is finished and can be born. She holds the cloth close to her face breathing in the sweet smell. Now the baby can be born. She can get it over.

Now things will change, it will all be all right. A few days ago the baby dropped low and became sluggish.

Yesterday there had been no movement. She had lain awake for hours last night waiting for it to move, feeling herself, pressing hard to make it respond. Her belly had been as rigid as a hill of chalk. Through the thick, coarse flannel, as she rested her hands upon her body, she was put in mind of Tradden and Old Marl beneath their thin covering of coarse downland grass.

"You all right?" Vinnie calls from across the yard.

Jaen smiles and nods.

"What you doing?"

Why can't they let me bide?

"Only seeing if these are aired."

The baby is dead.

She spreads the cloths back over the brambles and goes off across the yard. It is unusually quiet, there is nobody except Vinnie about. But if they see her go, they will think that she is going down to pick caterpillars off the young greens.

She hears her own voice say, "I can talk to you, Annie," and looks back at the house to see who is there, watching her. It is not the first time she has done it lately.

"Talking to myself again," she says aloud.

She has been doing a lot of queer things just lately, though Mrs Nance has not taken much notice, except to get from Nell Gritt, who is part wise-woman, part cunning man, reputed witch and certain whore, a small bag of herbs and powder to make into a remedy.

The baby must be dead, it is more than a day since there was any movement. Jaen gives a little hop to see if it will respond.

Between the Up Teg house and Keeper's Cottage where France and Annie lived, was a small stand of coppice. The ground around the boles and the pyramids of seasoning poles, was cool and green with fine-leafed spurge, and thick clumps of violets. Some of the trees had been there for generations and had cushions of moss at their roots. The very look of the cool green makes Jaen want to sit there. So she sits, soothing her bare swollen feet and ankles.

The baby's dead.

Jaen tightens her lips and a smile is in her eyes.

There won't be no reason to stop here if the baby's dead.

She leans back against the young pliable growth of coppiced hazel bush. Her mind drifts back home. Real home. Croud Cantle at the foot of Tradden. She goes out of the cottage, out of the yard and then she is climbing.

Climbing Tradden Raike.

On the lower slope there are the dog-roses and brambles. Blackberries just showing fruit. Up past the low growing juniper bushes. Up further. She can smell the medicinal lemony scent of mayweed as she crushes it under her bare feet. Harebells. There is always a breeze on Tradden making the harebells and waggle-grass nod, setting free the silk of star thistles and ragwort. She watches the gossamer rise on the warm air of the valley.

At the top of Tradden the Jaen that has drifted back home from Up Teg can see how the ring of chalk-hills enfolds Cantle. Safety. There is the Big House where Old "Sir" Henry who owns the village lives. The cluster of cottages, church, rectory and, close at the foot of Tradden, their own holding and cottage, Croud Cantle, home.

The homecoming Jaen on Tradden Raike is watching another Jaen as she runs along Raike Bottom and down Howgaite Path, her feet bare and small, her legs slim and her body flat except for neat, dry breasts. She runs into the yard, her red hair spilling from her mob-cap.

Ju is there, with her wild, red uncapped hair. Their mother, yet more red hair, stumps and thumps about with heavy pails of milk or water. Everything is back to normal because the baby will be born dead, and they wouldn't want her at Up Teg any more.

The Jaen in the coppice sees how simple it will be now that the baby is dead.

When she reached Annie's cottage, she called, but there was no one there, so she went to look for her on the common where Annie ran her hogs and geese. Although Jaen had been to Annie's place once or twice before, she had never gone beyond. This common was covered with clumps of closely growing birches. Here and there were a few large oak trees with shrubby undergrowth making it impossible to see very far ahead. Splay-legged and leaning back for balance, Jaen wandered about hoping to come across Annie. After about ten minutes she had to rest.

Once or twice she heard the crack of twigs and rustle of leaves and saw movement. There were a few hens roosting on low branches and a couple of red squirrels. She heard distant voices. She called, but there was no answer. She did not want to go back to Up Teg without seeing Annie, without talking to her. She had to talk to somebody about the baby.

It was impossible to talk to Dan; he would only say, there she was going on about summit foolish again. Nor could she talk to Mrs Nance. Mrs Nance would give her a look. "Saints! What you on about, Gel. You gets some blimmen funny ideas," and give her a dose of raspberry-leaf, and Jaen would feel a fool like she always did. Vinnie would tell her everybody gets queer ideas when it's near their time. "Cheer up, it won't be long now" – but Jaen did not need cheering up.

Right from the start she had not wanted the baby. Had unconsciously forbidden it to exist, at first when she had not needed cloths at the end of the month, and again when the dawn sickness started. Of course she had known well enough that those were the signs, but would not allow reality to escape through the membrane with which she surrounded the obvious facts.

For days it had not been true. The facts had not been named, so the baby had not been created – not then. It had been created when Bella's ferreting eyes had seen the dawn sickness. As soon as the word "baby" had escaped from where Jaen had repressed it, the baby was real.

And now it had all but gone away again.

Because she had lost her own first one, Jaen did not really like asking Annie if she knew what would happen, what must be done, but there was no one else.

She came out from the shade of the bushes and saw France going into his cottage.

"France."

He raised a hand and waited for her to come. His head was bare and where his frizzed jet-black hair stuck to the sweat of his brow, it formed minute curls. Like most men at this time of the year he had no time to spend trimming his beard so that it had become very full, emphasising his long, square chin, emphasising his full and sensuous mouth. Jaen had never realised what a fine and handsome man France was.

The first time that Jaen had met France it had struck her how different he was from the rest of The Boys. He was a Hazelhurst all right on the outside – but his nature seemed to be not like theirs.

"You looks hot, France."

"Nothing to what you do, you looks done in."

He told her to sit in the shade and went to fetch her some fresh water cold, which she drank quickly forgetting Mrs Nance's warnings about cramps and chills.

"I wanted to see Annie."

"What did you come all the way across here for then? You might a known she'd be over at Teg today; we starts on the top field in the morning."

Jaen had forgotten. The top field was ripe, the harvesting started tomorrow.

"You wouldn't a seen me except that I forgot a couple of blades I been sharpening up." France peered at Jaen as he idly drew a honing-stone across the blade of a sickle. "You looks a bit dicky to me, I'm surprised that our Dan let you out, or don't he know?"

"That sounds like I am the dog that turns the spit. 'Don't let her out, else she a be off again as soon as my back's turned.' "

France smiled, said nothing and continued stroking the blade with the long stone.

Jaen leaned awkardly back, eyes closed, resting against the cool flints of the cottage wall. Listening.

"I always like that sound, when it's done gentle. It makes me think if you kept it up long enough, the sickle would make a little tune."

France tucked up one side of his mouth in a half-smile and shook his head. "You'm a blimmen funny one and no mistake."

The way he said it made Jaen look directly at him. He was not scoffing like they did back at Up Teg, when she said something without thinking. If, back home, she were to say, "Listen, the doves is talking about the hens behind their backs," or something fanciful, her mother would behave as though she had not heard, but Ju would join in the fiction.

At Up Teg, she soon learned not to say such things aloud.

But France's voice sounded friendly. Jaen was taken unawares by the gentle merriment in his voice. She blurted out, "I came to see Annie because the baby haven't moved since yesterday."

And suddenly she was crying. Silently. Staring up at the clear blue sky, tears in a steady stream welled up and ran to her ears.

At first France looked awkward and embarrassed, then he said gently, "Come on, Gel, it'll be all right, you see if it an't. It's likely he's just gone a bit quiet before he's birthen."

Jaen pushed the tears away.

"I'm sorry, France, I didn't know I was going to cry like that. It was the relief . . . telling somebody. I was going to tell Annie. I thought she'd know what to do."

"You best let me walk with you back home. It a be breakfast time before long."

Neither of them spoke as they walked. Slowly, at Jaen's ponderous pace. When they were in sight of the house Jaen said, "You won't tell nobody, France?"

"An't nothing to tell."

Jaen snatched a leaf from a sapling horse-chestnut and shredded it, carefully as though it was important to preserve its skeleton whole. They were now going up the sloping clover ley that had been cut back in early summer and was now knee-high again. Vinnie was at the far side, tethering a goat. She waved and began to walk in their direction.

Jaen spoke quietly and urgently.

"I got to be honest, France. I don't want it to be like you said . . . just gone quiet before the baby's born. It's wicked and a sin, and especially with you and Annie not getting one of your own. And I don't wish it dead. But if it is . . . I got to be honest . . . I won't be sorry. And if you feel at all friendly to me, you will tell them it's best to let me go on back home."

Before France could reply, Jaen made a quiet, surprised exclamation, as her waters drenched the hayfield.

11

"I NEVER SEEN NOTHING so quick and easy for a first one." Nance Hazelhurst repeated her amazed comment to Annie and Elizabeth and the other women as they came into the farmhouse. It was not yet dinner-time and it was all over – "Like shelling peas."

Earlier, a message had been sent to Bella Nugent at Croud Cantle to say that Jaen had started birthen. Nance had sent the same message down to Dan in the far field, expecting that it would be evening before anything would happen, but within a couple of hours, Kath went with a second message to say that a girl had been born.

"Is it all there?" he asked and, on hearing that it was a small but healthy girl, he said, "I a come up at dinner-time."

Old Baxter paused in his work long enough to comment that it was a pity they hadn't got theirselves a woman as was better at bringing forth a few sons for a change.

Elizabeth, Annie and Vinnie had been to see Jaen and the baby, and were now rushing around catching up with the dinner.

"Put something aside for Mistress Nugent, she's like as not to come racing over here. I doubt she thinks I knows as much about mid-wifing as she – after all she had two and I only had seven."

"She a be a bit late then," Annie said.

"Who would have thought it though," said Vinnie with admiration. "I haven't never heard anybody be so quick – let alone a first one."

"Raspberry-leaf tea!" said Nance. "You a be sorry you tries to get out of taking it, my girl, when your time comes."

Elizabeth said, "I should a thought they had enough to do at her mother's place without coming traipsing all this way."

"Her mother don't like anything going on without her knowing," said Vinnie.

"She didn't know what went on last winter, with Dan," said Elizabeth.

"No different from what went on with you and me and Vinnie. It's a normal thing," said Annie sharply.

She and Elizabeth were always crossing one another. Elizabeth said that it was because Annie, being the oldest of the wives, thought she was more important. Whilst Annie thought that Elizabeth was always trying to make her look small because she was twenty-eight years old, and she and France had not got any children.

"It's normal when you known each other, but she hadn't never met Dan before. She was a complete stranger coming into the family."

Nance came in. "And now she an't! So you can shut up making trouble, Elizabeth. She's as much a Hazelhurst now as the rest of us."

"Your Dan was so cocksure he was going to have a son," Elizabeth said, not much put out by her mother-in-law.

"Ah, I suppose if he has got a failing, then it is to be a bit sure of hisself." This was about as near as Nance got to criticising any of The Boys aloud; their heighth and breadth and labour compensated for a few faults. The contribution of work she took for granted, as she did her own.

They came in from the fields for their dinner. Dan went up to the Yard Room.

"You all right?" he asked Jaen.

"Yes."

"Didn't take you long."

"No. She seems to have been in a bit of a hurry."

He smiled at her. "I reckon it was you, wanting to be here lying-in instead of out there harvesting tomorrow."

She never knew how to take him. Sometimes when she thought that he was being playful, he was being serious. And he never seemed to understand her. If she had said to him what she had said to France, about the hone-stone on the sickle-blade making a tune, Dan would probably have listened but then, thinking that she was making sport of him, said, "There's times when you talks like a two-year-old."

So, in spite of the smile indicating he was being light-hearted with her, Jaen turned the comment away and said, "An't you going to look at her?"

Gingerly turning back the wrap, she showed Dan the creature they had made in their moment of passion on a cold November evening.

Disappointed at the smallness of his daughter, whose hair was the distinctive red of her mother's family, Dan Hazelhurst grinned at his wife and said, "We shall have to try again then, see if we can't get a boy next time."

After he had gone, Jaen steeled herself to look again at the child.

Whenever she had thought about it over the past months, whenever she had imagined herself with the baby, picking it up, carrying it, Jaen had imagined it to be as it had been with Ju as a baby. It was a false picture that she created for herself, because the baby Ju she remembered best was a plump, curly-haired responsive eighteen-month-old child.

The baby that Nance had placed beside her was not that nice little Ju. This one had swollen slit eyes, no eyebrows and only a little cap of red hair. It was as skinny as a paunched rabbit.

There was nothing about this child that Jaen could take to.

Vinnie came heavily up the stairs carrying a bowl of fermity and a drink. When Jaen saw what was in the beaker, she made a grimace.

"I thought I should a been finished with raspberry-leaf tea."

"Miz Nance says it will pull you together again. I know how you can't abide the taste, so I put a couple of good dollops of honey in it. I'd drink it for you, Jaen, so she won't know, except that you have got to have plenty to drink for the babe."

Jaen smiled. "That's true sisterhood, Vin, seeing as you don't like it any more than me – and I expect you've had a pint or two already today." She drank off the tepid liquor.

"She let me brew my own today – so I took a licorice powder instead." Vinnie hunched her shoulders and laughed silently like a girl at having got one over on Nance.

"It gives me the runs, but I can't ever resist licorice." Ever since she had come into the room, Vinnie had kept her eyes on the baby tucked in beside Jaen. Nance had said the baby should not be picked up much till its back was set strong, but it was in Vinnie's nature to want to pick up every kitten and piglet and tell it that it was a poor little soul.

"An't she the most beautiful little creature. Can I hold her? Look at her hair. An't you lucky, Jaen, she an't got," Vinnie lowered her voice, "nothing of they," she pointed down. "Except maybe a little bit about the mouth. But that don't matter if she gets the sort of Hazelhurst mouth like Peter and France. Their mouths is all right. Not that I mean Dan's an't . . . but you know."

Easily and naturally she held the tightly-bound baby in the crook of her arm.

"Oh Jaen, just look."

The baby was doing nothing except turn its face naturally into Vinnie's breast.

"That's what I'm waiting for. Don't you think that's the most nicest thing in the world. Did she suckle strong?" Vinnie put the knuckle of her little finger to the baby's lips. "Look, look Jaen, she's hungry. Here, let me put her to you."

"In a minute, Vin, in a minute."

Vinnie thought she heard something in Jaen's voice like she was tetchy or something.

"They do say it hurt a bit when you start, but not bad."

Jaen drank milk and ate the stewed wheat and cream, whilst Vinnie sat by the dormer window on a low nursing stool, rocking and making a low humming.

"Where are they all?"

"The Boys and the labour, and Annie, have gone back to the sheds getting things ready to start cutting – you have to feel sorry for Annie times like these. France and she would give anything," she kissed the baby loudly, "anything to have one like you. Miz Nance is out looking for the eggs. Martha has gone back to let out the geese. She do seem sharp these days, but it is always hard for the mother when a little'n like Laurie gets taken. It's bound to happen . . . my mother used to say God picks and chooses only the best." She stopped short and drew in a breath.

"Oh Jaen. I didn't mean . . . That's just like me. I never was able to think before I said something. Don't you worry. This one's as strong as a little ox . . ." She stopped again and said dejectedly, "I am a blimmin stunpoll, Jaen. I'm that sorry. I sometimes wonder how people put up with me."

She laid a hand on the bedcover and Jaen covered it with her own.

"If it hadn't been for you these last months, Vinnie, I don't know what I should have done. You're such a happy thing, such a bright light. And I missed Ju that much."

Vinnie thought that Jaen wasn't just saying that, but she really meant it. Though why she should, Vinnie would never understand, when she herself was such a great lump, and Jaen was so clever.

Sometimes when they were working together at the tedious dairy jobs, jobs like scalding and scrubbing, Vinnie would get Jaen adding and working things out. Vinnie never doubted that Jaen's answers were right, you could tell that they must be by the way she looked when she was working the numbers out. Jaen would half-close her eyes and look as though she could see inside her skull . . . "sixteen and a half pounds at fourpence ha'penny . . . six and tuppence farthing . . . ninepence-three-farthings change out of seven shilling."

When Vinnie had asked if Jaen could learn her, Jaen had said she would, of course she would, except that she would have to think how to tell Vinnie, as she never knew how she had learned herself, except by going on Blackbrook market with her mother for eighteen years.

Vinnie reluctantly tucked the baby in beside Jaen.

"I shall have to get back. If you want anything, shout and I shall hear you in the dairy below. It a be nice and quiet for a bit. Get rested so your mother will see you nice and rosy when she gets here."

"I doubt she will come yet – they'll be busy back home."

Vinnie collected the bowls and made to leave the room, hesitated, then came and sat beside Jaen.

"What you said . . . about me being bright. I got to be honest. I don't always feel like that, it's just that you got to make the best of it, haven't you?"

Jaen nodded.

Vinnie went on, "Only I thinks too much of you to have you think false of me. It's Pete that makes me bright." She fiddled with the things she was carrying, obviously having something else to say.

"You and Peter are just right for each other," Jaen said.

"I wasn't going to say nothing today – it being special for you and that . . . but I have to tell you. We are getting wed, soon as harvest is over."

"Oh Vin, I am so glad about that. I expect that a mean a big feast – wedding and harvest in one."

When Vinnie was back in the cool dairy she thought about how lucky she was. If she hadn't sent Dan off with a flea in his ear, she might have found herself married to him, instead of getting Peter who was worth a score of the others – a hundred of Dan. It was a shame that such a sweet thing like Jaen was should have to get Dan.

Vinnie would have liked everybody to be content, and not have bad things happen. When you think about all the hardship. The months of labour going into growing a crop then seeing it get the blight or mildew, or seeing a year's work go down in half an hour of hail. And the old men who can't stand straight, and the idiots who do things. They make people laugh, they'm always a bit of fun. That must be as bad as anything, Vinnie thought, to find your baby was an idiot.

She makes a short prayer that hers will not be like that, but if that was what God said you must have, then there wasn't nothing you could do. But it always do seem such a waste. Vinnie can never make God out. He is so wasteful. He makes oak trees grow, then blasts them down with lightning; he lets cabbages fill out then sends a plague of caterpillars – but then perhaps He thinks the caterpillars should be fed, or perhaps it is just teaching people a lesson about Him being Master.

Vinnie cannot see that people are all that sinful to keep on being punished.

God is hard to understand.

But he don't need to waste the children surely. All the waste of children there is, makes your heart bleed.

Sometimes Vinnie thinks how nice it'd be, to be able to wake up in the night and not to have the worry of things. Like Martha's secret crying over little Laurie. It was all very well anybody saying to her, "You an't the only one who got a child in the graveyard," a mother was bound to feel sad when it happens. It isn't so bad for men, they don't never take much notice of their children till they'm able to fend for theirselves a bit – but for a woman . . . once you hold a child to the breast you are bound to get fond, even though it looks like it won't live the year out . . . even if turns out to have summit wrong.

Vinnie hurts for Martha's misery.

12

JAEN HAD SLUMPED into a fatigued sleep. She had spent a little time looking at the babe and trying to get some better sort of feeling towards it – like Vinnie had done. It hadn't even been her own child, yet you could see she was just natural and loving towards it.

She was wakened by a donkey whose braying she recognised, one of the animals from home, and the sound of her mother telling it to bide quiet. For a few seconds Jaen was nonplussed at finding herself in bed in the daytime. Then she heard some little mewing sounds from the baby. Jaen's heart lightened. Mother had come. At this busy time of harvest.

By the slant of the sun it was late afternoon, which meant that she had given up half a day to come to Newton Clare. Was Ju come too? She felt so free with the pressure on her ribs gone and her legs up and so elated at her mother's coming, that Jaen determined to show her what a good mother she herself would turn out to be. She picked up the baby and held it in the crook of her arm.

When Nance Hazelhurst opened the door, Jaen saw her mother, glowing, red; cheeks reddened by little broken veins and red showing on her brow and at the nape of her neck. Mother, robust and solid compared with her newt-like mother-in-law. Upright, wearing a fresh cap and neckerchief, she was handsome.

Jaen flushed with pleasure at the sight of the other red appearing from below – Ju's mop of wild red hair. Ju had come. Jaen swallowed a ball of tears, afraid of the bother it would cause if she let them fall in the presence of either of the older women. Her mother was no end of a Tartar and had no time for such weaknesses as tears.

"Here's your mother come to see you." Nance stepped into the room and looked proprietorially at the baby, establishing who was who, and what was what. "I'll leave you to it."

"Well then!" said Bella Nugent. There was only the low nursing chair so she sat on the bed.

Jaen, seeing herself the picture of motherhood, and wanting to please her mother and show her that everything was just as it should be, held out the baby for them to hold and inspect.

It was an easy meeting after all. To look at Ju with the baby, nobody would ever imagine that five or six months ago there was such a rift between her and Jaen that Ju would not speak and only came to the wedding because their mother had insisted that she be there.

"You sprung it on everybody quick enough by all accounts. Is it true it was all over in a few hours? I can't hardly believe it."

When Nance Hazelhurst had greeted Bella Nugent with the news that the baby was already birthen, it was a girl and it looked like the Nugents, Bella had wanted to know why it took the boy with the message so long to travel the few miles from Up Teg to Croud Cantle because she had wanted to be with her daughter in her labour. She found it hard to believe Nance's story of how Jaen had gone off walking early in the morning, showing no signs that her time had come until the child was nearly there. But now that Bella had heard the story from Jaen's own lips she had to believe it and, as they all had done earlier that day, shook her head in amazement at such a little bit of a thing like Jaen doing it as easy as that.

During the visit, Jaen did everything that was expected of a new mother. She spoke seriously and asked her mother's opinion and advice, she showed no doubts and disguised her anxieties with smiles. Jude was absorbed in the baby, talking to it as though it could understand.

There had been changes back home. Jude was now going to market regularly and there had been some arrangement with Mr Warren at the cornmarket to teach Jude to read.

"She got this notion in her head and . . . well, you knows Jude, she won't take 'no' for an answer, so I thought she might as well . . . seeing she was so keen and that. She promised faithful that it wouldn't interfere with her labours, and I got to admit, so far it haven't . . . but new brooms sweep clean, we shall see whether she's just as eager come November when it comes to going over to Motte on a Sunday."

Jaen could see that her home was slipping away from her, they were doing things that did not include her. Ju suddenly saying she wanted to learn to read like that; Ju seeming suddenly to have small breasts: Mother wearing a neckerchief Jaen had not seen before.

Ju, who had been so wretched and dejected that Jaen had not told her that she was pregnant, was now bright and cheerful, behaving as though nothing had ever been wrong between them. Suddenly she saw the reality . . . by turning into Dan Hazelhurst's wife, she no longer belonged to her mother and Ju. Dan Hazelhurst's wife was somebody to be visited from time to time. Between visits they would be doing things that had always included herself. Between visits Ju would be growing up, growing away. She could not bear to think of it.

The time went too quickly and they had to start for home again. The light was going and there were some tricky bits of track between Newton Clare and Cantle. Jaen followed their journey in her mind, wanting to be making it with them, wanting to see what had been going on there.

Her mother had got the baby sucking properly and Jaen persevered with holding it to her, trying to ignore the contractions and the soreness by thinking about Ju and Mother, about living here these last sixteen weeks or so, and things changing back home. Behind her back almost, things had been going on in her own home.

They had made changes in the work routine.

Ju had already stepped into Jaen's role on market days. To fill Ju's place, they had taken little Johnny-twoey away from bird-scaring and stone-picking.

Strange to think of that.

Little John Toose. She had scarcely ever given him a moment's thought. He did have parents, and there were many other Toose children, yet she had always thought of Johnny-twoey as a waif, living more like the stray dogs and cats who found enough at Croud Cantle to keep body and soul together. He had never done anything except earn a few pence like any five-year-old. He must have been growing up and she hadn't noticed. They used to leave Ju to see to the place on market days, when she was the same age.

Ju learning to read. Mr Warren had given her a magnifying glass and she had gone all round the Yard Room peering at things; she had even undone the baby's wrap to look close at its hands, and got a telling off for it. Poor Ju. And Ju was right when she had responded to the telling off by retorting that it wasn't so long ago that Jaen would have been just as interested. And that was true, but life at Up Teg didn't allow of such things. It was all so . . . tied down, so full of noise and people, men's voices from cock-crow to night.

Back home in the evenings, after Ju's chatter had ceased, there was at times only the click and whir of the spinning wheel and an occasional hiss and rustle of burning wood on the hearth.

She could not get out of her mind how Ju had filled out. Watching her today, Jaen saw that at twelve, Ju was almost a woman. It might not be long before she too might find herself like this; frightened and bleeding and hurting; pretending that she was like other girls, pretending that she loved the child she had so easily conceived and, almost as easily, expelled into the world. She watched her own pathetic attempt to make it feed and its own reluctance to turn to her as it had turned to Vinnie earlier. Unfathomable little creature. It had held itself still for more than a day, it had lulled her into believing that it was dead and that everything would be as it was before.

13

VINNIE AND PETER were married at the end of September. There had been a better harvest than anyone had expected; there was an abundance of apples so that plenty of cider was being pressed; hogs had fattened well so that good joints of bacon were cured and pork pickled.

It had been decided that Dan's daughter was to be named Hanna and, although the child was not yet christened, Jaen had gone to church and got herself properly cleansed of Hanna's birth, so that she might go to Vinnie's wedding.

The re-thatching of the cottage at Ham Ford that Dan and Jaen were to have was not far off finished. There had been a bit of moving around in the Up Teg household so that Vinnie could move in with Peter until they could have the Yard Room.

Old Baxter gave the instructions as to what they would have. "If there's one thing the Hazelhursts knows, it's how to have proper festivities." And it was true.

They chose Saturday for the wedding and it seemed that half the parish would come to the feast. Early in the morning, the horns of the oxen were polished up and beribboned, and paper rosettes and streamers were attached to both the beasts and the wagon.

Vinnie loved every minute of the preparation. Although she still had a fair time to go, her stocky figure looked already overwhelmed, but that did not stop her working like a Trojan.

All the women had helped in the extra spinning and Nance had got some weaving out-work done so that Vinnie might be nicely turned out. Peter had gone down into Rathley without telling anyone and had got made for Vinnie a pair of fancy shoes and a cloak.

She laughed and cried simultaneously, and kissed him in front of them all, and told them, "There an't a better man in the world than Peter."

When she climbed into the wagon, dressed in a blue-dotted skirt with full gathering, bustled back and aproned front, she did not look nearly so overwhelmed and near her time as she did in her working clothes.

"I don't feel like me," she said, patting a tucked neckerchief that Jaen had made and frilled cuffs from Annie.

"Well," said Martha, "you wants to try, because it's the last chance you'll have. By mid-day you'll be somebody else."

Had Vinnie been a vixen, a hind, a doe, or a female of any species other than human, she would have been her own possession to give to her mate. But Vinnie Norris was a young woman, and by giving herself to Peter several months ago without the permission of a male member of the Norris family, had done a thing that had to be put right. There being no other male of the Norris family to be in ownership of Vinnie, she was to be given away by her young brother James.

Since they had taken him into Up Teg as a child, Jim had gone about the place almost unnoticed, doing as he was bid by the family. And that was how he liked it. Vinnie liked to be at the centre of things, but Jim kept to edges and quiet corners and spoke when he was spoken to. Jim was small, and seemed only ever half-well. The Boys joked about him in their friendly way – "Careful when you step back else you'll squash Jim underfoot." He took it all in good part because he was closely attached to Vinnie, and Vinnie wanted to be a Hazelhurst. Today Jim would give her to them.

St. John's church, Newton Clare, had its foundations in Saxon mud and its walls built and rebuilt upon them several times since; those now standing were almost two hundred years old. The swaying oxen plodded largo, splendid and extravagant, drawing from villagers and cottagers the same comments as when the beasts were last got up fine for Dan's wedding at Cantle in the spring just gone. Everybody liked a show, and Baxter Hazelhurst was one to give it. The Boys wore their elaborately embroidered linen holiday-smocks, and the women looked well-fed and decently clad. The master of Up Teg sported a neat wig, high black hat and cut-away coat.

"Why look, 'tis the king hisself," somebody called to him. Baxter, loving his own exhibition, doffed his hat with two hands and replaced it on his head as though a crown, and bid Nance wave.

"And I feel like a princess," Vinnie told Peter. "One day we shall sit up like Master Bax and Mrs Nance, and you shall wear a tall hat."

Peter, liking Vinnie to be pleased, and glad himself that he had got himself a good, happy woman who thought he was superior to any other man, and who looked strong enough to give him a family equal to his father's, gave her plenty of squeezes and hearty kisses on her cheeks.

It took but a few minutes for the boy to give the woman to the man.

Luke's voice calling the new husband to "Gid her a kiss then, Pete," brought forth cheers and laughs enough to sound like a whole troop of soldiers.

"Mrs Peter Hazelhurst!" Vinnie announced herself to her new family.

"Come on, Peter, we shall walk back arm in arm."

"No, Gel," Baxter told her, "you get on up in the wagon. I an't got the oxes all polished up to go back empty."

"Thank you, Master Bax, but me and Peter a walk so as we can talk to everybody along the way. Me and Peter shall walk. I made up my mind to that."

Baxter Hazelhurst was about to lay down the law, when Vinnie went up and gave him a loud kiss.

"You done me proud, Father Hazelhurst, and I thank you. Now you and Miz Nance lead us off in the wagon, and we shall follow and everybody shall walk behind us. That way we shall make a longer procession for everybody to see."

Something came upon Vinnie Norris as soon as she announced herself as Peter's wife. It was like when butter comes; before that moment all the elements are there, gathering, not yet anything except separate, tiny globules of fat suspended in solution, then one turn of the handle and there is butter.

Before that morning, every element that was to make the young wife was within Vinnie, and had been waiting to turn ever since she decided that she wanted to be married to Peter. He had given her a ring and his name, and the butter had come.

"Say 'Mistress Hazelhurst'. Go on, let me hear you say it." As they walked she chattered and laughed excitedly. The sight of her lifted women momentarily.

"It's a shame her mother and father an't alive to see her happy."

"If they was alive it probably wouldn't have happened, and Pete Hazelhurst would a put it in some other wench."

And it was agreed that the ill-wind of being orphaned had blown Vinnie's way, the good of a share in the Hazelhurst fortunes.

Vinnie Hazelhurst was probably as happy as any woman in England on that September day in 1780, and Baxter Hazelhurst allowed himself to be won over and told what to do.

With Peter on one arm and Jim on the other, Vinnie, flushed and bright-eyed, ordered a procession behind them.

Last year, the Hazelhursts' near neighbour, Original Day, had put on a wedding for his last daughter which was still bright in the memory of the villagers of Newton Clare for its abundance and pleasure. There had been food, drink and music. It had rankled with Baxter that Ori Day should have outdone him. Ori and Baxter had been neighbourly rivals since they each became masters of farms at about the same time, and they had fared about equally, except that Baxter, by producing such an abundance of sons, considered himself to have achieved the advantage over Original, who had produced only daughters. Except at weddings, when the Hazelhursts often must travel to the woman's parish.

Baxter had always put on good harvest and holy-day feasts, but this was the first time that there had been a wedding at Up Teg.

"Now we shall show Ori Day what a feast means," Baxter had said.

He held back on the normal use of one of the barns and now planks of wood had been set up as tables to hold the food; large casks of best ale and cider were taken there and broached; extra benches had been knocked-up for the occasion and bales of hay brought in for people to rest upon, and everyone commented upon the vast number of pitch torches, bonfires outside, and horn-lamps, oil-dips and candles within. There was an abundance of light, even in the barn where it was thought to be a novelty, seeing as how nobody needed that much illumination to find their mouths for their victuals nor their feet for the dancing. But Baxter felt that the jokes of his neighbours about it being "better'n 'Day' light" were a satisfactory return on his outlay in expensive candles.

From early evening neighbours and friends began to gather. The Hazelhurst women and scullery-girls went back and forth between house and barn with baked fowls, pies and tarts which were in addition to the cold meats, cheeses, fancy breads, pickles, spiced hams and belly-pork. All the women up to their armpits in food – excepting Vinnie, who had kept on her wedding finery and presided over Baxter Hazelhurst's wedding day as though it was her own, and Baxter, still in his wig, ordered, pointed and rubbed his hands.

"We shall show Ori Day what a feast means."

And he did. As well as the usual fiddler for dancing, Original Day at his wedding feast had engaged a horn as well. At Baxter's celebration, there was added a tambourine and a drum.

Ori, after the first, hungry wave of eating had passed, had called all those who liked to see the feathers fly, to follow him into the yard where a pit had been made, and three good rounds of cock-fighting were put on for their entertainment. Baxter provided two bull-baiting dogs and set them about each other, followed by a rope-pulling contest, a story-teller and a singer of tragic and merry songs.

The bride loved every minute.

"Nobody in the four parishes an't never had a wedding like ours, Peter, have they?"

Peter agreed that his father had done pretty well by them.

Nance Hazelhurst, knowing her own weakness when there was brandy and rum about, at first decided to stick to cider, what with Edwin getting hair on his chest lately and wanting watching when there was the heady mixture of strong brew and music and wenches. But she soon decided that if he was going to do it, her abstinence would not put the stuns on him, and so settled herself down to enjoyment.

Another one to enjoy herself to the fullest extent, was Betrisse.

When they had gone over to Cantle in the wagon for Dan's wedding, They had said she might have a new shift for the occasion, because the one she already had was getting felty from washing. When it was nearer the day and her mother still had not got the cloth wove nor had the packman come, Betrisse had asked when she would get it.

"Saints child!" Martha had said. "Cloth costs money."

Why did They always do that – say something would happen, then forget, and then get cross for carking them about it?

Betrisse had contained her hot anger until it cooled down to pique, for she had learned that anger only got her a clout, then said sullenly to Martha, "I wished you hadn't a said about it. Then I wouldn't never a thought about it."

But she had thought, and she was learning, watching what went on, and learning. She knew that her father had times when he would do things you wanted . . . help make a kite out of an old rag, or get it down when it got into a tree, or bend a bit of ashwood to make a bow, or listen properly to what she said. He was best at listening when he had been to the Bear with the uncles.

"Pa, if I gets a full pile of stones out of the top field, will you see that Ma gets a shift for me?"

"My life child!" Luke had said. "It'd take somebody bigger'n you to get a full pile, as well as see to your other labours."

"But if I do."

"Ah, so be it then."

"Shake hands on it?"

Her father had roared with laughter. Betrisse was not quite sure why, They did that sometimes when she was being serious, especially Edwin. But Luke had shaken hands, and Betrisse had worked herself into the ground, and had felt pleased when she had shown him the stones.

"Faith! That's not a bad bit of work for a little 'n," he had said, and later when They did not know she was listening, he had said to Martha, "She got some go in her, that one. Now you see to it she gets a shift, and get a bit of decent pretty stuff."

"And what about me?" her mother asked.

"Come on then," he had said, "I a show you summit you can do to earn yourself a bit of ribbon."

Martha had said get thee behind me, tis Sunday, and had laughed. It was one of the Sundays when things were nice, when they did things like have a song after supper. Sometimes it was like that, and when it was, Betrisse wanted it never to stop. When her Pa and Ma laughed.

And now she had the shift. Boughten yellow cotton with a darker yellow buttercups pattern, and a little cap that Annie had made her.

Now, flouncing so that she could get full pleasure from the feel of the thin stuff against her bare legs, with the barn crowded, and full of talking, moving mouths and greasy chins, she went to her grandfather and told him, "This'n is the best wedding I ever been to in my whole life."

It wasn't prattle, she was serious and she wanted him to know. Theirs was not a society in which "please" or "thank you" was ever used, except to their betters, so that Betrisse had no way of articulating what she wanted to say to Baxter. Nevertheless it would have been "thank you" had she known. She guessed that he would likely laugh or say "yes yer onner", which she never understood, but she didn't mind, she wanted to let somebody know how she felt, and it was Granfer who had laid on the feast.

Mellow and unusually genial from rum and compliments, Baxter picked up his eldest grandchild and stood her on a high trestle in the midst of the food, beside the centrepiece, a decorated boar's head. "There Missie, now you can tell the whole a Newton Clare."

Betrisse looked down at Baxter Hazelhurst, her mouth set in typical Betrisse mould – not exactly saying 'No I shan't.' It wasn't fair making her say it to everybody. What she said was to Granfer, not for neighbours to laugh at. She looked around, and suddenly her insides clenched with excitement – she was higher up than anybody in the room. People were looking at her, and she was higher than them all. She had attention.

"Well, Missie? Go on, tell 'm."

Betrisse ignored him, absorbed in the scene from her new point of view. She could see right down the full length of the barn. There was Father and France and Dan standing together; there was Edwin, Peter, Granfer and they all looked at her with the nice smiles they always got when they was a bit boozy. She returned her gaze to her grandfather. Most children of rural labourers spoke with stumbling shyness, inarticulate from the many hours they spent alone from quite an early age, banging clappers at birds, weeding or picking flints from the earth.

But Betrisse spoke up, fluently.

"I been to Dick's wedding, and I been to Annie's wedding and I went to Dan's, and I went to Master Day's big feast, but this b'st the best 'n I ever been to."

Amused laughter and cheers came from Luke and her uncles, and Betrisse felt warm with pleasure. Baxter lifted her high once, then set her down. She wished for the wedding to go on for ever.

It was a pity that Betrisse was not the male heir that Baxter had wanted from Luke's firstborn child, for he was so pleased at the way she came out with her praise, that he might at that moment have given her the Up Teg seal from his watch-chain. It was not a true seal, but a coin that Baxter's great-grandfather had dug from Up Teg soil. He fingered it, thinking of the tableau that might have been staged if she'd been a boy.

Betrisse went to Annie who was seated on a hay-bale with Jaen. Annie said, "You'm a proper little poppy-show, young Bet," and picked out a few almonds from the boar's head for her.

"Is it always men who grow tall, Annie?"

"They don't all grow like the men in this family," Jaen said.

"But an't there any women who's tall enough to look down?"

Annie looked at Betrisse sideways, as Annie did when she wasn't going to answer.

"I don't want to grow little like you and Ma and Auntie Liz. I wants to be like all The Boys and Granfer."

"You wants to eat your turnips up then."

Sometimes Annie could be like the rest of them, treating her like Kit and Laurie. And there in the middle of the happy feast, she remembered that Laurie was dead, and she got angry with him again.

"What did Laurie die like that for?"

The quick turn-abouts in her niece's thoughts was part of Annie's liking to have the child about her.

"He got a fever, you know that."

"What did he get the fever for? I got a fever, and I never died."

"You was lucky then."

"I didn't want him to die. I liked him, and I was learning him to set a snare."

"You will have to learn Catherine."

"Kit might get a fever too. Fevers is no use. It's a waste of people. Laurie might as well a not come alive at all. I shouldn't a got to like him then. And he wouldn't a spoiled the wedding." She left them, angrily.

When the child had gone, Annie said to Jaen, "There's times when I think I'm talking to an old granny she's got such a head on her."

"She minds me of Ju. Not in looks, but Ju always got angry

about things like that. One time she jumped on a whole clump of gilly-flowers for fading and stopping their scent, then she went and propped them all up with sticks when she found out that they would flower again next year."

"There's times when I don't know what I should do without young Bet."

Jaen nodded. She knew what Annie meant.

Although a thousand years and more ago, the cross had found its way into Newton Clare, aggressive, thrusting itself at the pagan deities who had lived with their people and made life bearable, the sword-shaped symbol had never destroyed them. It had merely pushed those gods into the stealth and hush, the familiar part of the minds of their faithful – people who lived close to the earth and the elements.

On nights such as this, safe, welcome, and out of sight of churches built over their old shrines, beyond the grasp of hands with nail-wounds, out of hearing of such words as "sin", they emerge.

Germinal deities, soft and round goddesses; dark, square gods; antlers, maypoles; wreathed in vines they join their own kind. They breathe their spiced and mulled breath into the shades of their earthly representations, and the shades take on flesh and blood. For a few hours corn-queens and green-men reign over eating, singing, drinking, dancing, love, lust and blood-lust.

In the barn, children, unused to such unlimited and rich food, curl up in corners and sleep. Babies reminded by thudding feet and rhythmic drumming of pre-natal heartbeat, are as limp and drowsy as when they had floated in their amniotic ocean. The corn-women and the green-men, faces flushed, full of laughter, are freed of ploughs, scythes and flails, of yokes, hoes and churns. Away from sun, frost, hail, gales, pestilence, fever, aching limbs and breaking backs, they awaken for a few hours.

Men with rough and calloused hands grasp the hands and waists of neighbours' wives and daughters. Wives and daughters hitch up their skirts, throw off holiday neckerchiefs and loosen bodice laces.

Dan and Luke were in the midst of everything; sleeves rolled up and shirts open to the waist, they shone with sweat and male pride. They made exaggerated dips and arm-links, twirling their partners and making play of their great height when going under the arches of paired arms.

Several times, as Dan passed, he grinned at Jaen, beckoning with his head that she should come into the circle, but she indicated that the babe was still feeding.

From where she sat, with Elizabeth, Martha and Annie, Jaen watched.

"They'm two of a kind, our two," Martha said.

Jaen smiled in reply.

"I should a said all Hazelhursts was of a kind," said Elizabeth. "Blimmin gert oxes!"

Annie pursed her lips and raised her eyebrows. " 'Kind' and 'Hazelhurst' an't words that go together."

"Ah, but 'oxes' goes all right."

"Shh," said Martha, nodding towards Nance, who was sitting, using a platter as a tambourine, knocking it in time to the dance.

"Ah, don't worry, she's well away. I never know how she can abide drinking spirits like that; it's as much as I can do to hold a spoon of brandy in a bad tooth," said Elizabeth.

"Bejowned to her," Annie went on, "there's times when I hardly care whether she hears or not. Sometimes I feel I shall call it in church – like they do at weddings – 'If there be anybody who knows a reason why this man Hazelhurst shouldn't get wed, speak now or for ever hold your peace.' 'Yes, your Reverence, he an't kind, and that's a reason enough that he shouldn't be wed.' "

Martha's loud laugh was drowned by music and the thumping of boots. "If we had to wait for kindness before we took an husband, we a be a long time single maids," she said.

Listening, Jaen could not believe that Annie meant that France wasn't kind. On the morning when she thought the baby was dead, and she started in labour, he was kinder than she believed any man had it in him to be. It was just talk.

Often when the Hazelhurst wives were together, they began this odd sort of wrangling. Their deepest instincts were to side with one another, yet none of them had ever really been so outspoken as Annie had just been. Usually they sparred lightly, all of them being afraid of their mother-in-law. She could herself harangue and tell her Boys what she thought of them, but no one else dare do so.

They all, from time to time, had wondered about Mrs Nance.

There must have been a time when she still thought of herself as Nancy Douglas, glad to have the security that Baxter and Up Teg gave her, trying to be Mistress Hazelhurst, but a bit sad to see her natural family fading as surely as though bleached out with white-lead, as in their turn each of their own families had faded.

The group of wives dispersed when Betrisse, who had had a sleep and was ready for more pleasure, claimed Annie's attention once more.

The first time that Dan came to get Jaen into the dance circle, she had had the excuse that she was suckling Hanna. The second time he bent over her, took her empty breast in his large hot hand, and removed it from the sleeping child.

Gentle.

"Now 'tis my turn." He spoke low and close to her ear as he had done the first time they met. He was breathless from dancing, heaving his broad chest, milk-white below the weather-line at his neck. His own warmth and dampness turned the soft wave of his hair into curls, his dark beard and eyebrows glistened and, like all The Boys, the only teeth that he had lost were from manly contests with fists. He is a picture of strength and virility.

The look that he gives her, the odour of his body and the charm that he can summon up for a woman, is Jaen's aphrodisiac. Once in the circle she dances as she has not danced since May Days and Harvest Homes when she was a girl. But here she is not a girl. The Corn Queen dances to the Green Man.

As, in their turn, they reach the head of the chain of dancers, he does not skip her cross-armed back to their place in the dance, but twirls her out through the door. Luke and Dick give shrill whistles as they have done when other couples have danced with abandon off out into the night. Some pairs, who are not normally bonded, married or otherwise orthodoxly coupled, go out together under eyes turned blind eyes for the night. They all accept that when the old deities come to join a feast and there is darkness on the land, the laws of the new God of the nails and the cross are not enforceable – natural desire is innocent, sexual pleasure is beyond guilt. The kindly gods are abroad.

Half-way across the yard they stop, Jaen panting from the exercise and the unexpected spark that had lit her when he touched her so gently as he took the child from her. Warmth seems to flow from there, spreading outwards and downwards. The soreness from the child's hard gums on her still-soft skin becomes intense, but for now it does not plague her, rather it is the centre of a return of other feelings.

Dan tugs her arm. "Let's go indoors."

A second of panic. "No, let's not go in the house," she says. "It's fresh out here."

As they walk, his large hands enjoy her. They hear Vinnie's laugh.

"She b'st in high spirits."

Words form in Jaen's mind, but she does not speak them.

She laughs because she knows Peter, and Peter knows her. That's the difference. She's been living here since she was a girl. She knows Up Teg ways. It wasn't a stranger she wed today, she hasn't all of a sudden found herself married to somebody she don't even know. Perhaps I might laugh too if I wasn't so knotted up inside all the time, afraid of something I can't even put a name to.

Instead of answering, she slips her hand through his arm.

His hands feel rather than caress, but Jaen does not move away from his touch as she has done for months now. The man she gave herself to suddenly last year has come back.

Either he is being gentle, or she has become so used to crushing and carelessness, that it feels gentle in comparison. She wants to tell him that he might not have to complain of her giving him as little joy as a "blimmen pile of fleeces" if he would more often be gentle. Wants to tell him that she feels strange and alone being so suddenly away from home, in somebody else's house, an unfamiliar room, a bed that seems almost communal in its nearness to other beds; wants to ask him to be patient, and gentle, gentle, until she gets used to living with such a crowd of people, to the breathing of his brothers close by in the night, to the trying to please him, to please his mother and father, to please everybody.

Wants to let him know that she is trying hard to like holding the baby, to like feeding it, trying hard to want it.

But she does not tell him, knowing that when such words are out, the sound of them will act like rennet in milk, separating the unarticulated feeling from what comes out in words, so that the meaning is run off as whey leaving the words as something that they had not been until they were said aloud.

The grass is long and beginning to turn from summer greenness. The Corn Queen who has been conjured to life for this wedding feast is persuasive. Jaen looks straight up, from beneath him. Dan's shoulder, the branches of a cherry tree, a few bright stars and the dark sky. She feels the glacier that has lately encased her emotions melting, breaking up. If he will just be gentle. Just be a little . . .

Ah. But the Green Man is always urgent. He has a function to fulfil. Now, now – before age neuters him. Now, now – before there is a battle. Now, now before he must leave and hunt. Now, now – there may be other males, and he must be the one. Now, now, now.

When Dan had seen her with the child asleep at her breast, when he had felt the softness of her and had seen her flinch from the tenderness as he pulled her bodice about her; when he had seen how small she was dancing, giving him her neat dry hands to make an arch for the dancers, he knew that if he was gentle with her, he might again find the girl he lay with at Pewsey's Farm last year.

He lies beside her, resting on one elbow, caressing her; he sees the gleam of her eyes but does not know that she is looking past him. He sees all that he wants to see in her look and quietness.

A thousand years before this, the Green Man coupled with the earth so that the Corn Queen would give life to another spring. Now, now.

Still looking up through the branches, Jaen feels the Corn Queen leave her and return to the barn. Hot tears in a steady stream flow silently into her hair.

If only he had been gentle, not so urgent . . .

He had intended to be gentle. Intended to give her pleasure.

He is heavy upon her sore breast.

The glacier flows back.

14

BETRISSE, PLAYING the game inside her head where she was Annie's child, held her imaginary mother's hand and watched her real Ma dancing with one of Granfer's hired men. Ma and him holding one another by elbows, shining wet faces, Ma's cap almost off, both of them their hair sticking damp. Betrisse knew that her mother's hands would feel warm and slippery to the man when she made him hold her by the waist, holding her hands over his as she twirled down the line of dancing people. Ma, unaware that she had faults in the eyes of the firstborn of this new generation of Hazelhursts.

Back in the winter, Betrisse had heard something that had bored into her subconscious. She had been sitting reluctantly in church, cold, wearied by flat words, cross at the unfairness of things and prepared to take it out on the toes of her boots all the way home; but on reaching the church door after the service, she saw flakes of snow falling, huge flakes like soft goose-feathers, the unexpectedness of which had thrilled her.

"Oh Mu-Mawh . . . look! It snows greatly. Oh Pu-Pawh do see!" The clear voice of a girl of about six, about her own age, had rung out paralleling Betrisse's own "Lors Ma, 'tiddn half snowing."

"Snows-greatly", child of the gentry, had been shushed by a nanny and bundled into a carriage, leaving Betrisse the gift of her tortured vowels to try out secretly.

Annie became Mu-Mawh. With her straight back, erect head and a way of looking down the line of her nose; with her dry hands and the irritation she almost always had in her voice for everyone except her niece, Annie passed for gentry in Betrisse's imaginary world.

She had no Pu-Pawh as yet, the only one half-way suitable was

Vinnie's brother. Quiet-spoken and not always showing off hisself like Pa and the uncles, Jim Norris would have done, if he'd been a bit older – and a bit taller too. Pu-Pawh would wear a high wig, but even in a wig as great and heavily piled up as Snows-greatly's Pu-Pawh's, he would not really do. Connecting the phrase "lost at sea", that she had picked up somewhere, with Annie's description of Emworthy Bay, Betrisse had decided that "Pu-Pawh was lost at Emworthy". As he was only lost, there was always the possibility that he might one day be found.

Of course, Annie wasn't always Mu-Mawh, but when she was needed, Betrisse could always call her forth, expanding and embellishing, weaving new experiences and observations into her secret life.

(Mu-mawh?) "Can't people have a feast like this unless they gets married?"

"A course you can. You been to Harvests and May Days enough."

"Oh I knows that," (Mu-Mawh) "I been to a lot of them, and Christmasses."

Annie smiled, the child had for a moment sounded like her father – Luke's contempt at anyone stating the obvious: "Oh, I know *that!*" She'd give them a run for their money when she grew up.

"I don't mean that kind of feast, I mean one like this, one that's just your own like this one's only for Vinnie?"

"And Pete."

"Peter's only *here* – it an't his feast. Vinnie got give bits of lace and everything, and she walked in front and it's her feast, only her'n. Can't you get your own feast without getting wed?"

"Ah. Now that's a question and a half!"

That was an "Annie" answer, and Betrisse felt irritated but turned it into an obscure gentryism so as not to let that other world retreat.

(Mu-Mawh?) "What means a question and a half?"

"It means summit we should all like and can't have. Like fresh meat without the slaughtering, like bread without the toil of growing the corn, like butter without the churning. We should all like the feast part."

"I'm going to get one."

"I'm glad to hear it."

"I shall."

"I believe you. What you going to call your feast?"

She had not thought about this.

"Couldn't I call it St. Betrisse Eve?"

"You have to do something before you gets to be a saint."

No other name worthy of a feast-day came immediately to Betrisse.

"It don't matter. I shall find out what it's called when I'm a lady." She looked seriously at Annie. She trusted Annie with her most delicate and precious possessions – her dreams. Only Annie could be trusted not to dash and destroy them. Her Granfer, her Pa and the Uncles would toss them from one to another until they were limp and tawdry. Granmother would not even think them to be worth a moment of attention and Ma would seem a bit afraid and slap them down like flies. Vinnie would pretend that she was taking Betrisse serious. Jaen was still too new in the family for anything yet.

Only Annie was interested enough in Betrisse's dreams and fantasies to treat them with any delicacy. She had a long memory stretching back to when she too had thoughts that were all fragility and swirling colour, like membranes of soap held between the circle of a thumb and finger. It is possible to hand over a soap-bubble, if the recipient wants to take it.

Annie returned the serious look when Betrisse said, "I mean *really*, when I'm a lady."

"Then you could call it Lady Betrisse Day."

"I could couldn't I?" She looked at the pictures just behind her eyes. "And I could have the feast at Emworthy and everybody could have oysters straight up out of the sea."

It was closer to dawn than midnight when Vinnie's wedding feast finished.

Jaen, in the Yard Room, listens to the ale-heavy breathing of her husband and the milk-satiated breath of The Child, and is overwhelmed with guilt and anguish that she wants neither of them. She wants the sound of Ju's light, twitchy sleep. She wants to be herself.

Annie, her head low and knees raised as Nance has said that she should, listens to France sleeping and wonders why it is that some women fall so easy, often when they don't want to. She longs, aches, pines to become pregnant. There are times when she feels exhausted because she is so obsessed by it. For ages, she has imagined that she would have a child that was a replica of Betrisse, but now she is willing to think of any kind of a baby; she could always try to mould it into another Betrisse.

Betrisse watches her own pictures as she dresses her family in high wigs, hats and gowns like gentry; she makes them talk quiet like gentry; she makes them take notice of her.

She will have a box pew. To herself.

She will take little sweet cakes to eat there.

She will learn to talk like the Snows-greatly girl. She cannot yet see how she will do it, but there must be a way as there was when she did the deal over the stones to get her father to buy the yellow-buttercup cloth for her new shift.

What a waste Laurie was.

Vinnie had said, when she was told, God called the best ones to heaven first. He might just as well have not sent Laurie down to earth at all if He wanted him that much, and He had plenty of others, He didn't have to have Laurie too.

She still cries sometimes. Silently, because They said she had to stop making such a fuss, if she was good she would go to heaven and Laurie would be there. And she ought to be looking after Kit better than she did. But Kit was not Laurie. Her mother said it had been a blessing in disguise having Kit and Laurie together. Betrisse often sits in the far recess of the inglenook listening, not understanding. What if she doesn't die until she is very old – will Laurie know who she is?

15

AUTUMN

NANCE SAID ALL ALONG that Vinnie would not go to her full time because she was so big.

"I was just the same with Luke and France, and so was Martha with Kit and Laurie." With her privileged position as midwife and law in her own house, Nance had set herself up for the confinement with a herbal remedy of her own creating – a flask of rum, brandy and honey mixture as a suspension for a pinch of marigold and mint. Her testing and tastings had made her flushed and expansive and slowed down her usually jerky movements.

"There's twins all over the Hazelhursts, and I back it's what's come to her through our Pete. There's twins there."

But Nance Hazelhurst was wrong.

Vinnie went her full time and, though what Vinnie had did indeed come to her through Pete, it was not twins. Annie helped Nance birthen a feet-first baby.

Vinnie had taken to the stripped-bare bed in the early hours of a gloomy October dawn. She laughed and chattered to Peter, telling him to get on out of it and let her get on with getting him his little'n.

"Don't expect to see'n at dinner-break, but I reckon you shall be a father at supper."

She listened to the comforting sound of cattle squelching the mire, their lowing and the clumping of wood and leather as the dairy workers began their day. Rain fell through the grey murk making it such a benighted dawn that one could scarcely tell when the new day had come. But Vinnie was a Jack-o'-lantern, seeming to give off her own light.

Annie came as the extra pair of hands always needed when a woman was in labour and men wanted food on the table, but after a while she saw that the men could better manage without her than could Vinnie. Jaen and Kath did the cooking and baking. Jaen was silent and withdrawn, speaking only when she was spoken to.

For the first part of her labour, Vinnie was her usual self, excited at having another great event so soon after the last. But as the hours and hours passed she lapsed into silence that was broken only by exhausted grunts as she tried to send her child out, and the repeated comment that she knew '"summit was wrong". It was true, the baby would not come.

The natural light outside the lamplit room seemed hardly to change all day. The rain stopped and the mist thickened to grey fog which deadened all sound except that which came from the kitchen below. By supper-time, Peter still was not a father. Neither was he by dawn of the following day.

Myrtle, who was a good girl to have about on such occasions, stayed up with Annie the whole night so that Nance could snatch moments of rest as they waited for the long labour to progress. When Nance said that there wasn't nothing she could do except wait because it was a britches baby, Myrtle patted and comforted Vinnie, telling her that she'd a come out feet first herself, and there wasn't nothing wrong with her as anybody could see.

When the child had at last slipped its feet into the position where its head should have been, Nance purged and greased and massaged then finally mixed a concoction that caused Vinnie to have several long and powerful contractions one after the other.

At last two small feet were born, followed by knees, then the bouncy little male organs, that looked as though put on as an afterthought and were too large for such small legs.

"Bless us, Vin, we'm getting a boy!" Nance said, and Myrtle called down the news to those assembled for their dinner-break. Peter started to clatter up the stairs, but Nance told him to bide his time a bit . . . which was as well, for it took the women a long time to adjust to the whole child when it eventually made its tortuous entry.

Nance crossed herself and said at once to Vinnie, "Take an hold of yourself, Vinnie – it's got water on the brain, girl."

Annie, white with fatigue and tension at getting the child to be born at all, turned on her mother-in-law in an explosive whisper.

"God take you, Mistress, but you'm not only a hard-hearted old woman, you'm a fool too. Couldn't you a just waited till she got her breath back?"

"Always best to face up to things right away."

"Not after thirty hours in labour."

"I knows what I'm talking about. It don't help avoiding what must be faced."

"Then you might at least have given her some of the remedy you been stewing yourself in for hours. She's in need of it more than you," Annie said fiercely, quietly.

"I don't want no lip from you, girl."

Because of Vinnie, Annie held back further words of her anger, except, "Don't you 'girl' me!"

"Let me see him." Vinnie, gaunt and deflated so that even her normally pink, plump arms appeared fleshed with coarse, saggy, grey dough, propped herself up on the rustling straw bedding.

"Give him here, Annie; if you puts him to the breast now, I shall easy give up the afterbirth. It's summit he can do for me after taking so long to get here." She was smiling.

"No!" said Nance. "It an't going to live, Vinnie, no more would you want it to, so you best . . ."

"Let me see my babe."

For all her weak and exhausted state, for the first time in her life Vinnie commanded.

"He's mine, and you nor nobody else can tell me what to do with him. He's mine and Peter's. But most – he's mine!" Vinnie gave Annie the impression that she might almost have rehearsed her words, or at least thought about a situation when she might have to stand up to Mrs Nance, so unhalting and fiercely did she say them.

Annie had wrapped the baby in a woollen cloth so that its hugely swollen head was well covered, but immediately on taking the child from Annie, Vinnie unwrapped him and held his face to her breast. He did not respond but she continued to hold him there, supporting the poor misshapen head and seemingly not finding anything amiss as she inspected every part of him.

"Look at them gert big hands – just like mine, he a be able to help with the milking as soon as he can walk. Look at his hairy little back – he gets that from Pete." She gently laid her hand over his plump and obvious organs and said in her usual laughing way, "And they'm so sweet – no mistaken about they, is there. I shall call him Peter Norris . . . you'm Peter Norris Hazelhurst, but I shall call you Norry, like my own Dad . . . that's your grandfather but he's gone to heaven now."

She looked directly, defiantly at Nance and her voice became strained with the effort of trying to sound natural.

"Master Bax won't have no objections. He a no doubt want to wait for a better one to carry on his name."

Annie recognised Vinnie's mounting hysteria, under control.

"Let me have him, Vin. I'll swaddle him proper."

Nance looked from one to the other. She was losing control of the situation.

"Leave him be and put him in the rush-crib till we finished cleaning her up, then I . . ." she was interrupted by a loud, held shout of "No-o-o!" as Vinnie's last contraction, which came unaided by any sucking by the child, released not just the placenta but Vinnie's streaming, silent tears.

Whilst Nance performs the ritual, secret burying of the afterbirth, Annie holds Vinnie about the shoulders and rocks with small movements in the way of all women comforting one another, and cries too, but her tears are unseen – they stream dry and bitter into the dry and bitter pool within her, of tears already shed.

She cannot understand why, after all that she has seen in just this one family alone, in just a short three years or so – Martha's sadness over young Laurie's short life and swift death, Jaen's obvious misery with obviously unwanted little Hanna, to say nothing of her own miscarriage and what she has seen happen to Vinnie as well as what she can see here and now . . . why does she still ache to conceive?

Why?

It seems such a great muddle.

Why? What is supposed to be the meaning in a babe like this one?

I could run the world better than that.

And unfair.

Unfair that France and Peter, and all the rest of them, have a natural powerful urge to make a child which gives them such high old pleasure, whilst her own natural, passionate urge and Vinnie's and a lot of women's results in hard labour, pain and often misery, yet still the urge to conceive is overwhelming.

Nobody you can take your grievance to though, not a case for the magistrate or the squire. Annie smiles faintly but is not aware that she does.

She will do anything. She will take France twice a day and sleep on her back with her knees raised; she will drink the concoctions of old wives and cunning men; she will take powders containing dried urine from pregnant mares and wear lockets and charms. She will go on visiting Nell Gritt who would have been burnt at the stake before the enlightened times of the eighteenth century.

Would she do violence because of her need?

There are times when she feels extreme enough.

Do men, when their needs and desires are unfulfilled, foment and pine and long and agonise?

Perhaps that is why some men take a woman by force, men you would never think it of? Her father had . . . Annie had never known who the girl was, but even though it had happened twenty-odd years ago, the terrible face of him and the terrified face of the girl entered the four-year-old Annie's memory and had been embedded there.

France has been like that – once or twice. No, more times than that . . . during the year after she miscarried. Then, his desire for a child was very strong . . . his anger and lust and unhappiness – though a married man cannot be said to violate his wife, he would say he had the right to take her however unwilling. Would she do that to him?

She rocks Vinnie. She cannot imagine an equivalent violation. Not even to satiate her longing.

But there are things that she can imagine herself doing, like taking Vinnie's child and . . . then what? She sees herself sitting in a safe cave, rocking the baby as she watches the sea lapping smooth round stones embedded in flat sand.

If no one else understands, Annie knows why Vinnie was so fierce with Nance who had called the baby "it". Vinnie's claim – He's mine! Knows why Vinnie held the unfair, encephalitic head with the same gentleness as she had held the wholesome little penis. He's mine! He is Norry, the baby that knocked Vinnie's ribs and disturbed Vinnie's nights, Norry whose movements were felt by Jaen months ago and compared to Hanna's.

Annie does not know the details but she understands why, and rocks and waits for Vinnie to assimilate the reality of Peter Norris Hazelhurst.

16

FOLLOWING THE REVELATION of the child that Vinnie had birthen, something settled its unquiet self, as it seemed, on the roof, where it squatted, voiding frustration, rage, gloom and fear which seeped into the fabric of the house, infecting them all except Vinnie and her child.

Nance had gone down and told Peter that he had got to stop Vinnie trying to suckle the child. Peter, without even a hat or jacket, banged off out into the dripping October weather. Dan was brooding and silent, then he too went off to wherever it was he always went when he was in his black moods. France flew at his mother, saying if she wanted to put the child down then why not do it honest, like kittens and pups, in a sack.

Baxter, thwarted again by the rag-tag-and-bobtail bits of women his sons got themselves mixed up with, struck France across the mouth and unbuckled his belt as he had done so very often since the first time – when the four-year-old twins Luke and France had set fire to a pile of furze ready for the house.

Now, France too unbuckled.

"You do, and you'll get the same!"

Baxter wound the leather about his fist but made no further move.

"You do. I warn you. You been whipping the hide off us for more'n twenty year and you an't going to give yourself that pleasure no more. I'm bigger, younger and a lot stronger, and I don't know why one of us an't stood up to you before."

As with Nance earlier in the day when Vinnie had made her stand, the master of Up Teg saw the first intimation that his authority was not almighty. And he felt afraid. If he was not master then what was he? He hurled a pitcher of cider into the hearth as a gesture, then he too glowered off into the dark yard.

Young Ed watched. He saw the first crack appear in the pedestal that had always supported his father. Awe of him began to slide from his shoulders like an unfastened cloak, leaving him unconsciously aware that he could not go on relying upon him.

Nance, picking bits of broken pot from the debris of the fire, said, "He won't forgive you, France. A man's got to be master in his own home."

"Goddamn it all, Mother! Not with a strap in his hand, nor not master of a man who's full-grown." France looked down at his own white knuckles. His hands still clutched belt and buckle aggressively. He relaxed and refastened his belt. "I had no reason to turn on you . . . it didn't mean nothing."

"It didn't mean nothing" was about as close to an apology or an admission of being wrong as a Hazelhurst could go. It was what he said to Annie whenever he laid hands on her for crossing him. Once she had shouted back at him, "It means summit to me," and he too had said, "A man's got to be master in his own home." The question "Why?" had risen for a moment, but was soon submerged and lay there fermenting, adding to Annie's resentment.

Annie, who had watched the scene through the scullery door, was glad that France had stood up to his father yet sorry that he had resorted to the same old solution. She hated to see men in that stance, like bulls or stags – except that in nature creatures were never malicious or rancorous in defeat.

It had happened too in her own family. There, her father's fits of fury stemmed not so much from being unquestioned master, as from the suspicion that her mother, then later as they grew up herself and her sisters, looked at men whom they should not in ways that they should not – the words sin and women were often synonymous to him.

Then a day had come when her father gave vent to his ire on a young travelling butcher and there had been a similar clashing of antlers as that she had just witnessed. Although it was ten years ago, Annie still felt the mix of fear and hysterical laughter rise in her whenever she remembered her father stumbling about the yard dripping blood. Most of it had been the pig's, though he did lose the sight of one eye. It did not stop his suspicion and possessiveness, though he did thereafter confine his outbursts to the source of his torment – the women of his household.

Myrtle and Kath, being the household scapegoats as well as its drudges, suffered more than usual during those weeks. In the night-time privacy of their cold isolation over the dairy, they agreed that it was just like They to make such a fuss about one of Theirn having summit wrong.

"Anybody'd think it was the end of the world to get a babe with water on the brain. And It can't last long anyhow. They never do."

"Well 'tis in a way like the end of the world for the Master, the way he's always on about They being better'n ordinary folks and that."

"And coming right after Luke's boy going sudden like he did, with nothing but a simple fever."

"I don't know what they a say if Master Richard's last one snuffs out. Did you see him?"

"Ah. Mistress been telling Missis Richard to feed him pounded raw liver to thicken up his blood. But if you asks me, he still looks unnatural, that bluey sort of white."

And so he was. The baby that had been pink and fat when he was christened and named Nicholas only a few months earlier, and had been admired for being a cherub at Vinnie's wedding, was slowly becoming a fragile, chilled-looking, pinched child.

17

WINTER

THE STREAM OF ILL-LUCK flowed down upon Up Teg right up till Christmas.

Ed, youngest of The Boys, whose Hazelhurst heighth and breadth at puberty was equal to most full-grown men – and superior to most of the ill-nourished, bow-legged and stunted men who worked the land – proud of his growing strength, was given to pushing and pulling excessively. A few days before Christmas, when axeing out roots for new drains, he all but severed the finger and thumb of his left hand.

Strange as it may seem, Ed's accident was the one bright spot for Master Baxter in those dark weeks. Before the flaming log on the ale-house hearth he can boast.

". . . near cut right through, if I don't rise from this seat again, and he walks in holding them together – two miles he must a walked like that – and asks Kath for summit to bind 'em back on." He drinks deeply to let the drama of his son's courage sink in. The other drinkers do admire Ed's manliness, but they would do so with greater generosity if Master Baxter did not always tell tales in a way that set his sons higher than those of his neighbours. Especially when Baxter himself seemed to be going down hill of late.

One bit of ill-luck following another.

It was the worst time of the year, the days were at their shortest. The dark time when people who still lived much as their peasant forebears had done, sat by the light of tapers and wicks, the women spinning, knitting and sewing, the men whittling tool-handles and doing small work. The dark time when the old people tell rhyming rules and knowledge, hand on family history and ancient stories into the keeping of the next generation.

Thirty days hath September,
April, June and November . . .

The mistletoe hung on the castle wall,
The holly-branch hung in the old oak hall . . .
Oh, the mistletoe bough,
O-oh, the mistle . . . toe bough.

Now, they often sit gloomy and silent in the Up Teg kitchen: Baxter, Nance, Dan and Jaen, Peter and Vinnie, the hired labour and servants sharing the same warmth – though on many evenings it is only the Up Teg women who are there; the log in the hearth of the "Bear" warms the older men, and Nell Gritt's pathetic mattress in her mouldering shelter has more appeal than some of the flock-stuffed ones at Up Teg.

Although it was weeks since Vinnie came downstairs from her childbed she still made excuses whenever Nance tried to get her to go and be "churched", chiding her that until it was done Vinnie was not "Clean and fit to meet thy Maker".

"I a go – but not just yet."

Jaen sensed that Vinnie was waiting for something.

Because the baby Norry could not suck, Vinnie's milk did not come. Nance behaved as though the child did not exist but, once given, the knowledge that she had passed down to her son's wives could not be taken back. So, without her help or approval, Annie did what she had seen the old woman do when she had got Lucy and Rachael going. Goat-milk at first trickled down a finger, then a greater flow with a leaky but effective teat of her own devising – Nance Hazelhurst had a well-placed faith in the milk of ewes and goats for any digestion that was not robust.

So, with that knowledge, and with Jaen expressing some of her milk directly into the child's mouth, he survived – he did not thrive, but he did survive.

Nance, whose word was law when it came to do with women's business, felt that the act of defiance when Vinnie had said "He's mine!" was swelling into rebellion.

Annie, Jaen and Vinnie were always fussing with It, but what could she do against their combined wills? They never neglected their work; the men were fed on time.

When she had started on to Baxter about it, he had turned upon her. "What do you expect me to do – tell them to put it out on the hillside like they used to in olden times?" The child was like a thorn that could not be plucked out because it could not be found – it was a constant bother to her yet there seemed nothing that she could do. Of all the decent, normal children that had been taken – her little Alice, young Laurie and . . . and it seemed likely, Richard's latest – this one was holding on.

One morning in the week running up to Christmas, Vinnie went off on her own and came back saying that she had been down and got herself churched.

"Well, that's good, Vin," Peter said. "We shall be able to go to the Christmas service together."

Ever since the day when the child had been born and Peter had gone off out into the night, nobody knew where, he had said nothing except what was necessary for work or food. Vinnie seemed not to notice, or if she did, was not affected by it. As far as anyone knew, he had never looked at his son.

The effect that the malformed child had upon the family was strange, particularly upon Jaen.

Hanna was now getting on for four months old. She was a healthy, solid baby with the striking colouring of Jaen – green-blue eyes, pale skin and hair that would grow to be the same red-gold as her Estover ancestors. But she was querulous and grizzly, it was difficult to know why; it could scarcely be hunger for she often cried whilst feeding, seeming to want to turn from Jaen even as she tried to feed.

Jaen would often have to steel herself before she could pick Hanna up. At first Nance had pushed and pulled Jaen into a more natural position, but in the end she gave up.

Exasperated, she said to no one in particular, "I don't know why she can't get a hold properly, anybody'd think she was having to give suck to a wolf."

Jaen was left to her own devices with Hanna, and to her own continuing loneliness and misery and her belief that there was something wrong with her. She was cold to her husband and she had no instinct to mother her baby. The unnaturalness of her feelings made her afraid and ashamed. She tried constantly to affect warmth and smiles for Dan and pats for Hanna. To outward appearance she had settled down as a Hazelhurst wife. She worked very well, and Baxter had stopped singling her out for criticism.

Her rejection of Hanna was all the more difficult for her to understand when she found herself cradling Vinnie's child and trying to wet-nurse him. She would let Hanna start feeding, and as soon as the milk flowed well, Vinnie or Annie, sometimes both, would try to get the second child to take. Compared to the rigid and writhing Hanna, Norry was soft and pliable, and Jaen sometimes put Hanna back in the rush-basket and cradled the new baby.

On the day that Vinnie was churched, she and Jaen had been doing their regular dairy chores of scouring and scalding. It was rough, hard work, especially in winter when the walls were so cold that the steam froze on contact and the feet of the women became numb and their hands chapped and raw. Jaen and Vinnie had never minded the work half so much when they shared it.

"Remember when I felt Norry quicken?"

Before Jaen can answer, Vinnie goes on. "I a have to let him go."

Jaen nods. It is becoming more and more of a struggle to get any milk into him.

"It an't just water on the brain, there's other things wrong, an't there Jaen?"

"He got more than his fair share of trouble."

"He an't never going to be able to take food proper."

Jaen guesses that Vinnie too has felt about the small mouth whilst trying to get him to suck from a finger, has discovered the unfinished palette and the oddly shaped jaw.

The thing that Jaen finds so difficult, to touch another person spontaneously, has always been easy with Vinnie. She dries her hands on her sacking apron and puts an arm about Vinnie's shoulder and draws her down so that they sit side by side on a draining bench.

"It wasn't wrong to try. It wasn't wrong. He's mine and Peter's son – she didn't think of him like that. She would have just throwed him away if she could. Just because somebody got summit wrong, don't mean you have to throw them away. I seen her looking at me and him, she thinks I'm like a cow with a dead calf."

Jaen says, "She don't think very deep."

"She don't feel very deep neither."

Jaen ventures her first explicit criticism of the family she now belongs to. "Perhaps we won't when we've lived with Dan and Peter as long as she's lived with their father."

Vinnie, who has been looking inwardly, looks sideways at Jaen. "Pete a be all right."

Jaen thinks that there is an implied criticism of Dan because she doesn't include him in her comment, but it is Vinnie being honest, and Jaen believes that Vinnie is probably right. Once they are living on their own, Vin and Peter *will* be all right. Like France, he seems a different man when the other Boys are not there.

"So, I'm going down to St. John's this morning, and get churched."

Jaen did not follow Vinnie's train of thought.

"If you a just let Hanna feed till you'm dry. I an't going to make no to-do about it, none of your milk and none from the nanny-goat neither, well, only enough so as it looks like it's milk. I shall tell Annie."

"What shall you tell her?"

"Only that . . . It wasn't true that my mother knew witchcraft, but she knew things and she learnt me a lot. I know how to do it so as he a go gentle, like going asleep. I shall tell Annie to feel in his mouth – if she an't already felt it. You felt it?"

Jaen nods.

"It an't a sin, Jaen. I an't just throwing him away like she wanted, before anybody tried to see if he was all right. I heard France shouting at her the night I had Norry – you know how the voices comes up through that floor. About thinking she was God or summit. I reckon that sometimes you have to, but you can't just do it like when you makes a mistake and burns the bread . . . you can't say, 'Oh Lor that's spoilt throw 'n to the pigs,' can you? You haves to see if summit can be done." She smiles at Jaen. "I don't half talk, don't I? Once I gets started."

"What about Peter?"

"I shan't say nothing to him. Not even when it's over. We a just start all over again."

She held Jaen's hand for a moment, then hastily kissed it. "Your Ju's lucky to have a sister like you. Come on, let's get this done so as

I can go down to St. John's and catch Vicar at Morning Service – won't be nobody hardly there today."

Later, when they were going their separate ways, Vinnie said, "I got to admit, it wasn't only just for Norry's sake. I wanted a little bit of time with him. You know what I mean?"

Jaen did not, but she nodded her agreement.

"It a be easier now. I got something to remember about my baby – not like Annie."

PETER NORRIS HAZELHURST
FIRST SON OF PETER AND LAVINIA HAZELHURST
DIED DECEMBER 23RD 1780 AGE NINE WEEKS.

NICHOLAS HAZELHURST
FIRST SON OF RICHARD AND ELIZABETH HAZELHURST
DIED FEBRUARY 1781 AGE NINE MONTHS.

18

WHEN MAY COMES ROLLING over the downland, from the west, for those whose limbs are able to take them to the top of the downs, who have leisure enough to spend time wandering and whose pleasure in wild flowers is discriminating, inclining towards the delicacy of harebells and tenaciousness of vetchlings and rest-harrows, rather than to exaggerated hollyhocks and sunflowers, or overwhelming rhododendrons – there is no place on earth equal to Hampshire to touch the senses.

Skies are boisterous with white cloud. The new grass has come, and hemlock and hellebore, willow-herb and tansy, eyebright, and yellow rattle, moneywort, lousewort, speedwell and bearded-bellflower are regenerating.

The vanilla scent of hawthorn hangs about lanes, lark-song spins up into the lively air, and leaf-mould rustles with the long chain of hunters hunting and the hunted being hunted – most of them living and dying both roles. Even whilst only fifty miles north of the county border there is still heavy fog and frost, in the Four Parishes of Rathley, Motte, Cantle and Blackbrook, if one were to climb to the highest point, one could see summer approaching Devon and Cornwall on its way to Hampshire.

Down the ages clergymen with Hampshire parishes, safe from need and with much leisure, have discovered and documented that which people with calloused hands, soil on their boots and toil in their bones, have always known.

Clergymen have been able to wander and study because tenants like Baxter paid rent and tithes. Because men like Luke and Dan grew more than their own requirements of food and timber. Because women like Annie and Vinnie and Jaen tended beasts, made dairy products, and gave birth to the next generation who would continue to provide for clergymen. Thus the clergymen will continue to be the recipients of acclaim for observing what is under their noses, and for turning nodding flowers, iridescent beetles, and chalk-hill butterflies into printed words.

In their letters to one another and their notebooks, vicars and friars have written their findings, presumably because they had greater faith in the durability of ink over voice – or perhaps they simply did not know that people other than clergymen had the means of handing on lore and knowledge. Accurate knowledge too, for not the lowliest rural worker would have said that swallows over-wintered beneath pond-mud, they would observe migration as surely as they observed bud-burst. Not understand, but observe and tell the next generation.

All the years when she was growing up as Jaen Nugent, she had been an observer. She had wandered over the hills around Cantle knowing where white violets grew . . . puzzled about why one plant should be white, watching bees dancing when they returned to the hive . . . wondered why, saw how each month had a predominance of one colour of flower, the white month, the blue, the yellow, gold, red.

Now that she was Jaen Hazelhurst it was distressing to her that she was no longer free to go wandering out onto the hills, so she grabbed at any chance to work outdoors. The repairs to the cottage at Ham Ford were still not complete, but she did have a sty there and had begun clearing the neglected land around the cottage. It gave her a good reason to be away from Up Teg for hours at a stretch.

Ham Ford Cottage and its little plot, like Up Teg and the rest of the Hazelhurst cottages, belonged to the Church. Around and about that part of Newton Clare village, Baxter now rented Keeper's, a similar sized plot and cottage in which France and Annie lived at the bottom of Keeper's Hill. Westcott, where Richard and Elizabeth were, adjoined Luke and Martha's One Acre.

The Up Teg house was on the far side of the shallow River Hammet, and shared Th'ammet, both as a boundary and as a source of good trout, with the Norris Land – which did not belong to the Church. It belonged to young Jim Norris, who it seemed had also been incorporated into Up Teg as surely as his land.

As soon as Jaen cleared a strip of ground, she planted it, bit by bit, and to find a haze of green where she had sown carrot-seed, or to pull back straw from a head of chard was her most absorbing pleasure. Her feelings for Hanna had not changed, though she had got used to feeding and having the baby with her constantly, but there was always a moment of hesitation whenever it was necessary for her to do anything for the baby.

The guilt that she felt because of it made her life a misery.

Yet there was Vinnie, always looking on the bright side of things, but not so bouncy as she had been a year ago and no longer a girl. Vinnie had become a woman who, no matter what trouble came to her, was still able to think "you poor thing" about another person, and mentally put her arms out to comfort.

"An't it a pity I never had no milk come in, Jaen. I reckon I should a liked to wet-nurse." Often when there was an hour between the regular farm work, Vinnie would go down to the place at Ham Ford to help Jaen with clearing the ground. There she would pick up Hanna and walk about talking to her.

"Your mother's very busy growing stuff for you, so you a just have to do with me giving you a bit of a cuddle up."

"She's better with you than me, Vin."

"A course she an't. It's just that babes likes summit different to look at. Don't you, little Goldy-girl? See Jaen, she's laughing at her Aunt Vinnie's funny face. An't that right, Goldy-girl? I'm summit funny and different."

And so Vinnie would take Hanna close to her and the baby would respond to arms that were less tense and a voice with no fear.

Occasionally during that spring and summer, Jaen got almost to the point of telling Vinnie how she felt about Hanna, but how could she say to another girl of her own age, almost a sister, "Vin, I can't take to Hanna. There's something wrong with me that makes me not want to be her mother. There's times when I would do almost anything if she wasn't here." How could she even hint at such a deviant side to her nature, to such warping, worrying frigidity towards her own child? how . . . to Vinnie of all women? who had wanted Norry so much yet had . . .

Had . . .

The knowledge that Jaen and Annie had about Norry's quiet death was now buried so deep that it no longer even flickered behind tell-tale eyes if his name came up, or somebody mentioned "last Christmas".

It was just the same with Annie. Perhaps worse. At least Vinnie did not have the spectre of "barren woman" hovering about her. Nor could Jaen talk to her mother – of all women, Bella Nugent was the last that Jaen could open her heart to . . . no, not the last person, Nance Hazelhurst was she.

Ju. She could have talked to Ju. The only one in the world she could have talked to about the terrible thing that was wrong.

If they were still at home – real home, sleeping close, arms flung about one another in the close little chamber over the kitchen, or curled up together in the apple-sweet roof space, there Ju might have helped unwind her sister's hard and tangled knot of emotions. Ju, who could run rings round anyone for knowingness, brightness and understanding, was not often free to visit Up Teg. When Ju and their mother did come on visits, it was with a kind of formality almost the reverse of servant girls visiting home on high days and holy days.

There was no question of Jaen going over to Cantle. Dan had said "no". No arguing. No! First grandchild be blowed. If Mother Nugent wanted to look at her grandchild, she had a good pair of feet and a donkey. Jaen's emotional fatigue was just too great these days to even begin to argue with Dan.

19

It was late September when The Boys finally finished work on the Ham Ford Cottage, and Jaen and Dan moved into it soon after. The day that she lit a fire on her own hearth Jaen felt happier than for many a long month.

Seeing her pleased look, Dan said, as he had when she had sat with him behind the swaying oxen on their wedding day, that they should be all right when they got going on their own.

Jaen still had to make her contribution to work at the main farm, which was a ten-minute walk directly across the fields – twice that distance when the land was wet and she had to take the pathway. There was, too, the extra washing now that their clothes were not done as part of Kath and Myrtle's chores. And, although they took some of their meals at the main farm if they were working near, Jaen's was the only pair of hands at Ham Ford to do the cooking and cleaning, the only shoulders to carry water pails, the only arms to carry bavins for the oven, and cordwood to the hearth.

But. There were such advantages. Less of Nance to tuck up her lip with dissatisfaction thus making Jaen all fingers and thumbs, less of Baxter pushing at his food suspiciously if he was in a bad mood, less of the sudden flare up of tempers.

There was space.

Only three people drawing breath under one roof was a luxury Jaen had taken for granted when she lived at Croud Cantle, and had found most hard to adapt to in the ménage at Up Teg.

There was quiet.

Even Dan was less prone to give voice to his opinions and denigration of other farmers, when there was only Jaen across the table from him.

There was for Jaen a partial return of her dignity.

Something of the kind of privacy she had been brought up to

accept as normal, and only later realised was peculiar to the female environment of Croud Cantle.

There were no people sleeping only inches away behind a lath and plaster partition.

On the first night in the little room under the tarred beams, Jaen smiled up at the mice and birds settling into the thatch for winter, as Dan reached the climax of his right to satisfaction.

They *would* be all right.

If she held on to that belief . . .

If she could keep Hanna at the breast for another year . . .

She and Hanna had never settled down to the business of feeding – not like Martha who carried little Rachael about almost as an extension of her own body, or like Elizabeth had been with Nicholas, easy as cats with kittens – but Jaen knew that whilst she was still feeding Hanna, she was safe, and would not have to face having another child who would rebuke her a dozen times a day for her unnaturalness.

Given enough time with space and quiet and being on their own, Jaen thought that they would be all right.

And so it was, on their first night in the little cottage, that she could smile up at the mice in the roof.

And so it was that Jaen Hazelhurst learned that to believe something is not enough.

By All Saints' Day, she suspected that she was carrying another child.

By St. Andrew's Day, she was sure.

When she realised it, she fell into a well of despair, but eighteen years of training by a straight-backed mother who despised weakness and any kind of behaviour that smacked of "making a peep-show of yourself" had veneered Jaen's behaviour with pleasantness and her countenance with cheerfulness.

Only Vinnie and Hanna sensed the sham.

Hanna began again the bouts of grizzling and whining that became worse now than they had ever been.

Vinnie thought that Jaen was trying to hide physical troubles, fatigue perhaps from all the extra work she had now they had the cottage.

"You looks tired out. I'll see to my Goldy-girl for an hour, I haven't got nothing to do till supper. You put your feet up and have a bit of a rest."

Jaen held back her automatic response: "Oh, there an't nothing wrong with me." Vinnie probably had plenty to do, but Jaen was in such need to be on her own that she let Vinnie sling Hanna in a shawl and take her off.

She does not put her feet up, but goes out of the cottage and follows the path beside the Hammet and closes her mind.

The Hammet runs shallow, filtered to a brilliant clarity by chalk-hills. Although oak leaves still hang on tenaciously, rustling, falling singly, rocking as they go, the rest of the trees and hedges have given up most of their foliage. The air is as clear as the water.

It is a year and a half that she has been Mistress Hazelhurst, and there have been very few hours when there have not been people, people, people, coming and going, upstairs, downstairs, all about the yard, down in the meads and fields and in every room at Up Teg, walking, talking, clattering, arguing, banging and clanging. People.

Sometimes, in the dairy, there was an hour with only Vinnie there, but that was not outside. Not like now. She could cry with the relief of being alone.

She does not know why she has always had such need to walk away from dwelling-places and people. No reasonable person walks the raikes and paths over such rolling great hills as Tradden or Beacon unless they have a necessary journey. The gentry will sometimes ride out for pleasure or to hunt, but it can be nothing but eccentricity that sent a hard-working farm girl wandering out, looking closely at every live thing that has its place on the chalk downlands of the Cantle Valley. And when Ju was old enough, Jaen had taken her too.

Bella Nugent's girls is queer, and no mistake.

Jaen listens to the crisp underfoot sound of Ju and herself going along Tradden Raike. A flash of dull red.

Look Ju! See him – it's that woodpecker.

The day is mild for November, but the sky in the west is becoming as clear as Th'ammet. Blue and icy. The moist spongy compost gives up the scent of fern, an aroma of decaying vegetation that smells much like the smell given off by new spring shoots.

Dead leaves smell lovely, don't they Ju? Why do our flesh smell so bad when 'tis rotten?

Jaen smiles, vaguely, momentarily aware that she is closing her mind to what is back there, waiting for her return. The cob-walls, limed . . . white. Shaggy thatch, unmatched reeds . . . the new-found, soon-lost quiet.

See, Ju? The alders and hazels got their catkins showing like they always do, even before all the other leaves are down.

The warmth is going from the day. In Th'ammet, with a ripple of its filmy tail, a sleek trout gives itself away to Jaen's observant eyes. She bends to sit on a rotten tree stump, slow careful movement, but it sees her and vanishes.

Don't be impatient, Ju, he'll come back. It's a good trout place, just where the water swirls away like that.

Her eye is caught by bunched buttons on graceful stems, sulphur-coloured toadstools growing from the decaying log.

Her closed mind does not inhibit knowledge gathered like grains of wheat since she was a child. Among the gleanings of seventeen years, some bits of knowledge, tagged red.

Laburnum. Nightshade. Yew. Arum. Death-cap. Hebona. She knows the rules. Don't never put one near your mouth. Don't never touch. They a kill you stone dead.

The colour is vivid and magnetic. Jaen reaches to break off one of the caps. The sun is low and clear and frost is not many hours away. Tomorrow the sulphur caps will be black slime. She holds the brilliant cap and sees tomorrow . . . white, smooth, pure. The miserable muddle of her life obliterated, like a midden beneath a heavy fall of snow. The nightshade thought. The death-cap idea.

Ju!

Foetid. Rank. Rot and putrefaction rise from the pale gills of the fungus, and for a second time the trout that had returned to its place, darts away as Jaen retches violently, again and again. She expels nothing in her convulsions – except the infected notion of escape that the beautiful sulphur offered her.

It's time I got home. Vinnie will be back with the baby. Dan won't be late, he knows I set a rabbit stew over the fire.

She retraces her steps alongside Th'ammet.

An isolated clump of hog-weed rattles and its few remaining seeds fall into the stream that flows south. As she walks, she sees their journey behind her eyes. She follows them bobbing and swirling, floating in still water then being blown on until one seed beaches high and dry and begins to grow into another isolated clump, where the Dunnock Brook flows past Croud Cantle – home.

Ju will be seeing to the goats and donkeys.

Mother will be . . .? In Jaen's vision, Bella Nugent is always stumping away from the deep well with heavy pails hanging from a yoke, straining against the weight to keep her back poker-straight.

Jaen reads the message in Bella's clenched jaw and frown-lines. *You made your bed, my girl, so you must lie in it.*

Back at the cottage, Vinnie has not yet returned with Hanna. Jaen puts the bellows to the glowing logs, stirs the rabbit broth and lights a few tapers.

20

MORE AND MORE, HANNA'S GRIZZLING frayed Jaen's nerves till she would put her hands over her ears and shout, "Stop it-stop it-stop-it!" making matters worse and the cries louder; then she would hear a note of distress in the cries and try to pacify the baby by rocking and patting.

Sometimes it was as much as she could do not to pick her up and shake some sense into her. Then, when the child fell asleep with a tear glistening on her golden lashes, Jaen would almost collapse with remorse.

"I don't mean it. It's just . . . it's just . . ."

Then Hanna started getting teeth and with them the wretchedness of the red-gum; she seemed to cry for half the day and most of the night. Nights were the worst. Jaen began to dread the child's first whimper after Dan had gone to sleep. He would turn furiously and pull the covers over his ears. Hanna, half asleep, would begin to make miserable distressed sounds. Moving gently so as not to disturb Dan further, Jaen would dip a finger into a salve Nance had made up, and rub the hot little gums. In spite of Nance's assurance that it had worked on every babe she'd had to do with, it never worked with Hanna, and every muscle in Jaen's body seemed to stiffen as, fretful from tiredness and in pain, the baby awoke fully and began to cry again.

"God and damnation! Why don't you stop her?"

"I tried everything. She don't never seem to stop."

"Why don't you give her some of Mother's stuff?"

"I did, I don't know what to do. Perhaps there's something bad wrong with her."

Many times recently, Jaen suspected that any day they would discover that Hanna had some defect that nobody had noticed, deafness, blindness, or that she would develop the neck growth and brain fever that caused madness. Always deep within her the feeling that she would be paid out by God for the day when she had hoped the baby would be dead. Now she had added to His black list those thoughts when she had contemplated the poisonous toadstools.

God never let you get away with sins like that. Little Laurence had died, then Norry – she sometimes wondered if that wasn't the way God was punishing her, showing her what her sinfulness meant, letting her see Martha's and Vinnie's sadness over babies they had never, for a single second, wanted to be dead.

"Well, I can't stand it no longer. You had better do summit about it. I got a day's work ahead of me, I needs my sleep."

Jaen would wrap herself and Hanna in a shawl and go down and sit in the inglenook rocking and dozing.

December, and getting on to three months into her pregnancy, she steeled herself to tell Dan, choosing a time when they had all had a night of undisturbed sleep and he was just leaving for Up Teg.

"You can tell them up there I shall be a mother again come June time."

He held the door ajar for a second, his thumbnail white he gripped the latch so tightly. Then he slammed off out.

And Jaen watched him go off with long-legged long strides. Watched his large body, his broad shoulders, strong arms which she had thought, when she had first met and loved him, would buttress and protect her for ever. Now, seeing him thumping his boots into the frozen ground, Jaen knew that he had never spoken truer words than the ones that still seemed to be hanging about the porch.

"You won't never be a mother if you lives to be a hundred!"

About the middle of December, Bella Nugent had sent a message with the carrier to say that she and Jude would pay a visit to the new cottage on Christmas morning and, so that she would not find herself in any position of disadvantage, told the man to say ". . . that's if Master Dan and Jaen didn't have any other arrangements set up."

On his next call at the Croud Cantle farm, the carrier brought the message that Miz Jaen was pleased as a cat wi' two tails, and would have good hot vittles ready for them in the forenoon.

When Nance had learned that Jaen's mother was paying a visit to the Ham Ford cottage she told Dan he must see to it that there wasn't nothing for Bella Nugent to turn up her nose at.

"There's summit about Bella Nugent that makes her think she's a cut above the rest on us, so don't give her no chance."

So Dan bought two new low chairs with arms, a footstool, and a bright copper kettle; then a two-branched brass candle-holder for the table, and a pewter candlestick which he set in the window; he made a fancy fretted rack with hooks on which Jaen could hang her ladles and knives, and a shelf on which he made a pattern of dots with a red-hot poker for her jugs and bowls. Nance gave them some patchwork chair pallets, and four blue-patterned plates. Jaen had been working on a large knotted-rag hearth mat with a lot of bright colour mixed in, which although she had not finished stitching the backing, she put down before the hearth on Christmas morning.

Jaen stood and looked about her, pleased and satisfied at the feeling of comfort and plenty. Again she recalled Dan's wedding-day phrase: "We shall be all right when we gets going on our own."

If we'd had a bit of time to get to know each another; if he could have come riding over to Croud Cantle a time or two; if I hadn't a felt so out of my depth; if there hadn't a been all the haste in marrying. If.

If it hadn't a been for the baby and now another, and probably more after that. Even if Hanna hadn't a been so peevish but nice and easy like Martha's and Elizabeth's was.

If a few small things had a been different.

There were times when she felt she didn't hardly know the man she found herself married to.

If it could be more like this. Everything nice and orderly, Dan looking pleased, Hanna asleep and quiet. Comfort, warmth, the smell of apple-wood, roasting meats, the copper kettle and pewter candlestick reflecting flickering flames and glow from the hearth . . . if they could a had a few months like this, then she might have been as keen to have a baby as Vinnie.

The day was bright and bitterly cold, drawing the fire to glowing brilliance behind two spitted fowls. Dan was in a good mood. He brought in a good pile of best apple-wood to burn, and a holly-bough for the mantel; he broached a jar of parsnip wine Luke had sent across and hung the hams from Jaen's summer pig where Mistress Nugent could see their quality.

21

CHRISTMAS AT HAM FORD COTTAGE

DAN WAS THE PICTURE OF a well-satisfied family man. Standing with his back to the fire, slapping his buttocks and drawing on a long-stemmed pipe, he said, "I got more improvements in mind."

"You got it very nice." A compliment indeed from Bella Nugent. "I reckon you might like it if you got some red tiles down here. It'd save no end of dirt and that."

Jaen and Jude exchanged amused glances at the thought of the red tiles in the Croud Cantle kitchen, the daily washing, the rebukes for footmarks, the exclusion of hired labour from the red-tile area.

"Dirt don't matter. But I was thinking as it might be warmer underfoot with some decent oak planking down." And although he had not, until that moment, given any thought to whether underfoot in a farm-worker's cottage there should be any kind of a floor other than the normal stamped earth, Dan reduced the use of red tiles to a notional list that might be headed "Inferior".

But knowing that the Hazelhursts were a bigoted lot in their opinions on any subject, and that Jaen hadn't by no means got herself mixed up with the best in the herd of they great lot of oxes, Bella put his ignorance about red tiles down to where it come from.

Hanna, being petted and nursed by her grandmother and young aunt, was told that she was the most pretty and good little creature in the world, and wasn't she just about as bright as buttons.

"Her gums is all up from her teeth, but it don't seem to bother her," Bella said, and did not miss the beginnings of a glance towards Dan that Jaen started, but withdrew quickly.

Her face arranged in a bright smile, Jaen told her mother that the naughty little thing had them about all hours of the night. Above all else, Jaen wanted to show her mother that she was settled and competent – above all that she was competent. And she wanted Ju to understand that Hanna's aunts on the Hazelhurst side did not have the same claim to kinship as Ju herself. So when Jude asked if she could take the baby out in the fields, Jaen hugged her very tightly as she tucked Hanna inside Jude's shawl.

Bella sat in one of the new chairs and missed nothing.

Whilst basting the fowls, Jaen suddenly rushed from the room. She had not intended telling her mother about the expected new baby, but Bella had recognised the signs.

"Ah well," she said, "I dare say you'm well looked after by this husband of yourn."

If the talk between Dan and Bella, about Nance's recommendation that Jaen consume near-raw livers for "peakedness", was anything to go by, one would believe that Mistress Jaen was an extremely cossetted woman. She smiled apologetically when she said how even the thought of it made her feel quite bad, but she did keep trying.

Although Jaen felt strung-up and edgy, expecting that each small sound from Hanna would develop into the wail that made her want to run and run and never come back, the Christmas dinner was a success.

Good food and plenty of mature country wine as potent as brandy worked the usual spell upon the two camps so that each came to admit that, well, when all's said and done p'rhaps there was summit to be said for th'other lot; they wan't all that bad after all, not once you got to know they a bit. Dan amused Jude and Bella by getting Hanna to respond to him by dipping his finger into the good gravy and letting her suck at it.

"Well, will you just look at her!"

"An't she a reg'lar little glutton."

"She a be a little porker if she haves much more a that."

Jaen prayed that the saltiness would not hurt Hanna's sore mouth and spoil the day. She had worked hard at making the Christmas visit memorable for Ju and Mother, holding it all up by her smiles, by the picture of cheerful domesticity she and Dan and Hanna presented, by responding to Dan's unexpected complicity in putting on the show.

Then Hanna let out a cry. It was as much as Jaen could do not to hit out at the child, but it was over in a second, and she regained her composure without ever having lost her smile during the short battle with her emotions. When her mind again began working upon what her ears were taking in, she realised that Ju had asked if they might not take Hanna with them. They had come in the donkey and cart, she was old enough now, wasn't she, now she could take solids, and it would give Jaen a bit of a rest, and let Mother and herself have the fun of looking after her, and washing her and that.

Ju, mature in some respects, still eagerly girlish in others, was stumbling on almost as though she had rehearsed her speech, trying to persuade Dan to agree. But it seemed that Dan did not need persuading.

Jaen felt that they must know at once how joyful she was.

That they must see that joy, and the guilt, written upon her face.

"Oh, you wouldn't want all the bother of her now she's getting her teeth . . . she an't never dry hardly a minute . . . you got to be always mashing and mixing up bits and spooning her with goatmilk and that . . ."

Bella blew away with mock indignation Jaen's weak protests.

"And what makes you think I don't know nothing about a sixteen-munts-old baby girl?"

And so it was settled.

The visit was cut short so that they should get Hanna indoors at Croud Cantle before the night air came down, and soon after the meal was eaten the red-haired grandmother and red-haired aunt began their journey, stealing away like thieves with the red-haired baby, concealing their glee at their good fortune.

The fourth red-head, properly, wifely capped, was overwhelmed with relief.

The short, slight figure of Jaen stood beside the renowned Hazelhurst heighth and breadth of Dan as they waved and watched the donkey-cart carry away the reason for them being bound to one another until death.

22

ON BRACK DOWN

THE BLIZZARD that laid down thick snow and ice like a carpet across the county, was said to be the worst in living memory and, although living memory picks and chooses the events to recall and relate with high drama, that winter was, for the thin-skinned county of Hampshire, indeed extremely severe.

On Boxing Morning, Dan went up to the main farm but Jaen, briskly, housewifely, put on thick woollen stockings and shawl and said she must go out and get in as much furze and bavins as she could find in case they was snowed up for a long time.

It was not much of an excuse to go walking out on such a morning, there being plenty of fuel of every kind at the main farm. It did not occur to him for a moment to suspect that she was off out for the sheer pleasure of walking abroad, alone, almost light-hearted. Normal people gathered to themselves every moment of rest and shelter, and Jaen could easily have found good reasons for working by the comfort of her own hearth. Had he known what pleasure was in her as she set off, he would have said that she was soft in her brain.

"Just as long as you'm back in time to get my dinner on the table."

Jaen went in the direction of Brack Down because that way she could return across Cuckoo Bushes Common where she could quickly gather the fuel she was ostensibly out to collect. It was still early in the day. The wind had dropped and the air was still. The cloud-pack that had been driven furiously over the chalk downlands during the night had gone; in the north, another pack was assembling. But for now, as Jaen's boots made holes in the unhandseled snow-cover, her skirts smoothed over the holes behind her.

The sky was blue as wild chicory, and appearing iridescent so clear and icy was the air.

She played her old game of closing her mind to everything except what immediately fed her senses. For the present she had no worries, no problems to return to. Guilt did flicker an occasional threat to her relief at being free to walk, but she was beginning to learn how to deal with guilt – as she was beginning to learn how to deal with other anxieties. She put the stuns upon it with forged cheerfulness and buried it alive.

Once or twice before, when out wooding on Cuckoo Bushes Common, she had walked briefly on the lower slopes of Brack Down, but this was the first time she had climbed it.

As she breathed in on the summit, the air was so cold that it seemed to sear the back of her eyes and she constantly had to blink away the tears that formed. But she welcomed the sharp pain and felt that she was being cleansed by it.

Brack was not as high as Beacon Hill, which was the highest down of the quartet of chalk-hills that surrounded and protected her home valley of Cantle, but there was a bleakness and bareness here that reminded her so much of Beacon. Although she and Ju had roamed all the other downlands around Cantle like two creatures who might well have had a dray or a burrow there, she had seldom taken Ju upon Beacon Hill.

When she was quite young, before Ju was born, looking up at Beacon from the yard, a mystery was solved for her. In church the Reverend Archbold Tripp told of things that would make you jump with fright if they ever happened to you – turning people into lumps of salt, fingers writing on their own, magic bushes and voices; and of places that were so strange that you could not even make pictures of them inside your head. But one day looking up at the high mound, the five-year-old Jaen suddenly realised that Beacon must be the kind of place where Moses went when he got given the stones with the orders on.

As she grew older the words which streamed forth from Mr Tripp became familiar, she could become totally absorbed into the sound of them; the phrases were spells; the intoning of psalms and creed raised her spirits in the same way as lark-song, but she never understood any of it. She learned how to cope with mystery – she reduced it to the mundane so that it was less fearsome. So she decided that when He would "come again in glory to judge both the quick and the dead", then He would probably come on Beacon.

And when struggling to create a picture of a Kingdom having no end, then the shining line of sea that could be seen from Beacon in high summer put boundaries about infinity so that it was no longer lurking hysteria.

When she was firmly on the valley floor, it was never clear to Jaen whether there was a difference between prayers and wishes. On the highest point of Beacon, it did not matter.

Since leaving her home valley, she had been penned and hurdled by events and people. Sometimes she felt as though she was at the bottom of a well, and longed to stand where there was nothing above her except . . . except whatever, or whoever, was there.

And now she had found Brack.

Like Beacon, Brack is another place of isolation. Where something exists. Some Thing. Some other Thing than herself. And here on Brack the same sense of a presence. It, or another of its kind, exists. Beyond understanding, but not frightening. She is out of the well. She does not know whether she is thinking or whether she is speaking aloud.

> *I will make a pact,*
>
> *There's something wrong between me and Hanna, and I can't take to her no more than she can take to me. I can't help it. I can't do nothing about it.*
>
> *But if you let it happen so that she can live with Ju and Mother, then I will be good to this baby and be a proper mother and wife.*

There is no Voice, nor do any of the stunted junipers burst into flame yet remain unconsumed by the fire. But she knows that the pact is made.

When at last she moves her body aches with cold. Her hand clutching her shawl about her is mottled purple and stiff. Boots and feet are fused by the chill of compacted snow.

Slowly she turns full circle.

White, white everywhere.

She feels as virginal and pure as the landscape.

A fresh start.

Jude and Bella have removed Jaen's mistake, her sin.

Yes, a fresh start.

Only hedges and trees show where tracks and lanes run. The turret and small spire of the church indicate the centre of Newton Clare village in the triangle formed by the Rathley, Tupnell and Winchester roads. On the far side of the valley two trails of smoke come from One Acre Cottage and Westcott, where Dick and Elizabeth, Luke and Martha live in enforced neighbourliness. Below, on the side of the valley where she stands, Ham Ford and Keeper's Cottages, both tucked into the lee of the downs, one either side of the River Hammet. Central to all of The Boys' cottages is Up Teg, where she can see people moving about, and someone riding a horse away from the house, dogs chasing, the sound of their barking drifting up as though from another world.

There are other farms, other fields, other clusters of cottages, the church and the inn. The whole is Newton Clare.

It is to that place she now belongs.

Where are you from then Mistress Hazelhurst?
I comes from Newton Clare.

Until now, she had thought of the village not as being Newton Clare, but as Up Teg. From Brack, Up Teg was put in its place, it was not so intimidating.

She had a pact to be a good wife and mother, she would be. She would do her best to belong to them.

Are you from around these parts Mistress Hazelhurst?
Yes, Ham Cottage in 'Clare.
A course I was born in Cantle, but now I'm from Newton Clare.

Lower down from Brack's exposed summit, the creatures that live on its slopes are everywhere. Although touched by bright sunlight, the snow is becoming crisp and hard, it is no longer virgin but patterned by pads and claws. Clusters of coal-tits descend upon food, bending stems with their group weight, the scarlet of aggressive robins flashes brightly in the sun as they give short shrift to any creature they can manage to stab at; foraging rabbits and squirrels warily ignore Jaen in their scrabble for food whilst there is still time.

The bank of cloud that had earlier looked like a grey and distant range of downs, is closer now, looming over the northern part of the county. Like all her kind, workers whose life is the land, and land is their life, she is in awe of extremes of weather. It is the enemy against which there is no defence, and from whom no retribution may be extracted. Her stomach clenches with apprehension. She has never seen such cloud, such strange threatening light. Wild animals, hours ahead of humans, had sensed the approach of Arctic weather when it was still far off.

Now alarm touches Jaen and she hurries back down to the shelter of the valley.

It is only when breathlessly she reaches the safety of Ham Cottage and her body begins to warm up, that she realises that somewhere back there, perhaps on Brack, or perhaps whilst pulling down snapwood branches on the common, she has started to miscarry.

By the time Dan comes in for his dinner, it is over.

Cleansed and virginal.

She is once more an empty vessel.

23

HANNA DID NOT SLEEP under her parents' roof again until she was a serious and useful girl in her ninth year. Jaen kept her part of the pact. Not consciously, but without Hanna there as a constant admonishment and rebuke for her unnaturalness as a mother, Jaen settled into trying to be Dan Hazelhurst's good wife.

The original intention was that Jude and Bella would return with Hanna to' Clare after a few days, but the roads across the downs, and the raikes and paths out of the valley villages, were snow-blocked and frozen for weeks. One day Dicken Bordsell arrived at Ham Ford, extolling his virtues as an intrepid and dutiful servant of Master Bella, and giving the message that the little Miss was doing just fine with The Master and Young Jude afussing after her.

"How can you abear letting her go, Jaen?" Vinnie asked.

"It a be good for her, and Mother; and Ju's just like a second mother herself."

Annie said little about the sudden decision that the child be taken to Cantle. She did not like to admit it, even to herself, but she had the feeling that neither Dan nor Jaen had ever really taken to Hanna, and was not surprised when the weeks and months went by with ever more reasons for extending the child's stay with the grandmother.

"She's going to stop a bit longer over at Cantle," Dan told Nance after the Easter visit.

"That don't surprise me one jot or tittle!" was Nance's response. "Bella Nugent likely thinks the child wouldn't be brought up fancy enough here. She's a queer one and no mistake."

She wagged her head at queerness of things generally at Croud Cantle. "If you was going to get yourself mixed up with somebody, why didn't you find somebody with muck on their boots?"

Dan let her trundle on, not listening, and when she had run down, he said, "It's because Jaen's expecting again."

"Lor, summit must a got in the water, that makes three on 'm. When's she due?"

"November time."

"Ah well, one a month after harvest. Martha's October and Vinnie's about Christmas time . . . that's if'n she an't getting worked up over nothing like she do."

Baxter, who, because his lungs were giving him trouble, tended not to cut into talk so much of late, said, "Let's hope one on you manages to make a young cock this time, this place is like a hen-coop. What's a matter with you all? An't none of you got the strength to give your women sons?" then lapsed into wheezy preoccupation.

But Vinnie wasn't getting worked up over nothing, she was soon growing fat and prominent. This time though, she and Jaen exchanged none of the girlish confidences in the dairy. They both still did most of the butter- and cheese-making but it was in a very work-like way as they each had other responsibilities.

Jaen's garden plot was expanding and flourishing under her knowledge and hard work. She had a good flock of geese and a large, healthy hog foraging about on Cuckoo Bushes.

Peter had put his foot down and said that it was about time they had a place of their own. Baxter made no objection, for he found Vinnie's exuberance too much when he wanted to listen to his own wheezing and subside into self-concern. There were no cottages available close to Up Teg and no land that could be spared to build upon, so it was decided that they should add on to Keeper's Cottage and make a pair of it, France and Peter sharing a wall but each having his own separate door, path and fence.

The Boys all acted as rough labour for the skilled builders and carpenters, so that by the summer Vinnie and Peter were installed – Vinnie named the extension Coppice Cottage.

She was in her element there, and had the makings of a good farm wife; she could turn her hand to anything. She was a bit slap-dash, not caring too much whether breeches were scrubbed often, reasoning, "Well, they only gets all dunged up again," and hens were welcome to go into her kitchen and clean her floor of bits of dropped food.

Peter had long ago realised that he had made a good bargain when he married her. Baxter still had not come round to considering Jim to be master of his own Norris Land – it was farmed as part of Up Teg. He expected that with Vinnie so pleased with herself and the cottage, Jim might feel obliged to let things bide, for he seemed happy enough in his quiet way. To Nance, Vinnie was the pick of the bunch.

"Looks an't nothing, Vin. You got a good pair of arms on you, and you an't got an ounce of scrawn left."

The three new swelling bellies made Annie and France more distant and difficult with one another. Not that they spoke of it between them, but each for some unexplained reason was drawn to Jaen's company – particularly France.

With the settlement of Vinnie, the Up Teg women were now ranged on either side of the main farm. To the west, Elizabeth and Martha and easterly Jaen, Vinnie and Annie. Recently Up Teg had starting going in for sheep in a much larger way than hitherto, and were now running a fair-sized flock on the slopes of Keeper's and Brack. France, being the one most interested in shepherding, and with the greatest knowledge of lambing ewes, looked after them.

It would have made more sense for Annie to have worked with France, but she couldn't abide being with sheep.

"Sly and awkward creatures. They knows all right what they'm doing when they starts running off, looking at you out a the corners of their eyes, gives you the creeps."

She preferred to work with calves and cows, spending many of her working hours, eyes half-closed with one cheek pressed against the side of the animal as she milked it efficiently. She could turn a breech calf and calm down a frightened, calving heifer. All the meads and cow-sheds were at the main farm, which meant that she worked a fair distance from France on the downs which lay behind their own cottage and Jaen's.

When France was out tending the animals he usually went by Ham Cottage where he would stop for a few minutes, or on his way back bring in one of the rabbits he had knocked off with a sling. If he had nothing, then he would call in to say that he was empty-handed. If Jaen was alone, he always said, "Tell Dan I stopped by," which usually she did not because it never occurred to her to do so.

Ever since the day when Hanna was born and he had cared for her, Jaen had taken to France, felt easy talking to him.

One day in the spring after Hanna had gone to Cantle, he stopped and commented on how well her early potatoes were coming on and said, apropos of nothing, as though he had been carrying on an imaginary conversation and then had spoken out loud:

"I don't reckon us humans is a great deal different to other creatures."

Jaen did not reply but smiled, and waited to find out what he meant.

"There's some ewes that don't take to their lambs, same with some sows – an't nothing, far as I can see, you can do about it."

He bent down to his working-dog and ruffled its coat. There was a moment of hesitant silence. Suddenly, it came to Jaen that he was trying to tell her that she was not to blame for rejecting the child. She flushed because she did not know how to reply, so she filled the silence by telling Gyp what a good dog he was.

"It have done me a deal of good since I been shepherding. Gid me a chance to think about things." He smiled up at her. "It an't no good shepherding if you don't like being on your own."

"You'm different from the rest of The Boys, an't you, France?"

He did not appear to have heard her but continued, "Being up there," he flicked a hand in the direction of Brack, "and looking down on this here, it . . . like puts everything in its place." He paused. "All this time, we been thinking it must be Annie. But perhaps it an't, how can you tell? It came to me the end of last summer when I was raddling the rams, it came to me . . ." He left the sentence unfinished, obviously finding it impossible to put words to his fears. "I shouldn't ought to be talking like this to you."

"I don't see no harm, France, we all needs to get things off our chests sometimes. There an't no harm talking things over. After all, we'm the same as brother and sister."

He looked directly at her. She returned his look and her cheeks reddened. But it was France who lowered his eyes first. Then, briskly, he slapped his thigh at the dog and began walking away.

"France?"

He turned in her direction, but did not look fully at her.

"Do you reckon a lamb is sometimes better off with another ewe?"

"Ah. If you can get the ewe to take it. Usually they won't. Nature's a queer thing."

He waved at her.

"Tell Dan I stopped by."

Now she realised why he always said that – to be open and natural about his frequent visits, so that Dan would not hear of them second-hand.

24

TWINS RAN IN THE HAZELHURST FAMILY, and Martha suspected that she had been honoured with that blessing weeks before she gave birth.

Deborah and Alice.

Even though the babies were strong and healthy, neither Luke nor Baxter was much impressed.

Baxter spat his annoyance at the fire, where it hissed.

"Guard in Heaven! If there wasn't enough 'oomen start a nunny-convent already, without having another brace."

When Nance picked up the new Alice, her eyes moistened, and thereafter she always made much of the child, petting it and chucking it under its chin. Martha assumed that Luke's mother was getting soft and sentimental in her old age, but was glad to have Nance always willing to take at least one of them off her hands sometimes.

Now, the small squat West Cottage housed Luke, Martha, Betrisse, Catherine, Rachael and the twin babies. Another room with a chamber above was to be added and during its building, Annie and France had Betrisse to live with them.

As all children were, Betrisse was put to work as soon as she was capable of contributing any labour however puny. Now, in her ninth year, she could comb and card wool for spinning, sew well enough to make simple garments, go wooding, fetch water from the stream, stone rooks and crows, glean, hoe, lead horses and fetch and carry, and when she went to live at Keeper's, Annie began teaching her the skills of milking and handling cows.

In November, when Jaen went into labour, Betrisse helped with the chores of keeping the fire going and seeing that there were plenty of wrapped warm stones for Jaen's feet whilst Annie and Nance helped with the delivery.

As with Hanna's birth, Jaen let the baby escape easily into the world. Although it was November and late in the afternoon, the air in the upper room was warm because the great chimney comprised part of one wall, and Annie's face was flushed in the light from several candles, from bending over the bed, and from conflicting emotions as she held the large, healthy baby for Jaen to see.

"You got a son."

Nance smiled and nodded with satisfaction.

"Well then, Gel, you done it this time all right. An't nothing wrong with this one. He's a Hazelhurst all over, Dan's father a be pleased."

They named him Daniel, and he was as different in stature and colour from his sister at Croud Cantle, as it was possible to be.

About a month later Vinnie, although not pleasing Baxter by adding another hen rather than a cock to the coop, pleased herself and Peter.

They named her Clarice.

Nance said, "That's a fancy blimmen name."

And from that time, although Clarice was entered in the family Bible and the parish records, the tough, healthy twig of the Hazelhurst family tree became "Fancy".

The following spring, although it was the time when they were most busy with sowing barley, getting ewes and lambs onto the lush first shoot in the water meadows, and when every breast-plough and harrow was in daily use, Baxter gave a supper.

In the forenoon, Alice, Deborah, Clarice and Daniel were taken to St. John's to be christened, and in the evening a supper was put up to celebrate.

Although it was not such a lavish affair as a harvest supper, being restricted mainly to the Up Teg family, close neighbours and one or two skilled monthly-men finishing off the cottage renovations, there was a sense of occasion in the large farm kitchen, which smelled of spicy foods, meats, cider, cheeses and ale.

"Quiet!"

Baxter, at the main table, cut through the fog of talk, belch, laughter, clang and clatter. Nance could judge almost to the mouthful at what point he would get up on such occasions; having fed his belly he came to the course where he fed his vanity.

Although breathlessness from the farmer's lung caused him to have caved in a bit at the chest, he was still a large and imposing man as he stood looking down the makeshift tables. His awareness of his own effect and his sense of timing and drama would have stood him in good stead on the hustings, the stage or in the pulpit.

The room was quiet. He spread his arms wide.

"Go forth and multiply! That's what it says in the Bible. And what that means is, if you belongs to a tribe, it's your duty to make sure that your tribe goes on for ever."

Nance, still at the stage when her party-bibbing caused her to be a mere four or five seconds behind in registering what was being said, suddenly realised that he was saying something new. She turned her head slowly up to look fully at him. He placed a hand upon her head as though about to bless her.

"Your mother here, and me, have had six of you, Hazelhursts to a man." The tone of sentiment in his voice developed, bordered on the maudlin. "Our sons." He paused. "Luke and France, come as a pair more'n thirty year ago." He spread his palm at Dick. "Richard, come the following year." He continued moving his hand, indicating each one of The Boys as though no one in the room knew who they were. "Next one – Daniel, then Peter and Edwin. Six fine sons."

There was a bit of shuffling. Eyes glanced a bit sideways. Shiftily. Trying to see how others were reacting, but not wanting to catch anyone's eye. Everyone knew how The Master of Up Teg always liked to make a show at weddings and harvest suppers and the like, but he usually did it with trials of strength, extravagance and the telling of loud stories and jokes. Perhaps this was the first sign that he was becoming an old man, meandering and pathetic.

"Six fine sons . . . and now a fine, fine grandson."

He pushed back his chair and went to where Jaen was sitting with the baby Daniel.

It was a good scene; every eye was upon Baxter, wondering what was coming next.

He lifted the baby from its mother, and laid a blessing hand upon Jaen's head.

"This here gel come quiet enough into our fambly and she have give us the next generation." He fingered a lock of Jaen's red-gold hair that showed at the front of her cap. "You'd a thought that anything as showy as this . . . and so inbred too when you thinks of

Mistress Nugent and her other daughter with their redness . . . anybody'd think as it'd show up somewhere in any of her little 'ns. Yet Young Dan'l is pure-bred Hazelhurst and no mistake about it. The first of the next line of this fambly of ourn, this here tribe I been on about."

At various places about the table, Martha, Elizabeth and Vinnie looked inwardly and felt resentment cause their breath to go shallow. In her place, Jaen too, felt resentment.

Martha and Elizabeth were left for ever thereafter with crow to pluck. Laurie and Nicholas had not come up to scratch. Fever and thin blood – their sons had not proved to be pure-bred Hazelhursts.

Vinnie's resentment centred on the way it seemed that what Master Bax was saying might set the women against one another, and it wasn't fair because, if they said anything, it would look as though they was jealous of a little baby. She knew that the Norris blood was a good as the next, and if the Hazelhursts was as good as they reckoned, then it was the hand of God that had made Norry the way he was and nobody else.

The passive set to Jaen's features gave no indication of the embarrassment she felt at being so unjustly singled out as an example of acceptable Hazelhurst motherhood, nor of the indignation she felt on behalf of Vinnie and the others. Vinnie caught her eye and, with little movements of her shoulders and brow, indicated, "I don't know what he's on about . . . don't feel bad about it . . . it an't your fault."

Still holding Young Dan'l, Baxter reached into his weskit pocket with two fingers and took out the coin that had been handed down together with watch and chain from his great-grandfather. He held the coin up like a talisman.

"Summit tells me that this here little shaver is going to carry on the line, so I decided to let him take the Up Teg seal right at the beginning of his life. It a be like a charm so that he will grow up manly and strong. You might say it's my way of handing things on to him."

Now it was the turn of The Boys to look puzzled.

"When we was younger, me and France used to talk about if you might split the seal in two and gid us half each," said Luke, trying to appear not very concerned, "but we never thought not to have it at all."

"The seal don't signify," said France.

"I never said it did signify," Luke said sharply. "All I said was I always thought it'd be handed on down through the line – it a been talked about often enough – how your father handed it over with his dying hands, that all I meant – not that it signified anything."

"Signify is all it do do," said Peter. "It don't matter who got it. It an't as though it's a paper nor nothing. It an't nothing but an old coin, and Great-grandfather started the handing down to eldest sons."

"Old and gold and rare," said Dick in a chant that suggested that it had been said before. "We heard that time and often enough."

"It still don't signify nothing to do with this family. I don't know what you'm getting all hot for," said Peter.

"Nobody's getting hot," said Luke.

"You'm getting hot," said Dick. "You'm half afraid you'm being done out of son-and-heir rights."

"It got nothing to do with eldest son rights," said Dan, not liking an argument going on unless he was in it. "It's . . . like Father says – 'tis a charm, and it is his own, and if he wants to gid it to the baby, 'tis his to give."

"Nobody's denying that," said Luke, "and I don't want it particular. It's just breaking a tradition that was started a hundred year ago."

There was a moment's lull, when Annie spoke up, sitting erect as always, appearing to look down her nose disdainfully.

"I don't know why you'm all making so much of a bit of metal. It's like if you puts a crown on a king's head, it an't the crown makes him king – it's everybody agreeing that he's king that makes the crown signify. Same with that," she nodded to the seal; "it don't matter who gets it – it's who's *agreed* to be head of the family that counts."

Annie had often made them feel like silly bickering children, so as usual when she effectively put a stop to their wrangle, they totally ignored her.

All the while they wrangled, Baxter still nursed the baby in one arm and held the coin up in the other hand, almost as though he was playing see who can jump the highest, as he used to do when they were young boys and he held up a prize high over his head.

Edwin and Jim Norris and the hired labour, aware that this had nothing to do with them, continued quietly helping themselves to large slices of meat and enjoying the interesting turn of events.

The children had been given piled-up platters and were happily savouring the food and the partyfied atmosphere. Of the four, only Betrisse listened to the talk from the adults' part of the room – although she concentrated her gaze upon her food, she missed not a word.

The Up Teg women watched the men. They sensed unease. The dominant male of the pack was weakening. The young blood, whilst still appearing to support his role as leader, was each nudging for position.

Up Teg had been lived upon and farmed by Hazelhursts for generations. They built barns, sties, milking-sheds upon it; they kept cottages in good repair, improved and extended them; they hedged and ditched, re-seeded the clover leys and tended the water-meadows regularly. They worked the soil and kept it in good heart with dung and ashes. They invested their labour and re-invested any gain from sale or barter of what they took from the land.

But in legal terms, this meant nothing. Like most other farming families in the 'Clare valley, the only claim they had to their farm was what their rent and tithes purchased from the Church Land Commissioners. It was a strictly commercial agreement. The Hazelhursts paid for the use of so many acres and so many cottages for certain specified periods for certain agreed payments.

Up Teg did not exist except as a name of the farmhouse in which the family were gathered – and as an idea that had been fostered by several generations of Hazelhursts. Because of that, there was no tangible inheritance, nothing for an eldest son to claim apart from the animals and the equipment. Without land, both were useless as a means of providing a living. The Church held them in the palm of its hand or, as it sometimes felt when particularly heavy tithes were taken, in the grip of its fist.

They all realised it. Baxter had become head of his tribe because his father had given him the seal, not because he inherited a birthright. But Annie was right – it was not the seal that had made Baxter accepted head, it was the recognition that he would make best job of it. He had been a good choice for under his patronage the size, and the idea, of Up Teg had grown.

It had grown to the limit of its boundaries. There was no more land that could be taken into the arms of Up Teg. On the north side of Th'ammet, the carcase of the valley that had been swallowed almost whole by the Church had been regurgitated in small parcels to tenant farmers in the same way as Up Teg. They all held on tenaciously to their leases. Up Teg had reached its limit. It had reached equilibrium – the right amount of land, supporting the right number of people, with little fat to spare.

In Newton Clare, there was not much other than the Norris Land that was independent of the Church.

For the moment the Norris Land had become almost indistinguishable from Up Teg. Its boundaries were north, the southern bank of Th'ammet; west, Teg Path; south an ancient hedgerow, and on the easterly side Norris's petered out irregularly at the Ham Lane ford.

Of all the farms in the 'Clare valley, only Norris's was its own, but at present it was merely a few clover-leys and water-meadows.

"Right!" Baxter said, "you had your say, now I'm going to finish what I set out to do. By reason of the way it was found – bright and shining as the day it was minted, showing this face . . ." He turned the coin like a priest showing a relic so that they could all see the profile with its wreathed head. ". . . ('tis a Roman king so I been told, centuries old, yet clear as a new portrait) – and where it was found . . ."

Young Dan'l heaved a great sigh and squirmed. Baxter handed him back to his newly-approved mother.

"Found on the face of Up Teg land under a flint as though somebody had just hid it there a moment before . . . and found on the day he was wed, by my great-grandfather, Daniel, Francis the eldest of seven sons. By reason of these things, it was long ago taken as an omen and a thing of special properties. And so I believe too. For since that day, no man have gone hungry on this land, and every son have had sons to hand it on to."

None of The Boys knew what to make of it. He'd had trouble with his lungs for years, especially at threshing time, and it had got worse lately since they had been going in more for sheep; he could not go near the shearing pens without dragging his breath into his lungs.

Peter was the one to speak out. Lighthearted.

"You an't thinking of dying nor nothing, are you?"

"No I an't!"

"Only a jest. Why make all this to-do then like you was on your death-bed?"

"I wants to see the charm working on the next in line (God grant I be spared). You'm a great fool if you can't see that having such a token do signify. It shows whoever keeps it he got the responsibility of his generation on his shoulders. Knowing that, he makes more effort to live up to it. This place is going to need somebody strong to go on holding it together . . ." He wagged his head at his sons who looked as though they would protest.

"Wait till I finished . . . I an't talking about the next twenty year – I'm talking about a time when you'm my age. I reckon I done a good job bringing you lot up so I an't got no fears about things going on the same as now. Why, there an't no man in a hundred miles got a fambly of sons of the like of theece."

He walked back to his place at the head of the table, still holding the head of the Caesar like a talisman.

"When I sees you gathered round my table," he placed his blessing hand upon Nance's head again, "I sees what a marvel it is that this little bit of thing that was called Nancy Douglas ever birthed such a great herd a giants. You done all right, Gel."

The Mistress of Up Teg, mother of remarkable men, had been patted before now when the Master of Up Teg felt the need to demonstrate family sentiment. Tomorrow the pat might have more force and no sentiment behind it, but for now with warm fumes of party spirit having put her in a mood of serenity, she nodded acceptance of the public tribute and waited to hear what else he had to say.

"I been thinking about it lately, and it seems to be fitting the first-born of the generation to follow on after you, and him being Daniel and son of Daniel, that he should have the . . ."

Betrisse could contain herself no longer.

"He an't the first-born! I am. I'm the oldest! I should ought to have the . . . thing!"

Her father pointed, threatening with his finger. "You bide quiet when your grandfather's talking."

"No! I shan't! It an't fair. He an't hardly been born yet, and I shall be ten next year. Granfer said it was for the first-born to look after the rest. I shall be grown up before he even knows how to scare crows proper. I can do milking as good as Annie already. I could plough as good as Ed, if they'd let me."

Martha, with a baby in each arm, tried to flick a warning hand at her eldest daughter. "You heard your father – bide quiet else you a get a clout."

The other children were seated close to Betrisse, on the inglenook bench. Her sisters, seven-year-old Kit and four-year-old Rachael, knew when Betrisse was heading for a leathering; there hadn't been any since she had been stopping with Annie and France. They edged further into the recess and concentrated on looking into the fire, with watchful ears.

Their cousin Lucy also began to feel apprehensive even though she did not know what was going on, except that suddenly the children's corner became the focus of adult attention. She slid unobtrusively down onto the hearth with a wad of meat that had become unswallowable in her cheek.

Half the trouble with Betrisse was that when she was little and engaging, Luke would laugh at her forwardness and call her Miss Saucebox. Nance had warned him. That one got the makings of a real handful. He'd be sorry.

Betrisse's unbroken spirit and simple sense of fairness urged her. She stood up.

"It's only because he a boy, an't it?"

Luke began to rise but was hampered by being on a bench close to the wall, and hemmed in on both sides. His move only served to make her have her say louder and faster. She knew that she was in for it so she had no more to lose.

"You wouldn't a cared if it'd been me died instead of Laurie and Nick. Would you? Would you? You'm only letting him have it because all the rest of us is girls. I would look after the farm. If you gid me the gold thing, I'd be a better farmer than anybody."

Her father had extricated himself. She watched him pick and squeeze his way towards her. Began to lose her concentration. She hurried on. Her eyes started to brim with tears of hurt.

They thought a little baby was best.

"I'd do it better than a silly baby. He don't know anything. He might even die. I won't die, I'm strong. I an't never had no fevers ever. It an't fair giving it to a baby!"

In watching Luke, she did not see her grandfather as he drew from the leg of his boot the whippy cane he always carried to speed up slow animals.

It came hard and stinging across the back of her legs.

A reflex action. She saw herself doing it. Slowly it seemed, so that it was like watching another person. She watched a hand, her own hand that held the wooden platter, come up. It took slow aim at the hand with the cane. The cane that was about to sting her a second time. She heard the thud of her platter upon her grandfather's knuckles. She saw the flash as the gold flew from his other hand.

She was quicker than they were.

She was out of the door and did not stop running until her chest began to hurt.

Part Two

CHANGES

I

EMWORTHY BAY

AT THE HEAD OF A CREEK, close to Chichester, lies a small, busy inland harbour.

At low tide the extent of the large area of mud-flats is revealed. When the sea is at its lowest point waveless pools and small lakes are left, their surfaces riffled by wind and disturbed by stranded or foraging creatures.

The bars of land are smooth and in places vegetation, that seems not to know whether it belongs to the sea or to the land, colours the mud brilliant green.

Whilst the sea has gone, here and there, events that in their day were dramatic and tragic come up for air and show rotting ribs; at the very lowest tides the skeletons of larger vessels, still with their masts ahoy, surface. Then people stand watching and looking inwardly they see how fearful it must have been when she keeled over and went down like a lead weight, so close to land – but it was dark, and the waves were like mountains and bodies came with the flotsam for days.

When it is low tide, it is easy to see the usefulness of the many small flat-bottomed boats and barges about, as they negotiate the shallow, narrow channels. Then too there are work-worn rowing boats, the wheelbarrows of the shallows, beached at drunken angles, looking fagged-out. A few masted and rigged ships, the wagons and coaches of the sea, lie stranded in more dignified positions awaiting the return tide and deep water.

This is Emworthy Bay.

And that is how it is at low tide.

But now it is high tide.

It is April; the air is calm and the sun looks as though it can be relied upon.

The woman holds the girl by the hand.

They have travelled forty miles to the glitterish sea and are not disappointed.

"It's just like you said."

"I know. And I must a been years younger than you when I was here," Annie says. "Everything . . . everything just like I remembers it, just as though it were yesterday."

She stands easy, as though some tight thread in her that has kept her puckered and strained has been drawn out and left her soft and smooth. Her back is still straight, but not rigid. She still looks down her nose, but lately she unconsciously inclines her head as she speaks, exchanging her previous haughty demeanour for gracefulness.

The journey of forty miles and several weeks, has changed Annie. France would have recognised her as the attractive woman he once held and made pregnant.

"It's blue though," says Betrisse thoughtfully. "I had in my head that it would a been more silver – being glitterish."

"It was silver, the last time I was here." She laughs easily. "First and last time, till now."

"But this is just as good," says Betrisse enthusiastically.

"Oh, just as good. It's lovely."

"Better."

"Yes better – I likes the blue. It's still glitterish . . . but it's blue. Look!" Annie points.

On a twin-masted ship, figures can be seen busying about; a sail is being unfurled, the breeze catches, it flaps, then billows.

"What they doing?"

"Putting out the linen to dry."

Betrisse looks up at Annie, and knows that it is a joke. Annie laughs. In the weeks it has taken them to get here, Annie has altered – she has been laughing a lot. Betrisse would like to jump up and kiss Annie for being so happy. Instead she rubs her warm, flushed cheek against Annie's dry hand, and surprisingly Annie squeezes her tightly and gives her a quick peck on her bare head.

"We are going to stay, an't we." It was not a question. Betrisse was sure of Annie, but she just wanted to hear it said.

"I said we should."

"I know, but they might find us."

"We a face that one if it ever comes. I doubt anybody would think we should go so far."

"And you told your sister you was going to Salisbury."

"Yes."

"And that packman who knew you."

"Yes." Annie squeezed the small hand that was becoming moist they had been holding on to one another so long. "I an't daft you know."

"I know you an't, Annie. There wasn't nobody thought it was a tale you was telling, was there? They a all think you took me off to Salisbury."

"Most a them places we worked at along the road . . . they wouldn't likely even remember seeing us if they was asked. Must be hundreds a widows and girls working a few days. A lot of it is tramping labour – picking watercree."

"And stringing beans and hops."

They repeat to one another what they have said before.

"They wants dirt-cheap labour, and they don't care who does it. Never you fear, nobody took no notice of us. Just tramping labour. So long as you don't ask for nothing and moves on, nobody don't want to know on them sort of jobs."

"The hops and beans was nice work. The water was cold though doing the watercree." Adding in a rush, in case Annie should think she minded the clear, cold streams where watercress grew, "But I never minded the cold water, and we had plenty of cree to eat."

"Oh Bet, Bet, my little duck. Cold water half-way up your legs, your back breaking, your skirts sopping wet and cress and bread for dinner . . . and you says you never minded."

"I didn't."

"No . . . I don't think you did. You never grumbled nor made no fuss, never once."

"No more I won't. Never. Not now we come here."

"Good! No more shall I."

Since they had come there, the tide had turned so that the waves now lapped a few inches further from the patch of sandy shingle where they stood, leaving stones, pebble and shells gleaming with salty wetness. Annie noticed something, picked it up and dried it on the corner of her shawl.

"Here," she held it out to Betrisse. "This is my token to you, saying, 'I, Annie Saint John, shan't never grumble nor make no fuss as long as we lives in Emworthy.' "

"Which is for ever. What is it?"

"It's a shell of a oyster."

"It's beautiful! I never thought oyster was like that. You never said it was shiny and all over colours." She twisted it to catch the light. "I thought it'd be like a snail or summit. How do the oyster stop in?"

"There's another half to it. Let's see if we can find him."

They were wearing the rough clothes that they had worked in for weeks, the hems were frayed and stained from the watercress bunching, so neither of them felt restrained at grubbing about on the wet shore.

When she got close Betrisse was fascinated to find that in with the sand and stones were small shells with many different shapes and patterns and colours. She picked them up and inspected them closely, showing Annie each different individual.

"Can I keep it?" she asked.

"It don't belong to nobody."

Before long her apron pocket was weighted with her prizes.

Annie discovered a complete oyster shell, its hinge intact.

"Here," she held it out to Betrisse. "Have this one instead."

Betrisse delved into her bodice where she had put the half that Annie had given her first.

"No. I'll keep this one. It's the proper token you gave when you said your promise. I shall put it with my other one. Yourn's better than this though."

Annie, like a child, plopped large stones into the sea.

"You got another token?"

"Mmm." Betrisse pulled a small knotted rag from deep down in her bodice, and undid it with her teeth.

"There 'tis! See, it an't as pretty as yourn, is it?"

In her moist, grimy palm, gleamed the golden coin with the wreathed head of a Caesar.

"Betrisse! You got his blimmen seal."

"No it an't. I got *my* seal. And it don't matter even if we lives in Emworthy – when I'm grown up, *he* won't be chief of the family . . . I shall."

"How did you get it? You never went near the house again."

"It was in my apron pocket. I found it there next day. It must a flew there when . . ." she sucked in her lip, "when I hit him with the platter."

"You shouldn't a done that, Bet."

"I know. If I'd a had the time to a thought about it I wouldn't have. It wasn't really no different than when a wasp stings you–you just jumps and slaps at it without thinking."

"And the seal just flew into your pocket?"

"It must of. It couldn't a got there no other way, could it?"

"I suppose it couldn't, not unless it was by a spell."

Annie pinched her bottom lip between finger and thumb and tried to look serious.

"You can't hardly take it back now."

Betrisse looked sharply at Annie, then saw that the pinched lip was to restrain a smile.

"You'm laughing, Annie."

"No I an't. It an't no laughing matter, but . . . I was . . . just thinking . . . I should a liked to a seen their faces when you took that there precious seal out of that dirty bit of rag."

"You are laughing, Annie."

Annie was.

Her laughter that had been tamped-down for five years smouldered through a layer of unhappiness, unfulfilment and feelings of inadequacy, and burst into flame on Emworthy shore. It was ages before she could stop. At last she crossed her arms across her stomach and heaved a sigh, but still little hiccups of laughter shook her.

"Oh Bet! They'm all so daft. If only they could see that their best man might be a girl."

Betrisse looked seriously at her aunt. "I wants to give you a token too. I can't give you the Thing, else if I ever got to go there one day when I'm big, and tell who I am – they might not believe it if I can't show it."

"You could give me a shell too."

"No, you can't have two tokens the same. It's got to be summit that's nothing like a oyster."

"I tell you what I would like."

"What?"

"That bit of cloth you had the Thing in."

"That's only a bit of old rag."

"No it an't – no more than my token is a old dead oyster's shell. A token is what people means by it."

"Like what you said by the crown?"

"What d'you mean?"

"At the christening. You said about a crown don't matter, it's people saying he's the king that makes him king."

"Ah . . . I'd a forgot that." She went silent for a few moments. "I wasn't really meaning crowns when I said it."

She fell silent again; at last she pulled Betrisse gently towards her and looked her fully in the face.

"Listen child. I hope I shan't never pester you with my ideas and that, but I'll tell you this because I thinks it is important and I hope you'll remember and not make the same mistakes as a lot of us do."

Betrisse caught Annie's serious mood and held it, looking directly back.

"I wasn't meaning crowns so much when I said that – I was meaning wedding bands." She looked down at her own. "When I had this give me, I believed it was a token to show that me and France meant to do what we said. You a understand one day."

"I understands. You mean, when I give you this cloth and says I shan't never make no fuss nor grumble now we'm here, it means . . . oh! I know what it means, I can't just get it right."

"It will mean that you got every intention of doing what you says. It don't mean that anybody expects you to be perfect. Tokens means people *intends* to do what they say, and even when they slips up, they goes on trying. Lord, I sounds like some old preacher."

She pulled the ring from her finger and held it on the flat of her hand.

"It wasn't only France. It got so as it never meant nothing to me neither, so what's its use."

Suddenly, she flung the ring far out, to where there was mud below the surface of the water. It made only a small plop and a ripple of rings as it sank into Emworthy mud.

"There!" she said. "Now give me your token."

Betrisse did so – feeling a bit self-conscious, but nevertheless solemnly.

Annie tucked the cloth into her bodice.

"I just tell you summit else we ought to agree on. Don't let there be no holding back between you and me. If we wants to laugh or cry, we shall do it."

"But not grumbling."

"No, no, we said not grumbling nor making no fuss. We can show proper anger, and get it over."

"Can I call you 'Mother'?"

"No!" Annie's tone was stern. "You got a mother."

"She beat me – you know how she used to beat me."

"She thought it was for the best."

"She beat me with a strap."

"Only so your father wouldn't beat you harder. It was her way of trying to save you."

"She never did though! He still beat me."

Remembering the dreadful sight that she had witnessed, Annie pulled the girl to her and rocked her gently. "I know, I know. And nobody will ever beat you again. Nobody. Ever. Long as I live."

"And *he* watched. I'm glad he lost his poxy seal."

"I told you before – we might a been working like tramp labour, and living with them, but we don't talk like they."

"But I am glad though. If it had been Laurie that spoke back, even threw a platter at him – he would of only just said 'respect your elders and betters'; then he would a told everybody Laurie was growing into a real little man."

"Is that what you wants to grow into?"

Betrisse did not reply.

"Can I be Betrisse Sinjen then?"

"It's Saint John really. Sinjen is the way it come to be called over the years."

"Betrisse Saint John. Don't that sound real nice? Can I be it?"

"I dare say it'd be better. I don't reckon many people from 'Clare is likely to come down here, but if they did, 'Hazelhurst' might make them prick up their ears."

"I shan't call it Sinjen – I shall be Betrisse Saint John."

"All right. But that's all that is changed. We don't want to start off with a pack of tales that will only find us out. I am still your aunt." She considered for a minute, then added, "But if people thinks we'm mother and daughter, it a stop a lot of curiosity."

2

FOR THE FIRST WEEK AFTER Annie and Betrisse disappeared, Luke and France, sometimes with Edwin or Richard or hired men, rode about the downlands and the lanes to try to discover them. France rode over to Annie's old village where her sister still lived.

"She never said much. Only that she had stopped on her way, and thought to stop a night here."

Annie's family had been split up for so long that her sister had scarcely remembered Annie's existence until she appeared one evening, saying, "I expect you don't remember me."

"And I never at first. I never knew her from a stranger. She and the girl slept in the corner there. All she said was that they were on their way to Salisbury or Old Sarum or somewhere that way. She left early. They went on the Stockbridge road, so they must a been going somewhere that way."

It never crossed anybody's mind that Annie had been fly enough to lay a false trail. After they had asked at every inn and coaching house along the road, they gave up. There was little else they could do.

They could have gone to see the magistrates, but that was to let others know too much about what wasn't their affair. Nothing so dramatic and shameful had ever happened in the Hazelhurst family and they agreed upon a story, that France's wife had gone off on something to do with a relative over Salisbury way.

"It an't none of their business," Baxter said. "And if anybody asks, then tell them – it's her affair and none else's."

To cover Betrisse's absence, they agreed to say that Annie didn't know what she might find when she got to wherever she was supposed to be going, and had taken Betrisse to help out if needs be.

Now two of the Up Teg granddaughters had been let go. True,

Hanna was brought over to visit whenever time and weather and state of the roads allowed, but gradually they became discounted from the Up Teg family. Jaen seldom called Hanna anything but "Child", and Martha never spoke of Betrisse at all.

At the eventful Christening celebration, Jaen already knew that she was pregnant again. By the time Young Daniel was just over one year old, Young Baxter was born.

3

NEWTON CLARE

FRANCE BECAME MORE AND MORE SOLITARY. Because he was a good flock-master, they gradually increased their buying of ewes in lamb to fatten for the good market in mutton. A bit of pig meat was available to everyone who had a few rod of garden, but fat mutton, for the town-dweller's table, needed good clover and grass meadows, or free-ranging downlands like Keeper's and Brack.

Old Baxter expected something out of every Up Teg acre of land and every Up Teg person living upon it. He held the working of them in his head, and whilst he held the reins, water-meadows were properly and regularly flooded at intervals between November to March, giving France a good run for his sheep and then later a mow or two of hay. He saw to it that every seventh year the pasture was turfed up and dried for fuel then re-sown with red clover for the heifers and milkers. Horses were never slip-shod nor hay badly stacked.

But his breathing slowly became more difficult and he often had to admit defeat and suffer Nance's goose-grease plaisters, balsam steam, and days when he could not walk his acres and see that everything was in order.

Eventually he got rid of the oxen, so no more Hazelhurst processions were made. The grandchildren as they came along each had their Christening-day supper, but never like in the olden days. There was always present at any Up Teg gathering, like a shade or spectre, the remembrance of the occasion of losing the Up Teg seal. Original Day too was feeling his age, and gave up competing in the neighbourly rivalry for top place in Newton Clare.

On the night when the gold piece was lost, and the next day – and on many occasions after when somebody had a new idea of what could possibly have happened – they searched for it. Even some of the newly-laid flooring planks had been levered up, and the fire douted and the ashes searched.

That night seemed to be a turning point in the fortunes of Up Teg.

Sometimes France would go off up Keeper's and Brack and nobody would see him for days. Before he left he would always stop as he passed by Ham Ford Cottage, and Jaen would stop whatever she was doing for a few minutes and they would pass the time of day about sheep, or beans or the babies, and when he was gone she would be left feeling remorseful that such thoughts about Dan's brother should fly into her head.

Later, she would try to make up to Dan for them by putting her arms about his neck. But the action always ended with her feeling more guilty than ever for the fancy that it was France's black and curly beard that pressed against her face in the dark.

Strangely, now that Annie was gone, France had less need to visit Nell Gritt. He still took her a sack of whatever vegetables were in season, and the occasional rabbit or hare, but often not for the usual service that she rendered to the men of 'Clare – and as a consequence, to their wives.

Since the time, a good few years ago now, when the wild bull had reduced Tad, her new young husband, to a child, Nell had become a kind of rustic hetaera, confessor and safety-valve for the village and, as she grew out of her youth, she gained an unwanted reputation for knowing old secrets. An apothecary, a doctor or even a Cunning Man, could be consulted openly by women, but they went to Nell almost furtively.

Likewise some husbands who had too many mouths to feed already, or men like Dan who had strong appetites and wives reluctant to feed them, or others with desires like France . . . passion for close kin . . . sisters . . . thou shalt not. More openly went youths like Edwin bursting with manhood, not minding if they were seen coming from the direction of Nell's corner of the Common.

Cuckoo Bushes, the wasteland, no man's land.

Belonging to no-one and everyone.

Common property.

Cuckoo Bushes.

There, women often waylaid her with half a pie or knuckle of bacon "for poor Tad" when she was wooding on the common. She would listen. Often that was all they needed from her, an uncritical ear, someone who would not look away, but listen and nod. Some went to her because they thought that she must have knowledge that they did not. They did not know that her barrenness was within her, that she had no secret that rendered her infertile.

But she gave them hope if they were childless, or hope if they wanted to be empty of the one they carried, or hope that they might stay barren for a while. They never got anything from her but words – no concoctions, no devices, none of the tampering service offered by some of her kind.

She was the recipient of secrets, an exchange mart and reservoir of bits and pieces of valuable knowledge about the mysterious workings of women. She often wore a sprig of some bush or a bud or cone or mast, which she would give to a woman who begged it for a charm.

"That there an't got no power, only what theece gives it theeself."

And if it did not work then none could blame Nell Gritt, for she had said that they might find such things for themselves, that she had just come across it lying there, and that it waddn't "nothing only two ole oak-galls that growed into one another."

Her voice was always quiet, her dialect broader even than the rest of her broad neighbours.

"Waal, if 'twere Oi . . . I reckons I might try the Cup of Roots but added in, a garden crocus bulb ground fine." Adding, with a laugh so that they would not pin too much reliance on the abortive power of a garden crocus bulb ground fine, "Ah, but then it b'issn't Oi, 'tis thee, and thee's the one must say whether 'tis a trick tale or no."

". . . black hellebore – waal, so Oi bin tole – made up into pellets like . . ."

". . . peppermint with honey . . ."

". . . be thee sure 'tis what thee do'st want? Ah. Well. Young rundles of ivy leaves spread with honey. But 'tan't no blessing without chick or child – so be thee sure, for 'tis a tender place to be putten ivy leaves."

She lived her precarious existence from day to day. She was an open secret. Her shanty was on common land, but that would be no obstacle to her being sent from the parish should she ever be an embarrassment or burden.

No matter how much they despised her, ostracised and feared her, communities like 'Clare needed a good woman like Nell Gritt. An unobtrusive woman who presented no bastards likely to threaten private or public purses. An independent woman who never came begging for anything or asking for help to provide for the man she had been bound to within the sight of the God of the nails.

In any case, there was no help.

Those who cared had not the means, and those with means cared not to discover that help was needed by such as Tad and Nell.

Nell Gritt was not a warm-hearted whore. She and Tad were of those at the bottom of the pile. They had nothing, never had, never would have. She had been a young wife, and now was an older one. She had a husband who needed looking after like a child. She provided for them both.

She was France's only confessor to his thoughts about Jaen.

"And don't tell me 'tis sinful thoughts, for I knows that."

"Thee casn't help thoughts, France," she said. "Only so long as thee *tries* to put them from thee."

"I tries. Times, when I stop out on Keeper's for days and never comes down. I sometimes won't even take the flock on Brack, where I can see their garden, because I know I shall end up sitting there, waiting to see if she comes out. And I makes up my mind to go down by the back path home. And until I'm nearly there I haven't got no intention of coming across the Common. Then it's like having a parched thirst, and the means to slake it and forcing yourself to go without. Then I suddenly finds that I've come to the Ford. And then I'm looking to see if she's there drawing water; then if she's working on their patch, or whether cooking smoke's coming from the chimney. I tries all right, but I gets driv without realising. Then 'tis all remorse."

"Poor France."

4

"You gets worst instead of better!"

Dan, hungry and tired, had again come in to a delayed supper. Sometimes he looked furious enough to give her a good leathering, knock some sense into her. But he seldom gave her more than a passing angry knock.

When he had first taken a fancy to her, although she was pretty, he had not thought her more desirable than many another pretty maid he had taken unawares and seduced with his good looks and playful charm. His mother had always said that all the Hazelhursts could charm linnets down out of the trees, but only Dan could make 'm sing as well.

He knew it. He had been confident that she would return his kiss. What had surprised him was her passion. And now where was it?

Occasionally it seemed to flare up, and when it did, Dan would feel quite light-hearted believing that she was getting better. Better from what, he did not know, but it made him hopeful that their marriage might stop being the scrappy, unsatisfactory affair that it was. When he was feeling buoyant and hopeful, he might make up a treat for them.

"Why don't us go for a treat a Sunday. We could go to Morning Service – you wear that new blue skirt – and we'll take the wagon . . ."

Occasionally they might even go. If they did, Dan would be led into imagining himself a few years hence, head of a family of sons, perhaps living at the main farm.

"We shall be all right. Father is as pleased as a dog with two tails now he can see the line succeeding. What we should a done was to call the first one Baxter, but then it's only natural I wanted to call him Dan. Still, Father's lived to see another Baxter Hazelhurst."

It was as though Jaen had lapses of normality, but that her usual state was one of wretchedness when she could scarcely hide her dislike of being touched by him.

"What be a matter now!" Exasperation in his voice.

"Nothing. It's just . . . I wish you would . . ." Then she would remember the pact about being a good wife and mother. "I wish the children didn't come so fast one upon the other."

"You wouldn't want to end up like Annie, would you." It was not a question, but an assumption. "Threatening people with a sickle . . . running off in the dark . . . stealing her own brother's child because she was so eat up with wanting a child of her own."

You wouldn't want to be like Annie?

You wouldn't want to be like Jaen!

"I only meant that they seems to come one a year." She might have said about the bother of wet-nursing, but that would have been being dishonest, for she always felt a sense of relief when she handed the child over to be fed by a village woman.

" 'Tis a blessing for the farm that they do come so often. I seems to be the one with the male seed for this family. Can't run no farm without men and boys coming on."

Jaen did not give voice to the thought, that she and her mother and little Ju had done pretty well. And now, by all accounts, they were doing even better, what with Ju's idea that they make products especially for selling, and not simply taking the stuff that was surplus. But Dan would never have it that Croud Cantle was a farm. "Fairy Acres", "Pixie Farm".

Jaen's best times were always when Bella and Jude visited. It was usually on a Sunday but sometimes they came on a Holy Day as well. They would leave Croud Cantle in the charge of Dicken Bordsell and the boy Johnny-twoey for a few hours. Perhaps a packman or a journeyman or a carter would carry a message beforehand: "Master over Croud Cantle says, God willing, she a be over on Sunday fortnight hence, if it won't be no hurt to the Master here."

Although she was pleased to see her mother, it was Ju who caused Jaen to anticipate the visit with so much pleasure. There was usually a moment of hesitation about Hanna, perhaps *this* time they would not wish to take her back with them. But she senses that they have become so used to Hanna, that they accept her as their own.

Jaen says, "Hello Child. You'm certainly growing."
The Child says, "Hello Jaen."
Then, when told to do so, "Hello Father."
Dan says, "Well Child, don't you think they'm fine little fellers?"
Hanna, well-nourished, sturdy and looking more like Jude than Jaen now, nods her red head and looks solemnly at the babies who are her brothers and plays with their fingers. Jaen watches her, trying to feel in herself something alive for The Child. And she does. She finds fear and guilt. What she looks for is that which she believes is natural for a mother to feel.
An instinct Vinnie would call love.

Why don't I love you, Child? Why will it be like a ton weight off my chest when I sees you going off down the path by Th'ammet, and why will it wrench my insides when I sees Ju going off too?
And why don't I love you, Dan'l, like Vinny loves Fancy?
And why don't I love you, little Bax, and you the one that's inside me?
Why can't I just be like anyone else and be pleased?

In the recesses of her mind lurks an unformed thought about Dan being as willing as herself to let The Child stay away year in year out – but, it is a subconscious thought.
She looks away from her children and sees that Ju is watching her closely. She smiles brightly at Ju.
After a visit from Bella and Jude, Jaen would often go for weeks seeming well enough, then Dan would come home of a day to discover that she had been off wandering, leaving the little ones with one of the girls, hardly seeming to know where she had been. Other times she would sit, staring into the fire, then jump when he spoke.
Smiling brightly. "Lord, I was miles away then, Dan."
If Dan was bewildered by her moods, so was Jaen herself. It wasn't just her attraction for France – though that did not help – she felt sometimes that she was living in a dark cave or a well. When she saw France it was like someone letting in the light.
She tried to talk to Vinnie.
Smiling brightly. "I reckon my brains is going soft, Vin.

There's times when I don't know whether I'm going or coming. Dan gets that cross. And I don't wonder."

But stable, practical Vinnie had no experience of what Jaen felt. "I know. 'Tis just the same with me. I had to make Pete put up a tethering post for Fancy. Once they'm on their feet you got to have eyes in the back of yer head."

Smiling brightly. "I shall need some in my elbows soon – I got another one on the way."

Placid, dull, contented Vinnie saw, as did Jude, something behind Jaen's brightness. Only once did she venture to hint to Jaen that she knew a bit about the use of alum and certain oils that could make a cottage fill less speedily with children. Jaen said that she did not like alum, and Vinnie left it at that.

There is only so much close friends can do for one another, and for the rest it often means standing by helplessly. And Vinnie had her hands full. What with Peter and Fancy, and her work at the main farm and their own plot. As well, being the one living next to France, she had undertaken the care of his cottage.

Jaen and Vinnie saw one another often enough, even though they only worked at the main farm at the busiest times such as planting, sheep-washing and harvesting. Vinnie always called out when she was going wooding so that occasionally they might go together. Vinnie was placid, and happy, and when she found that she was again pregnant at the same time as Jaen, she tried to rally their old intimacy.

When Fancy was four Jamie was born, by which time Jaen had Young Dan'l, Young Bax, Francis and Richard.

5

THE LONELINESS THAT JAEN had always felt living in 'Clare worsened, particularly since she could see nothing that would change it. For a while there had seemed to be a chance.

At one time, Ed Hazelhurst had started riding over to see Jude. At first, Jaen hardly dared let herself think of the prospect of Ju's marrying Ed and coming to live close by.

There would be the problem of The Child, of course. But soon in her imagination she settled all that. The Child could still go on living with Ju. She was much happier with Ju. Or they might share her. Hanna could come and see them quite often – that would be all right. She would get to know her brothers . . . they could work together in the fields. Ju could teach them all to read and write. That'd please Dan. He didn't approve of Mother allowing Ju to learn such stuff, but he would like it no end if the boys learnt. He always said that they should get some schooling – if Ed married Ju, then she could teach them.

All that mattered was, if Ju married Ed, then it would be like it was before; she would have someone to talk to, someone who would listen, talk back, ask what she thought about things. If only Dan would have taken her seriously it wouldn't be so bad. She used to try to talk to him at one time, but not now. She had been put down too many times, laughing at the very idea that her experience had any value.

"A couple of women growing a rod or two of peas for Blackbrook market and a crown of rhubarb to sell to the apothecary, and they thinks they can run a place like Teg!"

She pinned a whole new future on Ed's interest in Ju.

The next time that Ju and her mother brought Hanna over for

her duty visit, Jaen could not but help showing her disappointment when Ju made it plain that if there was any interest it was on Ed Hazelhurst's side, for she'd as soon marry the packman. "At least with the packman I should get a free supply of coffee beans – I got a regular passion for drinking coffee since I tasted it."

"I wish it had a been true, you'd a been such company, Ju."

She could see how unbelievable it must seem that she should feel so lonely in a cottage filled with the great chest and shoulders and voice of Dan and the clatter and voices of her boys, and the maids who sometimes came to help out.

By the time Young Dan'l was five years, and Bax a year younger, they were as lubberly and as large as bull-calves. Three-year-old Francis seemed to be twice the size of his cousin Margaret, who at the same age, looked as though a puff of wind might blow her away; and Richard, even when he was still on all fours, seemed to need more space than all the farm dogs put together. When Vinnie with Fancy and baby Jamie came into the Ham Ford cottage, they were like nine-pins tumbled in a box.

Ju was now quite taken over by learning her letters. She had changed their way of farming and had built up a good market trade. She had every hour of her day filled with things that interested her. She was so clever. Why would she want to marry a bunch of muscles like Ed?

Jaen had felt the loneliness grow back over her like thick ivy, shutting out the light, undermining her.

Throughout her childhood and girlhood, she had been ill-fed with any affection apart from Jude's, but Jude's love was a kind of adoration, which pushed Jaen into an adult role of giving at an early age. That hunger, for an affectionate arm about her or a pat upon her hand, was below her level of conscious desire. She was not aware of being rejected by Bella – she longed for such small caresses but did not know that she so longed for them. When she met Dan she was hungry for affection.

But it had been like feeding a starveling with fat pork. What she had needed was a more digestible kind of affection such as Dan's older brother now seemed to offer. Compared to the sweating, heaving Dan, France, with his quiet solitariness and the safe messages that were sent only with his eyes, became her fantasy love.

She had seen how harshly he sometimes used to treat Annie; she saw and heard him being as "Hazelhurst" as the rest of The Boys; she had seen the real France, but she ignored him, preferring the fantasy France, the quiet shepherd who had been kind on the day when Hanna was born.

Tending the flock on the downs behind Jaen's cottage, France saw her leave and walk along the path at the bottom of Keeper's Hill. She was alone; one of the maids from the main farm was temporarily at the Ham Ford Cottage helping with the little boys who seemed to be everywhere at once, and the baby who could move so fast on his knees that he often had to be confined by a tether for his own safety. Had Jaen taken one of them with her, then France might not have walked downhill. But with each baby that she carried, the swelling of her legs became progressively worse so that if she walked, it was slowly, and little boys were too much to cope with.

"You looks well enough, Jaen." He used to call her "Gel", and his using her Christian name had been the first change in his attitude towards her that she had noticed.

She sat on a tree that had recently been felled. The smell of the fresh sap rose and mingled with the crushed moss and wood sorrel where they had walked.

"For a mother of a brood like mine, I'm fair."

In his mind he said to her that it was true that she was fair, and that when he had seen her, almost nine years to the day, wasn't it, the day she was wed? – on that day he had been ashamed of his thoughts when he had seen her come from the Cantle church on Dan's arm.

This was not true, but he had made it so whilst tending his sheep and thinking of her. When he had begun to love her, he had gone over every picture of her that was in his memory.

His memory now held a great many retouched pictures.

It was true that she was fair. Her face was peach-coloured, her lashes only slightly darker than the pale gold of her eyebrows. Her light bone structure gave her face a fragile appearance, small almond-shaped chin, small nose and wide-spaced eyes. The bright smile she was accustomed to wear so often had caused small creases to form at the corners of her eyes – there were no creases on her brow. It appeared that the bearing of children in quick succession had improved upon the features of the girl who had left the Cantle church less than a decade ago. The ravages were hidden – almost hidden for, even this early in the day, her feet showed swollen and shapeless beneath her skirt.

"Are you all right these days, France?"

He nodded.

Asking questions outright like that when there was no one else there, was part of a change in their relationship that was taking place. A kind of verbal dance they did, where one would step forward with a comment and retreat, the other would bow and nod with a reply; but their conversation never joined hands and went twirling off – they each were aware of the danger there.

Perhaps Jaen feels protected by the movement of the baby. She takes another step.

"Don't you ever think of going to look for Annie? Don't you want . . . ?"

"No!" Sharply.

The dance halts in mid-step.

Whilst she has been seated, he has been crouched with one knee on the ground idly picking off sprays of crab-apple blossom that have flowered even though the tree is cut down; now he picks off the little pink buds and flicks them away one by one towards his dog who jumps to catch them.

"Don't do that to flowers."

He looks at his hands with surprise and says "Sorry" without thinking why.

Then, more gently than the first time, he says, "No. We never would a made a go of it. She was desperate for children; I don't think nobody can really blame her for what she done."

"That's not true. What about Martha? You know what it done to Martha, never really knowing where the girl is, if she's all right or no?"

He begins picking at the blossoms again so she reaches for them. He gives them to her.

She sits holding them like a posy before her unborn quiet child.

"Can I ask you summit?"

She smiles. "I don't know till you ask me."

"It's about your first one. The little girl."

Her voice comes out shriller than she intends.

"What about her?"

"I was only going to ask, is she going to live permanent with your mother?"

The question that asks itself of her daily, the question she puts aside not wanting the answer.

He sees the distress that shadows her face as she looks around for an answer.

"Ah. It an't no affair of mine. I shouldn't of asked."

He thinks that her distress is that she wants the little girl. Suddenly the answer to the puzzle of why the child does not live with her and Dan, comes to him – it is that Dan is not the child's father and he will not have it under his roof.

It is no affair of his, so he tries to suppress his anger and his younger brother's insensitiveness to the fragile golden woman he has loved by watching her from the top of the downs.

"Now you'm at it." He nods to the crab-apple blossoms that she has broken off and lie strewn upon her skirt.

"Oh!"

His sheep-dog comes and sits close, taking their attention upon itself, giving them a small breathing space. France now sits with his back against a bole facing Jaen and fondling the dog's ears.

"I was always grateful to you that day when she was born."

"It an't going to happen again today is it?"

She smiles, starts to take a step into the conversation but retreats again for a few moments.

"That day . . . I thought the child was dead . . . I hoped it was. It don't sound sense to say it, but I thought if it was . . dead . . . I could go back home and start all over again. I thought everything would come right if I could start again."

By making that confession, she has given France permission.

At first, two solo dancers in their verbal dance.

"I can't think of you like a sister no longer."

Still solo, Jaen says, "I never wanted the Child, but she was as much my fault as his. First off I thought after she was born I was sure that I must take to her, natural. But I never did."

"Sometimes I sits for hours on Brack, waiting to see you come out of your place."

He tries to catch her gaze, but she is looking inwardly, continuing as though he has not spoken.

"Like mother, like child. My mother never took to me. I think that it an't something that can be helped, but nobody never tells you it's possible not to take to your own child."

"I can't help myself."

"When they took the Child over home to stop for a bit, I went up on Brack and d'you know what I did? I promised I should be a good wife and mother if only the Child I couldn't take to stopped away." She suddenly looks directly at him. "Do you think that was wicked, France?"

"No!"

The force of his reply brings a lump to her throat.

Keeping a good distance between, he sits beside her upon the felled tree. There are no longer any barriers to what they may say to one another. They link verbal hands and move with slow steps.

"Why did you marry our Dan?"

"Because of the Child a course . . . they said I should. Not Dan, but he wasn't unwilling."

"I had an idea it was he what might of sent her away because . . ." to complete the sentence he must admit to what has been buried in his mind about her – part of his fantasy.

"She's Dan's child then?"

"Course she is. It's why we got wed."

"It's only that I never would a thought he'd have let no child of his own go to somebody else."

"If she'd a been a boy he wouldn't have, but she wasn't really a good enough prize for finding himself tied to somebody like me." His obvious tenderness towards her makes her open with him.

"He should of married somebody different. I never realised how different it'd be. Mother brought us up hard, but we never had no father nor brothers. When I was old enough, she would always let me have my say about everything to do with our farm." She smiled wryly. "She never always took much notice, but she never gave me orders, not once I was growed. It's been hard being told what to do by Dan."

"There an't nothing wrong with that. I reckon most husbands has a year or two of aggravation before wives gets settled down."

She is not listening.

"I *have* been a good wife to him, like I promised that day on Brack, except that I haven't never felt nothing warm for him."

She has implanted an enduring image in France's fantasy. Dan fathered their children, but that is her only link with him. She is free to be loved by France.

"Do you think I be wicked, Jaen?"

She frowns a little in puzzlement.

"You'm my brother's wife," he says. "The Church says 'tis incest."

"I never been able to understand how strangers can suddenly become brothers or sisters just because of marrying into a family."

"Bible says it is a sin."

She can see that they are leading one another into a quagmire that must suck them down. She feels as heavily pregnant as though near her time. She feels tenderness towards him, a chaste and thankful love. A safe, ideal love. How can such love be a sin?

The child lies between her and France, protects her from wrongdoing, and gives her permission to love her husband's brother like this. Unfleshly. Chaste love.

> *. . . Permission . . .*

She says, "It says 'n all, it's a sin to love somebody when you'm already married," and reaches to touch his tightly crimped beard that she has felt a hundred times in her fantasy.

France lays a hand upon hers, holding it to his face.

"I don't see no road out of that one. For you'm married, and I'm still Annie's husband. But I loved you even before she went off."

> *. . . permission to ignore the rules of the Church of God of nailed hands . . .*

"I wondered if you did. I hoped in my heart you did. Many's the time when we met accidental, it wasn't no accident."

> *. . . permission to love her brother . . .*

"I love you, Jaen – there an't no oddsing that."

She sees that his love is not unfleshly.

She experiences again the relief she felt that first time when she had reached out to Dan, but this time pure and unphysical.

"Then we both be sinners, France."

Jaen's next son does not stir when she returns his kiss and so breaks her promise to the spirit of Brack.

6

OYSTERS AND STOUT ALE

FOR THE FIRST YEAR OR TWO, life for Annie and Betrisse was harder than it had ever been at Up Teg. The main work to be had in Emworthy was that which surrounded the fishing fleet of cutters, smacks and flatties, and the importation of French wines. The importation business was not one that a newcomer would be aware of or would be employed in, it being carried on unobtrusively and with look-outs posted. However, those who were engaged in that business were proud of their reputation as handling only the finest wines from the best vineyards of France, and guarded it jealously.

Therefore, Annie had no option but to take whatever work she could get from the oyster people. Menial jobs, heavy humping of baskets, sharp shells, salt water. Annie was used to hard labour in all weathers, but now she became familiar with working in lashing winds and freezing sea-spray.

In the early days, she was often given work because of Betrisse: those who employed her got four hands for the price of two. The only pence a ten-year-old might earn was from petty jobs, but her labour added to Annie's made better economics because they were able to get more work. At first Betrisse was indignant that nobody would give her separate work.

"I an't a child. I used to do proper work back There. They'm just getting me for nothing. It an't *fair!*"

"Nothing an't fair, Bet, which means you got to use your noddle. If you can't beat them, you got to join up with them – and *then* beat them at their game. Don't worry, it'll come."

Although Betrisse did not know just what Annie meant, she had complete confidence in her. Ever since that day after the christening party, when Annie had stood up to Luke, when she had looked like a lunatic, or a wild animal, or an avenging angel, according to how you saw her; ever since the day when she threatened to slice Luke with the sickle she held over him if he did not stop the strapping; ever since the night when Annie had broken into the hen-house, where Luke had left his audacious daughter to learn her lesson on docility, subjection and filial obedience, and Betrisse and Annie had begun their long walk to the coast – ever since then, Betrisse never questioned Annie's faith in their future.

When they got to Emworthy, they had only enough money left from working their way down country to provide lodgings for a few days, but they never wanted for a bite to eat or a roof over their heads. Often it was of the very basic, but sufficient to keep them going.

Most of the work came in with the tide. Annie would wait about, looking for somebody wanting a pair of hands.

"I'm strong and I'll do anything – and you gets the girl for nothing. You an't got nothing to lose giving us a try."

They had come there on a whim, on a fancy and upon the image that Annie had kept in her mind and then shared with Betrisse. Sometimes when the sky was bruised, steel-grey with approaching snow, smudged with mustard-yellow and with that same yellow on the horizon, when the sea was flat and icy, Annie would take a moment from her work and look, then smiling broadly say, "Still like living by the glitterish sea, Bet?"

Betrisse would return the smile. "Better'n they old turnip fields back There."

And for them, it was.

They kept their promise to one another and never complained of their situation. When they were reduced to the meanest shelter they would nullify any discomfort by talking about and planning for better times. They were great planners, great talkers about what they were going to do. If on some January night they were chilled to the marrow, they would sleep in every garment they possessed and take warmth from one another, Annie wrapping her arms about the girl, talking low until they were warm enough to sleep. Annie never talked down to Betrisse, but asked her opinion, and took notice of what the girl said.

"Well, think about it. Don't say yes just because I thinks we ought to – 'tis your life as well. You got to learn to stand up for yourself."

Of course they did complain and grumble, but their expressions of discontent were only over things like being taken advantage of in their work, or the fleas in the lodging-house; for the rest they were happy together.

Neither of them ever forgot what had brought them to the coast.

After their initiation into the shellfish business by way of drudge, they graduated to other work, no more congenial when the winds cut their cheeks and salt-water stung the hundreds of small shell-cuts on their fingers, but better paid.

When the fleet returned, some of the vessels tied up in an area known as The Slipper, close to where Annie and Betrisse lodged. The catch would be landed, and the sorters would start on it. It was at this work that Annie and Betrisse were best. They became skilful and fast at sorting scallops from oysters. And Betrisse became particularly fast and good at judging which of the oysters were ready to be laid in the ponds for marketing, and which needed to be sent down-harbour for fattening.

As well as the better pay, the smacksmen always had fish that had been dredged up with the shellfish, to give away. They lived simply but well. Fish seven days out of seven, hardly ever two days the same – frizzled on a hot griddle, speared over glowing wood, stewed in a dish of cider and, their favourite, a suet pudding containing a pool of steaming oysters at its heart.

Although they had come to this busy little village on a fancy, they could scarcely have discovered a more suitable place as a refuge. Because of Emworthy's second, illicit, industry, once she was known and seen not to have any business with the Excise men, Annie was accepted. Nobody wanted to know where she was from or why she had come there. Annie Saint John and her girl were good workers who kept their noses out of other people's affairs, and abided by the established rules of the community. If a cutter brought in net bags that held a catch of bottles as well as shellfish, Annie ignored both origin and destination.

Here, they were as safe from discovery as they would be anywhere. If strangers came, the word went round and those who wished to could dissolve into the background until it was known who the newcomers were, or they left. No one who was the least threat to Mistress Saint John and her girl ever came. And had they done so, after a year or two only a close member of the Up Teg family might have recognised Annie.

It seemed that the only feature that she retained of her Mistress Hazelhurst identity was her short stature and her upright carriage, but even there she had lost her stiff-necked and haughty stamp. She walked freely with long strides, swinging her arms. She had come to terms with her maternal longings – she was not free of them and would ask to hold any baby – but she had Betrisse. In spite of all her long hours of hard work, Annie's silhouette became fuller and more rounded.

"Lor, a diet of fish and stout ale must suit me. I begins to look like a loaf."

Loaf or not, there were men who looked twice and thrice at Annie Saint John, and in her mid-thirties, an age when women were often staid matrons with as much gum as tooth, Annie looked ten years younger than they. And if a man should pay her a rough, smacksman's compliment – a bottle of French wine perhaps, or what remained of the specially baked sea-bread, or a share of his bed, she would turn down the last good-naturedly but accept the two former in the friendly spirit offered.

People liked Annie Saint John.

And if, by the time that they had truly exchanged husbandry for fishwife skills, Annie was scarcely recognisable as her former self, the child Betrisse no longer existed at all.

Betrisse Saint John, by the age of twelve, was a head taller than Annie. By the age of fourteen head and shoulders taller. She had developed into a woman with a small high bosom and round hips. Between one winter and the next, she had grown so that she and Annie were no longer able to share a pair of boots or pattens.

"Lord, you'm getting to be a Hazelhurst, Bet."

That name had never been said aloud more than could be counted on the fingers of one hand in the years since they left Newton Clare.

"Annie! Don't you never say that."

"No. I wasn't thinking. But look at it like this, that if you was going to inherit anything from them, it might as well be their looks."

"And have to bend down to get into a room?"

"Think about it as being able to look down on ordinary folk."

Betrisse pulled herself up to her full height and patted Annie's head playfully. "Do you remember Vinnie's wedding?"

"I can guess what you'm going to say," Annie said.

"Go on then."

"About you standing on the trestle?"

Betrisse laughed. "Was it that plain to see?"

"The old man lifted you up and told you to say something, and that look you sometimes get came on you."

"What look?"

"Your 'No! I an't going to' look. With your little lips pinched in defiance."

"I had gone to him to tell him what a beautiful wedding it was, and he wanted me to stand up and tell everybody and I wasn't going to. Then I looked around and saw everything like it must have been for Them – looking down from their great height."

"And you started to make a display of yourself."

"Oh Lord yes – I dare say I did." Betrisse went quiet for a few moments.

From time to time, they had made little moves towards talking of the past, but Annie had always felt it better to change the subject because of the agitation the child always began to display. Now the time seemed right to talk.

Last winter they had moved out of lodgings and now rented a narrow half of a narrow house close by The Slipper – a room which was virtually a scullery with a hearth and a row of hooks in the open beams. There was a small room above, reached by a climb of rickety steps.

The house belonged to a smacksman, Edward Scantlebury, whose aged father, and Scantlebury himself when ashore, lived in the front kitchen. The arrangement suited them all well, for the smacksman was more often than not at sea and let them have the rooms for a small rent in return for providing the old father with a meal, and keeping an eye out for him.

Four walls that they could call their own, were what Annie and Betrisse needed to allow them to feel that they now truly belonged to the village and the community of shellfishers. That a smacksman, who might have business to keep from the knowledge of the Excise men, accepted Annie and her girl as tenants, put a seal of approval upon them.

Now it was summer when they could usually take their food and eat it by The Slipper, where there was always something going on. Their new home was not far from their old lodgings, where they had long ago ceased to cause comment upon their habit of eating by the sea whenever the weather was fair enough.

It was probably because of their new-found security in the rented rooms, and because they had an established routine of work and leisure, that they felt safe enough to venture into the past. Or perhaps it was that they lived like sisters – true, twenty years between them, but certainly equals.

"Do you know, Annie, since this last spring, I've found myself thinking about standing on the trestle more than once. I suppose it might be because I've shot up tall all of a sudden, and I remember that feeling of looking down. There's plenty of men I'm on level eye with now. You don't think it's possible for a woman to grow as big as . . ." she faltered "Annie, I'm not like my father, am I?"

"We'm all a bit like our fathers, Bet, and it's foolish to say we an't."

"I couldn't abear to be like him."

"He wasn't bad. Nobody is."

"When I was little I used to . . ." She found difficulty putting into words her store of formless memories and emotions. ". . . he used to be nice. It was Him who always made so much of me. More than Her. I could get things out of Him. If I showed off, he used to laugh often as not – sometimes when She clouted me, He would tell her that it was just high spirits. I shan't never understand how He could . . ."

Annie too could not understand how he could bring himself to beat the tender child so much with hard leather, but she did not want the girl to grow up with a ghoul locked inside her – as the lascivious-featured ghoul of her own father was locked in her own memory, jumping out upon her from time to time. She had often thought that he would not have had power to terrorise her half so much if she could have told somebody what she had seen her father do to that girl.

"Perhaps Luke was afraid."

"Afraid!"

"Oh, I an't defending him, 'twadden ordinary chastisement, there was a beast in him that day. But he must a felt shamed. There he was at the Christening supper, in front of the whole pack of them, and you had shouted at the old man, and you wouldn't take no notice of your mother, then Luke told you to stop and you wouldn't take no notice of him. And then when you ran off and nobody could find you. I dare say I wasn't the only one who was frightened to death that night at the thought we might a found you drowned in Th'ammet."

She closed her eyes and shook her head at the memory.

"It don't excuse what he did to you, but I do reckon he might a been afeard of what you might grow up to be."

The sun, sinking into Portsmouth Harbour, glittered on the little triangular waves where the sea was riffled up by the breeze. That same breeze which carried from the dunes a heavy scent of evening primrose. Betrisse, watching a chaos of gulls she had tempted into riot with a morsel of bread, seeing inwards. Almost dispassionately now, she could retrieve the scene in which the small Betrisse's hiding-place had been discovered next day.

"It's the coldest I ever was that night."

"Luke was beside himself when they couldn't find you."

"So he beat me black and blue."

"Like I said, when people gets afraid, they do some things they regrets after. I dare say he leaped ahead in his mind and saw you when you was twenty standing up to them, saying 'shan't!' Men like Luke has a great fear of women."

"Ha!"

" 'Tis true. Dan's the same, and the old man. It's a like they'm not sure of theirselves."

Betrisse raised her eyebrows in exaggerated disbelief.

"Oh, I know all about they being domineering and that, and I wonder whether that an't just the trouble. If you watches men with a herd of beasts, they'm all shout and stick, making panic where there wasn't none, but women a get pigs penned or cows into a barn in half the time by just telling them 'girrup, girrup'. If a herd runs off when a girl's in charge of moving them, it don't make much matter to her, but if it's a lad, he a lose face and told he an't no better than a wench."

"I don't see what that got to do with it."

"I don't know hardly how to explain, but right from when they'm little, boys gets showed how they got to be top dog as you might say, they gets a stick put in their hand as soon as they'm big enough."

"So did I."

"Ah, but you wasn't told you was King o' the Castle. And I reckon it's because they'm told that, and that women is lesser creatures because they can't provide for theirselves . . ."

"Like you and me." Betrisse got an answering wry smile from her aunt.

"Ah . . . but you got to see how it all goes together. Even though they sees every day of their lives that there an't much they can do as we can't, they been given the responsibility for us."

"And that's why . . . my . . . why Luke leathered me like that."

"I think it's bid fair it could be. There was a little bit of a thing like you – a girl – his daughter – defying him before everybody, and he was supposed to be King o' the Castle."

"And you reckon he beat me because he was afraid?" Disbelief in Betrisse's tone.

"I don't know, but I've found myself doing it before now. I once near broke the back of a dog what turned on me – a yard dog who'd always been a docile old thing, then one day he bared his teeth at me and I turned on him. I turned on him because I was afraid of what might happen. I never thought about it at the time, but remembering how I felt, it was because I thought a lesser creature was out of my control – and I panicked with fear."

7

AT HAM FORD COTTAGE

When things began to go wrong, Jaen knew that she had only herself to blame. She thought she might return to Brack and try to regain the sense of being protected, but time and again she heard her mother's words: "You made your own bed, so you must lay on it".

And she said to herself that it was true.

It had been in her own hands to have said no to Dan; he didn't take her by force, did he? She had wanted him. Same with France, she hadn't done anything to stop him when he said that he loved her. At the time, all that she could think about was the pleasure of that moment. After . . . ? Afterwards she had to lie on her bed of guilt and anger at herself, bed of regret and misery at her own weakness. Why was she so weak? She dipped herself in a pool of guilt about Ju, Dan, the Child . . . France.

Then, over a period of time it began to occur to her that there must be a flaw in her, something born in her.

That must be it, a thing in her nature that she could not control. When she thought of it, it frightened her in the way that dark, lonely places are frightening, where an unimaginable creature lurks, waiting to leap.

Perhaps that was why their mother was so stiff and tight, always having to keep a hold of herself, never daring to let herself go. Was it something they was born with, like their red hair? Was that it?

She began to think about Ju, and the times when they had both done things for no other reason than that they wanted to, on the spur of the moment, not thinking of the consequences – just because they wanted to.

They had always been wandering off together, suddenly deciding to go to the old ruins on Winchester Hill, or somewhere like that, wherever their capricious thoughts led them, and they would stay in their fantasy world forgetting time and work until reality returned and made their hearts leap. Then they would race back home, and work twice as fast and hard to put things right.

Once they had jumped into Chard Lepe Pond and lay in the water without clothes. It had happened that they had suddenly felt like lying in the green water and hadn't thought twice about it. Yes, it did seem to be in their nature to be like that. Ju and her reading and writing, it was something she suddenly thought she wanted to do, and she had got her way.

And their father . . .

Tomas Nugent.

She had one image of him, ah such a wonderful picture to carry in the memory – the handsome man in a beautiful blue coat. She had been a very small child, and he had stayed only a short time, but Jaen remembered him.

He went as abruptly as he had come and their mother never mentioned him. It was only in the last few years that she had come to realise who the handsome man had been. That was after the whole dark story of him had come out.

She gradually panned the assorted ore of thoughts and was left with a residue of one nugget of truth – she had inherited her father's self-indulgent, capricious nature.

Tomas Nugent who had loved Mother and married her not long before Jaen was born. Then he had suddenly gone off and left them for five years. As suddenly he had come back.

That was what Jaen remembered.

He had come back and the days had been light and warm. A man, his blue coat hanging from one shoulder, taking the pins from Mother's hair, and Mother laughing, with her cap off and her great mass of thick, golden-red hair, unpinned and tumbling down to her waist.

That image and memory was a glowing charcoal in the midst of grey ash.

Then suddenly, he had left again, for ever.

Ju had been born a few months later. Jaen had not connected the two events at the time. Ju had been glowing charcoal too.

It had all come out a few years back. Their father had run off with a girl of twelve or thirteen. One of their own milkmaids. Then he had run away from her too, and had been drowned at sea. They had found this out years later, since Jaen had come to Newton Clare, when the girl, who was now a woman, had turned up in Cantle.

Once she began to think of it, she knew that she was right, her weakness was in her nature – born in her.

She only hoped Ju was different.

8

On a day soon after Jaen's encounter with France, Jude brought Hanna to visit her parents. Bella did not come and, as it was an occasion when Baxter desired to see a pew full of Hazelhursts in church, Dan had taken the older boys there. Once Hanna's duty of answering Jaen's stilted questions were over, she went off with one of the Up Teg child-servants to look at the Ham Ford animals and to poke about in the outhouses. Then Jaen had the rare pleasure of having Jude to herself.

Jude always looked full of health and vitality. Of the two, Jaen had always been the prettier, but now that they were women, it was Jude who caught the eye. Like Bella, she held herself erect, but with an extra tilt to her chin that might be thought of as too above herself in a girl who worked barefoot in the fields of a tiny holding, a speck compared to Up Teg.

Like Hanna, Jaen, Bella and their Estover ancestors, Jude had the hair. Red and gold and strikingly noticeable. Anyone who had the notion that character might be ascertained from hair-type, would have been interested in these four "Estover" women. Hanna's hair, like Bella's, was thick and flowing and solid. Jaen's fringed her face, light, pretty and curly, whilst Jude's sometimes appeared to be a wild, buzzing cloud that was always bursting from any twist or tie or cap.

The morning that Jude came was real March weather. The kind of day that, when they were children – Jude four or five and Jaen ten or so – Jaen would have drawn the back hem of their skirts between their legs and fastened it at the front waist, leaving their legs free to run in the blustering winds. Although Ju never really liked high winds, she did whatever Jaen did, perhaps going out to find primroses, or taking strips of rags to run streamers or to make sails that would billow in the winds that rebounded off the downs.

This morning, damp and glowing from the exertion of walking with the donkeys on the last, steep part of the journey down the sides of Keeper's Hill, with her hair stuck all over with celandines and tied on top as carelessly as a child's, Jaen sensed a change in her sister.

Ju had grown really beautiful lately, but it wasn't only that, she seemed soft, easy and sure of herself.

If only Ju need never go away. It would all come right again. Then France . . . No! She could not bear to think of France, not whilst Ju was here. She pushed France away.

Forget that now.

In the kitchen alone the sisters pressed cheek to cheek. Jude patted Jaen's belly.

Jaen hunched her shoulders. "I got some time to go yet, but I swells up so these days. Don't let's talk about that. I got some beans." She smiled with pleasure, knowing Jude's passion for a rare drink of coffee. They sat together in the quiet kitchen.

"Oh Ju, the peace of it. You got no idea."

"Ah, I dare say they make themselves heard when they'm all in here at once."

Jaen gazed into her bowl of coffee and saw the order and quiet of the kitchen at Croud Cantle, her mother's bright red-tiled floor which was treated like an object of ornament. The busy, quiet evenings with Mother k'chack-k'chack-k'chack at the spinning wheel, and herself and Jude combing and carding or perhaps in the orchard putting a maggot-wash on embryo fruit. Whenever Jude came, and they were sitting together, Jaen's memories were always of the two of them inseparable – until Jaen had proved traitor to her young sister. She pushed that thought away too.

Forget that now. Forget that unhappy time of Ju's withdrawal.

"I wish you wasn't so far away, it's so lonely."

Ju said that she wished so too, then she could visit more often, but Jaen was not sure whether she meant it or no. The thoughts she was trying to push away, pushed back. Ju was probably thinking Jaen hadn't cared much about loneliness when she had gone off with Dan.

Over their coffee-drinking, Jaen observed her sister as she passed on the Cantle gossip Dicken Bordsell provided, then it came to her . . .

"You got a young man, Ju."

At first Jude held back, but Jaen was sure that she was right.

Ju's soft, easy manner was love. Oh Ju. You could tell that Ju had met somebody who was more than just a passing fancy. When Jaen asks her about it, a bright flush springs to Jude's cheeks as she says the name, "Will Vickery", and Jaen knows.

Jaen knows, and she feels a kind of violence expand within her at the certain knowledge that Ju has been with the man. Whoever he is, this Will Vickery, he's not good enough. Whoever he is and however much Ju thinks of him, he's not worth half nor quarter what she got from his kisses and the few seconds of elation. None of that was worth it; worth losing the only things that had ever been your own, your own body, your own self. Even if Will Vickery was the King, what difference would it make? Ju could finish up with her legs swelled up and her insides feeling they was dragged down.

Jaen wants to cradle Ju as she used to, but that was years ago. She feels awkward. In her anger at the thought of Ju repeating her own mistakes, Jaen forces Ju to look at the ravages all her pregnancies have wrought; forces her to look at her thin hair, her waterlogged flesh. "Look at me, Ju. Go on look! This," she stands with the cap she has dragged from her head, "this is what comes of that," she runs her hand through her sparse hair, "comes of half a minute of enjoyment."

Jude stares at Jaen. Jaen does not move, hoping that she can get something into Ju's head. Jude does not respond as Jaen presses on with her angry advice but watches as her sister ties her cap and pulls forward the few ringlets that have helped to make-believe that constant childbearing has left her as pretty as ever.

At last though, Jaen has no more to say and goes to sit with Jude, and put both arms about her. It is a mature gesture. Now, they are two women, with equal knowledge of love and desire . . . except that Jaen believes that Ju can't see where it all leads.

The violence of her feelings calmed, she says quietly, "It an't worth it," and begins talking openly of her feelings, and of Dan.

She talks as though France does not exist. As though the only time she ever allowed her feelings to get out of hand was that first time with Dan. Somewhere – here, now – must exist the recent memory of her needful fingers raking France's virile beard.

Somewhere the knowledge of France's damp brow close to her own; his dry, warm hands; the admission that she was aroused by France with an unchaste look in his eye, his mouth heavy as he talks of the sin of his passion for her.

At the moment of speaking, her counterfeit truth was genuine.

"You need not go on so, Jaen, I haven't got no intention of marrying him. Him nor anybody."

Jaen wished that she could believe Jude.

They slipped back into talking of the years when Jude was growing up, when they had been at the centre of one another's days.

When it was near to dinner-time, Hanna came in and chattered in her serious way about the bits and pieces of work she had just helped the girls do; it was her usual way of filling in the time until she could go back home to Cantle. Soon after came the sound of light cartwheels, then chattering little boys. They burst in and filled the room. What Hazelhursts they were. When Jaen had come to Up Teg as a bride, Nance Hazelhurst had said that the one thing about marrying into this family was that they never wanted for a decent meal. And you could see the truth of that in all the fat little knees.

To see Jaen with them was to call to mind a wren with cuckoos in the nest.

Then Dan came in, ducking down in the low doorway and stooping when he passed under the beams. Jaen went to attend to the food and Dan came to stand astride the hearth. He could not help himself. Although he made no bones about not liking his wife's sister, he looked her up and down slowly, watching the rise and fall of her breasts, inspecting the curve of her back as he slapped the warmth of the fire into his thighs and stretched his arms. His thighs, his potent arms, his wide chest, sinews, biceps, illustrated the male, showed what Dan Hazelhurst was made for. He provoked the young woman into looking at him. Again and again she drew her eyes from him, always they returned to look him up and down.

Dan was as impressive and physically attractive in his middle years as he had been when young.

As Jaen cut up bread and handed the little boys their bowls she caught glimpses of Jude, noticed how in spite of herself she was captured by him. And glimpses of him. "Coming over all

Hazelhurst" was how she and Vinnie had described their way of looking down from their full height. Vinnie dealt with Peter by catching him around the waist and treating him playfully, telling him he needn't come the old giant with her. And for all the fact that they had been married as long as Dan and Jaen, Vinnie and Peter often behaved much like their children, tickling and chasing.

"An't it time you two growed up?"

"What for?" Vinnie would say. "We should only get like the rest of you."

Jaen heard Dan say, "Still not married then" in the challenging way he had with Ju. She did not hear the answer, but Ju had her defiant look on. Jaen hoped that she would not irritate him by asking him about corn-prices and things she seemed to know more about than he did.

He was very touchy at the moment about arguments that had been going on between The Boys about Dan's wish to go over to all one crop. He had been furious when Jaen had offered an opinion on being cautious.

If Ju got his back up now, he wouldn't get over it for days. Jaen suspected that, for all his protesting "I knows what I be doing of. I dussn't need theece to tell me," he knew that his new ideas of cropping were like playing hazard in a fair booth.

9

IN THE GARDEN OF COPPICE COTTAGE, Vinnie, with Fancy helping, was pinching out the tops of beans when she saw Jaen's sister crossing the ford on her way back to Cantle. Jaen's sister was alone.

"Wave Fancy, wave to Auntie Jaen's lady."

The child ran to the fence but Auntie Jaen's lady, riding one donkey and leading another, stared ahead.

"That's funny, Pete, she haven't got young Hanna with her."

Peter, sheltered in the porch, sunning himself and having a quiet Sunday smoke, said, "Well, what about it? Women always got to make summit out of nothing."

"When she come she brought Jaen's girl, and she've gone home without her. That an't nothing."

"I'll tell you one thing – it an't got nothing to do with you."

Vinnie went back to her task. There was summit up. She knew. Summit unexpected. Jaen would have said something when they met out wooding yesterday and Vinnie asked, "How's my little Goldy-girl these days?"

Jaen had said, "I shouldn't be surprised if they don't bring her over to see us tomorrow."

If Hanna had a been going to stop, she'd a had a bundle with her that morning. She didn't have a bundle; Vinnie had seen them as they passed along the lane at the back of her cottage. And going up the lane just now, not taking a bit of notice of Fancy . . . Jaen's sister never acted like that. She wasn't one to be all over you, but she always waved and told Hanna to say something. Hanna had been brought over from Cantle times enough over the last years, sometimes Jaen's sister and her mother together, sometimes just one of them, but they always arrived a couple of hours after sun up and left a couple of hours before dark. When she was little, Hanna would be riding with the mother or the sister, but these days she often came riding her own donkey.

There was summit up; there always was when people acted different from normal. Vinnie knew that she was not wrong. The sister was going home with the empty donkey, and she had not waved to Fancy.

10

SCANTLEBURY'S

At somewhere near the time of year when France had been holding Jaen's hand to his face, Annie was feeling the cold cheek of the old man Scantlebury, who did not respond when she took him his bowl of sops, and saw that he was dead. He had gone to sleep quietly, then drifted nicely into death, so that when Ted Scantlebury returned on a tide two days after the old man's interment, Annie could truthfully say that the father had gone on as peaceful as any good body could a wished for.

"I'm sorry I wasn't with him at the end." Annie was genuinely sorry, she and Betrisse had grown to like the old fisherman.

"You always done more for him than was agreed between us." Ted Scantlebury, always polite in his rough way, stood with her and looked at the place that had been allotted to his father's remains.

They walked slowly back to his cottage, which was Annie's and Betrisse's as well, by the payment of rent.

Annie said, "You a be wanting a new agreement now, Master Scantlebury: I shouldn't mind getting it settled soon as you feels like it, so me and Betrisse knows where we stands."

He drew his brows together.

"About the rooms," she added.

"Ah. Rent, you means?"

"Yes. Now the old man's gone. When you'm ready."

When he was ready, which was the day the oyster fleet was due out again, he went round to the back door, which it had been agreed should be for the use of Mistress Saint John and her girl. Although they rented a very small part of a very small house, it was because they had this separate entrance that Annie and Betrisse felt that they were not lodgers in the usual sense.

"I a come straight to the point," he said, accepting the stool and the drink of wine Annie offered. "I wants to make you a proposition – you don't have to make up your mind straight away, but if you don't want to take it up . . ." he trailed off and drank deeply of the wine . . . "That's as good a drop of May wine as I've tasted in many a day."

Annie held out her hand for the beaker and refilled it as he continued.

"I was saying . . . it won't make no difference to you stopping on here for the time being, but I should like to have your answer by next time we comes in."

Annie smiled at the man. Her liking for him had begun with the concern that he had shown for his aged father and had slowly grown when she observed other traits she liked in people: "A no-nonsense sort. A body knows where you are with somebody like that."

He was a middle-height, sturdily built man at the beginning of his middle years. His hair, which was rust-coloured, heavy and dead straight, he wore scraped back and tied tightly. Typical of someone of his colouring, beneath salt-water and weather-damage his skin was very light, his lashes which fringed very deep-set eyes were pale, as were his thick eyebrows. His hairline, which was inherited, rather than created by age, went far back giving him a lofty-browed appearance, a wide expanse for hundreds of small freckles. It was the freckling which Annie always said was what made him look honest – and his eyes a course.

"For somebody what's coming straight to the point . . ." she said.

"You'm right. It's just a question of which way to . . ." He plunged in. "Since the old Drag Anchor closed down, there an't been a decent inn at the harbour end, and I thought about opening up one. I don't mean a alehouse, but a good, clean place with a dormit'ry and one or two little sleeping cells for decent kinds of folk that has to put up for a night or two."

He peered at her, but she made no response except to say, "Go on."

"They two places," he indicated some cottages across the yard. "I got refusal of them if I wants. They an't much bigger than this, but the three on 'm together would make a decent enough size for what I had in mind."

"You means you wants to have these rooms back then?"

"No, no. I was wondering whether you'd care to go into business with me."

Annie looked with unbelief at him.

"In business?"

"Yes. It'd be a business arrangement. If I should take they cottages and have some alterations made, they'd be the . . . the sleeping quarters as you might say. This place would be the kitchens and eating room part. You and your daughter could have the room above here."

"And what would be my part in this here business?"

"To run it."

"Run a inn? My eye. I an't never done nothing like that in my life."

"Yes you have." Betrisse, who had been sitting quietly, taking in every word, leaned forward eagerly. "It an't any different from any other kind of cooking and cleaning, and we both done plenty of that. It only means it would be for more people. What part of the business would you be doing, Mr Scantlebury?"

No smacksman was used to being straight questioned by a young girl, but Betrisse's manner was polite and as straightforward as his own. He surprised himself at not taking exception to it.

"I wasn't thinking of nothing more than putting up the money and buildings at first."

Annie looked from Betrisse to her landlord.

"At first?" Annie said.

"Mistress Saint John, I an't getting no younger, and the sea an't getting no calmer. Apart from that I reckon, with all the foreign vessels that's coming to fish our waters, it won't be many years before this part of the coast is fished out. I'm looking a few years ahead, for what you might say is a nice little harbour to drop anchor in."

"You mean that you'd still go out dredging?"

"For a year or two more, then I should become a landsman."

"It still seems a queer sort of arrangement. Inns needs muscles, men and boys, stables, casks, there's no end of heavy work . . ."

Betrisse cut in. "Since when haven't we been able to move a cask between us? And in any case, you can hire labour can't you?"

"Oh Bet, don't get carried away. Master Scantlebury, I appreciates you asking . . ."

"Annie, we can do it!"

"Bet!"

Betrisse sat back, but it was obvious that she had not finished.

Annie resumed. "Mr Scantlebury, as far as I can see it, you – who an't never had no experience of inn-keeping – is asking me – who an't neither – to start up a inn. Since me and Bet came to live here, we have worked at anything that came our way, to get food in our mouths and a roof at night . . ."

"I know that. It's why I asked you."

"But inn-keeping!"

"Perhaps I shouldn't a called it inn-keeping. It an't inn-keeping in the usual way.

"You know what it's like when it's weather. Vessels can't get out for high seas – vessels with a few passengers aboard. Landsmen likes to sleep ashore when they can, and where's there a decent place to stay here? They an't all fishermen who's used to any old hole to curl up in. There's plenty like I am myself – taking it rough as part of the job at sea, but likes a clean and decent bed ashore."

Betrisse held back. She could see that Annie was tempted.

"What about when you finishes with the fishing then?"

"I should be the labour." He smiled and flexed his biceps. "Strong enough for hefting things about."

Annie smiled back and wagged her head. "I don't know. You see, Master Scantlebury, we always been used to being our own mistresses."

"We should still be, Annie. We could take on this job just the same as we took on all the rest. Was you thinking of paying us by the month or by the year?"

"Don't take no notice of her forwardness, Mr Scantlebury. She been like that since she was two."

"When you been dredging for shellfish as long as I been, you'm used to bartering with oyster-wives, but they'm usually a sight less decent a vision than your daughter. I was thinking, as we was doing business over more than a basket of scallops, we would have a yearly agreement."

"Would you give us a free hand?" Betrisse asked.

"A free hand?"

"To run the place our way?"

"I don't see why not, so long as it was respectable."

"*We* wouldn't run anything that wasn't." Annie's tone was sharp with this interjection.

"I know that, Mistress Saint John, or I shouldn't a had you under my roof in the first place."

"Well that's all right then."

"But . . ." He held out his empty beaker and Annie made a motion to fill it. "No," he said, "I wasn't meaning that." He paused, choosing his words. "When we says respectable, I hope we means the same thing."

For a moment, Annie looked puzzled; then Betrisse spoke up.

"Come straight out, Master Scantlebury. You means the French wine and brandy business?"

Scantlebury started momentarily, then laughed aloud.

"You, miss, would do very well in the Excise. The way you takes somebody unawares would startle an admission out of even a man who'd been in the business all his life."

"Like yourself, Master Scantlebury?"

"Betrisse! You never did know when to stop."

"That's true," Betrisse said. "I'm sorry, Mr Scantlebury." She grinned at Annie. "You can't blame me – 'tis the way I been brought up."

11

LINE OF DESCENT

TOWARDS THE END OF THE DECADE when Jaen's seventh child was born (a sixth son, George), Baxter took the long ride to Winchester to consult the Law and the Church, and returned with some documents which none of them at Up Teg could read, but which were intended to make Dan and his line eventual masters of Up Teg.

An assurance of Hazelhursts at Up Teg.

Upon his return the old man summoned the family into the kitchen of the main farm.

"Till I be gone on, you all stays on living where you be now. After the Almighty have seed fit to take me, then Dan moves in here. When he passes on, Young Dan'l gets the tenancy."

Bald statements. Until the Almighty did call him, even when seated, Baxter Hazelhurst was undoubted Master of Up Teg.

A moment's silence. They all knew that he had gone to get the tenancy renewed, but he had never indicated what his intentions were.

"And . . . what do that mean . . . for we then?" Luke spoke slowly, tight-lipped, angrily.

The father replied in a similar, deliberate manner.

"What it means . . . you got a interest in the land. And a roof over your head . . . and so have Martha and they little gels."

"And what about oldest sons?"

"You an't got none!"

"You knows what I means. You'm quite a one for forebears and descendants, and family name and all that, yet you'm passing over me what's next in line – along with France . . ."

"I don't want the place," France said.

"I waddn't talking about 'the place'. Not the house just."

Baxter pointed the same silencing finger as he had pointed when they were small boys.

"Bide quiet till I finished . . ."

Luke turned his head away from the old man, furious. "Be damned bide'n quiet, Father."

Old Baxter fought with his lungs. He would not be defeated by rebellious sons, but what he could not stand up to were the millions of particles of chaff and dust that had infiltrated his lungs over many years. He could not answer Luke for coughing. Luke did not even defer to his father's lungs but pressed on with his outburst.

"I'm the eldest son. If it was France it wouldn't be so bad, but Dan's a younger son."

"Only two years younger," Dan said.

"It an't nothing to do with years. There's France and Dick between theece and I."

Dick too was angry. Having no axe to grind so far as tenancy of Up Teg was concerned if it went to Luke or France, this new arrangement incensed him. Dan, Master of Up Teg! They were all of them better farmers than he was. Even France with his blimmen ideas about going over to sheep would have been more sense. At least France was level-headed.

None of them had suspected that they might end up with Dan as Master, even though they thought that the place would eventually go to Young Dan'l.

Peter opened his mouth to say something, but Baxter waved him aside, saying, "There an't no other way of me making sure of Up Teg for the next generation, and so on down, except by getting it handed on to Dan. 'Twadden only me, the Commissioners would have it that way as well, in case any of you lot lived to be a hundred. If it was to a been willed on down through you lot, Young Dan'l could find hisself seventy year old and still not Master."

There was a shuffling of feet at the extremity of that foolish argument.

France said quietly, "Same thing could happen if Dan lives to be a hundred."

Baxter held up a hand to silence them. "It's all done and settled. I meant to have it done whilst I still got breath enough to do it." A fit of dry coughing stopped him, and his statement stopped the rest of them. At once they realised what the years of their father's laboured breathing, his coughing and spitting into the hearth meant. His disease had come as a child comes, small and insignificant, had grown imperceptibly; then the hitherto unnoticed signs of full development appeared seemingly overnight.

Suddenly, they realised his mortality.

Saw that you'd have to be a reckless gambler to put your money on his having more than a year or two to go.

Baxter Hazelhurst was a dying man.

And, using the ruthless tactic of the sick of playing on opponents' feelings of guilt, Baxter forced acceptance of his plan to see that the Hazelhursts continued to populate Up Teg and the Newton Clare valley.

He had agreed with the Commissioners that, in return for a change in the tenancy agreement, the Hazelhursts would pay higher rents and a larger percentage of what they produced in tithes. The tenant and master of Up Teg would be responsible for the upkeep of all the buildings, the improvement of the land, drainage, and management of water-meadows, payment of Parish dues and the upkeep of any roads, tracks and footpaths that bordered the tenanted farm. Rent and tithes would be paid together every Lady Day, with a penalty for any delay.

It was a harsh agreement, but no worse than many landowners imposed upon their tenants. When they had taken the land away from the people whose right to it was equal to their own, the landlords took over the whip hand. And with that advantage, the entire burden of responsibility was removed from the owners and placed upon the tenant.

None of The Boys immediately realised the full implication of the new tenancy agreement, and when they did, Luke and Dick began to wonder who had the worse bargain – Dan who was responsible to the Commissioners, or themselves who would have to trust that Dan had enough brains not to ruin them.

With the new agreement, they were forced to behave as a family unit; if they fell out with one another – then they would have to fall in again.

But it wasn't over yet.

Baxter was now down to the details.

"Teg is your mother's home as long as she draws breath – that's understood. If Ed an't settled by then . . . well, the fambly must arrange about that when the time comes."

Ed spoke: "You can leave me out of it. I shall be gone."

Edwin, massive and brawny at twenty-three, had never come to terms with being the young'n of the family, so he felt compelled to prove himself better than all of them. He had become secretive lately, always going off on his own, returning often with bruises and a puffed eye, sometimes wearing some new noticeable shirt or waistcoat, fashionable, more suited to town.

He would offer no more information than that he had "been to the fair" at Blackbrook, Wickham or wherever "fair" meant booths and sideshows; and when Nance berated him for throwing money into the packman's purse and getting himself in with bad company, Baxter would tell her to bide quiet for he was only making a man out of hisself.

Had Nance known more about it, she would have realised that the shiny buttons and silky linings of some of Ed's garments were not tawdry purchases from a cheap-jack. But why would she think otherwise? Ed had very little money of his own.

So, with his reputation for not telling nobody nothing or, to put it as his brothers did, "close as a bull's arse in August", when he said "I shall be gone", he got the attention he sought.

"Gone? Gone where?" Baxter demanded.

"Anywhere it takes me." Dramatically, he took a small drawstring pouch from a pocket, untied it slowly and tipped four bright coins onto the table. A ray of deep-golden setting sun caught them and doubled their value.

"Where d'you get all that?" Baxter's hand made a move towards the coins, but Ed put his own over them then placed them before him in a neat line.

"Prize-fighting."

Had he said highway robbery, his announcement would not have got such a stunned reception.

Prize-fighting?

Prize-fighting!

"I'm joining a travelling booth in a fortnight."

Baxter started to his feet: "No son of mine . . ."

Ed too stood up. Like Baxter's disease, he had leaped from unimportance to significance.

"What you going to do, tie me to the table-leg like you used to?"

"I shall die before I let any son of mine drag the Hazelhurst name in the mire."

Ed smiled, satisfied that the playing out of the scene had gone better than he had ever imagined it would. None of them had been able to place four gold coins in a row. He had proved himself better than all of them put together.

And still it was not over.

"Theece needn't worry about dying, Father. I shall be gone before then. Prize-fighting's a decent enough way of earning your bread so don't you go talking about mire and that. I shan't use my old name – it an't much of a name for a fighter. Here." He took off his jacket and shirt.

"Lord!" said Nance. "Go and wash yourself, you looks like that heathen who used to show hisself at fairs for a farden."

"That won't never wash off. That's tattau. 'Tis under my skin."

The blue and purplish patterns on his back and arms showed up well against his white skin. His brothers gathered round him to look. On the biceps muscles of his arms were crude representations of a sturdy tree which were clear to all; what nobody in the room could understand were the words printed across his back.

"What in God's name do that say, Boy!"

"It says 'Lord Oak', which is my name from now."

"And well it might be," said the defeated father. "For, mark my words – he a finish up dangling from 'Lord Sycamore' along with the rest of the villains that travels along of fairs, and I shouldn't want nobody to hear no mention of the Hazelhurst name on no gallows hill. I only hopes you got the decency to take yourself off where nobody knows you."

"Never fear, Father. Lord Oak's next fight will be at the Goose Fair in Nottingham, where there's that much gold in prize-money that I shall need to buy a iron-bound chest and a pistol."

He achieved his moment of glory with his brothers.

12

THE FAMILY GATHERING about the new tenancy was the first occasion on which Hanna was with her entire family. Not that she considered that she was with her family – her family was "back home".

Sitting close to Vinnie in the crowded room, when the men were having their loud argument, Hanna watched them with solemn detachment.

"Have a nice plum, Hanny."

Vinnie polished one and held it up like a prize. Hanna took the plum and sucked at it. She made the gesture because Vinnie – Aunt Vinnie, remember to say "Aunt" – because Aunt Vinnie would look sorry for doing the wrong thing – like when Hanna had said she didn't like being called Goldy. Then, Aunt Vinnie had started to say "Hanny". Only John, back home, ever called her Hanny, but there was nothing that Hanna could do about it, she could not tell Aunt Vinnie again. Hanna put up with hearing Aunt Vinnie keep using John's special name and bringing him to mind.

John and Hanny. Hanny and John. She would be John's wife when she was a woman. Hanny Tooes.

Aunt Vinnie was the only one of Them whom Hanna did not want to be dead – Vinnie and Fancy.

Vinnie patted the poor little thing's hand. "I dare say you an't used to so many people all at once."

Hanna gave a nod that could be taken either way.

Grandmother Bella had taken her to harvest suppers, and they had harvests in their own barn, but the only time before this that she had been in a large gathering of people in a house, was when she and Jude went to Black Fair and they had stayed with the Warrens. There had been parties then, with people crowding one another, all squashed together, all talking and noisy and jolly and laughing. There had been such excitement in the Warrens' house.

They were all squashed here too – and crowded, and noisy but there wasn't nobody looking pleased. Hanna looked at her mother. Jaen was smiling. Always smiling, always strange and smiling. Hanna often wanted to scream at her, "What you smiling for, Jaen?" But she never did, for since They had made her come and live here, Hanna spoke only when necessary.

"Sullen little maid."
"Answer me when I speaks to you, Gel!"
"Be cust if I knowed such a long face in a chile."

There wasn't nobody to say anything to, nor nobody you wanted to hear.

Sometimes Hanna wanted to hit Jaen hard to stop her smiling. She felt a kind of excitement when she thought of it. Hit her and keep on and on and on. Hitting her. But there was something worse about Jaen than her queer smile. That was those times when she was being her ordinary self. When she came back from her dreaminess, when she stopped talking as though she was thinking about something else. When she was like that, Hanna could not stand the torment, because then you could see that she and Jude were sisters.

It made her insides burn and ache so much that she had to go somewhere where she could not see Jaen.

Once she tried to run back home, run far along Ham Lane, but she went the wrong way and was fetched back. "He" had put a switch across the back of her legs.

She never tried again. Not because of the sting of the switch, but because she had never been struck before and it made her hot with shame. She would never again let Him do that to her, treat her like you treated animals that wouldn't go into their pen, or like a spit-dog that wouldn't tread. "Their" children never seemed to mind much when he switched them, just jerked their buttocks together and said "aw". Then, they was a bit like little animals. Except the baby. The baby was nice.

Months ago, when Hanna had first arrived back upon the Up Teg scene, Vinnie had told Peter, "There's times when I looks at her little face, and it fair makes my heart bleed."

"You always was soft. I 'members when Jaen first come here, you was just as soft with her as you are with that one."

"I can't stand to see a child so pining and miserable. You'm right, her look minds me of Jaen – when Dan first brought her to Teg. They ought to let her go back."

"You wants to keep right out of it. She's Dan's girl and he can do as he pleases. You a only make things worst."

"I an't likely to, am I? But that don't mean I haves to have my heart broke from seeing a child with her'n broke too. I wasn't much above her age when I come to Up Teg. You was nice to me, Pete."

"Ah well . . ." Peter smiled at the memory of the hay loft. "That wadden the same."

"You put your arms round me."

"And me legs."

"Pete! You knows what I means – before that. I was that lonely and it was you was friendly and nice. She must feel just as bad. Your Dan never really wanted her, nor did Jaen. If they did they wouldn't of never let her go on living with the grandmother all they years. I shouldn't of."

At nearly seven, their own little girl, brown-skinned Fancy, was more than two years younger than Hanna and, like three-year-old Jamie, "wadden no trouble to nobody". Fancy went about her work of weeding, stone-gathering, bird-scaring and gleaning at harvest in an orderly way – quite unlike Vinnie. "I don't know where she gets it from, I was that hare-brained."

Growing up with Vinnie's good nature around them, Fancy and Jamie seldom needed to be wrapped around with arms and comforted as often as Vinnie would have liked. Peter, Fancy, Jamie and her brother James, were all fussed over by Vinnie. She loved to hold a baby or play with a child. Her desire to pet and cuddle was now much as it had been when she had gleefully taken the new-born Hanna from Jaen, so that when Hanna's stoical misery had made her heart bleed, she again wanted to take Jaen's Goldy to her. But the girl was almost as inside herself as Jaen had been getting the last year.

Jaen, concentrating on not allowing her eyes to rest too long upon France, withdrew into a world which was not quite substantial but was safe. There she saw only bits of reality, the bits she could cope with. She did not see Hanna.

"You don't want to take no notice when they starts shouting like that," Vinnie told Hanna.

Hanna made a smile for Vinnie.

She returned to thinking about getting away from Them.

If they all got a fever . . . if there was a fever that took the men . . . then there wouldn't be anybody who could stop her going home. Grandmother Hazelhurst might be . . . but Grandmother Bella could deal with her.

If I move a bit? Will Vinnie pat my knee or squeeze my hand?

The fever must only be a man's fever. Only the uncles. It mustn't get out to John, nor to Mister Warren, or Mister Vickery – Jude would marry him. No!

Sometimes she hated Jude more than Jaen and Him.

Images of Dan and Jaen, slain but unbleeding.

Black bryony. Henbane. Yellow-caps.

"Aunt Vin?"

Vinnie looks encouragingly at Hanna, who seldom speaks unless spoken to.

"Why does Jaen smile at nothing like that?"

Of all questions, it was the one Vinnie does not want to think of.

Vinnie briefly draws the poor little thing to her.

"I reckon she's pleased that you come home."

She polishes another plum for poor little Hanny.

13

EMWORTHY BAY

WHEN THE CONVERSION of the cottages into an inn was finished, the Saint John/Scantlebury partners looked for a name.

George. White Horse. Black Bull. Harbour Lights, even Smack-at-Anchor were sounded out.

"It ought to sound like what we intend," Betrisse said. "So that people won't think it to be like other places."

With a merry facetiousness that would have surprised them all at Up Teg, Annie said, "The Clean and Decent Place to Sleep Inn?"

Then Betrisse said, "Scantlebury's!" and it had sounded right.

"Funny, Bet, but that do have a ring to it."

"Must be because of Master Scantlebury being clean and decent hisself."

And, thinking about it, Annie thought Betrisse might not be so far off the mark at that. "Decent" was a word that he often used in conversation.

By the time it had been going for three years Scantlebury's was a busy place, and they were ready to expand.

There had never been any real setbacks because they had started in a small way and learned as they grew. They took no business from any other establishment, for what Scantlebury's offered was quite new. The alehouses and lodging houses went on providing the same rough welcome to rough people as they had always done. Scantlebury's took those travellers who, whilst they did not object to a plain and simple room, liked it sweeter-smelling and less verminous than the other accommodation offered in the town.

Their "clean and decent" standard was proclaimed in fine lettering on a swinging sign which hung from a fancy wrought-iron pole, above the entrance that had once been old Mr Scantlebury's house door.

SCANTLEBURY'S
A clean and decent place for
the night
GOOD PLAIN FOOD

Below that announcement, a portrait of a woman wearing a white cap and apron and holding a pile of clean linen and another with a steaming pie.

Right from the start, it was agreed that the day would come when Ted Scantlebury would eventually take more than a financial role in the place, when the right time came. For the first three years there did not seem to be a right time, then one trip he came in and slapped down his canvas bag.

"Right then, Mistress Saint John. I had my fill of seeing decent lads fed to the fishes. Tell us what to do."

Annie had gone on with her work, waiting to hear what had happened that had made him finally decide, but he never said. She guessed that it was to do with the conditions on certain other smacks in the fleet; guessed that some smack owner did not maintain a safe vessel and held his labour cheap; guessed that yet another youth might not have had hands strong enough to hold on in a rough sea, or that a rail was rotten or a rope frayed.

Whatever that final straw had been, Ted Scantlebury stopped going out with the oyster fleet and never seemed to have a day's regret.

Although his feelings for Annie had grown warm, he kept them to himself and always behaved correctly with her, almost formally. The only familiarity was his acceptance of her offer that he should use her first name.

"My name's Ann if you like."

"Ann."

The way he said it was agreeable to Annie.

"Will you call me Ted?"

"Thank you . . . Ted. But only outside of business. Me and Betrisse have always tried to keep off familiarities. It was her idea, she reckons first names is only all right for kitchen-boys and maids. She always says Mistress Saint John to me when we'm in Scantlebury's." Annie smiled at her partner. "I can't say as how I finds it too easy to call her Mistress too, but I'm getting used to it. She don't stand no nonsense."

Ted pulled a face and smiled. "I noticed that. I always feels it a liberty calling her Betrisse these days. If I hadn't a known her when she was a girl, I should a felt obliged to call her 'Madam'."

That was understandable, for womanhood had brought to Betrisse enough of Martha's blowsiness to make her soft and round, and enough of Luke's height to carry it well. Her hair when she had been a child was a bird's nest. It had the same tendency to crimp as France's, but she now mastered it with pins; only at her forehead and nape were there curls out of control.

Living as they had, with Annie treating her as an equal in spite of their being of different generations, Betrisse had learned to be resourceful and to use her intelligence. She seldom did anything that mattered without thinking first – even to the kind of skirts and necklines she should adopt. When Annie had suggested that a girl of seventeen might show a bit more bosom without being thought light, Betrisse said, "A lot of our clients who have been at sea might get the wrong idea about where they can lay their heads at night."

"Lord, Bet, if you deals with them like you did that flattie skipper, you remember?"

Betrisse laughed. She remembered.

The flattie skipper had mistaken a fifteen-year-old Betrisse's bare feet and ragged working skirt as an indication of the girl within, and had finished bedecked with fish heads and guts. She had some Hazelhurst about her, but not too much.

So, at eighteen, Betrisse had stature, common sense, and an air of confidence which, even if she had had no good looks at all, made her an attractive woman. But she did have good looks.

She also now spoke like a person of a quite different background from her own. It was this, her voice and accent, that gave her authority. She had set about learning to "speak" as she set about everything else, with determination to get what she wanted.

That voice and speech contributed to a person's authority had long been evident to her, and when some passengers on a damaged vessel put up at Scantlebury's for a few days, she realised that to lose her broad rural dialect would be of value to the establishment. There were ten of them, two of whom were women. Three were personal servants and the others persons of some standing. Big

House People, Annie called them. Good linen, good boots and good speaking.

One of the women was a companion or chaperone to the other, a woman with a girlish figure beautifully gowned in widow's-black.

"Tippie, have water sent up. At once, Tippie. And, Tippie – be sure that their sheets have been scalded and aired. And, Tippie . . ."

That voice echoed down the years.

Oh Mu-Mawh . . . look! It snows greatly.

Betrisse had never forgotten that voice. Its fine quality, its beauty, its authority and command.

The arrival of the woman was the first time in about ten years that Newton Clare had come near to them. When Betrisse told Annie who it was that they had in the best room calling for such amounts of hot water, for washing not only her personal linen but her body also, that their service was tested to its limit, Annie covered her mouth with her hand and for a moment appeared to be very agitated.

"Oh dear Lord! Pray she don't notice us."

"Don't be such a puddin', Annie. The only time she'd a been anywhere near us would a been in church, and to her we'd a just been 'the village' – and it's ten years ago."

"Well a course, you'm right; we an't nothing to her. You said that you knew her though, before she'd a even lifted her veil."

Betrisse gave Annie a wry smile. "*That's* the difference, she was somebody you noticed and remembered even when she was a little child."

The young widow, Countess d'Archard, *en route* to view her inheritance – money grown on tea-bushes by brown equivalents to Newton Clare "villagers" – stayed at Scantlebury's for four days. She left without knowing that she had shared a roof with a girl with whom she had once shared the wonder of snowflakes. She left also without knowing that she had planted two seeds of ambition in Betrisse Saint John – to speak as she spoke, and to make Scantlebury's a place which, in addition to their present good business, people would visit for pleasure.

"Annie, you heard about water-bathing? *Have* you heard of water-bathing?"

Annie did not reply, knowing that there must be something more to the simple question other than the stressed aspirants and the slightly halting speech.

"Snows-greatly asked me whether there was such to be had in these parts, and when I said that I an't . . ." correcting herself, "I had not heard, she told me how it is becoming the very thing for gentry and Big-House folk and such as they, to walk into the sea. Don't look like that, it's true – they do it for their health."

"She was talking of springs and sulphur-baths and that – I've heard of *them*."

"No, definite . . . ly, it was sea water. They go in up to their necks for minutes at a time and then . . ." This time it was Betrisse herself who had to smile. ". . . Well, they take a cup of it as a drink."

Annie flicked out a sheet for Betrisse to help her fold. "And then they'm sick."

"I don't know about that."

"A course you do. Salt and water is a 'metic, what else do anybody give to children what's eaten the nightshade? Salt-water to make them sick it up."

"Well, anyway that's what they do. It is the latest idea for youth and health."

"Then run and fetch us a bucket of the stuff, it's what I could do with."

"Annie! It isn't a jest. I asked her companion. She said before the Count died, she went with them often to Brightlingsea and Southampton to get into the sea."

"No wonder he died."

"It wadden the sea-water. He fell from his horse."

"And didn't all they cups of salty water never bring him back to health and strength?"

"You can jest all you like. But there's money to be made from it, and we shall have some."

They had finished folding the linen. Annie sat down. "All right, I know you got a bee in your bodice, so let's have him out; but you won't never persuade me to start no fancy schemes, not now we'm just beginning to get up on our feet."

"What it seems to me is that these kind of Big House people go from place to place that's got something special. London play-houses and balls, Bath has got warm-water springs, places with sulphur and salts-ss – not salt . . . and these people stay there for a few weeks."

"And you'm suggesting they'd come here to get into the sea and then drink it?"

"Yes."

"And they'd pay us. With all that stretch of water out there? What in the world would they want to pay us for when they could jump in it all day long and drink their fill for nothing? I know Big House people an't always that bright but . . ."

"Annie. What is it they want more than anything else?"

"Jewels? Fancy clothes? Carriages? Money?"

"Money! And they spends it on carriages and clothes and that. But most of all they wants money so they can have somebody to do things for them that the rest of us do for ourselves. If they wants to jump in the sea – they an't going to jump in by their own selves. They'll want undressing. Then dressing up in special sea-clothes . . . yes, special. They'll want to be kept private. And they would want to take their sea-water from special flasks in special little beakers."

As Betrisse was speaking, Annie's amusement dispersed. She pursed her lips and raised her eyebrows, then began nodding in agreement and understanding. "And they would need somewhere Clean and Decent."

"Clever Annie. They'd want something Clean and Decent *and* Special."

"And I'd hazard a front tooth Betrisse Saint John knows what 'special' it is that's going to make our fortune."

"This!" Betrisse produced a crudely illustrated broadsheet depicting a row of persons, of whom only capped heads might be seen, the rest being encased in black coffin-like baths. "The companion gave it to me. We should start off with one at first; we could build a small place onto the wash-house so that there's plenty of hot water."

"What do the wording say?"

"I don't know, but summit to the effect that it is a health treatment for skin and joints."

"And what, if it's summit a lady might hear, is in that there box they'm laying in?"

Betrisse tried to make her face very solemn. "Well 'tis like the sea-water, summit we got plenty of at Emworth Bay."

Annie's shoulders began to shake. "I thought it might be. So, along of their jumping in the sea, then drinking some of it, we'm going to offer people a lay in a box of Emworth Bay mud."

Betrisse too began to allow her false seriousness to fall into humour. "Ah now, it wouldn't be any old Emworth mud, you couldn't get even the nobility to pay for that. It'd be . . . *clean* Emworth mud. We would not be taking their money for nothing. We should sieve it and warm it . . . and then let them lay in a box of it."

"And should we have a broadsheet like that?"

"That's a most important part of the plan I was thinking of. And that's summit – something – that's a puzzle to me. I thought perhaps Ted might know how you gets – get – that kind of thing done."

"Long before we gets to that point, we got to put the whole idea to him. What shall I say? 'Ted. Bet thinks we should try to get a better quality of person . . .' "

"Not better – just extra to what we already get."

" '. . . we should try to get more people to come to Scantlebury's, and so Bet thinks we should offer them a box of Emworth mud to lay in.' "

"Summit like . . . something . . . like that, yes."

"Bet? Are you trying at copying her way of speaking like you . . ."

"Yes. Like I did when I was little. That's part of the change too. If we do get these people coming, and I an't – have not – any doubt they will come, then we should have to have a bit more fanciness about the place. I'm going to learn to speak like they do, and I shall dress up for it too. Not for fanciness sake, but because it is what is needed. Like we always keeps the doors painted, boils the bedding and that, it's the sort of thing that makes Scantlebury's a bit special. So, when you hears – hear – me not talking ladylike, then you got – haves – have to tell me."

"And be you going to say 'pish-tush' and 'fie' or 'fee' and 'praying' everybody . . . 'pray hand me the blankets, Mistress Saint John.' 'Cause Lors Bet, you come to the wrong person here."

Quite to Annie's surprise, Ted Scantlebury took up Betrisse's idea seriously. He read the broadsheet aloud to them.

It proclaimed that immersion in mud was a *VERY WONDER*. Noble lords who had attended a spa where this treatment was offered, avowed themselves *MIRACULOUSLY FREED OF GOUT AND OTHER NOXIOUS AILMENTS*; gentlemen declared that *STRENGTHS* and *POWERS* that they had thought *LOST*, were *NOW RETURNED* to them; and titled ladies were thankful to have been given the *SECRET* of *YOUTH* and *BEAUTY*.

"Well!" said Annie. "I should never have believed it if it wasn't put down in writing by such Big House folks for all to see."

"I don't know about the mud cure," Ted said, "but we shouldn't be chancing much if we offered . . ." he thought for a moment then quoted as if on the broadsheet he held "Scantlebury's warm or natural sea-water immersion."

Annie gave him a sideways look. "And what do that cure pray?"

"He never said it cured," Betrisse said.

"No, I never said it did anything."

"That don't seem quite right to me," said Annie. "Not selling something people can get for nothing theirselves."

"They should come of their own free will, Annie. We should never compel anybody to jump in the sea, should we, Ted?"

In the face of the combined amusement and enthusiasm of the other two corners of their triangular partnership, Annie capitulated, and they agreed that they would make no claims other than that Scantlebury's offered, in addition to Cleanliness and Decency, "*SEA-WATER IMMERSIONS*".

Ted was a man capable of turning his hand to almost anything, from earthing the soil-pits to putting colour-wash on walls. His years at sea had taken him to many towns around the coast, and had widened his outlook, he was interested and interesting. He also knew a great many people and had numerous friends and acquaintances. So when Betrisse asked him about "learning to speak", he not only thought it wouldn't do her no harm and might do her a bit of good, he knew the very person to show her how to twist her tongue round. "And if you wants to, I shouldn't mind learning you to read."

Learning to read was a bit more than Betrisse had bargained for, but she saw the skill might have its uses and agreed to try it out, although she never really took to it.

It was a "Captain" Jetsam to whom Ted took her about the speaking. Ten years or so older than Ted, the "captain" still had, like Ted, the eyes of a man who has spent a lifetime looking at a horizon; his cheeks were bright red with broken veins and he wore his hair tied and pig-tailed. A seaman. Until he spoke. Then one was at once nonplussed upon hearing the accents of a gentleman. It was believed that he had long ago gone over the side of his vessel, taking an Excise Officer with him. But in Emworthy, people were allowed to live with their secrets – particularly if Excise Officers were involved.

The idea of replacing Betrisse's broad accent with something more ladylike – or gentlemanly as it had to be – pleased the old man, and he vowed he would have her fit for society inside a year.

"I shan't be wanting that," Betrisse told him. "Only so as people will take notice when I say something."

14

CHANGES
Up Teg

As upon that winter a decade ago, when Laurence had died, and Norry was born with "water on the brain", then Norry and Nicholas had died, and Ed had nearly lost a finger, and there were violent humours in their midst – so again in the present winter, the hag of misfortune chose Up Teg to settle upon.

Luke, slithering down Keeper's Hill on a dark night and holding a bag of game, slipped upon rimey grass and hit his head on the flint-strewn bank of the River Hammet.

Had it happened twenty yards further upstream or down where there were shallows, the outcome might have been different. As it was he was knocked unconscious at Deep Run. There, Th'ammet is wide and deep, like a dark deep pool. There trout may live untaken by an entire generation of men, and so grow to become legends. There the banks are steep. There, after eleven hours' floating face-down, Luke was found by Peter.

"He never let go of they pheasants." It was one thing that Peter was never to forget, Luke holding onto the meal that he had been out to get for his family. By the time the ground was thawed enough to dig Luke's place in the churchyard, the pheasants were well hung and provided meat at Luke's solemn feast.

15

HANNA WITH HER KIN watched Luke's remains lowered into the gravelly hole, unmoving and unmoved by the dispassionate words of the curate.

"*This our Brother . . .*"

Since the last Hazelhurst had been brought to the churchyard, there was a noticeable change in the composition of the family.

Had Betrisse been there, Luke would have had five daughters watching his burial. Kit was now almost fifteen, Rachael eleven and the twins, Deborah and Alice, eight.

Equal in number, but younger in age were Dan's sons, ranging from Dan'l who was the same age as the twins, to four-year-old Gregory. George, the baby, having recently found his feet, had been left in the care of a girl back at the farm.

Richard contributed only Lucy, who at twelve was in many ways already a replica of Elizabeth, and six-year-old Margaret looking as fragile as Laurie had done. But that look was deceptive; Margaret had a robust constitution and worked hard.

Looking at the way the hands had been dealt to himself and his brother, Richard wondered what game the Lord played that gave Dan such an advantage.

It was taken for granted that the grandchildren belonged to the husband, and were always attached to the father's name: (Luke's Kit, Richard's Lucy, Dan's Young Bax), except for Fancy and Jamie. Fancy and Jamie were Vinnie's.

Vinnie's Fancy was now eight, and Vinnie's Jamie five.

Hanna was attached to no one.

"*I am the Resurrection and the Life . . .*"

France had no one attached to him.

It was a year since Ed left, and almost eight since Annie and Betrisse disappeared. They had gone as effectively as had Luke, and were only brought to mind by most of the family on such occasions – brought to mind, not tongue.

The family which accompanied its eldest son to the churchyard was greatly changed from the one that had attended Vinnie on her wedding day. Now, there were half as many children again as there were adults.

At the time of Luke's burial, Hanna had been back with Jaen and Dan for near on two years, yet she felt as isolated and as much an outsider as ever.

At first after Jude had left her with Them, night after night she had gone over every word that had been tossed between Jude and Him: Jaen keeping on saying, "Let her go back, Dan, let her go back," over and over . . . Him saying, "I says she stops here!" Gradually, over the months, the scene had frozen to a vision of Jude leading the empty donkey back home.

If they called her a sullen little maid, they were short of the mark; it was not sulkiness that gave her that expression, it was hatred, the uncomplicated self-regarding hatred of childhood. She looked down at her father's feet and invoked them and him into Luke's cold pit.

" . . . *Earth unto Earth* . . ."

Her spell did not work for Dan, but within the month, the Hazelhursts were to be found standing at another graveside, and saw James Norris go underground to meet his Maker. As was the custom, every one of the family went to view its departing member laid out in their best embroidered smock. Luke's discoloured and saturated face did not disturb Hanna, but she thought that James looked less weasel-faced now he was dead.

An infected tooth had caused his body to swell and increase in size. His death at twenty-six or -seven from the infection, increased too his importance. In life he had gone about his work almost unnoticed except by Vinnie.

In death he was noticed. More Newton Clare people attended James's burial than had attended Luke's, and it was the presence of villagers paying their respects to the last of the Clare Norrises that forced upon The Boys the realisation that James Norris was looked upon as a landowner. Which of course he was – owner of land that had come to be accepted as part of Up Teg.

Nobody in the family actually spoke the thought, but over a

mulled tankard at the Bear and Ragged Staff, it was pounced upon as an interesting fact that Norris Land must come to Vinnie and so would belong to Peter. And Peter had a son.

Deborah whispered to Alice. Alice looked and saw their red-haired cousin had tears running down.

"Look at she!"

"Aunt Vinnie. Don't! I can't abear to see you cry. Don't, Aunt Vin. You'm kind and it an't fair for your brother to die like that. Don't cry . . . please don't cry. I can't abear it."

Hanna's words form behind her sullen little maid mask, but she does not speak them. She slips her hand into the placket-pocket of her skirt and fingers the small brass object she keeps always close to her, always hidden from Them.

"*This our Brother . . .*"

Her only possession. Everything else belongs to Them, her skirt and boots, her stockings and shawl even though she had knitted them herself. The bell though, belongs to Hanna.

Before Jude had gone home without her, Hanna distraught and crying had made her promise to tell John a message. "He a know I wouldn't have gone away from him, but you got to tell him that I couldn't help it."

Tears for John flowed with those for Aunt Vinnie.

Hanna had bought John a china bluebird from Black Fair, his only possession. He had brought her a bell as small as a thimble. Not long after Jude had left her with Them, he had come. He had come to see her, grinning.

> *"I come on my own, Hanny, and I never got lost once.*
> *"I got summit for you, Hanny."*

And when there is a new moon she holds the bell, knowing that at the same time John will take down the bluebird as they have secretly agreed.

> *"If you thinks about it, Hanny, it an't all that different to when you used to be in the house with Miz Jude and the Master, and I was in the outhouse – 'tis only that we'm a bit further away."*

"... *Dust unto Dust* ..."

"What's that gel crying like that for? She never hardly knew Jim Norris."

"It's what comes when you brings a girl up to nine thinking she's summit special."

16

JAEN THOUGHT THAT JUDE might come for a visit that Christmas.

"Oh Child, I could do with cheering up after these last weeks. I hopes Ju is going to come and see us. You a be glad too."

Hanna nodded, which could mean anything. Jaen had made a great effort to make friends with her daughter, but Hanna would not give an inch in bridging the chasm that was between them.

If you hadn't a give me away in the first place, I wouldn't a known no different. But you did. Then when I was used to Grandma and Jude, you made me come back.

Sometimes Jaen would catch a glimpse of the girl working in some dark outhouse, and catch her breath. "Lord Child, for half a minute I thought you was Ju." Hanna would look up, hold Jaen's eyes for a second, and then return to her work.

Dan seemed to look upon her as a useful pair of hands and appeared to expect more of her than the girls whose parents received wages for them. She worked in the dairy at Up Teg, in the fields and in the Ham Ford cottage. In matters of her labour Dan could not fault her.

"You turned out to be a decent help there, Gel."

When she worked at the main farm Nance would dart into the dairy, or down to the pigs or wherever Hanna happened to be working, and watch her for a minute without being seen.

"I can't make that one out, Husband."

"She works like you'd expect a girl to what had been living with Bella Estover."

"She's deep. Never hardly says a word."

"Pity there wan't more females like she then."

"Well, she don't get her closed mouth from the Hazelhurst, I'll tell you that for nothing!"

These days Nance had the upper hand and made the most of it on every occasion. He could try and call after her the last word in an argument as much as he liked – it didn't do him no good.

"Nor . . ." a cough from years' flailing and winnowing. "yet . . ." A spit from flooding the meads in January fogs. "from thy fambly . . . Wife." Heaving lungs from a lifelong struggle to make the land give up food, and from fighting the elements which were for ever ready to destroy what had been grown or reared.

"You wants to save that breath, you a need it one day."

None of them could make Hanna out.

Jaen was concerned for her, blaming herself for the girl's obvious unhappiness. She looked half-starved, thin and dark marks under her eyes. Anybody would think they never gave her a decent meal; you couldn't go about telling everybody she was fed the same as the boys but she would never eat properly.

On the few occasions when she had tried to talk to Dan about it, he became exasperated and spoke roughly.

"Why not let her go back, Dan? She an't happy."

"No more an't I. Your whole family behaves like they was summit special. She's a farmer's daughter and the sooner she gets that into her head, the better it a be."

"You can't deny she works hard, Dan."

"I never said she didn't. But she got fancy notions put into her by your mother."

Jaen knew what he meant; she had been vexed by it herself often enough. "There an't no harm in washing yourself."

He looked contemptuously at her. "Every blimmin day? She's worse than you. That's your mother's hand and the sooner she gets into our ways, the better. In a few years' time she a be a farmer's wife, and there an't likely to be many about as will put up with what I puts up with."

Once Jaen flared at him: "You was willing enough for Mother to have her when she couldn't earn her bread."

He had raised his hand, but did not land the blow. Had he done so, it would have removed a speck of Jaen's guilt about the girl.

The old intimacy with Vinnie had long faded to a relationship that was not much different from that shared with Martha and

Elizabeth, except that because the Ham Ford and Coppice cottages were close they saw one another frequently but briefly.

The only person Jaen can talk to is France.

It is for him she goes looking the day after Jude's Christmas visit. Long before she needed an excuse to go out so that she could meet France, she had imposed upon herself the chore of going wooding for the hearth and the oven. It was a task which she could have given to one of the village girls who came in to help, or to one of her children, but it was the one and only reason she had for going out on her own. Her small freedom from the uproar and congestion of the cottage.

Whenever she goes to meet France, she ties over her cap a bright-red kerchief which she tucks into her pocket as soon as she sees him. He knows the times that she is likely to go looking for snapwood and furze and watches her cottage from his vantage point on Brack or Keeper's for the spot of red moving towards Cuckoo Bushes. They meet in the most dense part of the common where amidst thick rhododendrons they are well concealed.

There are times when she meets France only because she feels that she ought. No great enthusiasm. Simply, France a be waiting, and she goes, so as not to disappoint him.

At other times when she sees him, a small figure on the downs walking with his sheep, she feels a leap of joy that he exists, that he is gentle, that it does not matter to him her legs get swollen and she has half a dozen tedious, niggling ailments, that she is the mother of a houseful of children. He will run his thumb across her lips and say, "You'm a witch, Sister Jaen."

Brother France and Sister Jaen.

The spice of sin is at the core of their attraction to one another. In church, where the Up Teg family sometimes attends together, France will come in after they are seated so that he will have to push past Jaen to reach his seat, touching her as though unavoidably. If he catches her eye, she knows what his message is.

Under the eye of the vicar and the Almighty, they sin in thought. Brother lusts for his Sister, Sister tempts herself, remembering.

Then we both be sinners, France.

Today, as soon as she sees him she bursts into tears.

"Leave him, Jaen." He has said it a score of times. "Let us go off together."

She has sometimes wondered how serious he is. He surely knows that she will never go with him. It is a fantasy they share. Jaen's many fears and guilts are a burden enough already. She knows that she is too afraid to add to them. And . . . a devil you know . . . Eleven years she has known Dan.

"No, France . . ."

"Brother," he insists.

She shakes her head, preoccupied. "He sent Ju away and says she must stop away from us, and never come no more. Oh France, I should die without seeing Ju sometimes."

He guides her to a place where they have sometimes sat and she continues.

"Ju does so get his back up."

"It'll blow over."

"No. He meant it. If only she wouldn't goad him so. She don't realise what it does to a man to be more knowing than he is. He thinks Mother brought us up to think we'm better than folks, but it's just that she made us always stand on our own two feet, like she did herself."

France has heard it before, her defence against the charge of trying to poke her nose into what is no concern of a woman. He has a certain sympathy for Dan; Annie was not above giving her opinion when it was not wanted.

"She said terrible things to him. About us having so many children. And that he worked the girl too hard. Once she started, it was as though she couldn't hold back."

"I can imagine. She never struck me as being tender and nice like you."

"You hardly seen her."

"I've seen her. Many's the time I've watched her when she's been to see you, she unties her hair and strides out like a man."

"Ju?"

She is silent for a minute.

"I shan't be able to abear it, not seeing her. But it's The Girl that worries me." She starts. "What was that?"

They listen.

"Only rabbits."

"I must go. I still got the wood to get."

"A minute more. I got some bundled up ready so that you can pick it up on your way home."

France, the gentle brother of her fantasy, who gives her kisses and says that she bewitches him.

"I don't know what I should do without you."

"You won't have to do without me. Now your Jude can't come to see you, you will have some love to spare."

"I can't give you Ju's."

He remembers the arrogant shoulders, the flying red hair, the strong steps.

Jaen begins her walk back.

"I'll come to the bottom of the track with you."

"No, there might be people."

"I'm your brother, an't I? Why shouldn't brother and sister be walking on the common together?"

On some banks in open places the frost has not gone from the grass and their footsteps sound crisp on the morning air. The scent of moss and decaying leaves drag Jaen back fifteen years, and into the spinney close to Chard Lepe Pond.

If only time had stopped there, whilst she and Ju were still all in all to one another. Stopped, when the only worry was forgetting they still had the scalding to do, and guilt was no more serious than stolen preserves or a naked swim.

"Don't you ever feel guilty, France?"

"What about?" He knows. He smiles. She asks him frequently.

"You know what I mean. If we should be discovered together. Every time I come here, I thinks to myself, 'Luck can't go on for ever. This is going to be the time when Dan a be watching us and will burst out of the bushes.' "

"Don't that add pleasure?"

"No!"

As they come near to the edge of Cuckoo Bushes, he runs his hands over the shape of her bosom, as he always does on parting, and then feels her lips with the ball of his thumb.

"You bewitched me, Sister." He gives her a teasing little tug towards the path that he will take to get back to his flock on the downs. "Come. Walk up the track with me. And let's keep walking and talking till we have left them all."

"And live in the hedge-bottoms?"

"It'd be more like living than it is now."

"Not for a woman."

She means not for a woman with bad legs, and with things gone wrong with her body that a man's body will never experience, though he has contributed to their cause. But as the woman who ties on a red scarf, and is so desirable that she bewitched her husband's brother into a sin against his Church, she stops short of the truth.

Although he often sleeps without a roof over him, it is she who understands the reality of hedge-bottoms. She has often wondered how and where Annie and Betrisse live. Especially more recently when she has seen the starveling families who daily pass her window as they trudge along Ham Lane in their search for some work to alleviate their dire poverty.

In her imagination she has seen them among the agricultural workers who trail throughout the county looking for work – and there is none. When they lose their hiring, they lose the crumbling walls and broken thatch that has been their shelter. They know the hedge-bottoms.

Times are hard.

And when have times not been, for the people who eat their bread with earth on their hands? Jaen does not have to dig far into her memory for the fact of thin childhood meals, turnip stew and little else for weeks on end.

Lately, times are harder than ever.

Even protected women like Jaen can see that.

Along Ham Lane flows the growing stream of dispossessed cottagers, of uneconomic estate workers, of paupers who until recently were cowherds or dairymaids.

Men who have prided themselves on a straight furrow, or a well-laid hedge. Women who were mistresses of ten fine skills and could make a rabbit stretch to feed a dozen. Hard-working families, holding about them their last shreds of decency, before they become infected by the widespread rumour that they are feckless and work-shy. Then, when the infection catches and saps them, then they hide in hedges and leap upon a person with whom they have no real quarrel, except over possession of a coin that will buy some bread or wheat gleanings.

Are they more alive because occasionally they indulge their passion in the hedge-bottoms? True, France is never so aroused as when he meets her in damp mists or chill frosts.

Jaen's fantasy though, of the gentle flock-master who says he is bewitched by her, does not include walking away and sleeping in hedge-bottoms.

> *"The Hazelhursts have never gone short of much; even when times is hard they always seem to do all right. There's always that to think of . . ."*

France can see that she is beginning to withdraw from reality as she does sometimes.

This is when he loves her the most. His passion that was first aroused by her pretty femaleness and her fecundity when compared with his barren wife, became spiced with the idea that that very passion was against the Church and God. But now the passion was changed to love – gentle, compassionate love that he had not known to exist until he was a man in his middle years.

She does not blink, and though she walks surely she looks to the side and sees something about eighteen inches from her and chews the inside of her mouth.

"Ju's learning village children to read, back home. She's got a room in the village and sits them on benches."

He wants to take her with him to the top of Brack where nothing can harm her.

She returns to the present and looks at France. "I should a give anything to a done that."

"Read?"

"I could do numbers in my head right from when I was little. Mother showed me how to count up to a hundred. At first she used to put eggs in rows ready for the market and tell me 'one', 'two', 'three', and by the time Ju was born I had found out how to go on after a hundred."

Her gaze is upon events and people France cannot see.

"People on Blackbrook market used to get me to cast up numbers of things. They'd say things such as 'if I had seven hens and they lay every day for a month, how many eggs?' and I could tell them straight off almost without thinking." She smiles at the distant child. "And they'd say, be that June or February? and I should tell them that February hens don't lay well and take away a number from the June total. And they'd tell Mother that I was a little marvel."

She sees the unfathomable expression of Bella and interprets as she did at the time – disapproval of a child getting above herself.

"Eggs was always easy – I could picture them, in rows."

She watches Jaen the child who stands with her mother, Bella Nugent, selling the produce of Croud Cantle, and receiving a tit-bit from a housewife or a trader as a reward for demonstrating her skill at casting up rows of imagined eggs.

"I should a loved to learn how to write down numbers."

France sees her drifting away again to whatever world inside her mind she returns to.

"Ju said he wasn't no good as a farmer. That was the worst she could a said to him. That's what made him say she wasn't never to come again. She said he was a fool to talk of putting every foot of land down to one crop."

"So he is. But you can't tell Dan. Nobody can."

"Ju did."

She picks up the bundle of firewood he had made ready for her.

"I don't know what the Child's going to do."

"She a survive."

"I don't know what I shall do."

"Talk to the girl. Like she was your sister."

Walking back to his flock he thinks about the red-gold heads that have come in from Cantle, disturbing him. First the one, then the proud striding sister, the third is still not a woman but he can imagine what she will become.

Nell Gritt's shelter is not much better than a hedge-bottom. He goes to her after dark when her hair could be any colour he likes to imagine it.

17

FROM THAT CHRISTMAS, there was no contact between Jaen and Hanna and Croud Cantle – the place they both still thought of as home.

Whenever a packman called at the Ham Ford cottage, or a journeyman was engaged to do something at Up Teg, Jaen always asked if they had been through Cantle recently. Had they done so, then she would feed greedily upon the morsels of information. It was a travelling butcher, Gilly Gilson, who had been "doing" the pigs at Croud Cantle ever since Jaen was a girl, who told her about the deterioration of her mother.

"Ah now, Miz Jaen, you mu'nt upset yourself; we all has to get old."

Mother old? Yes. How strange that Mother should be old.

Realising that Hanna held a headful of memories of life at home since she had left, Jaen tried to get solace from trying to make her tell about them. At first Hanna gave short, factual answers, but gradually she began to gain comfort in talking about her years there.

As Hanna grew out of childhood, she grew into a relationship with her mother. It had never occurred to the daughter, before Jaen began relating stories of her childhood years, that the life that Hanna had led on the Croud Cantle smallholding was in many ways a repeat of that of her mother's.

"Did you used to go to Harvest Home up at the Estate?"

"You mean in that big barn at Manor Farm?"

"Where there's a cock-pit outside?"

"I never liked cock-fighting. Grandmother likes it, but I never."

"Nor I. If they chooses to fight in the barnyard, that's their affair, but to put them together where they haven't got a chance of honest retreat, then I thinks that an't fair."

"And did you dance the maypole on Cantle Green?"

Oh bride, oh bride come visit this cott,
The door stands wide, come stay,
And bring to us your fair-maid's wish . . .

"I was May Queen once. It must of been about the year of 'seventy-five. It seems a hundred years since. Ju was little and wanted a crown as well, so I made her one and she was cross because it still had some prickles on it."

Hanna picks up her small brother, George, who has been absorbed in rolling small logs across the floor, and waits patiently for her mother's gaze to return.

Oh neighbour, neighbour a token I ask
And I'll make a wish for thee.
But if I leave with empty hands,
Thou'll get no good luck from me,
O-oh no good luck from me.

They talked only when Dan, and those of her brothers old enough, had gone out into the fields or up to the main farm. Hanna now did most of the work that village girls had in the past been hired to do, so that for hours at a stretch, there was often only Gregory and George in the cottage with her and Jaen.

Hanna adored George. Although he was a real Hazelhurst in every other respect, he had hair like his great-grandfather's – always one in every generation they said – like France too, the tight crimp and curls which Hanna loved to twist about her finger as she played with him.

When he was born Hanna had been at her most miserable, then at the moment when she happened to be alone with Jaen and she had seen the baby slide easily into the world, the icy lump of resentment against Jaen began to melt. Hanna felt unique. Only she in the entire world had seen George appear. She laid claim to him. As she wrapped him in a cloth, Hanna felt such a surge of emotion that the tears which she had withheld for months fell upon him.

Of all Jaen's children, he was the one most petted. As Jude had once carried Hanna about in a shawl slung round her, so Hanna carried George. Young Dan'l, who was becoming aware of his responsibilities as future head of the family, did a fair job of making a rocking-crib for George and so took a bit more interest than he had in the others, and would sometimes work the rocker.

As well as being the most petted, this baby was the most content. Jaen was more at ease with him than with the other six, he was not wet-nursed or pushed aside by a new sibling. In part this was due to Nance Hazelhurst.

"Look, Gel," she said. "Six sons is about all any man can expect. And you got a girl too, which is more than I had. If you wants to keep your health and strength, you can't keep on having all these little'ns so quick one after the other."

"I don't get myself that way." A rare flash of spirit for Jaen.

"Nor don't you seem to do much about it."

Jaen did not reply at first.

"Didn't your mother tell you nothing about oils and herbs, or is she one to wait till it happens then jump off the table and hope for the best?"

Nance thought, "I don't know why I'm bothering to ask – Bella Nugent don't look like she even knows what causes big bellies."

Jaen had felt ill at ease with Nance Hazelhurst from the day she arrived at Up Teg. Bella Nugent was no easy woman to have for a mother but at least Jaen knew where she was with her. But with Nance, Jaen was never quite sure how to respond. If Bella Nugent was straight-backed and forbidding, at least she was always like that. Nance Hazelhurst, however, could at different times be prim or coarse, harsh or maudlin, and her darting, newt-like way of coming and going, Jaen found disconcerting.

"No. But Vinnie . . ."

"Vinnie's mother was reckoned to be a spell-maker, so you don't want to put too much faith in what Vinnie tells you."

"I don't think Dan would . . ."

"What our Dan likes nor don't like an't the question . . . Anyway, don't you worry about that. I a deal with our Dan. I tell'd him before that you looked like you had thin blood. Now you got legs. I a tell our Dan, don't you worry about that. If you has any more babes, you'm going to end up with green-water and before he knows what happened, you'm going to be six feet under the churchyard."

Once, long, long ago it seemed, breathing mulled fumes on Jaen's wedding day, Nance Hazelhurst had put her dry, brown arms around Jaen. This time, unfortified, she did not feel sentimental and was aware of her son's wife's many faults, so she simply laid a hand on Jaen's knee.

"Baxter don't say much, but he've changed his mind about you. He a go to his final resting place easier in his heart that there's all them little boys to carry the Hazelhurst name. You been a good girl, but you don't have to keep on. Don't try none of Vinnie's potions, a inch of fleece off a newborn lamb soaked with goose-grease or good oil will gid you a good chance of being all right."

She passed on to Jaen a technique of protection that has served women longer than bronze has served the men. Then she patted Jaen's hand and darted off, leaving Jaen feeling foolish that after all these years of being a married woman, with her own place and children, Nance had spoken to her as though she were a girl. Nevertheless, she took heed of Nance so that George remained her last baby.

"Child, I'm going to tell you something your grandmother ought to a told me, and what all girls of your age ought to know so we can do summit to look after ourselves. And I expects you to tell any daughters you gets one day."

Hanna listened, nodding gravely – as she listened to whatever fact or fancy Jaen offered.

18

CHANGES
Scantlebury's

WITHIN A YEAR BETRISSE SAINT JOHN'S accent was not, as Captain Jetsam had vowed, fit for society, for she still retained her country vowels, but as well as giving her a wider vocabulary, he made her aware of her grammar, word endings and clarity. He would take her out and make her speak against blustery winds. "Use the lips!" "Open the mouth!" "You are mumbling, mumbling like a peasant. Cast your voice out . . . out."

Betrisse, facing onshore winds, opened her mouth against them. She cast her voice out, out over the waves and noisily shifting shingle, and gained a voice in the world. A voice that might have been born with a note of authority in it.

Annie said that she began to sound like a lady, but Ted Scantlebury said, no, she sounded better than that, for ladies spoke in such an affected way that nobody took them serious.

"You can't say that about Betrisse."

And certainly you could not.

When the Saint John/Scantlebury partnership sat down to work out how they were going to describe Scantlebury's on a handbill, they looked at first for ways in which they might in a small way compare with the established health resorts where sulphured water or warm springs were a gift of nature; but they realised very quickly that if they were going to make something of Betrisse's idea, then it could not be by competing with places that already existed.

When again they were considering the detail of the expansion of Scantlebury's, and the addition of the "Sea-water immersions", Annie still had reservations about taking money for nothing; and it was her observation that, "There really an't nothing here" that sparked off Betrisse's train of thought and became the basis of "A week at Scantlebury's for rest and restoration", or "A few days at Emworthy to prepare for the social round".

"That is what we must sell, and what they need. To have nothing for a week."

"Oh I'm sure that will sell like hot pies," Annie said.

"It will," said Betrisse. "Young people like Snows-greatly can buy anything. Theatres, balls, house-parties.

"You remember when Snows-greatly left?" Betrisse mimicked the voice. " 'Tippie, tell them that I shall mention this place to others. The peace of it, Tippie . . . oh, the tranquillity . . . the little white rooms. It is quite like a retreat to a nunnery I am sure. It has made me quite refreshed.'

"Oh Annie, think what a novelty it might be to them to come to a place where they go early to bed, sleep in simple rooms, where the women may leave off bones and lacings and the men their wigs."

"I shouldn't pay you for it," Ted Scantlebury said.

"That is because you have it already. People with nothing to do except do as they please might think it a great thing to deprive themselves for a few days. And they might truly feel better for plenty of rest and some plain food."

"It's a fact that the young Countess did get a glow on her, whilst she was here," Annie said.

It took two years before "A Week at Scantlebury's Spa" had a place in the rounds of some of the young, rich and idle. Betrisse was proved right. People would pay to be deprived. Young ladies especially took the immersion in the sea seriously, and found that by allowing the breezes of the southern coast to touch them, they acquired a pretty pinkness to their complexion. The gentlemen, living on a diet of well-cooked fish and simply-cooked vegetables and taking only cider, found that their digestions began to improve.

The mud-baths scheme from which the new venture had originally sprung was abandoned when it was discovered that Emworthy mud was not easy to filter. The smell even a few bucketsful produced would not have persuaded even the most scourge-seeking persons to immerse themselves.

Few stopped longer than a week, and eventually the young went on to other novelties, but by then the benefits of "A Week at Scantlebury's" or "A Few Days at Emworthy", were established among their elders, and Emworthy settled down to providing a few wooden seats and cobbled paths and small shops selling bits and pieces made by net-makers, carvers and makers of model smacks.

"It don't hardly seem right, Ann, the way some neighbours is taking good money from our visitors for a few shells and pebbles put up in a box."

"Oh, I reckon you'm wrong, Ted. 'Tis doing the visitors a favour, making them notice things they'd tread underfoot and not see."

Ted tucked up his lip and considered. "It's still selling boxes of bits that an't worth nothing."

"Ted my dear, you'm the nicest man I met, but you an't much of a one for business."

Ted Scantlebury looked closely at Annie in a way that he had never looked at another woman.

"What's being sold to visitors," Annie went on, "is a bit of a memory of Emworthy, or a few minutes of talk when they get home. They a put the box on a shelf and their friends will ask about the shells and the visitors will have five minutes of pleasure talking about summit they really don't know anything about. But that don't matter. It's been an honest enough deal; you got to look at it the same way as selling summit like a . . . picture."

Ted came close to Annie and gave her an awkward but gentle hug.

And Annie did not move away.

"You're a fair wonder, Ann; you runs rings round me. You got such a sensible head on your shoulders. You seems to be able to cope with anything from cooking to mending a fence. It's the way you just get on with things. I have a great liking for you, Ann." He flushed at the unaccustomed expression of his thoughts. "You'm what I should call . . . a . . . an all-weather woman . . . No, more like a sort of . . . a woman for all seasons."

He gave her an awkward but gentle kiss and still Annie did not move away.

She patted his arm in acceptance of him. " 'Tis what most common women are, Ted."

Part Three

JOURNEYS

I

BETRISSE SAINT JOHN'S RETURN journey to Newton Clare, a dozen years or so after her furtive, miserable exodus, could not have been more different.

It was not until she was settled in the coach on her way to see solicitors in Winchester that her mind turned to the changes that had taken place since the day she and Annie had stood together on the shore at Emworthy, the lapping glitterish sea soaking into the frayed hems of their skirts. Betrisse laid a hand upon the large brooch upon her bosom. Annie's token. The broken-edged oyster shell was now clasped and edged with silver and with a silver pin and chain to hold it secure.

Hidden, hanging on a fine silver chain, and lying between her breasts, is the only tangible relic of her life as Betrisse Hazelhurst. The gold disc with the Caesar's head. The Up Teg "seal".

At the age of twenty-one, Miss Saint John is tall and as straight-backed as Annie Saint John, who is now known in Emworthy as Mistress Scantlebury. Mistress and Master Scantlebury have just waved a tight-smiled farewell.

"I shall come back soon, Annie."

"I know you will, Bet, I know."

Both women, although having a fleeting thought about how long "soon" might be, know that she will return.

As they stood watching the horses being harnessed and the coach made ready in "Scantlebury's" yard, Betrisse held the baby Leonard and talked to Annie through him.

"I promised my baby brother that I should not stop away from him for long. I've got to be here to make sure that his first words have the sound of the Big House about them."

Sharing him as they had been doing since his birth, Annie took back the child from Betrisse and gazed at him as though it was the first time that she had set eyes upon him. They caught one another's eye and both laughed, and said in unison, Betrisse relinquishing for a moment her acquired way of "talking like Big House folks", "My but an't he a fair miracle."

And so he was.

France Hazelhurst, had he known, would have agreed, for it had not occurred to him until it was too late that Annie was not barren. Annie had conceived the baby in her forty-second year, only weeks after adopting Ted Scantlebury's name and sharing his bed.

When Leonard Scantlebury was born into the midst of the prospering trio of Ted, Annie and Betrisse, he brought with him an abundance of pleasure and joy. They all doted upon him and he thrived upon threefold love and care.

An elderly couple who were seated opposite Betrisse, and had observed the great fuss that was made by the entire staff at Scantlebury's when she entered the coach, wondered at the drawing together of her brows as she moved so as to get a last glimpse of the waving people, and then a last glimpse of the sea.

Betrisse keeps her gaze fixed upon the passing scene, not wanting to become too much involved in the inconsequential exchanges that are inevitable inside a coach. How strange, it is only at times like this that one is able to see how many changes have taken place. On the few occasions when she had thought about the things that must have altered at Up Teg, it was only that her sisters would be growing up, or a moment of wondering how many more children had been born, whether Uncle Ed was married or James Norris.

Now she knew.

It had been Ed who had told her.

The very road that the coach was riding so smoothly over had brought Ed Hazelhurst, with his small entourage, to Emworthy on his way to put on a show at the hiring fair in Chichester.

The elderly couple see a faint smile flicker about Betrisse's mouth and are sure that she is going to meet her lover. But the smile is for the remembrance of meeting Lord Oak.

The responsibility for greeting guests as they arrived, seeing that they were comfortable and fed after their journey, was Betrisse's. She, like everyone in Emworthy, had seen the notices that had been posted everywhere showing two huge men in a bare-knuckle fight, and she had heard that one of the men was the famous Lord Oak, a giant who had fought bare-knuckle and wrestled his way to riches, and now had bonded to him a number of young giants who entertained at fairs with tournaments of wrestling and fighting with bare knuckles and shows of strength.

Ah, that meeting. No wonder Betrisse smiles.

Lord Oak had announced himself at Scantlebury's with a shout.

"Ho!"

An unnecessary announcement, for Betrisse was only a few feet from him.

"Uncle Ed!"

The words of astonishment were out before she could stop them.

He had looked the tall young woman up and down in the manner he obviously always used with young attractive women, but with puzzlement. Not the befuddled puzzlement of many men whose way of life involved being punched daily with bare fists, for he had never reached that state; his boast was that he had never lost his looks or his brains. It was true of his brains, but of his looks – bent nose and a scarred lip – it was a matter of preference in the observer.

Puzzlement, for he had not been called "Ed" for years, certainly never "Uncle Ed".

Then Annie had appeared carrying a pile of linen.

There was instant recognition.

"My God! 'Tis young Ed!"

Annie had paled with the great flood of different emotions that passed through her, the most dominant of which was fear.

"Well, well. Annie! So this is where you got to. They always said you'd a went off to Salisbury."

He had transferred his attention back to Betrisse, whose upright stance and calm expression belied the succession of images that sped through her imagination, belied her violent thoughts, and fear of a Hazelhurst presence. Overriding all this though, was the thought that, for all that they had built a new life, for all their prosperity and security, she would have run off again without a second thought rather than be claimed by Luke. And if they bound and forced her . . . her jaws had clenched at the image of herself at bay . . . of herself wielding a whip as he had done, a knife . . .

His voice had been full of amusement.

"And you'm the little gel? 'Uncle Ed' you called me. Well, then . . . an't that something to think about. Lord Oak have got a little niece as well as a sister."

"No sir." Betrisse put the full force of her Snows-greatly voice into her reply. "Lord Oak has no niece. Nor Edwin Hazelhurst, not since the day his brother burnt red stripes into his child's skin when he beat her."

"Why Gel, you'm magnificent!" Then Lord Oak pulled his brows together. "Did Luke do that? It was never mentioned, only that he had chastised his wayward child. And you had took her off somewhere, Annie."

Small as she was compared to her tall niece, Annie had stood protectively before Betrisse and spoke up defiantly. "We shan't never go back. Never!"

Again, Betrisse's travelling companions see a smile flicker as she gazes unseeingly at the chalk downlands. Superimposed upon the grassy vista, she sees herself and Annie when the huge prize-fighter says, "Ah, and I can't say as I blames you, for wild horses nor hunger wouldn't get me back to live under my father's fist."

As Annie said later, "I don't know if it is him that changed, or me. Or perhaps he was always a decent understanding youth and I never noticed."

Her observation was after an evening when the three exiles from Up Teg talked of their successes and pleasure in their new lives.

"I hated that old work," Ed Hazelhurst told them. "Fighting the Almighty to get a few bushels of summit . . . never a fair fight with Him. The years and years we should get close to harvest and there'd be some pestilence or blight come on the crop, or a great hailstorm."

"You have not come from these other fights untouched," Betrisse had said, nodding at his collapsed nose and lip and eye scars.

"They was give when I was new to the game, and they was give in fair contest."

Gradually, as they talked, they began to trust one another, slowly at first, circling round, testing the water so to speak, until each had the measure of the other; then they broached the topic of Newton Clare. Ed had never been near the place since he left.

The first years away he travelled from fair to fair, mostly in northern parts. The Rathley man who had first persuaded Ed to take to the roads had travelled with him ever since, arranging the contests and shouting the spiel. He went back home from time to time, thus keeping Ed informed of what news and gossip there was of "back there", but never breathing a word to anyone there of his partnership with Edwin Hazelhurst.

And so it was that Betrisse learned that Luke was dead.

"Things is not good there. But it serves him right –" "him" being Baxter Hazelhurst, Master of Up Teg. "He was so fixed in his mind about there never being nobody but him and his living on Teg land that he good as sold his soul to the Church lawyers."

He did not know the details of what his father had agreed, but it was rumoured that the Commissioners had got him all hands down.

"Now they changed their minds, and there an't nothing the old man can do. They'm going to sell house and land over his head."

2

EMWORTHY TO WINCHESTER

IN THE JOLTING COACH Betrisse feels, as she has done on many occasions since that day when Ed Hazelhurst happened by chance to choose "Scantlebury's" at which to break his journey, other jolts – excitement, apprehension and the thrill of the commission entrusted to her.

When he arrived, Ed had assumed that Annie and Betrisse must be servants, and for a while they let him believe that this was so.

"Don't tell him nothing," Annie had told Ted and Betrisse. But as Ed revealed to them his own prosperity and attitude to "back there", Annie revealed to him the extent of their success.

Ed was a true Hazelhurst in that he was not afraid to boast of the apparently never-ending stream of women he had loved and who had lost him, and the gold that he spent and that which he had safely tucked away.

"It was a hard and tough business," he had told them. "And it wasn't nothing like this. I slept 'neath a good many bushes, using what bit of money we had for food to keep our strength up." He clenched his fists and flexed his arm muscles in a way that Annie recognised as Hazelhurst, but slightly self-mocking. "But I made more gold these last years than most men of our kind makes in ten lifetimes."

Ted was impressed, having seen "Lord Oak's Fighting Men" years ago. "Well, you got to admit, he have got something to boast about. It's a few years since I saw his show. We had to put in at Portsmouth. I remembers as though it was yesterday: wrestling . . . bare-knuckle contests – a fine sort of entertainment. Not the usual bit of roped-off fairground, like most fight booths, but put on in a public room. The place was overflowing. No wonder he can wear such fancy waistcoats."

During the week of the fair, Ed had travelled back and forth each day along the short road between Chichester and Emworthy, coming in to the owners' private rooms at Scantlebury's, winking at them and jingling a small leather drawstring pouch of coins. Except for Ted, they did not meet Ed's partner.

"Best if he don't come here. He's a good sort but he do like to gossip, and he'd let slip summit about you when he was visiting home, without even meaning. I shall tell him I found a couple o' ladies that have took my fancy." Masculine pride widened his broad chest. "He's used to my ways in that direction."

Betrisse said that meant he could be trusted not to give them away to anyone, for his partner was his closest friend.

Annie still retained some caution and, except for inviting Ed to take his supper with them, treated him as she would other well-to-do guests. Betrisse found him of absorbing interest. He had awakened her curiosity about her roots, and she dragged from him every morsel of information that he had about the years after Annie had taken her away, and what he had learned since from his partner.

Ted found him a good companion and, after accompanying Ed to view the wrestling contests and the exhibition of fighting, had said there must be summit in the air round Newton Clare to turn out three such successful moneymakers. Four, when you counted his partner, as Ed pointed out.

"It's because we wasn't risking nothing," said Annie. "None of us would be so free with trying out new ideas now – not now we got summit to lose."

The rumbling male voices of Ted and Lord Oak could be heard in the long hours as they made exchanges of fishermen's yarns and travelling-showmen's tales, the outcome of which good fellowship was a smoke and rum-fumed admission from Ed that, "You'm worth three of our France any day of the week." And with that Lord Oak was accepted as a reliable member of the runaway branch of the Hazelhurst tribe.

None of us would be so free with our ideas now we got summit to lose.

Annie had been wrong. There was something within the four of them that pumped the thrill of new venture through them. They formed a partnership of four, and Betrisse – as the one who can "speak" and read a bit and make a reasonable signature – is their representative. They will make an offer for the Up Teg house and any land the Church representatives will sell.

There is a short stop at Havant, but Betrisse stops close to the coach, as though to sit inside the inn would indicate to the coachman that there is no urgency to get on. Although she feels Emworthy dragging at her the further from it she goes, she wants to be at Winchester, to complete the business there.

She tries to imagine Up Teg as it must be now, but she cannot.

Luke is gone too.

She has held hatred of him inside her soft nature, like the pit within a peach. She cannot imagine the place without him. That Jim Norris or Grandfather are not there can be imagined. But – Luke is gone!

Ed had mentioned it almost casually, as though he had forgotten that his little ragged, wayward cousin who made much of herself and shouted, "I'd be a better farmer than anybody" at the assembled family, that the child they had searched for, over downs and copse and stream and tracks for days, and this formidable young woman were the same.

Luke's gone. Skidded down the bank at Deep Run and got drowned. Pete found him so I heard . . .

Luke's gone!

Had she heard that he had died in his bed, the hatred might have remained with her, but he had drowned in Deep Run and nobody had found him till morning. A bad way to die.

It was all even.

All settled between herself and Him.

When she heard Ed speak of Luke so casually, the kernel of hatred germinated but then gradually began to grow and change into a shoot of compassion for her mother. What was she like now? Martha.

Betrisse might well have caught the morning coach and arrived at Winchester the same day, but she found a dozen reasons to put off leaving, seeing that all was in order, anticipating, giving instructions. So, it is evening when she steps down at the King's Head in Wickham. She looks critically at the place, and before her box has been taken in, counts a dozen faults that she would not stand for at Scantlebury's. No wonder Scantlebury's is gaining such a reputation for high standards.

The King's Head is a fine imposing building – not a collection of cottages bought up piecemeal and dragged together like their own place – but its walls are smoked yellow, its hangings smell of years of cooking and dust and oil fumes. No attention to the detail of comfort. She hugs to herself the secret the King's Head does not know – that people will pay good money to be "Clean and Decent" and sleep in simple comfort.

Already she misses Emworthy.

3

UP TEG TO CROUD CANTLE

A FEW MONTHS EARLIER HANNA had made a journey. That the two cousins travelled by horse-drawn vehicles, was the only similarity.

Betrisse had left leisurely, with embraces and good wishes from people who loved her and who were concerned for her comfort. Although she soon missed her Emworthy family her mind was full of the important purpose of her errand, and what might come from it. She travelled with her mind stimulated.

Hanna . . . ? Hanna tries to eradicate from her mind any memory of her journey.

On that same evening as Betrisse eats supper at the King's Head in Wickham, miles away from the people she thinks of as her family, Hanna is preparing a meal to eat with those she thinks of similarly: Grandmother Bella, John and Rosie . . . Jude.

Rosie, who cannot hear or speak, lives at Croud Cantle now. She came to live here whilst Hanna was away. Rosie is a relation, but what the relationship is, Hanna cannot fathom. She has been told but it has not yet registered as either factual or important.

Because Rosie – beautiful, gentle, smiling Rosie – is deaf and dumb, it is to her that Hanna confides, silently, those things that she cannot tell anyone, not even John.

She is able to tell Rosie because Rosie has no language, and what Hanna knows is too full of anguish and passion to speak of aloud. In her mind words and images writhe like a nest of snakes. Each time she silently lets her mind open up in Rosie's sensitive presence, a few of the snakes slither away.

Silent Grandmother. Silent Rosie. Silent Hanna.

And when she is there, Jude's silence is worse than any of the others'.

Jude works, gives orders, makes decisions, runs the holding and the house as she has done for years. When Jude speaks she sounds normal enough, for her silence is a silence of her spirit. Jude's is the silence of the newly-dead, when the body is still turgid and warm but the soul has flown.

So, even if Hanna could forgive Jude for abandoning her to the Hazelhursts and try to speak to her, there is no one inside Jude.

Soon John will come into the house.

A man now, John.

When she lived here before, he was a boy; they played together, worked and told one another secrets.

Twenty now, John. With a lovely black beard that Hanna finds so dear to her. During the time that Hanna has not lived here, Jude has taught him to read. From the child who came to live on the farm in the way a stray animal would come, he has become part of their tiny society, part of Croud Cantle and the family.

Soon he will come into the kitchen, bringing with him the noisy clumping of his boots, the hust-hust sound made by the rubbing of the rough cloth of his breeches as his thighs move, and the smell of animal and grass and himself, and the sage and thyme that he has been trimming back.

He will pull a wooden stool to the table and sniff with pleasure at whatever Hanna or Rosie puts before him, tearing his bread with his strong, earth-blackened fingers, perhaps stirring in a sprig of one of the herbs that he has become so knowledgeable about.

"Taste that, Hanny."

She will take a sup from his spoon.

"What do you think on it, Hanny? 'Tis that cross of sage that have come out with mottled leaves. Do you like it, Hanny? Do you think I should grow it on?"

John Toose will bring life into the silent kitchen.

Jude is away. Hanna knows, with a certain part of her mind, where Jude has gone, but she will not allow herself to think of it.

Rosie looks at Hanna. She smiles and pushes up the corners of her mouth to indicate that Hanna must smile too, and when Hanna does not immediately respond, Rosie pretends a moue of disappointment. Hanna responds.

There are times when Hanna believes that Rosie knows what she is thinking, especially when the thoughts are being wretched, when the thoughts conjure up sound. The terrible crack of a dead branch breaking.

Then, Rosie's eyes glisten. She shakes her head as if to deny what Hanna is seeing, then, with her firm arms about Hanna's tense young shoulders, sits and rocks her. It is Jude that Hanna really wants. Whenever Jude makes a move towards her, the image of Jude leading the donkeys away . . . the memory of Jude forcing Hanna's arms from her neck . . . the irrational blame she lays upon Jude . . . that it was Jude who had abandoned her, always compels Hanna to be distant. The image of Jude and the empty donkey is vivid still.

Slowly, over the weeks, the nightmare comes less often, but when it does come . . .

"I made a pact to be a good wife and mother, Ju, but I never kept my part."

"I'm Hanna. Not Jude. I'm Hanna."

"Oh . . . a course you are. Hanna. Yes. You looked just like Ju standing there. Hanna. A course."

The crack! as the dead branch breaks again.

Grandmother Bella is now an old lady with hair the colour of heavy cream. She must be helped to move, and her mouth and an eye look as though they will slide from her face. Sometimes though, coming back momentarily from wherever she lives, into the real world, Grandmother will look up sharply at Hanna, and Hanna will catch her breath at seeing a glimpse of the straight-backed red-haired Grandmother who used to call her "Lovey" and who, with Jude, had been mother and father to her for eight years.

Now that Hanna is in her sixteenth year, anyone can see that she only superficially resembles Jude, only superficially looks like Jaen. Jude's face is intelligent and her eyes are always looking inside her own mind or out at something distant in space or time. Jaen was born pretty, with delicate features and an upward curve at the corners of her mouth that gave her the *trompe-l'œil* smile that fooled everyone – everyone except Jude and, later, except Hanna too.

Hanna looks like Bella – Bella Estover all over again. And, as Bella did, Hanna will eventually deal with whatever nest of writhing snakes she encounters. Though not as her mother did, by laying bracken over the snakes, leaving them to breed and then to be fed by her emotions.

And, as Bella did, she will live her life with no fancifulness. Not like Jude with her dreams and passion for change. Like Bella, she will settle her mind on practical matters. She has never had any understanding of what Jude used to tell her of the wildness of the two sisters when they were girls, nor what they saw in dreams and stories, why Jude was always reading things, and wanting others to read also.

Hanna, old head on young shoulders, has seen where that leads.

When Hanna was quite young, Bella would take her to look at the rows of preserves, the wrapped cheeses, the well-bunched rhubarb and other medicinal stems and roots, and cooking herbs ready for market. Bella had filled her mind with the business of producing. Neatness. Order. No room for fancies.

Look at that, Lovey, an't that worth everything?

Rosie and Grandmother Bella have made their slow journey out of the room.

In the kitchen, only the sound of the soft plopping broth in the iron skillet hanging over the glowing logs.

Broth plopping in the quiet kitchen.

"Ju, give the pot a stir."

Yes (Cannot say "Mother") . . .

Yes (Must not say "Jaen" . . . He has forbidden it).

"Yes, I have seen to it."

"Do you remember, Ju, that time when you was stirring the broth and the soot fell? And you beat it in like it was powdered herbs. And Dicken said that he liked soup that had a well-smoked bit of bacon boiled into it. Oh Ju, you was terrible good for keeping a straight face and me bursting to laugh."

I am not "Jude". I am not "Jude". I am not "Jude".

"Oh Ju. I'm glad when you comes to see me. I been that lonely out here."

I am not-Jude-not-Jude-not-Jude.

Why did you marry Him?

Why did you come to this awful place?

Why didn't you stop at home with Grandmother and Jude?

I could a been born there. And we could a lived together the four of us.

We could a run our farm together – without Dicken or any of the hired men . . . except John.

You never wanted Him. Only Jude you ever wanted. If you had stopped home and let me be born there, you would never a had all they boys. Your legs wouldn't never a swelled up . . .

The dead branch breaks with a loud Crack!

Into the silence falls men's voices telling one another "see thee in the marn'n".

John comes in.

4

WICKHAM TO WINCHESTER

BETRISSE WAS UP at her usual early hour, and by the time the coach was ready, she had become fidgety with waiting. Dormant doubts that had germinated during the night, now grew cotyledons as she watched the comings and goings in Wickham's wide square.

Annie's questions, which at the time Betrisse had brushed aside – about whether the lawyers would be willing to deal with a young spinster, and would they even be *allowed* to draw up documents? – began to put down roots of doubt. Could she manage? What should she do if they turned her away? It would be no good telling lawyers that it was quite unfair!

A local solicitor had made out notes of authority which Ted and Annie and Ed had signed or marked, and which were intended to give Betrisse *carte blanche* in any decision she might make on their behalf . . . but local solicitors were – local solicitors. It might be entirely different in Winchester.

She walks out through the front door of the King's Head, over which is painted a notice: "MANNERS MAKYTH MAN – Bishop William of Wykeham." She can read it, but is puzzled.

As she walks past the grand new houses that she now covets as she sees them, she thinks of "manners", and wonders, as she often does, why she lets herself think on such matters. Where do the thoughts spring from? She has enough on her mind without wondering why old bishops said such foolish things.

Manners. She has learned from Captain Jetsam how to be mannerly, but it is hard gold that is enabling her to carry out the Scantlebury/Saint John/Lord Oak plan.

By the time she has seen all she wants to see of Wickham, the coach is ready and they are away.

Milestones – Droxford Four Miles. Corhampton Three Miles. Cantle Three Miles. Blackbrook Seven Miles. Winchester Fifteen Miles.

Signposts – Hambledon. Winchester. Warnford. West Meon. East Meon. Alresford. Motte. Blackbrook. Newton Clare.

Newton Clare. Newton Clare. The horses' hooves beat out messages. Luke is gone. Newton Clare. Luke is gone. Newton Clare.

Then suddenly, the coach reaches a crest and there it is, Winchester!

Breathtaking to see it from the top of the downs.

The coachman draws in the horses, for he knows that passengers who have never travelled here before and may never do so again, always want a moment to capture the scene to take back home to those who will never have the opportunity of visiting the old capital of England. Such consideration of his passengers is usually worth a coin or two, or a pot of ale and a pie at the coach-house.

Winchester, the vast city that Betrisse thinks that she can manage on her own.

Red brick and grey stone. Grey roofs and red roofs. Hundreds of roofs climbing out of the valley or sliding down into it. Spring sun shows up the newly-leaved trees and the fresh-green overlay of the chalk-hills. Hampshire abounds in valleys. Valleys set in green downlands with a stream running through, a huddle of houses, a church, a few tracks and lanes. Newton Clare is just such, bounded by hills on three sides with the Hammet its life-giving vein.

But this!

She has never visualised such a city. Great buildings, perhaps they are the colleges she has heard of, but had never thought to be so large. Spires everywhere, how many people are there here to need so many churches? It is a Newton Clare of great proportion: not with a stream, but a wide river flowing through; the river is not forded, but has bridges built over it; not with a church, but a great pile of a cathedral squatting at its heart. Its stone looks warm and yellow; its grey slated roof gleams in the spring sun.

How many people!

The coachman has opened the door so that they may stretch their legs. Betrisse walks to where the land falls away.

A feeling of *déjà vu.*

She is at Vinnie's wedding feast. Dressed in a yellow shift with yellow flowers upon it. Her Granfer lifts her up onto the table and her perspective changes. Looking down upon everything and everyone in the barn, the small girl is assaulted by unwomanliness. None of you is better than me!

Lord Oak, her Uncle Ed, had first brought her "unwomanliness" to her notice for her to speculate upon.

"Why an't a handsome girl like you never got married?"

"Would you enter a one-sided contest with your hands tied and your legs fettered?"

He had roared with laughter.

"You got me there, Gel! Still the same as you was. 'It an't fair!' I remember you shouting it, then you hit him with the platter."

She smiled. She had never regretted that moment.

"I hit him with the platter after *I told him it wasn't fair."*

"I'll tell you summit. If it wa'nt for all this . . ." he slowly looked over her bosom, and shaped his hand in an imaginary caress of her hips, "well then I might of wondered if you should be wearing flap-front breeches."

"And have all my brains bunched up behind that flap, like men do?"

He had shaken his head with pleasure at her quick wit and the authority of her Snows-greatly voice.

"Ah Gel, Gel. If you was a man, and you did keep your amount of brains bunched up there, then the prominence of it'd be a permanent embarrassment to you, and you'd a had to kep your hands held before you in decent company. But you got to admit that 'tis a might unwomanly to be 'businessing' the way you do."

"What businessing?"

"Man's businessing."

"Man's business! You think that running 'Scantlebury's' is not womanly?"

Although he had not known the adult Betrisse for very long, he recognised the look she gave him, and saw that he was again running into the quicksand of her quick mind. But he was smitten by the glorious woman that had grown from the little maid who had picked stones before the importance of his plough and himself, when she was four and he twelve. And, as she ticked off on her fingers the list of work which was involved in the running of an inn such as Scantlebury's, he could see where she was leading.

". . . and what did Annie do back there but cook and clean and make a farthing buy a pennyworth. And Martha . . . milking and butter-making, sewing, spinning, carrying water, earthing the midden pit. And your mother? What about her?" Stabbing at him with her forefinger.

"All you lot, one after the other. A Clean and Decent Bed for the Night, Sir? Supper and breakfast for you and your six sons, Master Baxter Sir? Rooms for your harvesters, Your Honour? Believe me, there wasn't one job on that farm that Annie and me – I – could not have done. And made a lot less noise about. Running a place like Scantlebury's man's business? There is not a job in the land that a woman might not do better than a man!"

Genially he applauded, then said gleefully, "You couldn't a pole-vaulted Th'ammet like us men though."

Flicking away male immaturity. "Of course not! We should never waste ourselves on such foolishness. There's a ford for crossing the Hammet. Pole-vaulting. Can you imagine any grown woman being so nonsensical as to try to outdo another grown woman in getting over a river in the most difficult way anybody can think of? Hooking yourselves over on a bit of a stick! Pht! Women'd make a bridge or a sensible raft and row ourselves over six at a time . . . and we should have had sense enough to keep our backsides dry!"

Until she met Ed, she had never met a man to whom she would have given one moment's thought in the one-sided contest. He was the kind of man she would have given two moments of thought. But he was Luke's brother. Uncle Ed.

As Lord Oak he was more than her kith and kin. He was her kind. As they were now, and she unmarried, Betrisse was, in every respect other than body, the heavier weight. Once married though, he would have Church on his side, Law and Custom in his corner. Then she would have cried out, "It an't fair! It an't fair!" until she was known for a scold and a shrew.

As Annie had once looked upon the glitterish sea at Emworthy and formed a dream, an ideal, so then, as the coach winds its way down into the heart of Winchester, does Betrisse hold the gleaming city to her.

The thongs that hold her to Emworthy – ties that she has always supposed and wanted to be unbreakable – stretch. If she pulls, she will see that they have become as fragile as spiderweb, and they will release her.

And she can release Emworthy.

Annie is happy with Ted and fulfilled by young Leonard. Annie too is a woman inside the laws of the land but outside the rules of the Church. She is not a bigamist, but she is a woman to cast stones at. If Betrisse is able to have documents drawn up in the name of Saint John and without reference to the names Hazelhurst or Scantlebury, then Annie and young Leonard may have some security against men who could claim to own her. Not, Betrisse is sure, that Ted will ever do anything but continue to admire her and treat Annie as beloved wife, but security for a woman is as fragile as a cobweb in a field of bullocks.

Scantlebury's is established and will remain a solid "Clean and Decent" place keeping them in security and comfort. If it expands it will be Leonard who will do it. Ted and Annie are of an age when, in more common circumstances, they might be dandling their grandson rather than a first son.

The transformation from small inn to Scantlebury's was an idea of youth. Without Betrisse, the gadfly sons and daughters of Big House people will, in their tethered freedom between childhood and marriage, settle on some other capricious idea, Scottish mountains perhaps, the Isle of Wight, lakes or foreign places with fountains and public marble eroticism – anywhere that has not been fly-blown by their elders.

So, as the coach rattles over the street-cobbles of Winchester, the web-thin tie stretches.

This is where I belong.

She does not know what she will do here, but unwomanly ambition excites her. Call it what you will, self-confidence or arrogance, determination or stubbornness, the sense of her own worth that she has felt since childhood has never left her; the episode at Vinnie's wedding when Baxter had lifted her onto the table, and that other, at the last family gathering when her childlike belief in herself had been affronted, that sense of her own ability surges up again as the coach wends its way on the final mile or so of its journey.

I could do anything if I lived here.

She carried no specific images of herself except one of herself organizing, influencing, making changes. Why should Ed think that this side of her nature was unwomanly? He accepted her with a certain pride – "You'm the very little devil, Gel."

Why unwomanly to want to do some interesting thing? Why did men like Ed think that women were – or should be – content to have the blanket of domesticity thrown over them?

Yes . . . it was like that . . . smothered beneath a dull blanket – like Martha had been. Luke has gone. Has Martha's blanket gone? Even when she was a little stone-picker in the fields, Betrisse had wanted to do Ed's work, more interesting work, ploughing.

She smiles to herself at the sudden recall of herself as a small child and Ed as a youth. "Ploughin's boys' work. Maids an't no good at making straight furrows." She had to leap high so as to reach his swaggering rear with her hard, bare toes, but her very fury charged her muscles and manifested itself in a dog-leg furrow which dignity forced the superior young Ed to ignore.

Yet she had believed him – that girls could not make straight furrows – believed him because he was a boy, and he said that it was so. And the kick he received was because she had believed it true: maids would never be able to plough a straight furrow, and so were condemned to pick stones for ever. She had been desperate to take the plough and show him that she was as good as he was.

Why was it unwomanly to want to do that?

Of all the men that she can think of, from Luke and his brothers, to Ted Scantlebury and "Captain Jetsam", she can think of none who is her equal. And of all the women, from her mother and the aunts of Up Teg to the tough oyster-women and Annie, she can think of none less able than their men.

Womanly!

Why did I not think of that before? Nothing to be ashamed of.

Womanly, to be self-sufficient and capable, like Annie.

Yet . . . ?

Starting with nothing, Annie has made a better life than she would ever have had at Up Teg. She lives with the man she loves, has the child she wanted. Yet . . . she is owned still by France Hazelhurst.

Ted owns his share in Scantlebury's, Betrisse owns hers. Yet . . . France Hazelhurst owns Annie's. Betrisse's stomach clenches at the unfairness.

As those thoughts worked on one level of consciousness, she looked eagerly at the closely-built streets thronging with people.

The thought "this is where I belong" was fed by small crumbs – the great number and variety of shops, houses with stepped up entrances, stone pillars, the way that passers-by saw nothing remarkable in the startling and fashionable vehicles that were on every street.

She could scarcely wait to walk in those streets. So, as soon as she had secured her room and her bag was taken up, she went out.

The sun had settled everywhere, fresh as dew, making every direction she might take inviting. As the lawyer she was to visit on the following day had premises in High Street, she went in that direction, so that she would not on the morrow go out unprepared.

The street was wide and seemingly endless compared with Emworthy's High Street. She found the lawyer's premises, the impressiveness of which gave her a moment of apprehension, but no . . . to deal with such men would be a test of her ability as a woman whose future lay in a city. At the heart of the street, the butter-cross. Not as Emworthy's cross, a simple stone, but elaborately carved and looking like a spire that had fallen from some well-endowed church. She laid a hand upon its grey stone as though it were a talisman.

A solemn bell began to toll out the hour, then was mimicked in all parts of the city by jolly carillons of the less dignified time-keepers. Scores of chimes from every direction. She was impressed by the extravagance of such a surfeit of information on what hour of day it was. Yet people continued about their affairs apparently not hearing, at least, not listening, accepting as normal the multiplicity of bell-towers.

She turned down a narrow alleyway and found herself in the

shadow of the great cathedral. It was awesome viewed from the base of its walls. The stones that had appeared light and yellow from the hill outside the city, now seemed to have been thrust up with force from the earth. Do people kneel and pray in such a place? Yes, if God is anywhere he would be in a place like this. Betrisse kneels for a minute and lets her thoughts rise like steam into the vault high above. Condensed, there comes back a droplet of an idea. Suddenly she knows what she will do, and that she can succeed.

The vast windows that had appeared mud and slime coloured from without burst into colour as occasionally Betrisse's dreams do. Upon awakening from her coloured dreams, she has always felt that her mind and body were like a pan of milk at the point of boil. The bright sun throws the stained-glass in patchwork upon the grey flagstones. She tries to put her hand in the path of the rays to capture a piece of vivid blue. A black-frocked and buttoned man frowns and she leaves showing more dignity than she feels. She would like to unpin her hair and stand where rough on-shore winds can send it streaming free.

With the fizzing mood growing, she wandered the streets for hours. At one gate she stopped so long that a keeper dressed like a beadle asked her what she wanted.

"What is this place?"

"This is The College." His words implied "Is it not obviously *The* College? Hub of the universe."

The college. Surrounding a wide courtyard, yellow stone buildings, windowed, niched and statued.

To think that there were men who went daily in and out of that place and probably thought no more of it than she did of Scantlebury's. Yet only to walk through the gate must confer status.

On her way back to the coaching house, she stopped at another gate. Another beadle-like attendant.

"This is the castle."

A universe with two hubs. Three, for surely the man who had frowned when she had tried to take hold of the glory of the window there, would assert that the cathedral was at the centre, had always been, would always be.

A castle? She had never known that there was a castle here. Had lived her childhood not many miles distant but had never heard there was a castle close by. Again doubt that she would be a match for city people. People who went about their business when a hundred bells in a score of towers chimed, whose daily life was conducted in the shadow of a cathedral, a castle, and colleges whose gates were protected by men in pompous costume.

After dark, the city still continued in motion. She lay awake a long time that night listening, and had never felt so vulnerable, yet strong, so confident yet doubting. A runaway child of ignorant farmers, a work-scavenging girl, an oyster-drudge who happened to have learned a thing or two about putting travellers up for the night. A woman. A woman without a man, to have aspirations that men think unwomanly. Even Ed – the great Lord Oak – had said he could not have managed without his friend and aide to help and advise.

Next morning, however, her faith in her own ability was restored. The lawyer, accepting her credentials and the worth of the partnership, set in motion the sale of certain lands, rights and properties known as Up Teg in the village of Newton Clare, Hampshire.

She thought, why, it is all a scheme to put the likes of me in fear of agreements. Parties of the First Part is Them, and Parties of the Second Part is us, hereinafter is from now on, and when you have sorted our Rights and Dues, it is all quite clear. So with her faith in herself entirely whole again, she asked the lawyer, "Can you tell me anything of coffee-houses?" His superior manner and way of looking down his nose in no way perturbed Betrisse; it was little different from Annie's natural manner.

"Can you tell me of any central premises likely to be suitable?"

In the manner of his profession, where it is never wise to admit plainly, or immediately, that it was a fact that the weather is set fair, he did admit that he, ah . . . might be aware of . . . ah . . . certain premises. And, if she would return to his offices later . . .

As it was still early in the day, she changed from her new full skirt and fine bodice and jacket, to a plain skirt and top and strong boots. On the previous day, she had come to a river and a path leading to a hill which had aroused her interest.

The college gate-keeper had said it was Saint Catherine's, a bare mound of downland with tufts of trees on its summit and patches of gorse and juniper and white patches of bare chalk over its surface. On reaching a point on its lower slopes, she sat where she could look across the city, over the colleges, the flat-towered cathedral, spired churches, to the castle.

It was quiet here, where city-dwellers came only when travelling. She often sat alone in the open air at Emworthy. It was an odd thing for a young girl to do, but Betrisse Saint John, in many ways, was a trifle odd. Why else would she be sitting, wondering where in that mass of brick and timber and stone will she eventually settle. For by this time, she has no doubts that this place will be her home from now on. When she returns to Emworthy, it will be only to tell Annie what she has discovered here.

I feel like I have found my home, Annie. I reckon it must be the most interesting place in the world.

Annie would nod and say something like, well, you only got so many years Bet, just make sure you don't waste none. Annie would not ask whether it was suitable that Betrisse should think of leaving to live in such a place, if it could be done, or was wise, or if it was like a straight furrow and could not be done by a woman. Annie's attitude had always been, get hold of the plough handles and see if you can.

She slowly walks downhill and sits on a fallen tree and watches a kingfisher flashing from willow-stem to river-bed in an iridescent streak.

It's years since I saw a kingfisher.

The times we children tried to down them with pebbles for fishing in our part of Th'ammet. We always missed.

Through the dark barrier which has cut her off from any bright memory of her early years at Up Teg, gleams that one of village children hooking-off from their tedious clattering at crows or stone-picking, to idle beside Th'ammet.

Idling now, she lies back and looks at the spring-blue sky. She has crushed water-mint underfoot and now the warmth of the sun brings out the strong aroma. At Emworthy there is always the smell of the sea, the stranded, rotting weed, the strong stench of mud which is revealed each time the sea retreats, the smell of decomposing fragments in discarded shells. Rough, uncomfortable smells, exciting to encounter, but quite unlike the spring-meadow perfume of crushed water-mint.

Back. Back, back and over the dark barrier.

Kit will be a woman. So will Rachael. Kit might be a married woman. I have four sisters. Laurie would have been a young man.

It is like stepping into a dream landscape, familiar yet strange, and she finds that it is not easy to stay there for long. She draws herself back to think of her future in Winchester.

It was the droplet of condensed thought in the cathedral that started her thinking of the coffee-houses of London and Bath. Information implanted by several visitors to Scantlebury's had begun to germinate into an idea, and now that she had successfully done what had been entrusted to her by the Emworthy partnership, and her mind was clear of that business, she could allow herself to think of coffee-houses.

The more she thought, the more stimulated she became at what she might do.

This city was the most important in the county and still retained status as the ancient capital of England; it was full of colleges and public offices . . . teeming with the kind of men who frequented coffee-houses . . . To open up such a place would need only premises and the knowledge that she already possessed. It would be a much simpler scheme, far easier to run in every way than Scantlebury's. No rooms to clean, no beds to turn, linen to launder, no fetching and carrying, or the roasting of meats and brewing of ale.

In her mind's eye, she saw the place. And from that picture an idea exploded upon her. Not a coffee-house . . . yes that too perhaps . . . but another establishment, a place where women might meet and be at ease with one another in the way of men.

How fine to open a place where women might sit with other women, respectably, as she and Annie and the oyster-women used to do, at ease, confiding in one another their ability to make a better job of the world than their menfolk had. Just as she remembered groups of women at harvest time, exchanging irreverent opinions. Rough men had their ale-houses, gentlemen had their coffee-houses. There was probably nowhere in a city where women might gather as they did in dairies, or on field-edges or shorelines.

She wishes Annie was here so that she could test her ideas against Annie's commonsense.

Back in the High Street, she sees that the people who took no notice of the city full of the sound of bells were now standing about as though a parade was coming. Betrisse stopped too, beside a woman with two large market baskets.

"Always seem to have a good day for it. It's queer, an't it?"

"What is it? Is it a parade?"

"The Seshins," the basket-woman announced with pride, as though Seshins were hers, whatever they were.

"What are they?"

"The Spring Seshins. The Assizes. Here they come."

Like the rest of those lining the street, Betrisse strains her neck to see.

Led by a menial in lordly regalia, came the parade of Assize judges and officials. Whitely wigged, costly gowned, stiffly frilled and lace-cuffed, the Quarterly judgement on Hampshire's serious offenders paraded before the inhabitants of Winchester its bleak authority.

"An't you never bin to the Seshins? Oh, if you'm a stranger, you ought to go. It's the best show next to the fair. I never misses, not if I can help it. It's the one time I gets a woman in to help me (with the pies you know – I makes the best pies in Winchester) but when it's the Seshins I gets a woman in to cut up the meat and that, so I can be free to go."

By the time she left the basket-woman, Betrisse had much information about the Assize Courts, and decided that she would indeed like to see a great judge on his throne, with the barristers and the jury; so the next morning she was, as told by her adviser, outside the courts well before they opened.

Her new acquaintance was already there, apparently well-provided for the occasion with bread and a jug of something.

"You come then. There's a few murders."

"Oh!" Betrisse had not expected to observe such a dramatic event.

"The one today, he says she slipped and fell. I don't reckon she did."

"Why's that?"

"Well . . . they always do. You can't tell what happens really. If a man clouts his wife or a maid with a stick and there an't nobody else there, and it cracks her skull, and he says she caught her foot in her skirt-hem and fell . . . well." She opens her hands to demonstrate the obviousness of her reasoning.

The public gallery seats were cramped and hard, but there were plenty of people willing to sit upon them. The public seeing justice seen to be done, but in fact satisfying a desire for a good drama, and if in luck the ultimate denouement of the black cap and the splendid idea of a legitimate violent, public death.

Betrisse was soon caught up in the pageantry of an Assize court in session and thought that she might spend a whole morning here. Some boring defendants of mundane offences were despatched quickly – at least as quickly as the ponderous system allowed; then the public gallery shuffled its feet and re-adjusted its buttocks.

"This should be the one what done his wife in."

The circuit judge composed himself upon his throne, flanked by the Lord Lieutenant and various others who never found themselves in any other position in any court, except when seated upon the Magisterial Bench or in the Jury Box. The Sirs, Hons, Barts, MPs and JPs of Hampshire.

The court falls silent.

A name distorted by echo rings out.

Betrisse's sinews shrink; and she shivers.

The basket-woman nudges, believing that this young woman is thrilled at her first sight of a murderer, even if he has been charged with Manslaughter.

But it is the name that causes Betrisse's thighs to tighten, heat to spread over her head and shoulders.

"Call Daniel Hazelhurst."

And even before the tall, broad, manacled figure appears in court and is led to the dock, Betrisse knows that the name is no coincidence of baptism.

The coincidence is in the time that she has chosen to visit Winchester, the day that she has laid aside to watch an Assize Court in session.

As she draws in her breath, so does another woman at the far end of a row, the front row, as close to the well of the court as one can sit.

It is a face that is vaguely familiar . . . connected in a way with

Back There . . . yet not one belonging to any of the servants so far as she can remember . . . nor any of the women who came in at harvest, nor any of the occasional dairy-maids. She tries to place the woman.

As the accused man entered, the woman stiffened and leaned slightly forward. There was a man with her, older than she, probably about thirty years old. He had an intelligent, generous expression, not handsome, but the kind of looks that Betrisse found attractive in a man, a man who would be passionate but not forceful, and for a moment, when he covered the woman's hand resting upon her knee with his own, Betrisse would have liked to be the woman. But only to receive so sensitive a touch from such a man.

The woman was full of anguish.

Betrisse looked at her again and again as she stared at the man in the dock. Then Betrisse remembered. Back behind the dark barrier . . .

My sister Ju always said . . . When me and Ju was little . . .

Her Aunt Jaen's voice returned. Aunt Jaen's sister . . . Ju. She used to visit Jaen in the little cottage next to Annie's. Yes . . . it was she of course who had brought up Jaen's little girl, whose name escaped her.

Annie used to say that the whole of life was made up of coincidences: "You can't meet somebody in the street without it an't a long line of coincidences that got you there at the same time." And so it had brought Betrisse, right into the drama where members of her own family were centre stage.

The charge was not Murder, but Manslaughter. As Betrisse remembered her aunt, she was pretty with sad eyes and a lovely smile. Manslaughter. She had had lovely reddy-gold hair in pretty curls that sprang from beneath her cap, hair which the little Betrisse had wished for.

Manslaughter? The word was chilling in its implications.

Impossible to connect that word, let alone the act, with the dainty Aunt Jaen. It was hers and the uncle in the dock's baby who should have had the seal which Betrisse wore as a pendant beneath her bodice.

Never once did the Uncle raise his eyes towards his wife's sister; even so he must have felt her emotional presence. Daniel Hazelhurst, the woman, Betrisse, all linked to the victim of Manslaughter, yet isolated from one another – even the man with the quiet passionate nature was isolated because the woman appeared not to be aware of anything except the man who stood accused of killing her sister.

5

AT THE END OF THE FIRST DAY of the trial, Betrisse knew that she could not return to Emworthy until it was finished. When she came to wanting to tell Annie that she would not be returning at once, she wished that she had paid more attention to learning her letters. The message, a reason and reassurance, were summed up in a few words addressed to Ted and put on the Chichester coach: she liked Winchester and wished to look at it for a few days, but saying nothing of her true reason.

Most of the first day of the trial was given over to the reading of the charge and the case against the Accused. Betrisse could not believe that the details of a story such as one might hear recited on the streets or sold in crudely illustrated broadsheets could be true – certainly not of someone who had tossed her in the air at harvest suppers.

One of The Uncles, accused of the killing of one of her aunts.

Next day she went early to the court to secure herself a seat. Jaen's sister was there before her, the man trying to give her moral support. She certainly did not appear to need physical help, for she stood head-up and straight-shouldered staring at whatever lay behind her brow.

"You come then."

Betrisse was drawn back from her observation of Jaen's sister. It was the basket-woman.

"That's one of them." The basket-woman nodded at Jaen's sister.

"Who?"

"That fambly. The murderer's fambly."

The murderer's family. The full awareness of the fact came upon Betrisse.

Betrisse Hazelhurst. Not Saint John. That was the make-believe. Just as Annie Saint John and Annie Scantlebury were make-believe names. Annie Hazelhurst. Betrisse Hazelhurst. Daniel Hazelhurst. The Hazelhursts of Up Teg Farm.

The basket-woman is pleased to have someone to take an interest in, especially a stranger who has not been to an Assize before. "Did you see him – the murderer? Didn't he look a ghost? No wonder, if he got that on his conscience. Fancy being shut up in the cells for nigh on six months knowing you done your wife in and waiting to stand trial."

Six months ago. Since Ed's last news from 'Clare.

Nugent! The name she has been searching her memory for comes. Her grandmother often called Aunt Jaen, "Bella Nugent's girl."

Judeth Nugent.

As she watches her, the apparently rigid control, Betrisse senses again her terrible turbulence. Anger and grief are fermenting within Judeth Nugent like heat in a strawy midden-heap. One blow and the heap collapses in upon itself. She would like to go to her and say something. There is no comfort to be given to such a grieving woman. And it is ridiculous anyhow. What could be said? I'm Betrisse Hazelhurst. One of Them. A born Hazelhurst. A Hazelhurst still.

But instinct tells Betrisse to hold back, not to become involved.

The man with Judeth Nugent obviously loves her, yet is not wedded to her, she wears no ring. His love is very strong and he would take every bit of anguish from her, or is that Betrisse wishfully thinking, hoping it is true? There is a faint suggestion of Annie and Ted about the couple. Love out of wedlock? Certainly he loves her. But what of the woman? Her face is so set that there is hardly a crease or wrinkle to suggest any warm emotion. Betrisse is glad that Judeth Nugent has a lover.

6

CANTLE TO WINCHESTER

EVER SINCE THE BEGINNING OF WINTER, when they had heard that the case was to come up at the Spring Quarter Sessions, none of them at Croud Cantle, Hanna, John Toose, Jude Nugent, could think much beyond the day when Jude would set out for Winchester.

The silent Rosie has carefully watched lips as some explanation was tried. She nodded. She has understood that there is trouble and that Jude must leave for a while. She made an encircling motion with her arms and pointed to Hanna, and Bella Nugent, then the same motion indicating that she and John Toose would care for them.

"It's all right, Miz Jude," John had said. "I a see to everything. If I could go to Winchester in your stead, I should do it."

"Yes, Miz Jude," he had said. "I a see to Hanny, you knows you don't need to tell me that. Hanny a be all right with me. And Miz Rosie."

"Yes, Miz Jude, I knows you have to go, that you have to find out what they will say at the trial. It a be hard for you, listening to all that."

"But I don't know what all 'that' is, John, do I?"

"Hanny a tell you in time."

"I doubt it. She still thinks there was something that I could have done when they made her go back."

"When she gets honest with herself, she won't blame you. She knows there wasn't nothing you could a done."

"She tells you things, doesn't she, John? Things about what happened. Even before she came back here, when you used to go over and see her sometimes. Things she won't tell me."

Some things.

He does know some things, some few things that Hanna has

brought herself to tell him. She was telling him things years ago, when he had been allowed occasionally to walk over to see Hanna.

"Take me back home with you, John."

"They'd only fetch you back, Hanny."

"I could a run away. We could run away together."

"What should we live on? Nobody'd give me and you work. Two young'ns like us'd soon be finded out. The only roads I know is Blackbrook and this'n. We'd get lost. Wait a bit, Hanny, till I learnt my way about a bit more. Just wait till I can come and get you."

Over the years that Hanna had lived at Ham Ford, they had had this conversation.

"This is a horrible place to live, John, you don't know what it's like."

True, he did not, for there were things that she could not yet even tell John.

He did not know that Hanna could not bear to see her father at those times when he pressed himself close to her mother, when she was carrying in logs, or skinning a hare; could not bear it when she heard him at night, breathing like a bull. He did not know that it was from choice that she went to sleep with the maids in the outhouses.

With Judeth now gone, it meant that John, Rosie and Hanna had to work late. Once Bella Nugent had been helped into her alcove for the night, the three went into the dairy or storerooms. The lead skimming-trays and wooden dairy implements needed daily attention, the produce for market needed trimming and bunching, eggs collected and basketed.

The responsibility for Croud Cantle and the care of its inhabitants and workers is in the calloused and willing hands of John Toose.

It is dark now as Hanna and John walk back towards Croud Cantle, the small, ramshackle cottage that is elevated beyond its station by being called "the farmhouse". No rushlight flickers in the dairy. Rosie must have finished. John carries heavy sacks of vegetables, and Hanna carries a lighter load in baskets.

"It a soon be over, Hanny."

"What do you think it is like to be hanged?"

"Hanny! You got to stop dwelling on it."

"It's the only way I shall get rid of it all."

"What do you mean, Hanny? You won't never get no peace keep talking about it. You'm only hurting yourself."

"No John, you'm wrong. Every time I tells you about something, that bit don't seem such a nightmare. It's like having a splinter in you. It hurts getting it out, but it feels better after."

What she cannot tell him, is that which she tells Rosie in her mind. The splinters that have gone deep, that fester and still seep poison.

The store, lit only by an oil-wick, smells earthy from the root-crops that have been cleaned there. Abandoned cobwebs thick with the dust of years hang in torn shreds, pigeon and chicken droppings solidified in mid drip whiten wormy timbers. It is a place that John Toose has known since the first time he slept here as little Johnny-twoey the night he and Hanna both adopted Croud Cantle as their home, and were adopted by it.

Within its dusty, brown decaying walls, in the dusty dim yellow oil-light, John Toose would give anything to be able to go up to her from behind and put his arms about her as she works at the bench, to speak about them getting wed, to lie here gently with Hanny. But he knows that it will not happen yet. He has sensed that to draw her to him and press her against him, however gently, will cause the skin to grow over splinters.

That, and years of owning nothing but his inferior position as foundling and yard-boy, years of knowing his place in the scheme of even this lowly holding. For all that they weeded the same patch together, picked flints from the same field, clattered boards at the same crows, for all that she had given him a bluebird and he had given her a bell – Hanny is Master's granddaughter and he is still Master's hired labour.

But he loves her, and she knows it, so he asks her in words that she cannot misconstrue.

"Will it be all right if I kiss you, Hanny?"

After several seconds, she smiles and offers him her cheek. He kisses her like a sister. She smiles.

It is a long time since Hanna Hazelhurst has smiled.

Later when Hanna and Rosie have finished the house chores, they sit for a short while before retiring for the night. They watch the slow ignition of a solid log that will smoulder until morning.

Rosie rocks herself gently, just enough to make her head nod back and forth. She often does this when not occupied, it is as though she is saying, "Yes. I understand. Yes. Yes. Yes." Silently.

Rosie, I never took much notice of him at first. France.

He was one of The Brothers, they all used to come and go in one another's kitchens if they wanted anything. (Do you know what "brother" means, Rosie? How can you know? How did you first learn that?)

France was a shepherd. He had his own place, but most of it was used by Vinnie and them. He sometimes used to run his flock on the hill behind . . . behind the place where I lived then. It might a been going on for a long time, and I hadn't a noticed, but once I did notice, there was no mistaking.

He would take his flock to a certain place and stand there just looking down, and she would go out into the yard and look back up. It wasn't something that anyone would pay any attention to, France just looking down and her looking up at where the sheep was.

You would probably a noticed, Rosie. You knows how people speak to one another without words.

Once I noticed what they were doing, I realised that he used to come into the kitchen, excusing himself for a drink of ginger, or a pat of goose-grease for the chaps on his hands, when he could just as easy gone into his own place and asked Vinnie.

He would say, There's quite a decent branch got blowed down, Jaen. I a break it up if you wants to come and fetch some, or The sloes is ready, if you bring a basket I a help you pick a few . . . or blackberries, or dabchick's eggs, it didn't matter what, it was their way of giving messages to each other. (Like when you and me are in the dairy, Rosie, and you holds up a scoop and a press, meaning that you'm asking me to choose if I want to do the cream skimming or press the curds.)

Sometimes she would say, I can't do with any just now, I got quite a stock in already, France, and he would just nod and go away, which meant that she could not get out. Other times she would look straight at him, and she'd say, Oh, that's nice France, I a have to see if I got time to come and get some later.

I understood their secret messages. There didn't seem to be nothing wrong. It wasn't nothing to do with me what any of them did . . .

Oh but it was to do with me, wasn't it, Rosie?

I saw it all happening. But I didn't care what they did. Not at first.

I saw that when she went to collect the things that France had told her of, she always tied on her red kerchief. Whatever it was she went out to collect, whatever the direction, she always went on the path through the Common, yet she always came back with the thing that she had gone for, which I knew meant that he had got them ready for her and they had spent the time together.

I saw other things.

When I was getting snapwood one day, I saw . . . my . . . my father go to Nell Gritt's.

You won't ever know what women like Nell is for, will you, Rosie? Nobody is ever going to tell you to watch their lips whilst they tell you what they are for? Do you even know what happens with men and women? When you was little and you saw beasts hot and rutting, did you think that humans got like that too? I never thought of it, I thought people would be different. It an't surprising, when you think of how we lived here when I was little, just Grandmother Bella and Jude and me.

Rosie is making an infusion of chamomile which she always insists that Hanna drink before she goes to sleep. Deaf Rosie treads on a piece of dry twig but only feels the vibrations that the sound makes in her.

Hanna hears the sound with her ears – it sounds like a bough snapping.

7

WINCHESTER

THE FORMALITIES, THE RISINGS, the recesses, the coming and going of the Jury, the bringing in and out of the prisoner, prolong the case. Whilst following what is going on on one level of consciousness, Betrisse's mind is afire with speculation about the rest of the family. Suddenly, Her Family.

What were they all doing when it happened? This event that is being presented for this gawping crowd to savour. Where were her sisters? Who was it had come to tell her mother the day Jaen died? Where were the rest of The Uncles? Suddenly she is flooded with the awareness of more than twelve years of absence. The rest of the Uncles, of the six that now leaves only Richard, France and Peter.

Why, of all their family, is there no one here? Only Jaen's sister. No one, as far as she can tell, on Dan's side. There's not a man here to be tall enough to be one of The Uncles.

After the midday recess on the second day, there was protest and uproar when those who had waited outside to regain their seats found many of them already filled by a party of ladies and gentlemen with whom there was no arguing, for they had paid to be slipped in by another entrance. Betrisse was one of the many who was turned away.

She spent the rest of the day walking through areas of Winchester some of which she might not have ventured into had she not been preoccupied. Narrow streets and lanes where very old houses jetted out, so that their upper floors almost met across dark and filthy alleyways, in which stumbled and wrangled pale and filthy children, and where her good shawl and boots were eyed speculatively and were only protected by her tallness, her long-stride tallness, and her imperious manner.

At one and the same time, she wanted to be in the Court, to be with Ted and Annie, and . . . to go to Up Teg. To go back there, to see what had happened. There was no one there now who could lay a hand on her. Luke has gone. She belonged to herself now. That night, when she removed from around her neck the seal with the Caesar's head, she dropped it into the travelling bag. It no longer had any significance.

The next morning Betrisse went early to wait outside the Court.

When she arrived, Judeth Nugent and the man were already waiting in the shadow of the doorway.

The basket-woman too is there, and on seeing Betrisse attaches herself to her, then nudges and nods at the couple in the doorway. Betrisse feels shamed that the woman associates her with the sensation-seekers.

The time drags for the basket-woman; she moves nearer to the couple. "They say 'tis your sister he murdered." Judeth Nugent makes a slight movement, then looks at her feet, not humbly but to regain her control.

The man with Judeth Nugent stands, hands on hips, and looks down at the basket-woman and says aggressively, almost a whisper, "Would y' care to take yourself somewhere else? As far off as y'd a mind to go."

The basket-woman looks for a sharp retort, but finds none under the man's gaze, so she returns to Betrisse and shrugs her shoulders. Her voice hisses complicity. "Evidence today to say she was mad. Defence!"

Betrisse realises that the woman means her Aunt Jaen. Mad? Her silence does not stop the gossipmonger. "You wasn't here yesterday, was you? He says she attacked him with a cleaver."

She realises that Betrisse missed the excitement.

"A course, you never saw his wound, did you?" She proceeds to tell of the deep wound that the wife inflicted in her madness. "He won't meet Lord Sycamore. That wound is what makes it Manslaughter. They a find him Guilty a Manslaughter. Transportation he a get. Well, she must a bin mad to do that to him." This last sentence with her voice lifted so as to give a prod to the man who had asked her to take herself off.

The basket-woman, her tune changed from that of Dan being a

man who clouted his wife and would get away with it, old hand at the Quarter Sessions, was right.

That day a witness was brought to testify to strange behaviour that she had seen. The Defence barrister delicately brought to the notice of the Judge the condition of the witness, which being so near her time, he could scarcely have missed. But he, being a good judge, would have none of it. All other witnesses had given evidence standing, so, not to be seen to show favours to one side that could not be shown to the other, Nella Martha Gritt of Cuckoo Bushes Common, Newton Clare, Hampshire, must stand also.

So, Nell Gritt, several years after she had thought child-bearing impossible, stands presenting unspoken evidence of a child within days of its birth. A child that might just as easily be that of one Clare man as another (except Poor Tad's), including Hazelhursts, including the man in the dock.

Mistress Gritt of Newton Clare gives evidence of often having seen the deceased wife of the Accused.

"Yes, Mistress Hazelhurst often wandered abroad in all weathers."

"Yes, Sir, talking to herself and climbing bleak hillsides fit only for sheep."

"Yes, Your Honour, I knew the Accused very well . . . as a good neighbour of the same village."

"Yes, Sir, I knowed the whole family to be good respected people."

"No, Your Honour, I wadden aware of anything amiss between Master Hazelhurst and his wife, that would account for her to go for him like that. Only that she was a queer sort of person."

"Yes, Sir, no, Sir – only that she was given to walking abroad alone on the downs. Yes, Sir, and talking to herself, Sir."

She says nothing that is not true. Without consulting any of them, Nance Hazelhurst had sold everything she could lay hands on to engage a lawyer, and none of them had demurred. So when she went to impress Nell as witness, she made no bones about it, pointing out to Nell her precarious situation as a known whore, living on common land, with one child in the womb and Poor Tad, the bull-gored other child that she has cared for half her life.

"All you got to do is to be led by what they asks you. He won't ask you to tell nothing that an't true."

Just answer what they ask you, then you are not likely to find yourself hounded out of the Four Parishes with your two children.

Questions that might have given the jury pause for thought about the value of Nell Gritt's evidence were never asked, because no one knew that they should be asked.

Did you receive any monetary advantage from the Accused's family, Mistress Gritt?

Are you now living in a cottage with a decent roof, repaired by the labour of Up Teg Farm, Mistress Gritt?

Is it possible that the child that you carry was fathered upon you by the Accused or a brother of the Accused, Mistress Gritt?

Were you afraid to refuse Mistress Hazelhurst when she suggested that you give evidence of mental disturbance in the Accused's wife, Mistress Gritt?

But she was QUEER, Your Honour, I seed her myself. Same as I seed her plenty a times goin' with the Accused's brother. And I knows what she was like, for France Hazelhurst would often come to me for comfort he never got from her, even though he reckoned he loved her more'n life itself. At least so he said, Your Honour, Sir. And none of what I said is a lie.

And perhaps France did, truly, love Jaen.

One day his flock was found scattered and wandering. France was gone. What the family had felt uneasy about but had left unsaid, was now hinted at, but only to another close member of the family. There had a been summit going on between her and France.

8

WINCHESTER TO NEWTON CLARE

On the first part of the journey, the coach took the same route as when Betrisse came from the south, then, when it reached the high downs, turned right so to speak and headed away from the early morning sun.

Now that she had walked the length and breadth of Winchester, Betrisse saw from the coach window a city that was to her no longer only a pattern of stone and brick and trees spread across the valley; it was familiar now. It scarcely seemed possible that she had been living within its old gates and walls but a few days.

Now though, although she was still excited and drawn to the activity and interest of city life and did not want to leave it, she was glad of this respite to order her thoughts.

As she watched the cathedral, the colleges, the castle and all the huddle of red and grey roofs disappearing from view, she determined that, no later than when the trees were in full leaf, she would be back to start the life in the city that she was eager for. The prospect of legal problems, the ties of conventions and other obstacles that might lie in the path of a spinster with unwomanly ambition, did not deter her – before she had left childhood, Annie had shown her how to be self-sufficient and a free spirit.

But for now, she had a few hours in a jolting coach that would take her to Four Post Hill on the parish border of Newton Clare.

The original reason for her journey to Winchester, the purchase of the Up Teg property, had faded in the echoing courtroom. It was there too that she determined to go back to her birthplace to discover why she felt so very uneasy. Like the basket-woman, she thought that what had been told in Court was only part of the truth.

"I should give summit to hear what really happened, wouldn't you? Look at the size of him. His wife'd have to be a pretty big woman to have got the better of him."

Betrisse remembered Jaen in her wedding-dress, and Elizabeth saying she looked like a thistle-seed, and a puff of wind could carry her off.

Where were they all? When the Judge had spoken to the Jury of "the victim, a poor distracted woman" and of "uncurbed anger", Dan had wept openly, but no look of comfort was directed at him, he had been alone in the courtroom; when the verdict "Guilty as Charged" was given, he was alone; when the sentence of Transportation was given, he was alone.

She thought of the weddings, christenings, harvests and other gatherings, and of the last time that she had been at Up Teg, when the room had been overflowing with Hazelhursts.

On the last day of the trial she had particularly watched the people in the public gallery to see if he had any friend there but, apart from herself and the red-haired woman and her lover, it was obvious that there were only voyeurs and timewasters present. Right to the end, Judeth Nugent had sat very still, and even when the verdict and sentence were announced, did not appear to react.

Betrisse had thought, I should not like to be you.

9

CROUD CANTLE

HANNA WAS SURPRISED AT HER own lack of emotion when John Toose came to find her.

"Miz Jude says I should tell you. They gid him fifteen years. He a be transported."

"How old will he be when he comes back then?"

"Hanny, he an't likely to come back. They dies like flies on the ships taking them, and then there's terrible fevers in the places they take them to."

"How old?"

"I reckon he a be about sixty year old when he've done his time there."

"And little George will be about the same age as you are now."

"Hanny, put it out of your mind. He won't come back. Why don't you go and talk to Miz Jude?"

"Later."

"I have to say it, Hanny – you an't been fair to her. She's grievous hurt that you won't talk to her proper. Just answering her questions and that – not proper talking."

"Jude don't understand."

"Why don't you try and make her understand then?"

"John." With a small rebuke in her voice. "If Jude was to come and tell you I was . . ." she hesitates, wanting to explain to him. "Suppose she said that I really wasn't nothing like you think I am . . . Suppose she told you that I had got a lover in Blackbrook and he wanted to get wed to me . . ."

"Hanny!"

". . . or that I stole, or was free with village boys . . ."

"Hanny. Stop!"

She looks fiercely at him, "Suppose that, John."

"I should never believe a word of it."

"But if it was true?"

"It isn't, Hanny. I know you. I known you since you was a little baby. I know what you are like."

"Suppose though I grew up different when I was living at 'Clare?"

"Hanny, Hanny. I can see you here and now, you are just the same as ever."

"Supposing I was DEAD. And Jude told you it was all true."

"I still shouldn't believe her."

Hanna said nothing, but looked at him with raised brows. He looked directly back at her until he had absorbed what she implied.

"And if you thought anything of me, you would spend the rest of your life torn by wondering whether there was just a hint of truth in it, wouldn't you? It an't no good saying you wouldn't, it'd only be natural. And that's why I can't never tell Jude that Jaen wasn't like she thought her to be."

John fell silent for several moments.

"You'm right, Hanny. It'd be unfeeling. You can't talk to her about that, but you can start being nice to her."

If Hanna was ever a child, it was long ago. Still only on the verge of womanhood her manner is that of a much older woman, one who has been buffeted about by life. Hanna Hazelhurst has been buffeted.

"It came to me one day – when Jaen was flitting between being up and down like she was sometimes – that they was like twins who was split. Jude and Jaen. Jaen and Jude. When I was little, Jude was always telling me how Jaen used to take her out on Tradden and make up stories. Jude used to have such a light in her eyes when she told it, like they had found some magic place. Then, when she . . . Jaen. . ." she pauses and then makes herself say, "my mother . . . first began to be strange, she used to tell me the same things, about when Jude was little."

I was only thinking about that the other day, Ju. That day I met France and he had picked some violets for me. I told him of that place on Tradden where I used to take you to get white violets. D'you remember, Ju? Did I tell you about France?

I'm Hanna.

Hanna? All right, but I shall be sure to forget.

D'you remember I used to tell you that white violets was special because they gave up their colour to make God a cloak. Do you still remember that, Ju?

We used to pick them and put ivy leaves round them like a collar. Or sometimes it was snowdrops, and we would take them home to Mother. Didn't we, Hanna? I forgot. Why must I call you "Hanna", Ju? Who is Hanna? I get so mixed up with you. Why didn't Mother ever say, "Oh an't they pretty, or an't you girls nice bringing me posies"? She never though, not once, did she, Ju? I used to try to cast spells on her to make her say a kind thing to me.

France is kind to me.

I'm glad that Dan made you come and live here. I been that lonely since I come here. But now you have come to live it is nice. Mother will still have my baby to keep her company.

Do you like France, Ju?

He was kind to me. It was once when my waters broke. Dan is like Mother . . . "Oh come on, Gel, don't make no fuss." But France was kind.

It was better when Mother took the baby. I don't know why, Ju, but I couldn't abear touching it. When it was born, I looked at it and I thought . . .

How would Dan like it if he was gored by a bull, then instead of the wound mending it swelled up into a child. I asked him that once and he . . .

. . . when I looked at the baby, I thought, "That can't be mine, I never wanted no baby, it can't be mine." That's funny, Ju, when you think of it, for it had just come out of me . . . and I was thinking, "It can't be mine."

France . . . was always kind, Ju. Do you like France? Do you see that little George looks like France? George has got just the same hair. One day he will have a beard like France too. Do you like to feel a tight-curled beard, Ju?

(I'm Hanna. Jude don't come any more.)

Yes, Jaen, I like him.

That's good. He was kind to me the day that baby was born.

John Toose waits for Hanna to return from one of the deep reveries that she sometimes falls into. It has happened many times since she came back home. He puts an arm about her and waits for the stream of silent tears to stop. He is an intelligent and observant young man. His work with developing new strains of plants has given him the eye of a meticulous observer and a gardener's patience.

He sees that each time she goes back in her mind to her past misery, each time she cries, she has afterwards withdrawn a bit more from her ordeal. He knows she will get better and waits patiently for it to happen.

"You could still talk to Miz Jude a bit more. Miz Rosie nor Master can't talk. Will you, Hanny? She was grievous upset that time when your father wouldn't let you come back here."

Of course – it was her father who was to blame, not Jude; she knows it as she has always done.

Hanna wishes that she could make herself more of a replacement for Jaen, but she knows that she has always failed in this – as she failed Jaen for not being Jude.

10

FOUR POST HILL

At the crossroads where the coaches halted for rare passengers who wished to alight at Newton Clare, there was no inn or alehouse, just a cottage where the tenant would give shelter or a place to wait to those who would buy his ale.

Betrisse left her travelling-bag there and set out walking up the slight incline to the top of Four Post Hill, towards where it began its gentle slope down to the village.

There had been a time when she had thoughts of returning, or rather of being brought back, but that was years ago. And certainly she could never have imagined herself striding along the Rathley Road.

As some days ago she looked down upon Winchester, so now she looks upon Newton Clare. Unexpectedly something catches her, a pang of regret, or sadness as she halts and takes in the village.

How tiny.

How very insignificant and small.

Like the figures moving about the fields, small, small and insignificant.

The river gleams its course through the heart of the village, clearly showing the shallow ford, but at Deep Run where Luke had floated still clutching his catch, Th'ammet hides beneath a cover of trees and shrubs. Deep Run where Luke had floated facedown all night.

Along the Tupnell Road there is the church surrounded by a cluster of cottages. More cottages strung out, where in the gardens, each with its sty and hen-coop, figures move. It will be planting time.

She tries to remember the names of the other holdings and farms. Brack Farm, Tupnell, Church Meadow . . .

She allows her gaze to follow where it is being inexorably drawn.

Facing her, directly to the south across the ford – Up Teg. To her right, westerly – One-Acre Cottage where Luke no longer lives, where Betrisse no longer lives. Does Martha still live there? West Cottage – where Dick and Elizabeth lived. Do they still live there? The unchanging image of Up Teg which she has always carried with her had begun cracking at its flaws when Ed came into their lives, and continued its disintegration during the time she was sitting in the Assize Courtroom.

A black-and-white dog races around the kitchen garden, but no person comes out to stop its yapping. Keeper's Cottage – where she once lived for a short time with Annie and France – when . . . ? It must have been when Deb and Alice had been born.

Ham Ford Cottage where Dan no longer lives, where Jaen no longer lives.

Where are all those children?

Where are the Hazelhursts who did not sit in the public seats and watch a morsel of their family history being picked over by anyone inclined to do so?

On the other side of the ford are several figures bending and planting. It is the time of potato planting. Is that what they are doing? Yes . . . that is the right pattern of workers. Betrisse is pleased that she still remembers all that. Potato planting. Strong-arm dibbers ahead of children with seed, and a woman or youth to follow scuffing earth into the holes and treading firm. That was the Norris Land. I thought that bit used to be water-meadows.

The Up Teg fields appear greened over from the distance of Rathley Road. She follows in her mind's eye what will be the newly drawn-up boundary of Up Teg. The boundary that is in the process of being agreed between solicitors in Winchester and Chichester – with no reference to anyone in that valley she now inspects.

And that is it – Newton Clare. Small and insignificant, a speck compared to Winchester. That is the whole of it except for one place that cannot be seen from Four Post Hill. That place is somewhere in the spinney at the bottom of Brack Down.

Yes, Your Honour, Sir – Nella Martha Gritt of Cuckoo Bushes Common.

The place that she has had fixed in her mind as a harsh and dark place for longer than a decade, is revealed as a small patchwork of reddish-brown earth. Some fields, those at the foot of Brack and Keeper's whitish, where chalk is near the surface. It is the place where she happens to have been born. It is the place in which she has invested her small savings.

Why has she done that? When they discussed it, the Emworthy group had said that it was as good a bit of property as any other to own, as long as it was cheap – which it was. They had *said*. But, walking down towards the ford, Betrisse allowed herself to admit honestly to her own quite vengeful motives. But now Luke has gone.

II

CANTLE

HANNA WALKS BACK TOWARDS THE COTTAGE where Jude Nugent has returned to the welcome silence of her own home. The girl sees that her aunt has lost her tormented look.

Hanna is right about that. The muddle that had been in Jude's mind has gone. Those who took her sister away and killed her, then plotted to save the killer, have been punished. She listened to the case that was made out for the killer and knows that it was not true, knows that the poor creature who suggested that Jaen was mad had been pressed into perjury.

Bella Nugent sits as she always does now, in a half-life with only one side of her body working.

Rosie, Jude Nugent's half-sister, sews neat patches with neat stitches to make a bedcover to sell on the market.

"Jude," Hanna says. "John told me. He got transported then."

Jude nods. "Fifteen years! Only fifteen years. If you think of what those places are like you've got agree that it's a longer punishment than hanging. Fifteen years' hard labour the other side of the world, each day another day of remembering what he did."

Hanna wishes that she could make herself say something more, but it will not come. She takes the other end of Rosie's work and adds more patches. As John did, so does Rosie watch Hanna as she withdraws again to pick at the scab that is beginning to grow over her wound.

Hanna returns to the day when Jaen had said, "I should like to see Rosie. An't it strange to think that Ju and me haves a kind of sister we never knew of?" It had been one of those times when Jaen could not tell Hanna from Jude, past from present.

"Do you know, Ju, since I been married, I know what it must of

been like for Father. His nature . . . it isn't suited to being married to Mother, is it?

"He be all right if he a married a different sort of woman. So would Mother, wouldn't she? Mother ought to marry somebody steady. Dan's mother told me Father was wicked and sinful, but he's like his nature, an't he, Ju? Don't you think that 'tis a great pity that we can't repair they kind of mistakes, Ju?

"I dare say Dan can't help being like he is, and I dare say we should have been all right too . . . if I was a bit more, well . . . like Vinnie, not to care about things quite so much. And if Dan was the sort to be a bit . . . kinder."

12

UP TEG

THE HEDGEROW BORDERING the Norris Land was too high for Betrisse to see who was working there. For a moment she stood wondering whether to take the right-hand path and go first to One-Acre or to go on into Up Teg. The sun was getting up to an hour or so of its noon position. They would be coming in soon for their dinner-time break. She turns into the Up Teg yard.

Was it always this small and unkept? Was it always so quiet? or did she as a child carry her own noise with her, making dogs yap, chattering, banging things with a stick, trying to get people to notice her? Did you see that? Look, look how high I can jump. Did you see how far I make that'n go?

Her boots crunch through the dried surface of deep mud and dung as she makes her way around the house. The house is bigger than she remembers. It is a good property. She has always thought of themselves as very poor, but the house is substantial. She compares it to houses in Emworthy, and for the first time realises that to run this place, her grandfather must have been a good farmer.

Sounds come from the dairy.

The door is open and she looks in. As always on bright days like this, the light that enters the windowless building through the door flows into the dim interior, spreading like milk poured gently into a water-trough.

A wide-hipped woman scrubbing vigorously and humming to herself.

"Vinnie?"

"Lor dumble us! You made I jump. I never heard nobody come."

Vinnie has turned away from the dimness and faces the tall,

unknown silhouette of the woman against the bright sun. She peers.

"Vinnie?"

"Yes?" Cautiously. Drying her hands on her rough apron, Vinnie moves towards the door.

Betrisse backs out into the sunlight.

"Do you know me, Vinnie?"

Vinnie's jaw slackens. Her arms go out instinctively to enfold. "Oh my dear Lord yes." Arms are quickly withdrawn again, hands burnt against the style and quality of the dress, and the big-house voice of the tall woman.

Betrisse puts out both hands and Vinnie takes them and holds them to her plump neck.

"Little Bet! You haven't changed a bit." Then she laughs as she has always done, and wags her head as Betrisse remembers. "Little Bet – why, just look at you. I'm such a fool." Laughter and tears. Sensible Vinnie has never tried to hide her emotions.

And so Betrisse came back.

If Betrisse had ever imagined a homecoming, then it must have been different from the true event.

She determined to say nothing about Winchester or of Dan immediately or perhaps not at all. And nothing of Annie except that she was well. The discovery of any hint as to where Annie and Betrisse lived, was pre-empted by the use of the address of the Winchester solicitors on all documents and letters. Whatever the outcome of this visit, Annie must be protected.

"Can we go to your place, Aunt Vin? Before I see anybody else."

"Tell me first – is Annie all right?"

"She is very happy."

"Thank the dear Lord for one bit of good news."

They went quietly, on the blind side of the Up Teg house, and out of view of the workers in the potato fields.

Vinnie poured thick, sweet blackberry cordial into fresh cold water and Betrisse drank appreciatively.

"Bet girl, you become a real lady."

"And all honestly got – in case you were wondering. All got with these." She pointed to her head and held up both fists.

"I'm glad you did, though you could a easy got rich on what else God have give you. The best of Martha and Luke, both." Her hand flew to her mouth.

"I know about Luke. Face down at Deep Run. Is . . . Martha . . . ?"

"She's pretty well. Been a widow for five years, and I can't deny it, she looks better than she did before. A course it helps now the girls is grown. Kit is just like Martha . . ."

A slender, leggy girl of fourteen or so interrupted them, halting wide-eyed at the lady seated at the kitchen table.

"And this is my Fancy." Such pride and love in Vinnie's voice. Understandable, for Fancy was growing into a young woman with fine features and of such grace that it was difficult to believe that she was Vinnie's child – except that, as one could immediately tell, she had inherited Vinnie's greatest asset, her warm outgoing nature.

"I'm glad you come home, everybody ought to be in their own place. Right from when I was little, Ma have told me about you. It was sad to wonder if you was hungry and that."

"You were just a little baby when I was last here."

"A course," Vinnie said excitedly. "You don't know I got a son as well. Jamie."

Betrisse began to realise how difficult it was going to be not to tell about Ed, and what she had discovered in Winchester. Vinnie was too open and honest to be served with such deception.

"Aunt Vin. I can't tell you how I came to know, but I do know some of what has happened here since I went away."

She was saved from saying more by Fancy, obviously agitated and wanting to speak.

"Ma. I been sent by Granmother. She wants you to come. It's Granfer."

"Lors." She jumped up and tied a scarf about her head. "I a have to go. He's on his last, Bet."

"Oh. I had no idea. The news of you all is more than a year old now."

Vinnie started to say something, hesitated. "A lot have happened here. I can't tell you now. Miz Nance a need me. Fancy a stop here with you. Do they know down in the fields?"

"Pa's up the main house. Jamie went to find Uncle Dick."

When Vinnie got to the house the old man was dead.

Betrisse in the cottage, helping Fancy with her chores, an outsider at her grandfather's death. Fancy's Pa, Peter. Uncle Dick. Jamie. Strangers, with whom she shared ancestors and blood. Relations, whom she might have passed along the road and would not recognise. Family, whose house they had always thought of as their own, she now partly owned.

Suddenly, the names that had been behind the dark barrier became people. She felt chilled at what she had done. These were flesh and blood people.

And suddenly too, she acknowledged to herself why she had done it. Not to "save" the house from other hands as she had said to Annie; not as a good investment in property as she had agreed with Ed. The true reason was to have the upper hand of one man who was on his deathbed, and another who was finished long ago at Deep Run.

This sudden realisation came almost as an instant thought, whilst Fancy was telling her how ill poor Granfer had been.

"I wish he wouldn't die. He haven't hardly been out of his room since I was little. All he done all day was sit and try to breathe. He was just thin and quiet, and I used to sit and play finger-strings with him. And when Granmother sends me off out he always says, Only five minutes more Nance, like he was a little boy." She wipes away the tears that have been trickling down. "Hark at me, saying 'was', like he was already gone."

Betrisse was silent as she made up the fire. A thin and quiet man who played finger-strings? Baxter Hazelhurst asking for five minutes more play like a child? Fancy's Granfer must be an entirely different grandfather from the old Grandfather Bax. Was the difference in Fancy's gentle nature and her own "unwomanly" one? Nothing, except to see for herself the thin and quiet old man play finger-strings, would eradicate her own vision of the domineering man in the forefront of everything.

Soon a heavy tread of boots approached the house and then into the cottage.

"Hello, Gel. You come back at a bad time." Matter-of-factly, as though she had only been away in the next village for a month.

"Uncle Pete."

He gently claps a hand on her shoulder. "We'm glad you come home."

Then he tenderly puts an arm about Fancy. Betrisse is surprised at the gesture. "Have a good cry, Fan, and get it over. The old man is dead."

Fancy weeps silently into her father's soiled smock.

"All them years of fighting for every breath, and now he's free from his lungs for ever. Nobody could a wished him to a gone on like he was, he never wished it his self."

Betrisse wants to cry. Not for Baxter. Not for Fancy, though she is hurt by the girl's grief. Not for Peter whose father is dead, but for young Betrisse Hazelhurst who was born with a great sense of justice, and without the facility to be submissive, and was whipped for her nature. She could shed tears too for the woman Betrisse Saint John who, at that moment, would have given all that she had worked for to have had a father to put an arm about her, and say Have a good cry and get it over.

She is alone. Annie has Ted Scantlebury, and young Leonard who is the core of her life.

Have a good cry and get it over.

Betrisse Saint John does not cry. They would wonder for whom she shed tears. It is not *her* grandfather who is dead.

Fancy puts food out for Peter and as he eats he talks about taking down the coffin oak, and who he and Dick should invite to join them in the digging of the grave. Fancy comforts him, tells him Granfer a be in a place where he can get his breath. From time to time they glance and nod in Betrisse's direction, including her in their talk.

For thirteen years Betrisse has held this world behind the dark barrier, the world of Up Teg, peopled with dark figures. She has broken through and they have said we'm glad you come home, Bet; they have laid dirt-grimed warm hands upon her, put arms around grieving daughters and said have a good cry.

That night, Betrisse lies awake in a tiny upper room that is both familiar and strange. It was where she had slept that time when she lived for a few weeks with Annie and France. Now, the two cottages, Keeper's and Coppice, are virtually one. She has learned that France too has gone. They do not know where, only that he left his flock one day and has not been seen since.

Her mind is too active for sleep.

She has been up to the main farm. Met her sisters, and what is left of the once great Hazelhurst family. Of the seven men of heighth and breadth, only Peter and Dick, and the sparse remains of their father, are left on the farm.

She has been looked over by Nance Hazelhurst. Still a sharp and darting little woman as Betrisse has always remembered her, but now looking like some dun-coloured apple that, being forgotten in the warm corner of an airy attic, has become shrunken and mummified. And, one could believe, as hard and enduring. Betrisse felt nothing at seeing Nance Hazelhurst again – not even much interest.

She has been reunited with her mother.

Rolled in a patchwork blanket on the shelf-like bed, she has gone over that scene again and again, and felt each time the same mixture of emotions, has seen Martha's mixture of gladness and pain, forgiveness and anger, recriminations and tears of relief.

"Why did you go with Annie, Bet? He never hurt you that much surely. I was off my head with worry for you."

There were no answers for Martha. No explanations that would do. After all these years, Betrisse thought, she's relieved that she knows where I am. I supposed that she must have forgotten me, but she never has. And of all of them, only her mother seemed not to notice that she had, as the old lady put it, got money wrote all over her.

She has still not told them that she was in Winchester, nor has she given any explanation for her sudden return to Up Teg. They are quite in awe of her, so that it will take some time before anyone asks her blunt questions. In the late afternoon, a man on horseback had cantered into the yard, he had brought from Winchester the message of the verdict. The reaction had been puzzling. Only Nance made any comment: "Thank the Lord his father went on before he knew."

She has taken to Uncle Pete in the way she took to Ed. Family. Uncle Pete, Vinnie, Fancy and the lively little Jamie. Hazelhursts all. She is under their roof now, wrapped in Vinnie's ill-made but colourful patchwork. They are a family as Betrisse likes a family to be, two parents, a daughter and a son. Dick and Elizabeth too, except that they have two daughters, but they are the unit that Betrisse idealises.

On the walk from Keeper's Cottage to the main farm, Peter had said to Fancy, "You go on, Fan, and tell your mother we'm on our way. I wants to say summit to Bet before she sees the others."

They were walking through the little coppice that hid the Up Teg house from view. Ducking his tallness, holding springy brambles aside for her, he slowed his pace. At last he said, "We had a terrible happening here between Dan and his missis – do you remember your Auntie Jaen?"

Betrisse nodded.

"This a be a big shock to you . . . Dan's up for trial at Winchester." He looked directly at her, accepted her impassive silence and went on, "It's a long story, and nobody a ever know the truth of it. Jaen's dead, they say our Dan knocked her down. So he's up for Manslaughter, and his case a be coming up at the Spring Sessions about now."

She had been on the verge of telling him that the trial was over, but had not been able to bring herself to do so. It would have involved her more deeply in their affairs than she wished to be.

She had asked, "Did he do it? Did he kill Jaen?"

Lying in the dark, listening to the distant sounds of beasts on other farms, she recalls his slight hesitation before he continued.

"Do you remember Dan?"

"Yes, very well."

"She was only a little thing. It wouldn't take much."

He had gone on to tell her the bare bones. A row, Jaen attacking him with a knife, her falling and hitting her head on the clothes chest.

"She had got very strange over the years."

"Strange?"

"Wandering off, talking to herself. There was times when she thought she was back at her old home. She got very queer, especially after they brought the girl back."

"Which girl?"

"Do you remember their first child?"

"Yes. She went to live with the grandmother, didn't she? I remember they had a little boy too." She flushed a little at having made reference to the child that had been the start of her running away. But he did not seem aware of it.

"Ah, you wouldn't know a course – they had six boys."

"Six! And the girl?"

"Ah. Like little steps when you sees 'm rowed up."

They were through the little coppice now and within sight of the house. He indicated that they should stop.

"We don't never talk about it now. There was more to it than that." He looked at the ground and kicked at a clod of earth. "I don't know, no more do I want to know, but our France have got a lot to answer for."

"France?"

"Ah."

She recalls again the anger that there had been in his voice when he said, "I only tell you this because you are fambly – he was always hanging round her."

"France?" She had found it almost impossible to take this new information into the story that she had heard in court. France? whose ownership of Annie had run like a flaw through the weave of their lives and years in Emworthy Bay.

"France and Aunt Jaen?"

"Yes. Nobody said nothing till it was over – the accident. Then it came out that all on us had wondered about him always going to their cottage, but nobody said nothing. It seemed a vile thing to think of in your own fambly. You'm old enough to know what I mean."

There had been a moment's silence that seemed longer.

"Do you really mean that France and Jaen . . . ?"

He had interrupted her. "Nobody know the answer to that one. Excepting our France – and he have cleared off and good riddance or there might a been more violence done here. For if it was true what they was up to, then it was the next worst sin to murder. I think my mother knows more'n she lets on. She was down there just a minute after it happened. The little gel was there in the cottage, with Jaen lying dead and Dan pouring blood from his back. Mother brought him into our place for Vinnie to see to and the little gel was took back to her Cantle grandmother."

France's implication in it had been dumbfounding.

"That's the bare bones of it. But nothing like that an't clear cut."

She sees the first hint that day is on its way over Keeper's Hill. The soft breathing of children is all around her. Fancy and Jamie and two of the six little boys whose mother is dead. Martha has taken in two and Elizabeth the other two. Dan and Jaen's six sons – the next generation of Hazelhurst men. As it is now, it is a family of women. Nance, Martha, Kit, Rachael, Deb and Alice, Elizabeth, Lucy and Margaret, Vinnie and Fancy.

More usually it is the women who succumb; there are so many more things that may go awry during their childbearing years. Betrisse wonders how the Hazelhurst women have all survived – all except Jaen. In their working lives – in the fields and byres, men and women have equality when it comes to lost fingers, scythed legs, infected gums and festering and poisoned wounds, equality of chance of developing lungs that die before the rest of the body, of chaff from flailing or whinnowing. But in the childbearing years, the scales are weighted against women.

Yet here they all are, eleven women called Hazelhurst – thirteen counting Annie and herself.

Of all the seven men who had been here when she left, only Peter and Richard remain as heads of families. She wonders if that is why the old Master of Up Teg had become an old man begging for a few moments more of playing finger-strings with Fancy.

13

CROUD CANTLE FARM

THAT SAME NIGHT, another Hazelhurst young woman watches the sky lighten into dawn. Hanna, whom Betrisse forgot was a Hazelhurst woman.

She has scarcely moved all night. Now that she knows that the trial is finished, she releases the hold that she took upon her mind to force it to contain the thoughts that have threshed about trying to escape. On many nights they have done so and she has cried out. It is then that Rosie, not hearing, fails her. It is always Jude who has been by her side, almost before the cry has faded.

This night she has gone over every detail from the day when she first discovered that her mother's mind was straying, to the day when the other grandmother had bundled her out of the kitchen and taken her on that terrifying ride cross country. The old lady had stood up in the little cart and whipped at the pony till it was all alather and foaming at the bit. Crashing, jolting. Wheels rattling. A frantic ride away from the place they had forced her to live all that time. Where Jaen's head, crashing down upon the corner of the chest, had sounded like the snapping of a bough.

She knows now that it is that cracking sound, that and the smell of the pork she had been chopping with the cleaver, which she will never be rid of – never, even if she lives to be a hundred.

Nor will she forget the last look of terrible bewilderment upon Jaen's face as Hanna came rushing in from the outhouse. "Ju?" she said as she fell.

Slowly, like a leaf on an airless day.

During the time it took for her father's full-fisted, back-handed blow to fall on Jaen's neck – crack! – for Jaen to be lifted away from it . . . to twist . . . to fall . . . to hit the wooden chest – crack! – Hanna had caught her father wrong-footed and hit him across the shoulders. Slowly. Slowly. The blade that he had made her unnecessarily re-do twice that morning, slowly sliced its way through woollen cloth and then flesh. Slowly. Slowly. He fell and lay across Jaen. Lay across her but not in the way that he had intended when he came into the house.

"Hanna?" No more than a whisper.

It is Jude.

Jude has come from downstairs where she has been to see that Bella is all right. She has whispered "Hanna?" several times every night. Until this time, Hanna has ever only replied flatly, "I'm all right," and Jude has got silently under her covers.

"Jude?"

Hanna hears Jude catch her breath at her response.

"I only wondered if you would like some of Rosie's may-weed tea?"

"Mint'd be better. Can we sit in the porch?"

"Oh Hanna." Jude collapses upon Hanna's cot and tries to hold Hanna, but it is Hanna, taking Jude to her small bosom, who does the holding, the comforting. They sit not noticing the awkwardness of their positions, rocking and mingling slow tears.

Hanna has begun to try to return a part of herself to Jude as compensation for a particle of her lost sister. But she knows that she cannot; she is not Jude's Jaen any more than she was Jaen's Ju. She is Hanna.

The breach that opened between them when Hanna chose Jude for a scapegoat will never be filled. But they have begun to build a bridge across.

In the little light that comes before the true dawn, the hedgerow birds are singing out the boundaries of their territory. The cottage is quiet except for the soft throaty snore of the stricken Bella Nugent and the crackling furze beneath the singing kettle and fermity pot.

The delicate smell of warm mint steam pervades the porch where Hanna and Jude sit and watch the chalk-hills around the Cantle valley appear outlined against grey, then lavender then pink.

It is difficult not to think that the sky lightens too over a grave in Newton Clare that neither of them has yet tended, or that it shows up the outline of a prison-ship in the Solent.

"I'm sorry for what I done to you, Jude. I think I wasn't myself."

Jude indicates with her warm knuckles against Hanna's lips that it is over.

As much as it can ever be for the sister and daughter of the woman who died to the sound of a bough cracking.

14

NEWTON CLARE TO EMWORTHY BAY

As soon as Baxter's burial was done, Betrisse went back up Four Post Hill and waited for the coach that would take her more directly home. She had been at Up Teg for five days now and had sent no message back to Annie since the few words from Winchester.

When she started out upon the journey to Newton Clare, she had not intended to be there for very long, for she had been eager to return to Winchester and look again at the place she intended to rent and turn into her first tea house, and to look at two other possible places into which she might expand. She had no doubts about her success, as with Scantlebury's she had seen the possibility of a simple need, simply catered for. She had known also that she could tackle this alone. Her mind had been alight with the prospect of organizing the scheme. This was what her entire experience had been leading up to. This time, there was no being lifted up as Old Baxter had lifted her to get a downview – she saw exactly where she was going. This time no finance except her own. No ideas but hers. She would start small and quickly expand.

On the journey to Newton Clare she had, in her mind, budgeted, planned, refurbished rooms and decided upon the design of every cup, plate and spoon that would be used in her . . . she decided against copying the idea of the coffee-house – a hanging sign, much like the one at Scantlebury's, held the message THE SAINT JOHN TEA ROOMS.

Annie did not hear her come, so absorbed was she in the baby laughter she was blowing and tickling from young Leonard. Annie had everything in the world she had ever wanted. Betrisse would tell her the entire Up Teg story so that Annie could feel, as Betrisse now did, that France would never turn up and claim Annie as his wife.

"Well, well. Playing with the boys at your age, Mistress Scantlebury."

"Bet!" Not abandoning the child, she gathered both to her. "We was beginning to think you had gone for a soldier."

"I hope everything was all right. I was a bit worried in case my being away so long put too much on you."

What would she have done had Annie said that they could not get along without her help?

"Well Lord, Bet, you'll never guess. Ed have been helping out in the front."

"Ed?" The idea of Ed greeting guests and showing them to their rooms made her smile.

"You got no idea how good he is. He got the showmanship . . . like you. He can put it over, people likes him."

Ed appeared in the doorway. "May I show the lady to a Single, at the front, with a view of Emworthy Bay?"

There was no denying, he had the presence. Tongue in cheek with Betrisse, but she could see that he was made for such a life. Guests would never notice a small, humble menial man, but Lord Oak in his bright silk waistcoats would be attractive. Lady guests would adore him. She could see him picking up ladies and carrying them over the street mire to their carriages. The idea of him in her tea rooms flashed into her mind, and then she remembered. If Ed stayed, he would be the easing of her mind when she told them that she was leaving.

Scantlebury's was busy, so Betrisse immediately got back to work, helping Annie with sorting and folding linen. The laundry maids were in the room, so that Betrisse could relate nothing except that she had achieved their objective of becoming owners of the Up Teg house and a small strip of land.

If pique had been one of Betrisse's faults she would probably have shown it when she realised how well they had got on without her. But when she saw how established Ed had apparently become, and how quickly he had become popular, she was pleased.

Broaching the subject when he came in to carry off baskets of laundry, as unselfconscious as though it was a usual thing for a man to be seen doing, Betrisse said, "You ought to take up this kind of work in your old age, Ed."

"I reckon I should start now."

"And do me out of my position?"

"Ah, we could both come out of the same corner, Bet."

"Dear Lord," Annie said, "can you imagine being met at the door by them two?"

"Ah, Lord Oak and Lady Birch."

"Better than Ed and Ted as it has been this last week or so."

"Would you give up the fairs?" Betrisse asked more soberly.

"I been ready to give they up a year or two now. It's a young man's life. Time I settled down."

Annie closed one eye at Betrisse. "He's thinking of taking up farming again."

"Never!" So firmly.

"Well, taking up farmers' daughters."

Ed grinned. "That's more like."

"He an't slow. I sent him up to Tillett's for duck eggs and he comes back near betrothed."

"You haves to be quick on your feet in the fight game."

By the time Scantlebury's guests had been fed and settled, it was late. It was then that Betrisse revealed that she had been to Up Teg.

Unmoving, Annie and Ed heard her out. Ted flicked his eyes from one to another of the three, watching their reactions. Betrisse was matter-of-fact in relating how she had come to be in court and subsequently at the trial. How she had decided to go back to Up Teg, and what she had found there.

"It is all a terrible mess. Their only means of support is what they got from the Norris Land. It was the one bit that Dan did not have under his control. Vinnie had her way about how they should farm it, and there wasn't anything that Dan could do."

"How did it get to be so bad?"

"First, because of the Old Man being so taken up with things like this." She takes the Up Teg seal from a pocket. "He was obsessed with the continuance of the Hazelhurst name at Up Teg. If he had left them to have gone on running the farm as they had always done, it would not have been half so bad, but he would hand everything over to Dan, who was the worst farmer of them all. Then when things started to go wrong, it seems that Grandfather was too weak to do anything."

"Couldn't none of the others control him?"

"I think that they did try, at first. Uncle Dick told me of the terrible rows they had. He and Luke and Peter, trying to tell him that it was dangerous to put everything into one kind of crop. He said, 'Even the women could see it wasn't a wise thing.' " She looked at Annie, knowing that she would return the half-amused, pained expression that had always been her own silent response to "only a woman" or "even a woman".

"Yes, well. Dan's not a woman, so it an't surprising he'd think hisself too great to take notice of anybody."

Betrisse pursed her lips in a small smile for Annie. Annie might have allied herself to Ted and borne his son but the woman who had flung her wedding-band into the Emworthy mud had not gone.

Betrisse went on building for them a picture of the events, as she had been told, which had led to the dual tragedy. The one contributing to the other.

"Whilst Grandfather was able, he backed every decision Dan made. Uncle Dick said that his father must have realised that Dan was gambling with everything they got."

"They'd a been sitting pretty if it'd come off. It wouldn't a bin the first time the price of corn has give a farmer gold lining to his pockets." There is to Annie's ear a disturbing gambler's eagerness in Ed's voice.

She says, "You wouldn't of gone all out for one crop and nothing else?"

"They had the sheep and the Norris Land."

"It is as well they did," Betrisse says, "or they might all have been on the roads by now."

"What caused the crop to fail?" Ted asks.

"Smut, mildew and Dan Hazelhurst never taking advice from anyone." Betrisse's determination to try to show no emotion whilst she related the events, fails briefly.

"Soaking the seed in salt and water a stop the smut." A statement by Annie.

Betrisse nods. "That was how the tragedy of losing the crop was part of the tragedy of Jaen."

The night-watchman calls that it is two o'clock on a clear night, and Betrisse is transported momentarily back to the city where great bells announce the time, back to the busy excitement in the thronging streets, one street in particular where there is an empty ale-house on which she has advanced one month's rent, and outside which swings the sign she has envisioned painted over white and lettered in gold THE SAINT JOHN TEA ROOMS.

Betrisse is now bringing her story to its conclusion, relating it as nearly as she can to how Vinnie had told her. Ed has fallen silent and Annie's gaze is far away.

"If Jaen hadn't a just said it in front of the whole fambly, it wouldn't a been so bad. But she said, 'That whole crop out there have started the smut.'

" 'Smut, smut, smut. There an't a speck nor blemish of smut or mildew on a blade of it,' Dan says. 'You been on about smut since the seed was fetched.'

"It wasn't like Jaen to say much at all when we was all together, and I hadn't never heard her answer him back.

" 'I only said that if you was going to plant out the whole acreage with wheat, it ought to be soaked in salty water first to kill any old smut.'

"I never seen him so angered. I think he must of seen it already – the beginning of the smut that is, and couldn't bring hisself to admit. And what with Dick starting the whole thing going by asking Pete to have a look at the corner bit next to Norris's, he was probably already fearing the worst.

" 'Hark at her. She had a few years growing rhubarb for the 'pocethary on a ladleful of land that wouldn't hardly raise a flock of grasshoppers and she thinks she can tell me how to run a farm like this. Woman, you gets queerer every day. You'm going to finish up in the madhouse.'

"Bet Gel, it was like he had punched her in the belly. She seemed to crumple up and she just sat there staring at nothing with tears running down her face like anything.

"Well, of course she was right. It was like fire had been set to the fields. It was the frighteningist thing I ever saw. Day after day, our living for the next year disappearing before it was growed.

"There was a terrible fight between Dick and Dan when it did come to light. Dan was supposed to have told the hired lads to make a salt wash for the seed. They said that Dan had never told them to do it. Which was true, for he hadn't even bought in any salt.

"So you can see, he was already in a state.

"Well, on the morning before it happened . . . before, well, Jaen . . . she come in to my place, Jaen did. I could see that she was in one of her queer moods – she always had a sweet smile and although she would be looking your way, she never seemed to properly see you; it was like she was watching pictures in front of her eyes.

" 'Vin,' she said, 'haven't you ever noticed how George is the spit out of France's mouth?'

"And he was. He got that tight hair that do sometimes run in their fambly – like France and a uncle of theirs I saw one time. So I said to her, 'Yes, he takes after that branch of the Hazelhursts with the tight crimp hair.'

" 'No Vin,' she said, 'not Hazelhurst, only France.'

"She didn't seem to be really talking to me, but kept looking up to Brack where you could see the flock.

" 'I always thought it was a pity Annie never gave him a child of his own. So I got George for him.'

"Well, I tell you, Gel, I didn't know what to make of it. I know she used talk to him more than the others, and I can understand that. I'd seen them more than once, sitting on some old tree at the bottom of Brack, or on Cuckoo Bushes, but they wasn't doing anything except talking. But she worried me.

" 'Listen Jaen,' I said to her. 'You don't want to go about saying things like that, people might not know just what you meant.'

" 'There isn't anything to understand. George is the baby I got for France, and I'm going to tell Dan that we must give George to him, so that he can have a son too. We got more than we can do with.'

"It was the way she said it. I swear she didn't mean that France was the baby's father; it was like she was going to give him a present.

" 'France has always been kind to me,' she said.

"That was the last time I saw her."

The room at "Scantlebury's" fell silent.

Betrisse stared into space for a moment. "Jaen was found dead in front of her own hearth, and they say it was Dan who hit her – accidentally, not meaning to do it hard."

Betrisse could not bring herself to tell them any more just then. Later perhaps. Perhaps she would tell Annie at some time, but it was not a tale to be told except in low voices, between two people, as it had been between Betrisse and Vinnie. If Annie never heard the whole story, it would not matter; in fact it might be better if she did not hear, for the memory of Vinnie's relating the tragedy of Jaen's death remained fresh and chill in Betrisse's memory, remembering every word.

"I don't know whether she said anything or no. She was like that when she was in her strange moods; she would tell you something, and forget it almost as soon as it was out of her mouth. I can't hardly believe it, for she'd had six babies one after the other, and hadn't wanted none of them, poor thing – she wasn't likely to offer to have one – no matter how kind she said France had been to her.

"Anyway, on the day it happened. I saw him – Dan – striding down towards the house. Bet, it an't easy telling such ripe gossip about your own fambly. Well, he came down, and I knew what he was after; you can't live close as me and Jaen have and not know what is going on, if he wanted her satisfying him in the middle of the day, he'd just walk off and look for her . . . and not only her, the maids and the servants'd do for him. I've seen him take a hold of girls and try pull them just into the outhouse or anywhere and she having no more say in it than a puppy on a rope following its master. If one of us is about, the girls'd come and say Master Dan's hunting again, and next time he'd be a bit more careful. They was two a penny to him, the little maids that got hired out for keep by their famblies who have had to take to the roads.

"Nobody will know what happened, except perhaps that poor little Goldy of theirs. But, putting together what I heard and what I saw, I think it must of been that he was out hunting again, and Jaen tried to stop him because Hanna was in the outhouse. Or Jaen had gone queer again and started telling him about her having the baby for France.

"I heard Hanna shrieking and shrieking. I rushed down and through the ford. Miz Nance had been just by chance coming by with some furze in a little wagon thing she uses since she got such bad bones, and she heard it. The old lady bade me see to Dan – we could see Jaen's neck was broke – she had to throw water at the girl to stop her screaming. Then she drags Hanna into the wagon and driv off going like a rabbit before a weasel.

"Perhaps there was something more – I don't know. But the old lady would have it that the child was the cause of it all but she never have said why. Perhaps it's a case of the sins of the fathers visited on the

children, like it says in the good book. That never seemed right to me, because it wasn't Hanna's sin that got Jaen poddy in the first place, now was it?"

15

"I AM GOING BACK THERE"

It is only as she hears herself saying the words that Betrisse knows that she has made the decision.

Throughout the journey from Rathley to Emworthy, she had thought over every possible way of doing what she wanted to, and what she knew that she ought.

She wanted the full life of the city. She wanted the Saint John Tea Rooms. She needed to be successful, to be seen to be successful, to be noticed – to always stand as on the trestle-table at Vinnie's wedding feast, and see a thrilling prospect laid out below her. It was not enough for her to know that she could succeed – she needed to prove it.

Her sisters and aunts had been surprised that she was not expecting soon to be wed, nor was interested.

"Why, Bet?" her sister Kit had asked. "You could get yourself a gentleman if you wanted to. You got everything a man could wish for in a wife."

"And what should I get?"

"A husband." Rachael's tone had suggested that a husband was what Betrisse ought to have, want one or not.

"If as you say I've got everything, why on earth should I exchange it for a thing I have no wish to have? And lose my freedom into the bargain. It's a trick that's played on us that it's a prize for a girl to get a husband and lose her freedom "

Kit looked sharply at her sister, wide-eyed at the talk of revolution that Betrisse had brought.

Rachael, at coming eighteen years of age, wanted marriage above all else.

"It's all right you talking like that," she said. "You got money of your own. I can't say as I wants the kind of freedom we got here. Ha! I'm free to weed the fields, churn till my arm drops off, scour down the dairy, scrub breeches and smocks."

Betrisse's reply was spoken quietly and seriously. "And what do you think you are going to do once you are wed?"

"You don't understand what it's like living here. We been living like the poor of the village. You don't know what it's like. You got money."

"I've money of my own because I did all those kind of things – working my fingers to the bone, and scouring and scrubbing and . . ." In her urgency to make her sisters think, she almost let out, "and packing oysters and scallops". "and . . . kept the money I earned for myself."

Rachael gave Betrisse a look that said that there must be more to it than that.

"Don't you want to have children?" Kit had asked.

"I can have a child any time I like."

Her words seemed to freeze in the air before she realised that she was no longer in the free and outspoken company of Annie. Her sisters did not know her yet.

She had laughed. "No need to look like that, Rachael, I meant only that there are so many here, that I could take one under my wing."

And on the journey back to Emworthy she thought more and more of that idea. Six growing boys with no parents were a great burden upon Martha and Elizabeth and Vinnie. The older ones, Dan'l, and Young Bax and Francis, were hardly yet earning their keep, and the other three were still only crow-stoning and weeding and picking flints. As well as their domestic work, nowadays much more of the farmwork was being done by the Up Teg wives and their daughters.

On that journey too, she worked out her tea-rooms scheme to the last detail. Planning its development had shown her where her talent lay, and the prospects of a new and unknown life excited her. It had shown her, too, her weaknesses: the main one being lack of skill with numbers. At Scantlebury's they relied upon Ted to do an accounting once a year, but day-to-day income and outgoings were dealt with in a most haphazard way. So, she determined to set about learning, convinced that, as she had found with legal papers, once you saw through the nonsense, it was not difficult. That would be her first task, to become skilled in everything that would further her ambition, to be as self-sufficient in the city as Annie had taught her to be in the early Emworthy days.

Up Teg needed money to survive, and as soon as her tea rooms were set up, then she would be able to help. She could perhaps also help them at sowing and harvest and help with the bringing up of all those orphaned boys.

These were the things she wanted to do. To prove herself with the tea rooms, as well as do something about the terrible plight of those at Up Teg.

"Back?" Annie looks at Betrisse as though she is speaking a strange tongue.

"To the farm, to Up Teg." She mocks herself. "I'm going to put the place to rights. What about buying out my share of Scantlebury's, Uncle Ed." Teasing him with her lashes and smile in a way she could not safely do with any other man, except Ted.

"Done!"

"Will you not bargain with me, like proper business people must?"

Annie says, "Bet, you'm serious, an't you?"

Betrisse sits on the floor where she can hold her mother/aunt's hands. "It's time I went, Annie. I had already made up my mind I was going to leave and go and live in Winchester before I ever went to the farm."

"I should a made Ted go to Winchester, then it wouldn't of ever happened."

"Oh, so you wouldn't a minded me not coming back then?" Ted said.

"An't no fear of you going off." Annie smiles affectionately at Ted. "You knows which side of your bread got the butter on."

"When I was in Winchester, I realised that I was beginning to lose interest in running this place. That don't sound very nice, does it? It's nothing about you, Annie, or Ted, but it is something in me. I had a real desire to do something like we did when we started up this place. I don't know whether it is because I am made differently from most girls – I can't believe that I am – or whether it is because when you brought me here, I had a chance to *be* different."

"But why go to that ole place?" There is a plea in Annie's voice that suggests – "if you got it in your head to go somewhere, why choose to go *There*?"

Betrisse turns to Ed. "I will wager with you that had you been in the company of any other young woman telling her mother that she was going away alone, you would have heard threats and tears and a man would have been called in to forbid it. A shocking, dangerous thing."

She is back on the trestle-table again, looking down on Ed, on men. She wants to show him that she is as capable of standing on her own as he was as a young man. She watches herself doing it, but cannot stop. "A woman with no man for protection going off to make her fortune – and what does Annie say: 'Why that place?' Do you find it shocking, Ed? Do you believe that I shall come to a bad end?"

It is the first time that he has seen women behaving as though they were father and son. He *does* find it disturbing.

Ed is serious and his voice is low. "No, Gel. I think Annie have done a good job on you."

Betrisse sits with her head resting upon Annie's knee. The warmth of love between the two permeates the room. They are letting one another go publicly. Owing each other nothing and everything. Thirteen years of loyalty and love.

They are letting go.

Untwining their lives.

For thirteen years they have lived like two closely twisted stems of bindweed – to separate them it is necessary to have care and patience and a knowledge of the nature of the plant. Annie and Betrisse will separate, but the kinks and twists that have been formed by thirteen years entwined in independence and closeness, are permanent so that the stems might at any time be rewound, re-bonded.

"I need your money for my share, Ed, to get the farm going again."

"You can have what I got."

"No. Just pay me what my share is worth. If you are going after Tillett's daughter for a wife, you will need to buy a bed."

Verbally sparring with her: "I'm banking on her bringing all her own duck feathers, so I shan't have that expense."

Jolliness is now back on the surface.

It is Ted who asks the question.

"Why are you going to do it, Bet?"

"Go and live at Up Teg?" She pauses for a moment. "Because of all those little boys, I suppose. They need a foster-mother, and I'm the one best placed to be it."

She looks directly at Annie. Independent, free, a woman out of step with her own times, Betrisse still needs Annie's nod of approval.

Annie nods. There was never any doubt that she would.

Part Four

HEARTH AND HOME

I

ON JANUARY FIRST, OPENING DAY of the new century, Hanna Hazelhurst walks from St. Peter's Church, Cantle with a new name, a new wedding band and with her dear, loving John Toose.

Her two spinster aunts, Jude and Rosie, have followed every word, watched every expression on the faces of the couple as they made their vows to one another, and are satisfied that Hanna's life is mended. If there are any splinters left in the wound of the tragedy of her parents, then practical John will ease them out tenderly.

Only Hanna knows the absolute truth about her mother's death, and that is buried too deep for even John to know, although she has told him something of Jaen's strange obsession with giving George to the shepherd, France. What Jude knows of her sister's last months of life, and especially of her last hours, is one version of the truth. Jude has enough to cope with, living in a world where Jaen does not.

On the face of it, Croud Cantle is not much changed, though John is slowly building up their crops of plants and pot herbs. Town-dwellers, with their small garden plots, pay well for a plant of primrose whose flowers are tinged orange, or for a purple-leaved sage bush that is practical as well as pretty. But there are changes.

"Come on, Hanny, up in the wagon."

"Listen to him – giving me orders before I hardly left the church."

They smile broadly at one another.

"You promised you should obey me, woman."

"Tomorrow, John. I promise I shall obey you tomorrow."

"Tomorrow and tomorrow . . ."

"Ah you and your poetry. Jude's been at you again."

Hanna looks round but Jude has gone.

Silent, smiling Rosie watches the beribboned wagon move off, taking the new husband and wife back to Croud Cantle, where Hanna will kiss her Grandmother Bella and show her the shiny wedding-band. Grandmother Bella will stare at something that no one else can see. Hanna will talk about what provisions she will take to sell on the market, discussing as though Bella Nugent's mind is still alive. As though she is still the red-haired grandmother who had once shown Hanna love – the kind of love that both her daughters hungered and thirsted for, but which Bella never felt for them or, if she did, could never show them.

2

ON JANUARY FIRST, OPENING DAY of the new century, Betrisse Saint John stands on the bleak summit of Brack Down. It is a place she escapes to quite often. When she walks away from the farm she tells no one, gives no reason. If they say, "There she goes, off up there again" or, "What she want to go all up there on her own for?" she does not hear them. If she did, she would not care. On Brack she is free for a short while of their small minds, their fears and pettiness, their clawing need of her.

Kit and Rachael escaped to milk cows on an estate farm ten miles distant, and Rachael is now established in a rickety cottage on the estate. Her husband is blessed with an employer who provides no less for his estate workers than other Hampshire landowners provide for workers who keep them fat and idle and rich. In his desire to keep up with the rest, he provides an abundance of long hours, gives hard labour and poverty in plenty; he is unselfish in his distribution of damp walls and fair-handed with broken roofs. He keeps none of these for himself and his pretty family. He makes no distinctions – men women and children, he treats them all alike.

And Rachael Raper, *née* Hazelhurst, now feels that she has become fully a woman. When she is not working in the fields and garden, she has a man and two babies and a pig and a spinning-wheel to keep her occupied. In her spare time she walks abroad collecting snapwood and furze. She also now feels that she *is* someone, a person – she is "The Cowman's Wife".

Kit has not achieved such distinction. She went from field-milking to dairy to kitchen, where she showed her ability in a moment of crisis in the household. Kit was one of the few servants not to be laid low when the rest of the household succumbed. It was her chance and she took it. Kit is now Second Cook under a cook whose legs cannot keep going for very much longer on the chill kitchen floors below ground. Kit knows her worth and is just biding her time till she can bargain her skill for a decent wood floor.

Betrisse turns in the direction of Winchester. In her mind's eye she sees the busy streets, the bare trees in the pale January sun waiting to burst into green as she once saw them; the rooms on which she had paid an advancement in rent are, in her imagination, still empty and waiting for the day when she will bring them to life with plain drapes, plain carpets, aromatic teas, quiet talk and a discreet chink of coins.

There have been times – often prompted by her own harassment with the boys – when her fancy takes flight and she adds new and fantastic ideas to her establishment, such as facilities for children, little tables in summertime under an awning . . . ah yes, better, under a fig-tree . . . and somehow water trickling . . .

The dream is always changing, being embellished, becoming perfect . . . dreamlike.

Dreamlike. For, apart from the Up Teg house, and the small bit of land that surrounds it, she has nothing.

As always when she escapes to Brack, she gazes in the direction of Cantle and wonders about Jaen's sister. She hopes that the man who was with her throughout the ordeal of the trial still loves her. Although she can never imagine that pair living in a cottage, fussing over mundane and domestic matters – but then, there had been a time when she could not have imagined it of herself. She surmises that Hanna lives there, but will not enquire even from a packman or carrier, and she is not a woman easily approached with gossip – these days, there is more than a hint of Annie's way of looking at people – and best not to turn over old midden ground.

Nance Hazelhurst is dead. When they lowered her into her grave, she added very little weight to the wood and nails of the coffin. She did not seem to die, she gradually dried out like a little stranded newt. When the family stood at Nance's graveside, Elizabeth was still alive, but now she has gone too. During her years away, Elizabeth's was the one face on the dark side of the barrier that Betrisse could ever bring to mind, but now that she has gone, Betrisse cannot remember one feature of her.

Sometimes she looks towards the waters of the Solent where the prison-ships set sail for the other side of the world. Is he still alive? She can never imagine a thousand miles of sea. What if he did return? Part of his term has already been served. Part of her own term has been served. In ten years' time . . . Ten years. She will be thirty-six years old.

She closes her mind to the possibility of herself still living down there on the valley floor then, down there helping to fight the land and the weather and the small, often invisible enemies that will destroy animals and crops overnight.

A few miles further east along that same split coastline is Emworthy.

Whenever she climbs to the summit of Brack on bright summer days, Betrisse looks for the thin bright line of the glitterish sea. Ted writes twice a year. Mostly about young Leonard. Ed's schemes for making Scantlebury's into "something" are curbed by Jessie Hazelhurst, onetime Jessie Tillett, who brought to their marriage not only a beautiful duck-down quilt, but a deal of commonsense which Annie appreciated. Annie and Jessie get on very well, as do Ed (who has become Edwin again) and Ted. They usually send "something to help with the rent" or "a bit to help out when it comes to pay the Church Commissioners".

"Annie says you must come and see us very soon," Ted writes. "And so do we all. The Captain died . . ." The Captain? Yes . . . of course. I remember now. The Captain. What would he say if he heard how broad my vowels have become? But, as with riding a horse, she knows that she will never forget her Snows-greatly accent.

Betrisse always intends to visit Emworthy, but now is never quite the best time – perhaps when the lambing's over, or the harvest's in or the boys have got over their fevers or rashes or festered wounds.

The boys. Now – almost – *her* boys. She can see from here the smithy where Young Bax has gone to get their only horse re-shod. Like Dan'l too, he is a young man of all the heighth and breadth of his male ancestors. He has not been easy, he and Young Bax had been youths when she re-opened the Ham Ford Cottage and tried to make a home for them all together. That had been a mistake. Ham Ford was their mother's home. But, once she and Nance had sorted out who was the head of the family, and it came out that it was Nance, the old lady was quite agreeable to go and live like a dowager in the cottage, so that Betrisse and the boys moved into the Up Teg house.

At first, only Vinnie knew that Betrisse held the deeds of Up Teg, the transference of which to Betrisse Saint John-Hazelhurst had been a parting gift from Annie, Ted and Lord Oak. However, once Betrisse had proved that she had more to offer than money and labour, she told the Up Teg family that she was owner and that they need not fear landlords so far as a roof above their heads was concerned.

They were naturally curious about how she came by them and, although she gave Annie and the men their due in regard to the generous act, she never once gave one hint of where she had lived for the thirteen years that she had been lost to Up Teg, nor where Annie and Ed might now be found.

Her last view, before she descends to the valley, is of where the sheep run on Keeper's Hill.

Because France Hazelhurst had always been the Up Teg flockmaster, neither Peter nor Dick had enough knowledge to build up a good flock again. Now though, Up Teg has a run of fat well-fleeced ewes and lambs that are helping bring the farm back to life. This is the achievement of Si Baldwin. A quiet man who appeared sombre until he laughed.

"Talk the hind leg off'n a donkey once he gets going." "Lord, I never heard nobody like theece for argufying, Si Baldwin."

It must be three or four years now since Simon Baldwin-Edwards walked into Up Teg and asked to see the Master about a "raggedy lot of old ewes that looked like they had been running wild with the goats, and needed a decent shepherd". Betrisse had said, "It's Mistresses as well as Masters here, and the flockmaster's job is yours if you can swallow taking orders from a woman."

" 'Tis all one to me. Just so long as the one giving the orders is fair, and knows what is what, or better than me."

She is now beginning to understand more about what that meant. His talk in the house is like his visits there, always brief, but anyone who meets him out on the hills will likely "get their ear chewed down to nothing by Si Baldwin". He has a much-used phrase that Betrisse understands – "That's never right. Do you think that's right? I don't think that's right." It echoes her own "That an't fair!"